F
H57   Himmel, Richard.
            The twenty-third web.

Temple Israel Library
Minneapolis, Minn.

Please sign your full name on the above card.

Return books promptly to the Library or Temple Office.

Fines will be charged for overdue books or for damage or loss of same.

THE
TWENTY-
THIRD
WEB

THE TWENTY-THIRD WEB

Richard Himmel

RANDOM HOUSE
NEW YORK

Library of Congress Cataloging in Publication Data

Himmel, Richard.
The twenty-third web.

I. Title.
PZ3.H575Tw   [PS3515.I7147]   813'.5'4   76–53464
                                   ISBN 0–394–41089–0

Manufactured in the United States of America
2 3 4 5 6 7 8 9
FIRST EDITION

This book is for Thornton Wilder

THE TWENTY-THIRD WEB

Sunday, February 6
Eleven p.m., Zurich

Twenty-eight men sat in the darkened theater, their eyes fixed directly ahead on the outline map of the United States projected on a large curved screen. Each man had been positioned in the auditorium in a precise and predetermined pattern so that no two of them could talk to each other or were physically close enough, in the darkness, to identify each other. The bulk and girth of the men varied, spanning the spectrum of human sizes, but there was a sameness about them nonetheless, an anonymity of dark suits, plain shirts and nondescript ties.

The man on the stage, standing at a lectern to the side of the screen, was exceptionally tall, his long, lean silhouette backlighted by the exit sign behind him and edged by the spillover of light from the screen. The details of his face were hidden in shadows and further obscured by large dark glasses. He was dressed as anonymously as the other men but he wore no tie, his dark shirt open at the neck exposing a tight strand of beads with a tiny, barely discernible silver pendant refracting specks of brightness as he fidgeted, checking his watch.

Then it was time, the split second of the beginning. From a small remote-control transistor cupped in his hand, the man pushed a button signaling the projection booth high in the darkness. At first, his signal appeared to have activated nothing; there was no change on the screen. Some of the men shifted uncomfortably in the seats, anticipating a mechanical malfunction, but those with more trained eyes began to see flyspecks appear on the map, slowly becoming larger and taking a defined shape. The quick eye counted twenty-eight tiny spiders located at the geographical center of twenty-eight major cities of the United States.

Music started, softly and suddenly, coming from all dimensions of the theater, building in intensity to discotheque decibel, unidentifiable yet reminiscent of many composers and many themes. The mantis forms grew in size as the volume of the music swelled. Every man's attention was transfixed now beyond the screen, relating the arduous months of training to this moment. Instincts were alerted, catlike energies straining to be unleashed.

Then, at the peak of a crescendo, the music stopped, cut off suddenly as though all man-made power had failed. In the silence which followed, the spiders on the screen began to spin webs of intricate lace, stylized lines emanating from twenty-eight vortexes, fanning out to enmesh defined regions and becoming entwined with each other, beginning to form an interlocked network which would cover the map.

Again the music started, softly now, the spinning of the webs and the sound of the music a total audio-visual impact. To this was added the voice of a narrator speaking first in English, then in French, instructing the twenty-eight men to put on the headset receivers which had been specially installed at each seat. When they were in place, the man at the lectern deactivated the audio and switched the sound system, which began another circuit transmitting specific instructions to each man.

In the darkness offstage, a lone man stood hidden, observing the production, studying the shadow of the tall figure at the lectern, thinking his own unprogrammed thoughts. He knew the script, the sequence of events which had occurred and what was yet to happen. He had been through all the planning, the rehearsals, the dry runs, watched the honing process create this perfection. Yet he was as fascinated by the performance as though it was all new to him, all spontaneous. He smiled, pleased with himself, pleased that instincts had been valid, were being validated now. When all his advisers had labeled the man at the lectern a madman, he had agreed, listened patiently to the warnings, nodding his understanding but proceeding with this plan in spite of the warnings. He had seen a brilliance beyond the man's madness, a genius which his advisers were too short-sighted to detect. Now the brilliance and the madness were working together as the animated webs blanketed the United States in a plot orchestrated by frenetic music and programmed with scientific accuracy.

Instinct. In the final analysis, he had always acted on instinct. It was no different now. Instinct told him how to judge others, how to estimate their potential and capabilities and use them for his own purposes. He was remembering other times when there had been guns and bombs and guerrilla fighters in the desert. The same instincts which had guided him then were guiding him now. But now there were no guns or bombs, no hot days and cold nights; now there were computers and data and films and sound systems. Still, it was the same. Men were men, here in this theater or out in the field, and the same intuitive yardstick measured them. The man at the lectern had been a perfect choice.

This part of the plan now being explained was a work of conceptual and technical genius that could not fail. By itself it was a staggering plot, but only this man hidden in the shadows of the theater wing knew that it was a sub-plot, merely phase one. He had not trusted his advisers or his international part-ners to know his total concept, the eventual target. The time for that would come when both phases had succeeded, when it was too late for anyone to stop him.

He turned up the collar of his coat, adjusted the brim of the unaccustomed fedora he was wearing, and as the webs contin-ued to spin on the screen, turned and walked out through the stage door into the crisp Zurich night. Immediately a cordon of his guards surrounded him, a black-coated wall concealing him and protecting him as he stepped into the waiting limousine.

Inside the theater the web kept spinning. The words coming through the headsets made sense out of the fragments of previ-ous training; jagged bits and pieces were fitting together into a total mosaic of projected terror. The fiber of the web was the fine silk of human weaknesses, conceits, deceits and secretive lives. It was a computer-spun web, programmed by assiduous research into thousands of lives: little secrets, horrendous deceptions, routine behavioral data, lies said in passion, truths said in anger. All of these had been fed into a monster machine which had rejected, digested, stored and assorted them by a baffling rationale, directed by the mad mentality of the man at the lectern.

When it was finally over and the words and music had stopped, the completed picture stayed fixed on the screen while the man at the lectern pivoted into the darkness and disappeared. He groped his way backstage until he felt a doorknob, turned it and entered a small long-unused dressing room. In the dim light he checked his watch again and smiled as his body slumped, the tension over. He stripped off the dark suit and shirt, wadding them into a shopping bag, stretched his arms overhead and stood on tiptoe, inhaling deep mouthfuls of stale air. He leaned over the dusty make-up mirror, pulled the black wig off his head, fluffed his own much lighter hair free and loose, took off the dark glasses and rubbed the pressure point where they had made a mark on the bridge of his nose. For an unscheduled moment, he indulged in his own reflection. Even in this half-light his eyes were startlingly blue and his teeth bright white. He looked at his watch. Quickly he slipped into a worn pair of blue jeans and pulled a white T-shirt over his head, straightening the Schlitz label emblazoned on the front. Over this he put on a caftan and then his kaffiyeh, carefully adjusting it so that none of his hair was visible. Satisfied, he put on the dark glasses again and backed off so that he could see his full length in the mirror. As he pirouetted, the white robe wafted in the swirl of air. The narrow dressing room became the vast desert, the grit on the wooden floor was the sand of the Sahara and he was T. E. Lawrence. Looking at his watch again, he quickly stuffed the wig into the shopping bag, climbed through the already opened window and disappeared into the night.

Timed to the exact moment of his exit, the screen in the auditorium went blank. By a prearranged timetable and explicit instructions, each of the twenty-eight men left the theater one by one at four-minute intervals, turning in alternate directions, never looking back, disappearing into the night.

For the twenty-third man, the waiting seemed interminable.

Though the screen remained dark, he was seeing the projection that had been on it, focusing his attention on the twenty-third spider and the web spinning out from it, the center at the base of Lake Michigan, the radius of the web second in size only to the sixteenth web, spun out from New York City.

Monday, February 7
Nine p.m., London

LEONID TATOV rolled a six, his father a two. He considered his opening move for a moment. They were sitting at the back-gammon table of his father's town house. The younger Tatov had taken off his dinner jacket, loosened his black tie and un-done the top button of his stiff shirt. Normally, on a six-two opening roll, he would move from his opponent's twelve point and slot his own five point, leaving a blot. But it was important that his father trust him now, have confidence in his judgment, depend upon him to move with studied caution. The more con-servative plays were to move one piece to his father's bar point and from his father's twelve point to his own eleven point, or else to move straight out, leaving his father a four shot.

His father asked, "Was it hot in Angola?"

Tatov reasoned that more than anything his father respected a winner. He made the bolder, more aggressive play to his own five point. "Not all that hot. Not too bad, really. Damn primi-tive, no real comforts, can't drink the water. But we had our hands full. There wasn't time, really, to think about creature comforts."

The elder Tatov rolled a four and a one. He hit the blot on the five and considered the one move. "I think that things are finally going our way there. The Cubans have always been difficult to handle. A scurvy lot. You did well with them." He slotted his own bar point. "Extremely well."

"I would have liked to have kept them involved longer." He rolled a four and six, knocking out his father's bar point blot.

"It was long enough. We accomplished our purpose." He reentered on his son's five point. "You did well in Zaire, too. I had a call from de Rocheford. He made some remark about looking to my laurels. Quite a compliment coming from de Rocheford. I've always found him a rather cold fish." He looked at his son and began a smile. "Rather a new experience for me, one's position being threatened by one's own blood."

"We are an entry. All for the same running, for the same purse, right?" He covered his father's bar point.

"Frankly, you surprise me." His father's double ones were blocked except on his home board. "It's disappointing in a way. I'd always expected that you would take after your mother's side of the family, be their kind—not like the Tatovs. But it seems that you and I are a great deal alike, after all. It's surprising, considering that our beginnings were so different."

"Blood is thicker than the British public-school system," Tatov said, rolling double fours. "And I suspect that Tatov blood courses thicker than Dudley or Ashcraft blood. The fact that we're alike in many ways is something you'll have to learn to live with, Father."

"Yes, I suppose I will." He rolled a three and a two, studied the board. "I suppose, in a way, I might even enjoy it." It was an impossible roll; there was no safe move.

"You didn't really think that I'd turn out like my uncles, did you? I always thought that you disapproved of Mother's family."

"It is treasonous to disapprove of the titled British gentry, isn't it? I rather envy them their ability to understand nothing and endure everything with their stiff upper lips and blond good looks." Without moving his head, he raised his eyes to study his son. "You look like them, you know. Same coloring, same ruddy cheeks. I always assumed that you would turn out to be like them." There was no alternative; he had to leave two blots.

"Sorry to disappoint you, Father. You and I are alike. I have confidence that eventually you'll adjust to the idea." He studied his own advantage on the board, then turned the cube, doubling the stakes.

"Rather early, isn't it? Bit rash at this stage of the game?"

"I have the advantage," the son said. "I think that I am going to win."

"You might. Let me consider it for a moment." He studied his son's face rather than the board. "You haven't been to America for a while, have you?"

"No."

"Do you like the States?"

"Parts." He watched his father jumble the pieces, giving up the game. "What did you have in mind?"

"There's a favor you may be able to do for me there, something that keeps annoying me. It may be a waste of time, but I would feel more secure if there was someone there watching things, someone I could trust." He moved his chair back, and walked over to his tall wing chair near the fireplace.

"I'd have guessed that I would be going to Lebanon."

"Things are proceeding nicely for us in Lebanon. It's been costly, both in money and personnel. It's rather dangerous. Your mother would have a fit if I sent you there."

"You and I have always proceeded on the theory that what Mother doesn't know—"

"Leonid, you keep surprising me. But never mind, Lebanon is not for you. Curious about Lebanon, though. There has been no crusade this time to protect the Christians. No Richards, no legions of soldiers."

"Who are *we* protecting, Father, the Christians or the Moslems?"

"With us, that's never the point, is it? We transcend all that. In our world there is no religion, no color, no politics."

"Only money?"

"Money," his father explained, "is a symbol, nothing more. You will come to understand that one day."

Tatov decided not to press, to proceed at his father's pace. "What would you like me to do in America?"

"There is a curious thing about to happen there, curious in many ways. So curious that I am suspicious. Without evidence, I must say, except for an uncomfortable feeling." He lit a cigar and stretched his legs toward the fire. "One of our partners came in contact with a young American, a mathematical genius from what I understand, a computer expert. This young American had a very ingenious plan for stopping the flow of American dollars into Israel. It's blackmail, basically, but refined to a high mathematical science. They have been at it for almost two years, feeding information of a very private kind into a computer. There has been a rather large network of agents digging up sordid facts of various lives. It's all there now, in America somewhere, waiting to have the lever switched, to put the machine into motion. The concept is simple: confront an individual with a rather dirty bit of his life. The price of silence? Stop contributions to Israel. Like most good ideas, this one is very simple in concept."

"But not in execution?"

"I don't think the execution is difficult; that's not what bothers me. On the surface, no bloodshed is involved, no extortion of funds, no guerrilla tactics. There may have to be a little violence once in a while, just enough to put teeth into the threats, but basically it's a rather ruthless and elementary manipulation of people. Ingenious, don't you think?"

"What if someone blows the whistle and calls the authorities?"

"There is little likelihood of that. As it has been explained to me, the targets are not religious fanatics, not emotionally committed to Israel. The plan has been to attack businessmen mostly, men of means who are not emotionally or religiously involved."

Tatov considered his next question, not certain how far he could push his father. "From one standpoint," he said, "I can understand the immediate purpose of cutting off funds to Israel. But what is the ultimate purpose, Father, and what is *your* purpose?"

"Good question, Leonid. A good question. Nothing is as simple as it seems, is it? There is always a motive beyond the motive. I'm glad you understand that." He thought for a moment. "God knows, I have nothing against the Israeli people. As you know, I have many friends there. But as a political entity, Israel is a detriment to a natural realignment of world power, a shift of the spheres of supremacy. One tends to get emotional about Israel, but when one understands the totality of international finance, one can see that Israel is expendable. Indeed, I should say, must be expended."

"If that is the case, what makes you uncomfortable about this plan, Father?"

"The numbers involved." He took a deep drag on the cigar and let the smoke out slowly. "The numbers are too small."

"Meaning?"

"A fair guess would be that we're talking about a hundred to two hundred million American dollars. Agreed, it's a great deal of money, but not in the overall scheme of things. I worry because the stakes are too small."

"Why have you sanctioned it, then?"

"We have thrown one of our partners a bone, so to speak. We are indulging him in this private crusade because we need him in more important maneuvers. It was his price for supporting us in our larger planning. Of course we tried to show him that the risk involved was not worth the possible gain, but he was adamant. He knows his worth to us, and wouldn't yield during bargaining. In the final analysis, the plan may be very effective. It is a futuristic concept to work everything through a computer. Still . . ." His voice trailed off as his thoughts took over.

"Father, I think that in order for me to be effective, you should tell me everything, not just the things you think I ought to know." He sat on the tufted leather seat of the fireplace fender so that he could look directly at his father. "I'm no longer a small boy to be protected from the facts of your life."

The elder Tatov leaned forward toward his son. "You're quite right; I have tried to protect you." He thought for a moment. "Or rather, I assumed you would grow up to be one person, and instead you have turned out to be someone quite different. It will take getting accustomed to, rearranging my thinking." He leaned back again and looked at the ornamented ceiling of the room.

Leonid broke the silence. "Tell me about Karim Hasad, Father."

"You even know his name, do you?" He laughed. "Karim Hasad, besides being one of the richest men in the world, is also one of the most innately shrewd men I have ever dealt with. Granted, it's an Arab kind of shrewdness, but it's deadly effective nevertheless. He's too shrewd, for example, to trust this operation of his to a paranoid American mathematical genius. Zealots like the American are to be used for one's own purposes, not to be trusted with total responsibility."

"Meaning that you suspect that Karim is using the American as a tactical diversion to screen a larger maneuver?"

"Precisely. Mind you, I have no evidence; it's just a gut reaction. But I know Karim so well, all the devious patterns of his mind. He is using this young American to go after bigger game, but what it is I don't know."

"And that's what you want me to find out," Leonid said.

"Karim is a fighter. Basically he is a man of violence, with the instincts of a guerrilla. This plan—a caper, really—is too civilized for him, too intellectual, and the stakes are not high enough. If you had ever seen Karim at a gambling casino, you would understand that he does not play for fun. He gambles as though he had a personal vendetta against the casino. As global as his financial thinking is, he is petty in many ways. In his world thieves still have their hands cut off and liars their tongues cut out."

"Have you shared your thoughts with de Rocheford?"

"It was de Rocheford's idea, really, that you go to the States. He is as concerned as I am. It would not be good to have trouble in America at this moment. We have too much at stake here."

"If there is trouble, can it be traced back to Karim?"

"Don't underestimate Karim; he knows how to protect himself. I'm certain that this young American and his computer are being watched every moment. If there is trouble, all the evidence will be instantly destroyed. Karim operates like that. He knows what he is about."

Young Tatov stood up, fastened the top button of his shirt and began to fix his tie. "Do I go to Damascus first, or directly to America?"

"It wouldn't do to act that openly. Karim will expect us to watch him; we all watch each other, after all, but discreetly. It wouldn't do for you to knock on the door of his palace and request a briefing."

"What do I have to go on?"

"Only the name of the American," Tatov said. "We learned his name quite inadvertently. I have prepared a dossier on him, but at the moment that is all we have. We do not know the location of the computer nor the names of the intended victims.

"We haven't talked at all about them, have we, the intended victims?"

"Jews are always victims," his father said, "and they always survive."

"Even us, Father."

Tatov's face hardened and his eyes narrowed, as if he were trying to penetrate his son's exterior. "So you know that, too, do you?"

"Ought I to know the names of your American partners?" Leonid was putting on his jacket.

"You oughtn't even to know that we have American partners."

Leonid looked into the mirror over a low chest at the far end of the room. He adjusted his tie and ran his hand through his hair. The top of the chest was crowded with Russian icons and elaborately framed photographs of the last Romanoffs—a carefully arranged collection of lies.

His father came up behind him and looked over his shoulder, both faces reflected in the mirror, each man seeing himself and the other. "Tonight has been rather a milestone, hasn't it?"

The son turned, and they stood awkwardly face-to-face for a moment, then hugged each other. "Be careful, Leonid. Be careful."

Young Tatov broke the clutch first, smiled at his father and saw the wetness glistening in his eyes. "I'll be careful," he said. "Tell Mother goodbye. I'll send her a postcard."

"You have a late appointment tonight?"

"As a matter of fact, I do."

"A girl?"

"Yes."

"I'm glad," the elder Tatov said, thinking about his wife's brothers.

Wednesday, February 9
Ten a.m., Damascus

FROM THE BALCONY outside Karim Hasad's study, Leonid Tatov looked down into the courtyard. The bright sunlight caught the moving water in the center fountain. The light was refracted into fragmented sparks playing against the white stucco structure. Alternating Byzantine and Moorish arches lined the four sides of the house. The floor of the balcony was a mosaic of little tiles, deep colors forming a never-ending pattern of geometric intrigue.

A large, legless man sat in a wheelchair in the shadows on the far side of the fountain. Young, clean-shaven, his blue-black hair glistening in the light, he wore a short-sleeved white sport shirt, and the heavy muscles of his arms moved as he shuffled a deck of cards. What was left of his body was powerful, the power more menacing because it was immobilized by amputation. The man opposite him, picking up the cards as they were dealt, was also young, and obviously not Arab. He was barechested and barefooted, wearing only faded denim jeans, large sunglasses and a necklace with a silver pendant which shone in the sunlight.

The decision to come to Damascus, rather than fly directly to the States, had been an impulsive one, made on the spot at

Heathrow Airport. The information his father had supplied on the American mathematician was sketchy and gave no real leads about where in America Leonid might be operating. He knew from the dossier that the mathematician had parents in New Jersey and an ex-wife and small son in Chicago. His plan was to go there first, reasoning that since the man had lived there and because the city was centrally located, it was the most logical base of operations. But Tatov also knew that logic might not be applicable in this case or with this man. The dossier reported repeated instances of erratic behavior, irrational motives.

Tatov had not informed his father about his change of plans. He gambled on playing the innocent with Hasad, lying that his father had sent him, parlaying the little information he had into further knowledge of the plan. He explained that his father wanted to season him by introducing him to the operations of the international corporations. Tatov reported some of what he had done in Angola—information which Hasad already possessed; told the Arab that his father wanted him to observe this operation in America, and asked Hasad to brief him. For an hour he sat with Hasad in the dark study, fascinated by the man, baffled by his philosophies, intrigued with his stories of the wars he had fought. But when Hasad stood up, ending the interview, Leonid realized that the man had given him little more information than he already had.

"Sir, I know that I must appear stupid to you," Tatov said, "but where do you suggest I start?"

Hasad smiled indulgently, his eyes conveying his amusement. "At the beginning, Leonid, at the beginning."

Tatov played the game. "Where is the beginning?"

"It is time for my prayers. Wait for me out on the balcony. Contemplate there. Perhaps that is the beginning."

He had waited for a half-hour, looking at the sky, watching the two men play cards and counting the arches around the building. The beginning was here. Hasad had been ambiguous but deliberate.

"The son of Geoffrey Tatov is more fortunate than the son of Karim Hasad." Hasad appeared silently from nowhere to stand beside him. His voice was low-pitched and smooth, his English polished by the years at Cambridge. "The logic is indisputable. The son of Tatov is more fortunate than the son of Hasad; therefore Tatov is more fortunate than Hasad. Indisputable."

"I did not know. My father did not warn me."

"Warn you? Warn you against what? Warn you against a hopeless cripple that once was a powerful man? It was in the stars that the son of Hasad would be more powerful than the father, braver and stronger." He snapped his fingers. "Cut off. All that power cut off. No sons will come from this man. The lineage has been destroyed."

"But you have other sons."

"Not like this one, the first-born. The seed was strongest with this son."

"The other man, is he the American mathematician?"

"Yes."

"He looks controlled enough."

"It is before the storm."

Somehow aware that eyes were focused on him, the American turned toward the balcony and saw Hasad and Tatov standing there. He signaled with his hand, then returned to the card game with Hasad's son.

"Your father wishes you well. I have just spoken to him." Leonid held his breath and said nothing. Hasad continued, "In time, you will learn our ways. You will learn that one partner does not send a courier or an observer to another partner without first being assured that the man will be accepted and welcomed. That was your first mistake."

"I guess I've been a blundering idiot."

"You might have been killed. At first I thought you were a foreign agent. You do not appear to be your father's son. But then, as we talked, I began to see the father in the son. Then you spoke of Angola and of matters that only the son of Tatov would know."

"Did my father tell you the truth?"

"Your father told me what he wanted me to believe was the truth. Now, I think, you shall tell me what you want me to believe is the truth." Hasad looked down at his own son, then turned his back, resting against the balcony wall. "Begin," he said.

Leonid had to gamble that he could guess what his father had told Hasad. "The truth is that when I returned from Angola, I badgered the old boy for more action, to go into the field again. He told me about this plan, and thought it would be useful for me to go to the States as an observer. It would be good experience for me, and I could keep him informed of what was happening. I mean, we realize that you will be busy and won't have time to keep everyone current. I suggested coming directly to you for a briefing, but Father said it wouldn't do for me to knock at your door and ask for information. He thought you might be a bit suspicious of our motives. On the other hand, he had no information to give me other than what you had already told him. It was a bit headstrong, I suppose, going against Father's advice and taking a chance that I would be found out—as indeed I have—but the most sensible way to get the information, it seemed to me, was to go directly to the source."

He smiled.

"Am I making a dreadful fool of myself?"

Hasad nodded. "Yes" he said, "a dreadful fool."

"Sorry, sir. I bungled it, but I did try."

"Will you stay for lunch?" Hasad asked.

"Under the circumstances, sir, I think I had better not."

"You give up that easily?"

Tatov nodded. "When I'm in over my depth, it is best to give up." He waited for his host to give some indication that he was dismissed.

Hasad turned around, his back to Tatov, leaning over the balcony and watching his son again. "You acknowledge defeat, Leonid, and yet you have won. You do not deceive me. You now know the face of the man who directs the operation. You know that he sits here playing rummy with my son, and when he leaves here to begin his work, you will follow him. I told you before that the beginning was here."

"I promise, sir, that I shan't interfere. I will be an observer only. That is the truth."

"Remember your own words, Leonid. I warn you to do nothing. Even if the whole plan appears to be collapsing and you think you can do something to save it, do nothing. Even if you can save a life . . . do nothing. I warn you. I do not want the son of Tatov to end up like the son of Hasad."

"How did it happen, sir . . . with your son, I mean?"

"During the cease-fire when the fire did not cease, when the war which was not a war had supposedly ended. The guerrillas came from across the border, cowards hidden by the night. Three grenades and this . . ." He nodded at the legless man in the wheelchair.

"Were the intruders captured?" Tatov spoke carefully, measuring his words.

"Caught and executed at once. Except the leader. He escaped. But his time will come. We know who he is. He is called Shlmariah, the lion of the desert. His time will come. Students of the Koran learn patience—and inevitability. If you have patience, the inevitable is eventually inevitable."

Sunday, February 13
Seven a.m., Chicago

In the quiet aftermath, Livingston Stonehill was wondering when this had stopped being only a sexual relationship and had become this moment, a time of tenderness. From where he lay he could see the top of her head, silky black spilling over his nakedness, and the fluid curve of her back as she curled and nuzzled against him. With her finger she was tracing the line of hair where it began at his navel, then feathered out over his abdomen and bushed black and wiry at his pubis; back and forth, an endless pattern, lightly and lovingly—a child fondling a kitten.

What had been fantasies, virility dreams of a menopausal male, were possible now. There was the very real possibility that he would leave his wife, give up the life he had been leading, marry this girl and, in an as yet unknown way, live happily ever after. He thought again of the turmoil and hurt to the lives that revolved around his. The hell with it, he thought; it's my turn.

The delicate tracery of her fingers moved more urgently now. Then her lips followed the pattern of her fingers, skimming the same surfaces, sudden darts of wetness as her tongue punctuated the pattern. After all his years of loving, this is the way it should have been the first time. He looked from the top of her head to the window and the daylight just beginning. It was going to be one hell of a Sunday, he was thinking, all the men he had to be, all the things he had to do, so he closed his eyes and concentrated on the sensation of her fingers and lips playing against his skin. His sensual network came alive, blocking out all thinking, and he began to harden as her tongue probed. He erected suddenly as the wetness of her mouth engulfed him.

No matter how he fought, the same picture crept back into focus, the same recurring images that always ended in terror.

The picture began with the broad span of his office, the macrophallic forms of the Chicago skyline seen through the vast windows, the slick-line furniture, the giant modern paintings. Then the shot telescoped into a close-up of a man sitting on a sofa, an ordinary-looking man with an ordinary-sounding voice saying extraordinary things. Without warning, there was danger in his life. Where before there had been the comfort of the routine, the cushion of the familiar, now there was terror. The ordinary-looking man was making threats which Stonehill could not relate to his own life. These were elements in other people's lives—people in the newspaper, on television, in books—but not in his own. His kind were not prey to this kind of fear. Yet when it all had penetrated, he had been very afraid.

His hardness went limp in her mouth, and he opened his eyes to stop the picture projected in his mind. He touched the top of her head tenderly, apologetically, and her face turned up to him, wetness around her mouth, a look of hurt and surprise which changed to a slight smile.

"Listen, you'd better concentrate, or I'm going to get me a young stud who can keep his schmuck stiff."

He laughed as best he could and tousled her hair. "You'd turn a young stud into an old man like me within a week."

She crawled up, kissed him lightly. "You don't do so bad, all things considered." Then she moved back, her fingers tracing the same line again. "Not only that, but you have a very flat stomach and a very large prick."

"Go ahead, finish the sentence. I have a very flat stomach and a very large prick for a man my age."

"Was your prick even bigger when you were younger?"

"Was your ass even fatter?" he teased. He felt the nip of her teeth against his flesh and then, like an apology, the soft wetness of her mouth as she took him in completely. But the terror was still there, and no sensual expertise could overcome it. He guided her head away. "Forget it for now. Remember past performances."

"And be grateful?"

"And be grateful."

She jumped up. She really does have a fat ass, he thought. "Well, if I can't eat you, I'm going to have breakfast. Bagels and cream cheese. Are you sure you don't want any?"

"No way."

"What kind of a nice Jewish boy are you, anyway? Even the most goyish Jews break down on Sunday. One lousy bagel. Who's going to know? I wouldn't tell anyone, none of your swell friends would know." He shook his head, still smiling at the wonder of her, her lack of self-consciousness, her bright fresh face. "Not even half a bagel?" He continued to smile and shake his head. "I'm being a Jewish mother again, huh?" He nodded. "It's not so terrible being a Jewish mother. Maybe if your Jewish mother had been a real Jewish mother you wouldn't be fucking young girls on Sunday."

"I like fucking young girls on Sunday."

"Okay, so lie there in your mock-goyish splendor. I'm going

to feed this Jewish face." She perched for a moment on the edge of the bed. "You are something gorgeous. Sometimes I get an urge to show you off, to pin a label on you that says *He fucks me* and parade you through one of my mother's Hadassah meetings." When he opened his mouth, she put her hand over it before he could say anything. "If you ask me what the Hadassah is— Were you?" She took her hand away. "Don't you honestly know what the Hadassah is?"

"Go eat your bagel."

"As full as your life is, my darling, with high finance, high society and your artsy-fartsy philanthropy, you're missing a lot."

"But I have you."

"You can't fuck that Jewish dimension back into your life. It's too late."

"All this because I don't like bagels and don't know what the Hadassah is?"

"Symptoms," she said, standing up. She leaned over and kissed him. "But you're gorgeous and rich, and when you're rich and gorgeous you don't have to touch anything; everything comes to you." She shrugged her shoulders, and he liked the way her full breasts moved. "You want coffee or anything?"

He shook his head and she left the room. Now he was alone again and able to let the terror surface, and to begin seeing again the pictures in his mind.

The Stonehill Bank Building had been built in 1968. From the beginning, the concept had been to build a structure of quality. It was consistent with the bank's image that the building was not to be the tallest in the city, nor the largest nor the most innovative. It was to be a reserved statement of quality, with attention to detail, a symbol that stability still flourished. The building was one the bank could afford, a necessity to house its vastly expanded personnel and the huge new machinery which made it work. It was also a shrewd merchandising maneuver which thrust this conservative establishment into the modern mainstream where new, young money thrived.

On Friday he had been sitting at his desk wondering again

what would happen when he died. The bank was too vast, complicated and powerful now to be a family institution, and there was no young Stonehill working his way up from the tellers' cages. Livingston looked at the photograph of his five-year-old grandson and shook his head sadly. There was no chance that Stonehill Crossely would sit here. By the time little Stoney was ready, the corporate colossus would have taken over, and the Stonehills would be represented only by their portraits on the walls of the board room. And these days, when his internal confusions were surfacing more frequently and his lifelong defenses against these confusions were breaking down, Stonehill found himself reflecting that his grandson might grow up to be a happier man without the burden of succession.

Yet there might have been a chance if his daughter had not married Whiz Crossley, or if Whiz had been able to channel all that mathematical and statistical genius into conventional banking. And if the son-of-a-bitch hadn't had a perpetual hard-on.

The buzzer on his desk sounded, and he looked at his watch and then at his calendar. Eleven o'clock: Wilford Shaw. The contact had been made through a private bank in Switzerland. Shaw represented international money seeking local investment. Stonehill knew that "international money" could mean anything. It could be legitimate or Mafia or almost anything else packaged in secretive Swiss respectability. Most likely it was Mideast oil money. There was a lot of that around these days, and because the bank was not getting its proper lion's share, Stonehill had decided to see Shaw himself and put his presidential prestige to work. With another buzz he signaled his secretary to keep Shaw waiting the customary four minutes and then show him in.

As soon as he saw Shaw carrying a briefcase, Stonehill knew that he was wasting his time. He should have let one of his vice-presidents handle this; big money did not carry a briefcase.

As he settled into the sofa, Shaw said, "I'm glad you were able to see me personally, Mr. Stonehill. It was a bit of a hassle getting directly to you. I was concerned that my business not be shunted off on a subordinate. It's nice of you to see me personally."

Stonehill sensed a dud, a miscalculation of the importance of this man. "Your letter was intriguing," he said. "I wanted to talk to you first to tell you about our bank, listen to your problems, and then zero you in on the man here with the right expertise to help you."

"It was made quite clear, wasn't it, that I represent international interests?"

"Quite clear."

"International interests can include many things. I'm sure that you understand that, Mr. Stonehill."

"Perfectly."

The smaller man smiled, rubbed the bridge of his nose and fingered the identification tag on the attaché case beside him. "Then I am surprised that you are interested. You must understand that international interests could include Mideast oil money—Arab money, if you will."

"We are one of the largest banks in this country, Mr. Shaw. We have offices and correspondent banks all over the world. We are experienced with international interests."

"I know very well the size and the scope of your bank, Mr. Stonehill, but that is not quite what I meant. I question your experience with Arab money because it is my understanding that this is a Jewish bank."

Stonehill masked his reaction with a look of calm, indulgent compassion. This man, he was thinking, was no one, looked like anyone. He was middle-aged, of middle height and middle build. What physical characteristics would there be to remember about Wilford Shaw?

"A bank this size has no religion, Mr. Shaw," he said. "Our applications for employment do not even request information on religious preference." Damn it, he thought, I'm sounding defensive. "Other than a few specialists in our legal and trust departments, I doubt if we have many Jewish employees."

"But it was my understanding that you yourself are a Jew, Mr. Stonehill."

This time Stonehill did not bother to hide the annoyance in his voice; obviously he was dealing with an anti-Semitic crank. "It is quite true, Mr. Shaw, that I am a Jew, but I state again that religion has no part in banking." He started to rise, but when Shaw made a vague gesture he stayed seated.

"Don't write me off quite yet, Mr. Stonehill. There is a considerable amount of money that is available through us. The group I represent are cautious businessmen, and they feel that these matters are better discussed openly and in the beginning. Don't you agree?"

"Perhaps we ought to go straight to the business at hand," Stonehill said, reaching across the table for a cigarette. His eye caught the cluster of buzzers next to the cigarette box. "Would you like coffee or a cold drink, Mr. Shaw?" The other man shook his head, and in an overtly absent-minded kind of gesture moved the box and, in doing so, pushed the plaque of buzzers out of Stonehill's easy reach. "From your conversation I take it that you merely represent the group, but are not a direct part of it." Shaw nodded, and Stonehill continued, "Are you a lawyer, Mr. Shaw, or a financial consultant?" Shaw shook his head. "Real estate?" Again the head shook.

"I liken myself to the days of the Western migrations in your country. I am the scout, the advance man, making certain that it is safe for the covered wagons to move forward." He smiled, pleased with the allusion.

"You are not American?"

"Oh, indeed I am, both by birth and registered nationality. But I am more than that—a citizen of the world, if you will. My thinking is not confined to any single chauvinistic nationality. The world of money is apolitical, don't you think? It transcends geography—or at least the arbitrary lines on a map separating resources into nations. Haven't you found that the world of money is like that?"

"My thinking is not global like yours. This bank *is* chauvinistic; it is a Chicago institution dedicated to the development of the resources of this area. Investments in other areas are of interest to us only as they affect our corner of the world."

Shaw was looking indulgent. "They warned me that your thinking might be rather provincial."

"Who warned you?"

"The people I represent."

There was an awkward moment of silence, each man waiting
for the other to continue. "Are you sure that you don't want
coffee? I'm going to have some." Stonehill leaned forward to
reach the buzzers, but with the speed of a switchblade Shaw's
hand caught his by the wrist, immobilizing it with a sudden steel
force. "Perhaps," Shaw said, "it would be better for the moment
if you rang for nothing and for no one."

Stonehill felt pain and astonishment. He tried to pull his hand
from the vise of the other man's grip, but the pressure was
unyielding. "What the hell is this? What are you trying to pull?
You can't get away with anything here. This bank is staffed with
guards and has a very sophisticated alarm system. What are you
up to?"

Shaw smiled slowly, gradually releasing his grip. "I know all
about your alarm system and just how sophisticated it is, Stonehill. I also know that of the five buttons on this control panel,
the red one rings for your secretary, the blue automatically
locks your office door, the green alerts the guard room, the
yellow sounds an audible alarm and the silver directly alerts
police headquarters. I am also aware that there is a duplicate set
of these buttons on your desk, and a foot-pedal alarm underneath it. You see, I studied your alarm system and security
precautions very carefully. As a matter of fact, in my opinion
the system isn't sophisticated at all; it is really very naïve. Witness this moment: the entire system is ineffective. But you can
relax, Stonehill. I did not come here to rob your bank, though I
must say it would be rather easy."

"Then what the hell do you want?" Stonehill stood up
quickly, and just as quickly a gun materialized in the hand of
the ordinary-looking Mr. Shaw. He cradled it rather than pointed it, but the blue-black steel had the authority to stop Stonehill.

Nothing in Stonehill's life had prepared him for possible
violence. He had matured between wars, a little too young for
World War II, a little too old for Korea. He was horrified at the
fear hot in his gut, and furious with himself that he was immobilized by it. He could not seem to focus his office or the gun or
Mr. Shaw into any kind of reality. Instead of taking heroic

action, he found himself wondering if he would be on time for his business lunch at the Standard Club.

"You had better sit down, Stonehill. You don't look well."

He moved slowly, giving himself time to recover and become again the man he was. He crossed his legs, leaned back a little in his chair and adjusted his body to a more relaxed position. Without looking at the gun he said, "I strongly suggest, Mr. Shaw, or whatever your real name is, that you stop this game, put that gun away and state your business quickly. This is a busy office and I am expecting my next appointment momentarily."

Shaw laughed, exposing crooked, yellowish teeth. "It was my understanding that your next appointment was out of the building. Well, nice try." He studied the cluster of buzzers. "Now, let me see, it is the blue one, isn't it?" He pressed it. "Now the door to your office is locked and no one can enter until it's pressed again." He slipped the gun into his pocket. "Why are you so afraid of a gun? Your dollars do more destruction than guns." He relaxed more comfortably on the sofa. "I think that we have now established the climate of this meeting, have we not? And we have also established where the control lies?"

"You have the gun."

"You are probably thinking that I am some kind of demented crank. A nut, if you will." He shook his head. "Be assured that I am not. You were expecting a representative of a well-organized coalition of international interests, and I do represent exactly that. With only one difference. You were expecting this conglomerate to lavish millions of dollars on your Jew bank, all the legendary oil money to be laid at your feet so that you could make millions from our millions."

"State your business."

"You must not be impatient, Stonehill, nor must you deny me this one chance to gloat a bit. You represent two years of careful and exhausting research to our group. I have waited a long time for this moment, so you must indulge me. This is to be our only meeting, just this one time."

"I repeat, state your business."

"And I repeat, this meeting is under my control. I will determine the timing and the agenda. You might say that this is my hour. After two years this is my hour, and it will be no more than sixty minutes."

"You are a maniac."

"Satisfy my curiosity, Mr. Stonehill." Shaw paused for a moment. "Stonehill is a funny name for a Jew until one translates it back to the German. Steinberg. Even your first name translates back to German. Who would think that the name Livingston Stonehill masquerades a Jew banker?"

Stonehill felt his jaw square and his senses bristle. He was not a physical man, but he was intensely aware of his body at this instant, and he realized that, properly goaded, any man could be physically violent. Yet there was the gun.

"As I was saying, Mr. Steinberg, satisfy my curiosity. You live in this society not as a Jew, but as a nonsectarian, if you will. Your affiliations bridge the Jewish and Gentile worlds. As a matter of fact, few people think of you as a Jew. You don't even think of *yourself* as a Jew. That's true, isn't it?"

"Keep talking. Somewhere along the line some of this may make some sense."

"What I am curious about is this inconsistency in you, and it is precisely because of this inconsistency that you were chosen by our group."

"What inconsistency?"

"The inconsistency is that you have given millions to the Zionists and have pledged millions more to these Israelites. You are not a fanatic, and you do not identify with them. On the contrary, your behavior indicates a disdain for your brother Jews. It is said that there is no anti-Semite worse than a Semite. Our records show that on quite a few occasions—in private conversation, of course—you have referred to them as those Hebes in the Middle East." Stonehill felt the blush of truth rush to his face. "So it is inconsistent that you would be a large contributor to their cause."

"I don't have to defend or explain what I do with my money."

"No, of course you don't, and we know that it isn't all your own money. Much of it comes from the Livingston trust which you administer—all that money from your grandfather Livingston. Amazing how all that money accumulated from an immigrant Jew picking up scraps of junk. Only in America, isn't that the expression? Only in America."

"I know my heritage. Get on with it."

"It's my own curiosity. Why do you give this money to Israel? I know that some of it is due to the insistence of your mother. Charming lady, I must say. How old is she? Eighty-five? Eighty-six on April seventeenth. Remarkable, the way she still moves around. Still goes to Israel once a year, even at her age. What are you going to do when she dies, Steinberg? Are you going to adhere to her wish to be buried in Israel? It might prove an embarrassment, might it not?"

"Get to the point."

Shaw laughed. "Jews are always Jews, aren't they, no matter how high and mighty they think they are. It's curious, Stonehill. You have been eyeing the silver button—discreetly, mind you, but eyeing it. Let's weigh the possibilities. Can you press the button before I kill you? Possible, isn't it, very possible. I'll give you a Jewish parallel: the Jews in Nazi Germany. Jews like you, assimilated like you, Germans first, Jews second, just like you, Steinberg. And some of them were even named Steinberg; some of them were even your relatives. They could never believe that Hitler was happening to them. For a long time they looked the other way. And when they were herded off to a concentration camp to be eliminated, they still didn't believe that they themselves would die. They thought that if it happened at all, it would happen to other kinds of Jews. Until they smelled the gas in the chamber, they never believed it. And yet if they had seen the truth in the beginning, there were silver buttons they could have pushed. They could have fought, they could have let the world know. They might have died themselves, but they would have died knowing that they were saving the lives of other Jews."

Stonehill stood up and walked to the window without looking back to see if Shaw had drawn the gun again. Beyond the strong Chicago skyline was the water, murky green and icy. He was remembering as a ten-year-old overhearing the arguments in his house: his mother pleading for money to get relatives out of

Germany and his father accusing her of feminine hysteria, distortion of reality, and of being a victim of Zionist radicals.

"Steinberg," Shaw called.

"What?"

"I'll give you your chance; we will live history over again. Run for the button. There's a good chance that you can get to it before I kill you. Think about it. The odds are probably sixty–forty that you'll push the silver button before you die. But if you do push the button, there is no doubt that I will be captured. Not that if I am captured I will reveal anything. But there is a chance that through fingerprints they will find out who I really am, and if they learn that, perhaps the entire plot can be uncovered and hundreds of lives saved. I am giving you that chance, Steinberg—a chance to sacrifice your own life so that hundreds of others can live. Sixty–forty. What do you say?"

"You're a maniac."

Shaw laughed. "It can't be happening to you, can it, Steinberg? Let me assure you that it most definitely is."

Stonehill turned. The cluster of buzzers on his desk and the coffee table loomed as though spotlighted, but he did not move.

"Time has a way of running óut, doesn't it?" Shaw said. Now he stood up, walked to the window and stood beside Stonehill, looking out over the city. "Unfortunately, as much as I am enjoying this, it is time to get to the point, and that point is to instruct you to withdraw your financial support of Israel. Your instructions are very precise. Retract all of your personal pledges to the Jewish United Fund, as well as those of the charitable foundations you control, and demand cash redemption of all Israel bonds you and your foundations hold. It's really very simple; two or three hours of work and all of our demands will be met."

Stonehill turned, stunned. "You really are a maniac."

"You don't believe that, not really. You are an eminently practical man. You are also an international banker. You must be able to see the overall effect of this exercise. From you alone over the next three years, five million dollars will be cut off from Israel. Multiply yourself by seven or eight other men in this city, and then multiply this city by all the major cities in the

United States and think of the millions and millions of dollars involved—millions of dollars that will not be in the hands of the Israelites. Think about it for a moment, Stonehill. It's a simple but brilliant plan, and, if I may say so, brilliantly executed."

"You mean that you are doing this all over the country to other men, and to other men here in the city?"

Shaw pressed a button which illuminated the time on the dial of his digital watch. "Now, at precisely this moment, men like myself are talking to men like yourself. Or if not at this moment, perhaps yesterday or tomorrow. It doesn't matter; the plan is in operation."

Stonehill laughed. "You don't really think you can pull this off? You're more of a maniac than I thought."

"Think carefully, think financially and think what the lack of dollars will eventually mean to Israel."

"Then what? What's that going to accomplish?"

"Come, now, Steinberg, you cannot be *that* provincial. We are all after the same thing: the dissolution of the barriers to freedom of an international economy. As a whole, my group has no personal vendetta against the Jews in Israel. To them, the political state is the block, not the people. It may surprise you to know that there are even some Jews in the group—Jew money mixing with Nazi money filtering out of South America. Strange bedfellows? Not really, when you think about it. They are all eminently practical men, and money transcends individual preferences. They all understand that Israel must be eliminated."

"What makes you think you can pull this off?"

"Even here, in this bastion of provincialism, you must read the papers. Our credentials are formidable. Pick a revolution, any revolution. Or a South American coup d'état. The Munich Olympics. The Japanese airport. Need I give you a complete recitation of our track record? It is brilliant, Steinberg, brilliant."

"What makes you think you can coerce free people into doing what you say? What makes you think you can coerce me? Kill me? You know that won't work. There will be only more money for Israel that way."

"Every man has his price, or, if you will, his breaking point.
You have been carefully chosen for your vulnerability, as has
every other person on the list. We have been most thorough."

"And what have you geniuses figured out is my price?"

"Now you're talking like a Jew banker. Eminently practical,
as I said. You have your price."

"All right, what is my price?" Stonehill realized he was talking calmly now. The bastard was right; he was back in his
element, being practical, talking price.

"We considered your wife and/or daughter. We also considered your own person. We rejected your mother because of
her age and because she would love to die for Israel. With you,
your wife and daughter, there were two possibilities. Ransom,
first, but that would bring us money which we don't need and
would not stop the flow of money to the enemy. Second, assassination, and this was a very real possibility. For example, your
wife could be executed. If that didn't convince you, your
daughter, then her son, or perhaps her son first. We never did
decide because we have a better plan for you, one that will hurt
you even more acutely."

Stonehill walked away and sank down on the sofa. Shaw
followed and sat in the chair. "I don't believe this," Stonehill
said, "this can't be happening." Then he remembered the other
man's words and did not say any more.

The gun appeared again, this time leveled, poised to release.
"Forget the alarm, Steinberg. You'll be a dead hero for nothing.
We will only find another way to stop the flow of your millions,
and my life means nothing in terms of the whole plan. We have
sacrificed ourselves before."

He changed the position of his hand, withdrawing it to grasp
the arm of the sofa.

Shaw continued, "If I mention one name, I can put my gun
away and you will know your price." Stonehill said nothing.
The other man gave a cat smile: "Myrna Gordon," and as he
said it he returned the gun to his pocket.

While the sound of the name still hung in the room, the
telephone buzzed, and Stonehill looked at Shaw for permission
to answer. The man's face indicated nothing but victory. Stone-

hill picked up the phone. "Yes, Miss Andrews . . . I know . . . Yes, I should be through here shortly . . . Well, call the Club and tell them I may be a few minutes late . . . I'll call him back later . . . No, you go to lunch at your regular time." He hung up.

Stonehill thought about what he was going to say. "Myrna doesn't mean that much to me."

"Doesn't she? We think she does. As a matter of fact, we are quite sure that she does. Perhaps you don't know yet just how important she is to you."

"You can't blackmail me."

"Can't we? To be frank, we weren't certain. On the one hand, your position in the community is very important to you. And then there is the relationship with your wife; could that survive the scandal? Your relationship with your daughter would be over—you know how she is about such sordid things—and she certainly would not let you see her child. But we also wondered whether those relationships meant enough to you."

Out of control, he said her name. "Myrna. Poor Myrna."

"That's true. Poor Myrna. We would have to kill her, you know. If for any reason you do not cooperate with us, we will kill her." There was a pause, and he looked at his watch. "You'll be late for lunch and I have a plane to catch. I've done my job."

"Have you? I haven't made any decision."

"From your record we did not expect an immediate answer. Your habit is to think things through. We anticipated that." He brushed the shoulders of his jacket. "I should add that not only will we arrange the murder, but will do it so as to make it appear that you murdered her in a jealous fit. In this way all bases will be covered. You will have lost Myrna—and incidentally, I think she is much more important to you than you seem to be aware of—but regardless, the scandal will estrange your wife and daughter and her child, and perhaps kill your mother. And even if you beat the murder charge, which I doubt, you will have lost everything but your money. Our way is really much better. You will lose nothing. A banker should understand that. You will even still have the five million you have pledged for the next three years. With that you could build the Stonehill wing on to the Art Institute. You'd like that, wouldn't you? It would certainly consolidate your position on the board and insure your elevation to the presidency. As a practical man, you can see everything you have to gain, and you must be terrorized by all you have to lose."

Shaw looked at his watch again. "Time does run out. Perhaps we ought to be specific, Mr. Stonehill. Your first move will be to withdraw from the committee honoring your friend the Senator. Man of the year, isn't it? But we all know that it's just another Jew device to sell Israel bonds. I understand that Mark Mendoza is coming from Jerusalem expressly to talk at this dinner and wring your hearts with his stories of triumphs in the war, his ruthless raids across borders against innocent people. They call Mendoza the Desert Lion, don't they? The Desert Lion," he repeated, and laughed harshly. "Withdraw your support."

"I can't do that. The Senator and I were roommates in college. I'm committed on both a civic and personal basis."

"But you'll find a way, won't you, Mr. Stonehill?"

"There is no way."

"You say that now, but after you've thought about it a way will occur to you. It will be easy after that. The next steps will be relatively painless."

"What are the next steps?"

"That's better." The man smiled. "You're being practical now. The next steps are to withdraw your pledges. Not one dime to Israel under any guise. Is that quite clear?"

"You're a maniac."

"Perhaps, but that only makes us more dangerous. A maniac does not proceed with the logic of ordinary men; nor does he play the game according to the rules. This is a new experience for you, Mr. Stonehill. Guerrilla rules. Adjust to them."

"Never."

"One learns never to say never." Shaw looked at his watch again. "If we were to play the game by the rules, you would be warned if we saw that you were not cooperating. But we will give you no further warning; you will probably never be contacted again. You have one week to withdraw your support from the testimonial dinner for your friend the Senator. If not, the first reprisal will occur. But as horrible as the first one may seem, it will be mild in comparison to those which will follow. You have thirty days to comply with our complete demands."

"And if I comply?" Stonehill asked. "For how long?"

"Forever, Mr. Stonehill. Forever." He looked at his watch again. "You're going to be late for lunch. Shall we go out together, side by side? You can walk on my gun side. It may be safer." He reached down and pushed the blue button which unlocked the door. "Ready, Mr. Stonehill?"

They walked together through the quiet office into the elevator and down through the crowded main banking floor, Stonehill feeling the hard steel of the gun. Out in the street, he heard the man say that it was getting nippy out, but when he turned Shaw had disappeared among the hordes of people on their lunch-hour scurry.

Stonehill continued walking the short, familiar two blocks to the Standard Club. The wind was icy. Traditionally, like his father and grandfather before him, he never wore an overcoat. He walked with long strides at a quick cadence, acknowledging the "Hi, Livie" and "Hello, Mr. Stonehill" greetings with an automatic smile, unaware of identities.

At the club, it was a lunch like any other: the same table in the main dining room, the same cronies saying the same things. Except that he had a second drink before lunch. It was while he was sipping it that he wrote Shaw off as a demented crank, dismissing the last hour of his life as some kind of nightmare. He was even able to laugh at a story Sam Weill told, to answer questions about the Israel bond dinner, and to field some questions about the Senator's unpopular support of Mideast détente.

But the composure lasted only midway through lunch. Then the terror returned.

He had lived this way all weekend, in a kind of malarial stupor, cyclical waves of chills and fever interspersed with tranquil intervals during which Shaw was nothing more than an annoying crank and everything seemed to be the way it always was.

The smell of the bagels toasting wafted into the bedroom to bring him back to now, and now was no different than it had been yesterday or on that awful Friday. Myrna came into the room, a half-eaten bagel in one hand, a plate of bagels in the other.

"I made some extras just in case." He liked the way her breasts jutted, tight and full, and her naked innocence. She sat on the edge of the bed and offered him a bagel. "Want a bite?" He shook his head. "Listen, could you do me a favor—I mean a real personal favor?"

"I'll try." Maybe he did love her very much.

"Could you get a hard-on?"

He laughed. "Just like that," and he snapped his fingers.

"I don't want to get fucked again or anything, but I've got this thing about dropping a bagel over a guy's schmuck. Crazy, huh?"

Kissing her, he tasted the cream cheese. "Crazy."

"You want to try?"

"The hole in the bagel isn't big enough."

"I thought of that." She picked another one off the plate. "You see, I reamed this one a little, just your size." She picked up his limp penis and eased the bagel over it gently. Some of the cream cheese smeared on him, and stayed; she bent down and licked it off. He began to laugh, softly at first, then louder and louder until his whole body shook. Or were those tears, he wondered.

"I got to tell you, Livie, old fart or no, you really turn me on." She fell against him, laughing now too, and as they clung together rocking with laughter he felt the bagel tightening around him.

He came out of the bathroom toweling himself dry, still not quite accustomed to the asexual nakedness which had become part of their life style. "You are something beautiful to behold," Myrna said, and then smiled when she realized his apparent discomfort. "Hasn't anyone ever told you before that you're beautiful? It isn't unmanly, you know." She sat up in bed. "Livie, you seem distracted. What's wrong?"

"Nothing. I'm fine. All fucked out, but fine."

"Too fucked out for your tennis game?"

"No, I'll make it. I may be outclassed, anyway."

"Are you playing at the Racquet Club?"

"No. I have to drive out to Lake Forest to a friend's house. Well, not a friend, really, it's business." He pulled his tennis shirt over his head. "What are you going to do?"

"All the little-girl things I don't have time to do when I'm with you." She lay on her stomach, her head toward the foot of the bed. "There is something wrong, isn't there?"

"No, nothing. You worry too much. Your Jewish-mother syndrome is showing again." He sat on the edge of the bed to put on his socks and closed his eyes as she kissed the back of his neck. "As a matter of fact, this week *is* going to be a little rough."

She drew away. "That can only mean that your wife is coming back from Palm Springs."

"Only until Friday. She's flying in late this afternoon. The fund-raising ball is Wednesday night at the Art Institute."

"I wanted to talk about that. Would it throw you terribly if I showed up? I mean, there's this guy who keeps coming to the gallery all the time. He bought a couple of lithos, but mainly I think he's trying to make a little time with me. A nice enough guy, I suppose. Rich as hell, one of the boy wonders on the option exchange. My mother would love him, a nice Jewish boy. He wants me to go to the party with him. I told him that I wasn't sure. I thought I ought to check and see how you felt about it. I mean, I know this whole museum kick is important to you." She thought for a minute and then continued. "Shit, I don't even sound like me anymore. You see what love does. It makes women into male chauvinists. I'm not doing what *I* want to do but what I think will make *you* happy. Does that sound like me?"

He turned and lay beside her, nuzzling her hair. "I am an old fool," he whispered.

"Because you love me?" He answered yes without saying anything. Now she held him to her. "You may not know it, Livie, because you've been so hung up for so many years, but you do love me. Like an old-fashioned love affair. Just like the Late Show and all the old movies. It scares me sometimes. I didn't think people my age could love like that anymore. It scares me because I want to. I want to love like that, be possessed by it. I want to be one of those all-for-love ladies."

It was hard for him to say because he did not know how, but he thought about it and finally said, "I didn't know I could feel like this."

She clutched him, fingernails digging into flesh, then laughed and roughly pushed him away. "You just thought your prick would never get hard again. That isn't love, that's rejuvenation. That's me, the great rejuvenator."

"Maybe it started like that," Stonehill said. "Maybe that's all I wanted it to be."

She thrust herself against him, this time to seek comfort rather than to be the comforter. He wrapped his arms around her and held her hard as she cried. "I'm so fucked up," she whispered. "You've got me so fucked up I don't know who I am. Sniveling around to ask if I can go to a stuffed-shirt dance." She threw her head back and looked at him. "By the way, can I?"

He used to smile at his daughter like this, full of love, understanding and worldly wisdom. "If you don't let him lay you."

"Fuck him. I mean I don't want to fuck him. We're not even talking about fucking. I wasn't sure you'd want me to be there because of your wife and daughter. Would it embarrass you?"

"No, I can handle that. I may be terribly jealous, but tell him you'll go. You can't spend your whole life waiting for me to slip my key in the back door. I never asked for that and I don't expect it."

"You really don't understand what I'm talking about, do you? You can't get it through that thick upper-crust skull of yours that I am the truly liberated broad. Miss Liberation, in person. I don't do one damn thing that I don't want to do, except maybe go to the synagogue on Yom Kippur. If I didn't want to sit on my ass and wait for you to show up at the back door, I wouldn't do it. Can't you understand that? I'm not giving up a single thing because of you. I'm doing this for my own pleasure. It's what I want to do, more than anything. Is that clear?"

This time they both clutched, each one giving and absorbing strength. She whispered in his ear, "Forget the tennis game. Stay here with me. Please stay here."

"I love you," Stonehill said, and then after he said it, realized that it had not been so difficult to say. The words hung in the room like heavy smoke, and to cut it he said, "Besides, I've gotten it up four times since eight o'clock last night. That's my world record, and I'm going to retire a champion." He broke away, took his athletic supporter from his tennis bag and put it on, thinking that he could have done it a fifth time, then got into his tennis shorts, sat on the bed and began to lace his Adidas. "I'll call you later."

"What time does her plane get in?"

"Four-ten. I'm going to the airport. I'll call you when I get home, while she's getting settled."

"I may not be here."

"Okay, I'll find you later."

"I may go to Butch's and pick up a young stud."

"I'll still call you later."

"Haven't you got a jealous bone in your body?"

"Every bone," he answered. He slipped the pants of his warm-up suit up over his shorts, put on the jacket, zipped it up and looked for a mirror. "You ought to have a mirror in this bedroom. All you have is this lousy art. For a girl who works with art every day, your personal collection is horrendous."

"I don't buy any of it. An artist comes in, and if I like his stuff I'll lay him for a canvas. Can I help it if all the good artists are either dykes or gay?"

"You know what you ought to do?"

"What?"

"Go out and buy yourself an extravagant new dress for the Art Institute Party."

"If you're going to leave money on the dresser again . . ."

He took his wallet out of his tennis bag and put a stack of bills on the dresser. "Do it for me. Be ravishing."

"Take your fucking money and shove it, Stonehill. Shove it."

"Do it for me. Be so ravishing that all my cronies will covet you."

"You'll be running the risk that Mr. Stock Options will rape me before we get out of this apartment."

"Do it for me." He came over to the bed, leaned down and kissed the top of her head. "I'll talk to you later."

As he reached the door of the bedroom, her little-girl voice called out to him. "Livie?"

"What?"

"We're a damn unlikely pair, aren't we? But it works. Jesus, it sure works."

"You bet it works." He dropped his tennis bag and went back to her, and into her hair and eyes and the secret places of her body he kept mumbling the words, "You bet it works."

Sunday, February 13
Ten a.m., Lake Forest

SHELDON COLE played tennis the way he did everything else, with precision and a ferocious determination to win. The physical power of his body was no longer raw energy; time and money had refined that, and a professional tennis coach kept the power honed to a gentlemanly perfection. Stonehill watched him slam returns from the automatic ball machine, the sound of perfect impact after perfect impact resounding in the indoor court. Even against the inanimate machine Cole was fiercely competitive, his ego dependent on each shot, and he remained immaculate throughout the constant exertion—not a sign of sweat, not a wrinkle in his Gucci shorts, not a hair out of place.

He's come a long way, Stonehill was thinking. In the three years since he had last seen him, Sheldon Cole had changed from a tough, redneck, overmuscled thug to this sleek animal, tanned deeply and evenly, manicured and barbered into his own immaculate conception of what a gentlemen is. But inside he would still be the same, Stonehill knew. Now there was a tennis racket to fight with instead of raw fists, a public company instead of a street gang, a long, blond gentile wife instead of the dark, round Jewish girl he had been married to when he first arrived from Scranton. Stonehill had seen his kind come and go; inside, where it counted, Sheldon Cole would still be the same.

Cole saw Stonehill watching him from the side of the court and switched off the ball machine with a remote control from his pocket. "I didn't see you come in. Sorry I kept you standing there." They shook hands quickly, Stonehill feeling the power of his grip. "The doubles game fell through at the last minute and it was too late to call you." Cole's voice had turned softer; the singsong intonation of second-generation Jews had been trained out of it. "Hell, why am I lying? There never was a doubles game. I wanted to see you alone." He touched Stonehill's arm and led him to a group of chairs around a table. "How do you like it? It was just finished about three weeks ago. Those bastard contractors should have had it done three months ago. Three months late and three times as much dough as it should have cost, but what the hell."

"I'm impressed. I don't know many people with their own indoor court. It's beautiful." Stonehill unzipped the jacket of his warm-up suit. Though it was cold outside, the sun coming through the huge skylight dome was hot. "I haven't been in this house since Sewell Gardiner lived here. It looks a lot different."

"You bet your sweet ass it's different—one million three different. I bet that old bastard is spinning in his grave knowing that a Jew-boy from Scranton is living here. That bastard kept this whole area restricted as long as he lived. They gave me a hell of a time when I wanted to buy it. Covenants, gentlemen's agreements—you name it. But that didn't stop me, not once I made up my mind that this was the way I wanted to live."

"What about the neighbors, how have they taken it?"

"Fuck the neighbors." He smiled. "As a matter of fact, it's not such bad fucking with these neighbors. I've tried it with a few of them. There's no hotter pants in the world than a suburban housewife after her old man catches the eight-ten and the kids go off on the school bus. Their neighborhood may be restricted, but their cunts sure as hell aren't." Cole moved his chair closer to Stonehill. "Look, let's not shit around—how do we stand, you and me? Are bygones bygone?"

"What's on your mind?"

"Tennis for openers. We can play singles. The word is that you still hit a mean ball."

"For a man my age, you mean."

"What have you got on me? Ten years? Maybe not even that. It means nothing when you stay in your kind of shape." He grabbed Stonehill's arm. "Like a rock. I bet you still fuck like a rabbit, too."

"Okay, tennis is for openers. Then what?"

"I want to talk. We haven't talked for a long time." Cole looked behind him, making certain that they were alone. "My wife is somewhere," he explained. "What those shiksas don't know won't hurt them."

"How is Diane?"

"She's fine, fine," and he dismissed the subject. "Look here," he started, then changed his mind, then started again. "We've had our problems, you and me. And maybe it was my fault, maybe I got pissed-off at something you couldn't help. Maybe I was so pissed-off I couldn't see it at the time. You know what I mean?"

Cole had wanted to join a downtown club and a country club, and had asked Stonehill to sponsor him, using his vast business with the bank as a wedge. Gently, explaining the requisites, Stonehill had refused. Working through another group, Cole was finally proposed for membership and turned down. He came back to Stonehill, accusing him of blackballing him and threatening to withdraw his business from the bank. Again Stonehill had refused to be his sponsor.

"You're bluffing, Livie," Cole had said. "You could do it if you wanted to. I don't care how much class you've got, a buck is a buck, and you're not a dumb enough cocksucker to let all my dough walk out of here. You guys worship a buck as much as I do, and if you want to keep my dough you've got to play golf with me, eat with me, invite me to your house and let me fuck your friends if I want to. Is that clear?"

"It's very clear," Stonehill had said, standing up. "Call me tomorrow."

"That's better, Livie, that's better. You all have your price, haven't you?"

"Call me tomorrow and tell me the name of your new bank. I will have arranged for the transfer of all your accounts and underwritings, as well as the loans. Get new checks printed; in three days everything with your name on it will be in the dead file." He walked to the door and held it open. Cole did not move. Stonehill waited.

"Son-of-a-bitch. You think you're calling a bluff in a penny-ante poker game? We're talking about real money." Then he stood up. "Okay, but it isn't a bluff. I've got the royal flush. And you know what you got, Stonehill? You got bubkes. But you're probably too high-class a Jew to understand plain Yiddish. You got bubkes—nothing, not a fucking dime." He had streaked out of the room, not even looking at Stonehill as he left.

Cole had been right; he had been holding the big hand. In the last few years his wealth had increased ten times. His business acumen was brilliant, his timing perfect. The directors of the bank had sympathized with Stonehill, admiring his steadfastness to principle, but gave him a bad time nonetheless, pointing out alternate solutions and more diplomatic methods that could have been used to save the account. At almost every board meeting Cole's name came up in one reference or another, and each time there was a polite but embittered discussion on how the incident could have been handled differently, suggestions about how to court Cole again and regain at least a portion of the business which had been lost. Stonehill always remained silent during these sessions, sometimes wondering if the situation were to happen again whether he would handle it the same way.

When Cole had called him at home on Saturday morning his first impulse had been to hang up, but he had a responsibility to the bank and the board. He knew the tennis game was a device, and that the other two men making up the doubles game, both large customers of the bank, were bait.

It was Cole's trap, Stonehill was thinking; let him spring it.

"You're not making this easy for me," Cole said. "In my own dumb way, I'm apologizing to you. I'm not a man who ever apologizes, it's not part of my make-up. I'm saying to you that you were wrong, dead wrong, but that I was wrong too. I was pissed-off and hurt—hurt mostly, I guess." He put both hands on the binding of his racket. "What about it, are bygones bygones?"

"Let's play tennis."

"You arrogant son-of-a-bitch." Cole laughed. "You haven't got balls enough to say that you understand and that maybe you were pissed-off too. I take it back; you're not arrogant, you're scared. You're afraid that if you let your guard down with anybody but your own kind you'll get hurt."

"I can skip the analysis."

"Let's not both make the same mistake twice."

Stonehill thought for a moment, of many things, so it was hard for him to think of the right words. Finally he smiled. "Bygones. Good enough?"

"Good enough."

"What's on your mind, Shellie?"

Cole looked toward the door again; then, satisfied that they were alone, he said, "I'm going to ask you one question. If you answer no, that's the end of it, we play tennis period. Okay?"

"Okay."

"Have you been personally threatened in any way in the last week?"

Cole was looking at him intently, and by the time Stonehill looked away it was already too late; because he had not instantly said no, his silence said yes. No longer could he write off Shaw as a demented crank intruding on the smooth structure of his life. He looked back at Cole. "How did you know?"

The cocksure expression on Cole's face disintegrated; even his suntan bronze paled. In this split-second degeneration, Stonehill saw another frightened man; then Cole's defense tightened, and his face became hard and unyielding again. "You've been rich for so long, Livie, for so many generations, that you've forgotten what it's like out there, outside your bank and your private clubs. How do I know?" He leaned closer. "I know because I'm like they are; I think like they do. I haven't got Harvard smarts like your crowd, I have street smarts, like them. God help me, I'm just like them, whoever they are." He let his voice drop and sat deeper in the chair. "They forgot that I'm their kind of smart when they came after me. They looked at this house and my cars and my custom-tailored suits and the polish on my fingernails, and they forgot that underneath I'm just like them. After all I've accomplished, I'm still just like those motherfuckers." For a moment there was sadness and a bewilderment in his face; then he toughened again. "How did I know that they'd go after you? That part was easy. Once I put together the pieces and understood their plan, it was easy. And the plan is brilliant. They rob Israel of hundreds of million dollars without firing a gun or throwing a bomb. Somebody real smart figured this one out. It has guerrilla balls but it's more high-level than that. It's like forcing bankruptcy, merging corporations, fucking the tax laws, rigging the market or playing futures. You have to have both the head for it and the balls for it. And simple—Jesus, it's so simple."

Cole stood up and walked around the table swinging his racket. "You were easy to figure out, Livie. You had to be their number one pigeon. You're the perfect target, I saw that right away. When I went through a list of major contributors to the Jewish United Fund, your name was in neon lights."

"There are larger contributors than I."

"Yah, but that's not the point. They couldn't afford to touch the guys emotionally involved with Israel—the nuts who see it as the Jewish homeland, the fanatics who make religious pilgrimages there. Throw out the religious nuts and the guys on an ego trip who have a school or a forest named after them. They're bad risks for this kind of blackmail. They can be smart as hell and tough as nails about everything else, but they have a fervor about Israel that won't let them think straight. These guys are going to call the FBI or the State Department, or

Golda Meir, Abba Eban and Jerry Ford. They'd organize rabbis and congregations. And the press would eat it up, blast it over every front page and never let up. Those guys would defy the threats, and some of them would get hurt, even killed, but you know what that would mean: more dollars pouring into Israel, more than after the Yom Kippur war. And even the goyim would become indignant and reach in their pockets. Congress would respond by allocating more dough to Israel, more machines, more weapons." Cole sat down again. "No, sir. You don't touch that kind of bastard in this plan. I told you it was brilliant. You go after the major contributors who aren't emotionally involved—the intellectually involved, the socially pressured contributors. You go after the Jews who are Jews by accident, not religiously committed. You get my thinking?"

Stonehill nodded, feeling inadequate and suddenly old. He hated Sheldon Cole and was fascinated by the man's mind.

"So when you cross those bastards off the list, who's left with the big dough? Not many. So which are the smart ones, which are the financial men, guys who understand concepts and ideas? The only targets that this will work on are people who understand the concept of money. Let's say it like it is: you look for guys you can blackmail. What's the easiest way to blackmail a guy? Puss. Old-fashioned puss. It gets to us all and it makes us all vulnerable. And if it isn't puss, it's kids. Nobody wants his kid killed or messed up. And when you have both kids and a cunt stashed away, it's bingo!" He leaned toward Stonehill. "Bingo? It is bingo, isn't it, Livie?"

Stonehill did not know what to say, so he nodded.

"Son-of-a-bitch. Even you." Cole's laugh resounded in the arena. "I bluffed that, Livie. I didn't figure you for puss, not Mr. High-and-mighty. Not the dream couple, not the nonsectarian pillars of the community. I didn't figure you for puss. I didn't know how to figure you, but I knew you were on their list; you had to be number one. You're the perfect target. The higher you're up, the farther to fall. If I weren't part of this, I could enjoy it in a way. All the fancy clubs that want one Jew-boy, but not *this* Jew-boy," pointing a finger at himself. "All the fancy boards of directors who want one Jew-boy but not *this*

Jew-boy. The bigger they are, the harder they fall. I wish I was on the sidelines, watching."

"Christians to Lions. Jews to Arabs. Your kind of spectator sport. For a long time I thought maybe there was something decent behind your loud mouth, but you're a bastard, Cole, all the way through." Stonehill stood up and began zipping up the jacket of his warm-up suit.

"For Christ's sake, Livie, sit down. Are you so insulated that you can't see the danger?" Cole's voice broke slightly. "Don't you have any compassion?"

"Compassion for what?" But he sat down again. "I didn't think you knew that word, Shellie. Compassion is not a Sheldon Cole kind of word."

"What kind of goy blindness do you have, Livie? Can't you see that I'm scared shitless? I don't see why you're not. I believe that those anonymous bastards mean every word they say, that they'll make every threat come true. You can't sit on your ass and figure it can't happen. It *can* happen and it *will* happen. Don't you see that?"

The hard edge was gone from Stonehill's voice. "I've believed it and I haven't believed it. Now you have forced me to believe it again."

"Then for Christ's sake have some compassion. Lower your standards for one minute and try to imagine how I feel." He looked around again to make certain that they were still alone. "I'll confess something funny, Livie. They didn't get me on puss. You can't blackmail or threaten a man with something that everyone believes he does anyway. I have no reputation in that department to ruin."

"How did they get you?"

Cole took a long time to answer. "Kids," he said finally. "My two kids. Not the ones by my first wife but the two kids upstairs in this house. You ought to see them, Livie; you wouldn't believe that they're mine. I have two goy babies upstairs, all pink and blond and blue-eyed with little turned-up noses. You wouldn't believe how beautiful they are, you wouldn't believe that they're mine." He leaned forward, lowering the volume of his voice. "Do you know what they're going to do? Nothing

simple like kidnapping them or killing them—not those bastards. They're going to mutilate them, disfigure them, turn them
into some kind of freaks . . . but not kill them, they made that
very clear. They want me to see those tortured faces grow up,
they want me to watch their wrath carved on my kids' faces for
the rest of my life. Those poor kids, the only people in this
whole fucking world that really mean anything to me." Uncontrolled, a piercing sob came from inside him. He put his hands
over his face, muffling the sounds, hiding the tears of terror.

Cole regained control and wiped the tear stains from his face.
"You know what those kids will be like if those cocksuckers
don't destroy them? They'll grow up to be like you, Livie, beautiful and unscathed like you. They wouldn't have to fight every
inch of the way, to batter down closed doors. Like you, Livie,
all the doors would open automatically for them. They're born
rich and they're born beautiful."

"You have a distorted picture of me," Stonehill said, surprised at the tremor in his own voice.

Cole smiled and shook his head. "No, I don't. You have a
distorted picture of yourself. Can't you see that for my whole
life I've wanted to be you? Even before there was a you, I
wanted to be you. I hated my mother because she let me be
whelped in a ghetto, and I hated my father because he never
lifted a finger to get us out of it. So I fought my way up and now
I have all the symbols but I don't have *it*. Can you understand
that? What was predetermined for you, I had to get the hard
way. I fought for it all, like a street fighter. But not those kids
upstairs. They're born to it, Livie, the way you were. Now those
cocksuckers are going to take their knives and destroy the only
chance I have to . . ." He could not say any more. The tears had
started again and he let them come, an unchecked catharsis.

Stonehill could find no words. A different man would have
touched Cole's slumped shoulders to communicate compassion
and understanding, but Stonehill was immobilized by the code
of behavior which made any display of emotion unmanly and in
bad form. Only with Myrna had this inbred reserve begun to
break down. He thought about Myrna now, fantasized himself
back in her bed, submitting to her sexual abandon.

"You arrogant son-of-a-bitch, you fucking, stuck-up Jew snob." Cole's strength was coming back as he spoke, his shoulders straightening, his head lifting. "You haven't understood one thing I've told you. You're so God-damned insulated that nothing penetrates, does it? You bastards never change, nothing can touch that armor you're born with. You're all so—"

Stonehill indicated with his eyes and by standing up that Cole should say no more. Diane Cole was coming through the sliding glass doors onto the tennis court, her high heels clattering against the floor. Cole wiped his face with a tennis towel and set his jaw, his strength tenuously restored.

Central Casting could not have provided a more perfect woman than Diane Tugwell Fitzsimmons Cole as one of the featured players in the life of Sheldon Cole. She was the symbol incarnate of her husband's ambition, Stonehill realized now, just as he himself was a symbol of another kind to Cole.

She was squinting into the bright light of the tennis court, a fur coat slung over her shoulders. Her hair was long, frosted blond, and she walked quickly with the inborn grace of a fashion model. "Livie, I can't believe my own eyes. Shellie just said that he had a tennis game, and I didn't even ask." She offered Stonehill a white-gloved hand to shake and a cheek to be pecked, the standard ritualistic behavior of the Lake Forest animal. "Why didn't you tell me, Shellie? You know how I adore this man." Then back to Stonehill. "You continue to be the most attractive man I know, Livie. You were my first crush, and I've never really quite gotten over it." She moved to stand behind her husband, her arms around his neck, her lips touching the top of his head. "You were mean not to tell me that it was Livie who was coming to play tennis. I've wasted a half-hour on my hair when I could have been here with the two of you. Now I have to go to church; the Fairweathers are picking me up at any moment." She looked up at Stonehill. "It is divine to see you, Livie. You conjure up memories of old, marvelous times."

"Where are the kids?" Cole interrupted.

"In the playroom with Nanny. They're quite all right. Stop being a Jewish mother."

"I only asked, for Christ's sake."

"Livie, tell me about Maude," Diane said, "I haven't seen her for ages. How is she?"

"She's fine. She's due back from Palm Springs this afternoon. She'll be in town for a few days."

"Of course—I forgot you had a pad there. I hear it's super." She moved her cheek back and forth across the top of her husband's head. "She must be coming in for the ball at the Art Institute this week. I read about it in the paper. I also read about you all the time. You're doing some kind of thing for Dinky, too, aren't you?"

"Who the fuck is Dinky?"

"Your senator, darling," Diane explained.

"It's a fund-raising dinner for Israel," Stonehill said.

"He fucking well needs it," Cole grumbled, "after all that horseshit he's been giving out about the Arabs."

"The dinner isn't until next Sunday," Stonehill said. "I doubt if Maude will stay for it. Interferes with the Desert Classic. I was lucky to get her off the golf course long enough to come in for the party."

Diane asked, "When is it?"

"Wednesday night. Aren't you coming?"

Diane shook her head. "Those things aren't part of my life anymore."

Cole said, "Tell him the truth, tell him we weren't invited. Your old man donated a whole fucking wing and you weren't invited because you're married to me."

Stonehill felt his face go red and fumbled for a word, but Diane's timing was as impeccable as always. "How do you like Shellie's new toy?" She gestured to the huge arena. "The world's largest adult playpen." Her heels clattered as she walked around the edge of the court, the sun through the skylight spotlighting her beauty. "The only problem is that the other boys in the neighborhood don't ever come over to play with him."

"Fuck them."

Diane walked back to the table. "Explain to him, Livie, that it isn't because he's a Jew that they don't come over to play. That isn't it at all. Explain to him, Livie, that it's because he's such an insufferable bastard."

"Cunt!" Cole retaliated.

Diane laughed and nuzzled his head again. "Of course I am, darling, and a super one. But that isn't why you love me, is it, Shellie?" She looked up at Stonehill. "You know why he loves me, don't you, Livie? After all, you are my banker."

"I don't need your fucking money. Stonehill knows that."

Diane ignored the interruption. "And you knew my father and mother and my ex-husband, and you know what a beautiful, glamorous, Waspish life I used to live."

Stonehill spanned the generation gap between Boynton Tugwell and his daughter. Diane's father was a customer of the bank, a large manufacturer of farm machinery, and it was through this connection that Stonehill, as a young man, had met Diane. He was first aware of her as one of three children running through the large granite house on Lake Shore Drive, a child to be patted on the head. When he had made a perfunctory appearance at her debut some years later, he had been surprised by the dazzling woman who had emerged from the nondescript child. They had danced in the great hall and sat on the steps drinking spiked punch while she giggled a confession of her schoolgirl crush, teasing him because he had ignored her, taunting him as a woman taunts a man. He had been tempted, but remembered his responsibilities to the bank and to Maude, whom he knew he would eventually marry.

The society pages chronicled the progress of Diane Tugwell from her debut until her marriage to Kenneth Fitzsimmons. Together they were everyone's dream couple, beautiful and rich. The public idyll of their romance persisted even while the marriage itself disintegrated.

It was inevitable that Sheldon Cole and Diane Fitzsimmons would find each other, and when they did, their affair blazed on the tongues of LaSalle Street and Lake Forest. They loved and fought oblivious to the scandal they were creating. Cole set up financial security for the round Jewish girl he had brought from Scranton and sent her back to Scranton. Diane divorced Fitzsimmons and left him alone and bewildered, a pitiable figure skulking around cocktail parties, drinking too much, boring people with invectives against that Jewish bastard who had destroyed his marriage. His vapid good looks had begun to sag, he was no longer decorative or sober enough to be the extra man, and gradually he disappeared from the social scene.

The sound of a horn in the driveway brought Stonehill back to the present. "That must be the Fairweathers. It's time for church. Livie, darling, it's been divine seeing you again." She offered her cheek and he ceremoniously pecked at it. "My love to Maude." She turned to her husband. "The Fairweathers want to have brunch at the club. I haven't been there for ages. Will you be all right? Nanny can fix you lunch when she gets the children settled." She kissed him lightly and swept toward the sliding doors.

Cole called after her. "Hey, cunt." She stopped and turned toward him. "Come here."

She smiled, replaying a many-times-played game. "Come and get it."

Cole stood up, a smile twisting his mouth, and started toward her. "I said, come here, cunt."

"And I said, come and get it." As she started toward him the fur coat fell from her shoulders to the marble floor.

They met halfway, two animals clutching at each other with open-mouthed passion alternating with vengeance. Stonehill turned away, knowing more than he wanted to know. The threats to his world were compounding at a dizzying pace. He heard her call, "Goodbye, Livie," and the clatter of her heels. There was no point in answering; she was already gone.

Cole walked with his old confidence again, the stocky stride of a middleweight. "Come on, Stonehill, let's play tennis. I'm going to beat the ass off you."

Stonehill started to protest; there was so much that needed saying between them. But then he thought that perhaps Cole was right; hard physical exertion was what they needed to clear the air between them. Slowly he took off his warm-up suit as Cole waited on the court, knees bent, racket in position, ready to murder the first ball over the net.

Cole won the first two games easily, but the third went to deuce four times before he finally pulled it out. Then, playing to Cole's weaknesses, Stonehill took the next four games and won the set 8–6.

Sunday, February 13
Four p.m., O'Hare Airport

AMERICAN FLIGHT 786 from Palm Springs was posted as being forty minutes late. Stonehill waited in the Admiral's Club, sitting in the darkest corner he could find, drinking a Scotch slowly, trying to sort out the confusions in his mind. After tennis he and Cole had sat in the sauna trading information, guessing at the identities of other victims, discussing possible courses of action and rejecting them all. There seemed to be no solution but compliance, and compliance was impossible. There was no longer any doubt that the threats were real, the plot against them not simply terrorist tactics but a highly technical plan instrumented and implemented by frightening knowledge of each of them, both of their day-to-day routines and of the secrets of their lives.

Rationally Stonehill had to admit to himself that Myrna Gordon might not be an accident in his life. Cole had planted that doubt, and now it was festering. If Myrna was part of this Arab organization, she would make love and die for it as others had. With what he knew—and more important, what he did not know—about her, he could construct an airtight case against her. But emotionally, he believed none of this, only the renaissance that she had created in his life. It was an unending syllogistic dialogue: yes, she is, no, she isn't.

From the darkness near him a voice said, "How goes it, Sir Stonehill?"

Only one person had ever called him Sir Stonehill. He was forced to catch his breath before looking up. "Hello, Whiz. What are you doing here?"

"Don't blow the whistle. This is not the return of the prodigal ex-son-in-law. I'm catching a plane, nothing more."

"Where have you been? We didn't know if you were dead or alive."

He stepped closer, into the light. He was a tall young man, tight and sinewy, his muscular construction outlined by tight blue jeans and tight T-shirt with a Schlitz label printed across the front, the label distorted by his high pectorals. His eyes were bright blue, almost as intense as the turquoise necklace he wore. Light refracted from a tiny silver object dangling at the base of his neck. "Did you care? Did any of you care?" He held up his hand. "Don't answer that. Everything unpleasant between us has already been said. The coincidence of seeing you here threw me momentarily." He sat down opposite Stonehill. "I've been in South America," he explained, "with an oil company. I've just come from La Paz on my way to Los Angeles. Lousy trip. La Paz to Miami, Miami to Chicago, Chicago to L.A."

"You look different, Whiz—younger . . . better. More alive, maybe."

"I am more alive, more alive than I've ever been."

Stonehill, hesitated, then asked, "Are you married again?"

"No."

"Aren't you going to ask about Susan or young Stoney?"

Crossley shook his head, the little object on the necklace sparkling. Stonehill identified it as a tiny spider, meticulously crafted. "You're talking about people who don't exist for me anymore. You saw to that."

"No rehash, Whiz. Like you said, it's over. Susan is fine, she hasn't remarried either. Your son is a super kid, but you have to discount a grandfather's prejudice. He's like you in so many ways. Not the precocious kind of genius you were . . . I suppose we should be grateful for that . . . but bright as hell and . . ." Stonehill took out his wallet and opened it to a picture of Stoney.

His ex-son-in-law stopped him. "I don't want to see or hear anything. I've conditioned my mind to forget. It's blanked out, erased like data from a computer tape. I shouldn't have said hello. I should have seen you as just another face, with no connection to the past."

Stonehill smiled. "I'm glad you said hello, Whiz. Funny, now that all the bitterness is over, I'm really glad to see you. I feel better knowing that you're well and vital again."

"Are you going to tell her?"

"Susan? Tell her that I saw you? I don't know. I'm not sure that I ought to. I'll ask Maude what to do. She's about to land from Palm Springs. Her judgment is better about these things than mine."

"Don't tell her." Crossley's voice was a command, his jaw stiff.

"Maude?"

"Or Susan. This meeting is an accident that should not have happened. Erase it."

"I'm afraid I don't have your kind of discipline, Whiz. There's an excitement about seeing you again. I'm not sure that I'll be able to keep it to myself."

"Think about it, Sir Stonehill. My way is right for everyone involved."

"Perhaps your way is right, but I'm not sure that I'm not too human to be able to carry it off."

The hostess interrupted them. "Mr. Stonehill, 786 has picked up some time. It will be landing in five minutes at gate number seven."

"Thank you." He stood up. "I always wish it could have been different, Whiz. In many ways I miss you, and I think about you a great deal."

"You had your chance."

Stonehill nodded sadly. "We all have our chances. It's knowing when to take advantage of them, isn't it?" He held out his hand, but the other man did not take it. "Goodbye, Whiz. Good luck."

"Never more, Sir Stonehill. Quoth the spider, never more, never more." But Sir Stonehill was out of range and did not hear the incantation.

Maude Stonehill was one of the first passengers to come through the jetway. She was talking rapidly to another sun-tanned woman, walking quickly, not looking around for him.

Some of his resolve dissolved when he saw her. She was still a handsome woman, and he saw her as she used to be and as she was now. If she had been a stranger he would still be looking at her, admiring her sleek body, coiffed gray hair, bright blue eyes and slightly craggy face burned brown by the wind and sun. The vague sensuality he felt bewildered him. He dismissed it as the stimulus of the familiar, but he knew that it was more than that. Resolves were easily made when he was not confronted with real persons who loved him. Self-oriented decisions were easy when he was alone, but though these decisions were logical, and based on fact, they did not, he realized now, include the fact of love.

She was saying to her traveling companion, "Then I chipped on to the third green, and Ethel—"

He interrupted when she was almost past him.

"Livie." She was surprised. "Darling, I didn't see you." She leaned toward him, and in one practiced maneuver he kissed her lightly and transferred her cosmetic bag to his hand. "You know Catherine Allen, don't you, darling?" She made a vague gesture toward the woman beside her. "We're giving her a ride into town. She only lives at 1500. Did you forget my mink coat?"

He had. He always brought it when she came back from Palm Springs. "I'm sorry," he said. "The car will be warm."

"It doesn't matter, really." Then she seemed to see him for the first time, and a shade of concern clouded her face. "I'm glad to see you, darling. It's been a dreadful bore without you." Then to the woman beside her, "You do know, Livie, don't you, Catherine?" Stonehill and the woman grimaced social smiles at each other and touched hands. "I do wish you hadn't forgotten my coat. It would be the worse time in the world to catch cold. I have a million and one things to do."

"I brought the big car. I told Carl to keep the heater on."

Stonehill had planned the drive back into town as a time for being alone with his wife, in which he could test the sentences he had prepared and determine how much of the truth to tell her. He had even made certain that the glass partition between the front and back seat was closed to ensure a private conversation. He was hurt because he had expected that she would want this time alone together as much as he did, to reestablish communication. Catherine Allen would spoil that; they would sit in the back seat rehashing their adventures on the golf course, and he would be in the front listening to the hockey game on the radio and continuing his discussion about the Blackhawks with Carl. Their time alone would have to wait until they were home, and then it would be interrupted by servants and the telephone, which would mean a further delay until they were in the privacy of their bedroom. He had wanted to avoid that; it would be awkward. Even after all their years of marriage it would be more awkward than usual, adding the ingredient of the life he was living without her and what had happened these last few days. There would be time to decide if he should tell her about seeing Whiz again.

"Darling!" She stopped walking. "I almost forgot. Irving Feldman was on our flight. He was stand-by and almost didn't get on. He's frantic about something and desperate to talk to you—said he's been trying to call you since last night. He promised it would only take a minute. Wait here for him; he was sitting way back in the coach sections. Catherine and I will walk ahead and meet you at the baggage claim."

Before he could protest or answer, she started walking again, talking rapidly to Catherine Allen as though he wasn't there. Stonehill moved to the side of the corridor and leaned against the wall, watching endless hordes of people moving in both directions, his eyes alert for the face of Irving Feldman. One more element was being added to the picture in his mind, but Irving Feldman did not fit the pattern. By Sheldon Cole's logic, there was no way Feldman could be a part of this.

Irving Feldman was a character from a Saul Bellow novel: comic on the surface, miserable inside, deeply intellectual and deadly effective. Stonehill often kidded him about being the Jewish Abraham Lincoln, equating Feldman's impoverished West Side origins to Lincoln's log cabin. And just as Lincoln in later years used his humble beginnings to make a political or diplomatic point, so did Feldman. Now a brilliant lawyer, the head of a vast and powerful firm, Feldman would invariably interject into high-level negotiations a story from his boyhood, usually involving his immigrant father struggling with the new language, or his mother using her old-country wiles to hold the family together. But what at first appeared to be an indulgence became in retrospect a shrewd showman's maneuver to gain time, to hammer home a point of legality or to make opposing positions less tenable.

Now Stonehill saw him, approaching from the distance, a little man with stooped shoulders, heavy eyeglasses and a rumpled hat, carrying a briefcase in each hand as though weighted by the importance of their contents.

The little man squinted, then smiled when he recognized Stonehill, and walked over to him juggling the briefcases until he was free to shake hands. "What a trip. The last minute. Call the airlines. Call them back. My wife is shrieking and it's hot. I'm trying to pack. I have to break a date in Beverly Hills. Then I'm stand-by and have to fly tourist with screaming kids on both sides of me. It's not worth it. I'm too old for this. It's like high-class ambulance chasing. Who needs it?"

Stonehill was thinking, *Get to the point,* but he said only, "You look good, Irv. Looks like you had time for some of that California sunshine."

Feldman hunched his shoulders. "Not enough, not enough." He started walking, Stonehill falling in beside him, taking short steps so that he would not outpace the little man. "I called you all day, even from the airport. And late last night. No one knew where you were. I even called your secretary at home—what a megillah that was, finding your secretary. Never mind, when I saw your wife on the flight it was like a mitzvah, I knew that I would see you here."

"What's the problem?"

"What's the problem? What's always the problem? People. People are always the problem. You know that from your own business." Stonehill slowed; Feldman seemed out of breath.

"Let me carry one of the briefcases, Irv."

"Thank you. That's very sweet." Taking the case, Stonehill found it surprisingly weightless against the balance of his wife's cosmetic bag. "Did Mrs. Mandlebaum reach you from Florida?" Feldman asked.

"Mousey?" The surprise in Stonehill's voice was automatic.

"Mousey," Feldman echoed, putting a Hasidic chant to the sound of the name. "To you she's Mousey, one of your crowd. To me she's Mrs. Mandlebaum, and Mrs. Mandlebaum is a very important client both personally and the whole Mandlebaum estate. Otherwise you think I would have made this terrible trip?"

"What about her?"

"Who knows what about her? She's hysterical. She was calling you all day from Palm Beach. She wakes me up at five o'clock in the morning, she doesn't know from the time difference between Florida and California. She calls you and then she calls me. Such a tizzy."

Now it began to make sense. Mousey Mandlebaum would fit in Sheldon Cole's concept of the plot. "What's on her mind?" Stonehill kept his voice controlled.

"I couldn't figure out. She wouldn't tell me straight out. She was asking all kinds of cockamamie questions about breaking trusts and liquid financial positions. It didn't make sense. You'd have thought the Russians had just landed at Fort Lauderdale. I don't know what she was talking about, but I do know that she was just this side of hysterical."

"That's not like her. She usually keeps her cool." Stonehill was considering Feldman as a possible confidant. He wondered if Sheldon Cole would agree. Like Cole, Feldman had come up the hard way, fortifying education and experience with street smarts. There was probably not a smarter lawyer in the city. But he had an acceptance in the community and the country as a whole which Cole did not have. Feldman manipulated easily on local and state political levels, but his great asset was his influence and mobility at the federal level. He had been on presidential advisory commissions under both administrations, always remaining apolitical, the aura of the pundit from Chicago increasing with each assignment, even after the Nixon debacle. He had instantaneous access to all levels of the State Department, had been on a first-name basis with J. Edgar

Hoover and Allen Dulles, and still kept his contacts with the FBI and CIA intact. If, as he and Sheldon Cole had discussed, they needed a representative, Feldman might be exactly the right man. Stonehill decided to talk it over with Cole first, but he also knew that he would have to get to Mousey Mandlebaum before she had a chance to talk to Feldman.

"Maybe," Stonehill continued, "she's having trouble with one of the young studs she keeps around. That's happened before."

Feldman stopped, catching his breath, and looked up quizzically at Stonehill. "I've heard whispers about that. I can hardly believe it. Young studs. Such a nice, quiet lady like that." He shook his head sadly at the world. "That nice dowager, the pillar of the Jewish community."

"She's not even Jewish," Stonehill said, and then realized that Feldman must already know the whole Mandlebaum story.

"I forgot that. She's always so identified with Jewish causes that I forgot."

Stonehill knew that Feldman forgot nothing, but he waited for the next tactical move.

"Of course. I remember the whole story now. An Irish maid in his father's house. A terrible scandal that reached all the way from the South Side to Division Street, where my father had a tailor shop. Such a scandal. Well, it had a happy ending. From Irish housemaid to Jewish queen." He shook his head. "As my friend Harry says, only in America, only in America."

They began to walk again. "Her plane arrives tonight at ten o'clock from Palm Beach. She insists on a meeting at her apartment at eleven tonight. That's why she was trying to reach you; she wants you there too." They were going down the moving staircase to the baggage level. "I tried to talk her into seeing some of the boys from our trust department, but she insists that I be there personally. What do I know about trusts anymore? Nothing. It's a whole field by itself. Nothing like what I learned in law school. That's why we have the headache of ninety-six lawyers in the firm. Specialists, specialists, overhead, overhead. Who needs it? And who needs midnight meetings?"

Stonehill sensed that Feldman was manipulating him, and he felt some satisfaction that he was turning the manipulation to his own advantage. "Tell you what, Irv. I'll keep the date with Mousey, calm her down, find out what's really going on. I'll call you from her apartment and set up a meeting for tomorrow if she still wants it."

"Would you do that? Livie, you're a sweetheart. I'd really appreciate it. To be honest with you, I think it's more likely that she'll tell you the truth if I'm not there. You're her kind. Also it will give me a chance to do my homework tonight, make a few calls, and bring myself up to date on the Mandlebaum trust." He smiled his best humble smile. "I might even have to read a little law, who knows? Maybe better I should watch a Western on the Late Show and let you work it out with her. The worst that could happen is that I made this whole trip for nothing."

"While the time clock clicks against the Mandlebaum estate?"

"Of course, of course." They both laughed. "Call me tonight, Livie, any time."

Stonehill handed back the briefcase. "I'll see how it goes." He saw his wife waiting with a porter.

"And, Livie, I'm excited about the Israel fund-raising dinner that you're chairing for the Senator. It took some doing to get Mark Mendoza to leave Israel for this. You don't know what I went through. From Golda Meir, up and down. Fortunately, I did meet him once. He's a fascinating young man. Such a symbol of the fighting young Israeli. It's smart to get him here for this dinner. He'll attract the young people. But such a megillah to get!"

"I didn't realize that you arranged it. I thought Dinky did."

Feldman's owl eyes opened wide. "Dinky?"

"The Senator," Stonehill explained.

"Dinky. Mousey. You high-class people with your funny names. Never mind, the timing is perfect for Dinky. He needs this dinner to reestablish himself with the Jewish vote. It's very important for him politically. The people in Washington understand that, too. The Senator has a great friend in you, Livie, a real friend. Call me later." Feldman walked away chanting the names. "Dinky, Mousey, Dinky, Mousey."

Sunday, February 13
Six p.m., St. Louis

THE FLIGHT from Chicago to St. Louis was fifty uncomfortable minutes for Whiz Crossley. Fifty minutes of self-chastisement, alternating with uncontrollable binges into remembrances of his past and frustrating attempts to reprogram himself by blanking out his consciousness through autohypnosis. The encounter with Stonehill had been disastrous, temporarily destroying his discipline of alienation. The encounter had been unscheduled, not a deliberated part of the plan, and he could easily have avoided it. But on a whim he had indulged his ego, broken his discipline and thrown off the computer cadence of his timing, causing a defection he would not tolerate in another and could not tolerate in himself.

Somehow, seeing Stonehill again had not produced the expected reaction, neither refiring his furor nor reinforcing the steel structure of his vengeance. Stonehill had smiled at him, had been glad to see him, seemed concerned about him, interested in him. Crossley had been thrown off guard. He searched his memory to rekindle his rancor, flicking through pre-selected scenes of the past which always enraged him. But there was a gentleness about Stonehill now, a frank expression of compassion, human qualities which Crossley did not remember and could not accept.

Crossley activated the picture which infuriated him most. The hospital: he and Stonehill in the tiny, airless waiting room, and Susan in a room down the hall nearly dead from an overdose of heroin. Both men silent, each in his own way praying, and the hatred between them that hung in the air like thick smoke. Hours went by that way: silent hours of anguish, self-recrimination and recrimination of each other while Susan's life wavered. Each of them was alert to every movement outside the waiting room door, expecting the doctor, fearing the prognosis. At last Dr. Krause appeared, sweat on his forehead, his scant hair ruffled, his eyes red through thick glasses. He went first to Stonehill and put his hand sympathetically on Stonehill's arm. "She's going to make it," he said, his voice weary from the long vigil. "She's going to be all right."

Tears came instantly to Stonehill's eyes, a sudden, uncontrollable gush, a reflex catharsis of anger, hatred and love. He slumped into a chair, astonished at the violence of his reaction, and looked at the doctor through his tears. There were so many things he wanted to say, he could say none of them.

Dr. Krause turned from Stonehill to Crossley, and they glared at each other, until finally the doctor said, "If you were my son-in-law I'd beat the shit out of you, I'd beat your ass out of this town, out of this country . . . You don't belong anywhere in civilization. You're an animal. You're worse than an animal."

Crossley said, "It was an accident."

"Accident, my ass. When you take a needle to a girl's arm, that's no accident."

The words of his defense were in Crossley's mind. He had said them before to Stonehill, to Krause and to himself, but he decided not to say them again.

Krause was still raging. "I've known that little girl since she was born. I've watched her grow up. She was a beautiful, bright, uncomplicated kid until you made a mess out of her, until you fucked her up with your hippie ideas. The great unwashed Vietnam hero. Shit." He spat at Crossley's feet. "You're scum. Your father-in-law is too much of a gentleman to beat you bloody, but I'm not. You bet your ass I'm not. I'm going to run you out of town, Crossley—tar and feather you, if necessary. You get your ass out of here and out of that girl's life or I'll personally bring charges against you and make damn sure you rot in jail. Now get out."

Stonehill had recovered enough by then to speak. "Hold it,

Eddie." He stood up and touched Krause's arm. "I thank you
and I thank God that Susan will be all right. Now leave us alone
for a minute. I want to talk to Whiz."

There were tears in the doctor's eyes, a fast throbbing of the
veins in his neck. "If you don't kill that prick, you're an imbe-
cile."

When they were alone, Stonehill asked, "How much money
do you have in your pocket, Whiz?"

Whiz laughed harshly. "That's all you think about, isn't it,
banker man? Money, money, money."

Stonehill took out his wallet, pulled all the bills out of it
without looking at them and thrust them at his son-in-law.
"This is it, Whiz. It's more than you came with."

"You're not going to buy me off with a few lousy dollars. I
love Susan. Can't you stop thinking about money long enough
to understand that? I love Susan. Everything I've done is because I love her and want to free her from all your stupid,
stifling morality. My wife has a soul, and you and your money
are keeping it in prison. I want to make her free to fly, free to
live. Can't you understand that?"

The money was still between them. Crossley had not taken it,
nor had Stonehill withdrawn it. "Listen to me carefully, Whiz."
Stonehill's voice was tightly controlled. "You are going to take
this money, and you are going to leave Chicago directly from
the hospital, and we are never going to hear from you again. Is
that clear?"

"You can't buy me."

"You are not to return to your apartment, you are not to see
your son, you are not ever to try to see Susan again. Is that
clear?"

"You can't buy me."

"I don't want to buy you; I want to get rid of you."

"That's my wife in there, that's my son at home. I have
rights."

"You don't have rights anymore—you've lost them. Now
take this money and get out."

"Or what? Don't threaten me with an empty gun."

Stonehill shook his head sadly. "The gun isn't empty. Maybe

it's only loaded with money, but I'll make damn sure you wind up in jail even if it takes all of it. Jail, Whiz; think about your free spirit in jail. My money will buy jail for you."

"I'm going to see Susan." But Stonehill grabbed the younger man's arm with surprising force. For a moment Crossley was ready to strike, but Stonehill's hold was solid, and the fix of his jaw and eyes was intractable. "You wait until Susan is well. She loves me. You won't be able to hold her back."

"Get out now, Whiz, before I take Krause's advice."

Crossley shook himself loose from Stonehill's grip and slapped the money out of his hand. "You wait, Sir Stonehill. You wait."

By the time Crossley drove to his apartment building a uniformed policeman was at the entrance. He pressed the accelerator in panic and sped around the block through an alley to the rear entrance. Two more policemen were there. Stonehill had moved quickly. Crossley drove away, without a destination, and at that moment of outrage the plan to kidnap his own son and to destroy Livingston Stonehill was born in his mind, a specific act of vengeance, metastasizing later into an intricate web to destroy all Stonehills.

But at the airport, Stonehill had said, "Aren't you going to ask about Susan and young Stoney?" And he had offered to show him a picture of his son. Crossley had almost broken at that point; in spite of his resolve, he wanted to see what Stoney looked like.

Talking to Stonehill again had been a monstrous mistake, and he regretted it now as he sat on the plane. He tried to blank out the screen of his mind, dissolve the pictures projected there by closing his eyes and meditating, erasing the karma of his former life and transfixing himself back into the machine he had become, alien to any human relationship. But the concentration he needed was not possible on the plane. Each time he began to silently incant his mantra of meditation, an oversolicitous stewardess interrupted him. There was no way to transcend the mundanity of American Airlines.

By the time he was two years old, it was obvious that Clinton Crossley was an exceptional child, hypertypic, difficult to handle, capable of absorbing and understanding knowledge far beyond his physical age. The psychologist had reassured the parents that their son was gifted, not disturbed. At the age of six, it was clear that the child was more than gifted; genius seemed more appropriate. At ten, it was confirmed by a committee at MIT that he had already mastered most of the theory and practical applications of mathematical science, physics and chemistry. At twelve, he was a regular panelist on the Whiz Kids, had made the cover of *Newsweek*, clashed head-to-head with Hefner himself in a *Playboy* interview, and was the main subject of an in-depth study of genius which appeared in *Time*.

Crossley completed his doctorate when he was eighteen. When his number came up in the draft, he deliberately spoiled every plan to use his special talents, suicidally bungling his way to the Vietnam front. But when he got there, he was unequipped to cope with the other soldiers or the rugged life. The psychic shock of being outside the rarefied atmosphere of higher learning immobilized him for almost four months. He went out into the field in a glazed stupor, unable to communicate or to understand the simplest instructions. At last, when he narrowly missed being killed in an ambush, he approached the problem of his survival on a scientific basis. In short order he learned how to survive, how to become a leader, and how to make money in surviving.

Two years later Whiz was discharged from the Army, the seasoned man unrecognizable from the boy-genius recruit. For a while he floundered on the West Coast, vagrant, moving from commune to commune, finding nothing, fulfilling none of the unfocused, undefined needs of his emotions or intellect. Then he returned home and reinstalled himself in an academic atmosphere, this time at Tufts, outwardly a psychically injured veteran studying French literature, inwardly a guerrilla fighter, bitter and disillusioned, seeking answers for questions he did not know. He had turned on to drugs, not as a physical addiction, but as an experiment to expand the areas of his awareness to unbounded metaphysical experiences.

He had first been drawn to the sophomore Susan Stonehill by her beauty: the long, blond-streaked hair, the high cheekbones, the wild gray-violet eyes, the long, lean body. A classic beauty, her voice had the slight nasal quality of Eastern preparatory schools and her body moved with the pelvic thrust of a fashion model. Even in the campus uniform of the sixties, jeans and a sweat shirt, she had a radiance which set her apart. What intrigued Crossley was her apparent contentment with being exactly what she was, not rebelling against her establishment perfection. Crossley had conjured a free spirit trapped in that beautiful structure and waiting to be released, straining to soar with him to supersonic altitudes of the mind and body, finding peace and freedom in that stratosphere. His concept of her became an obsession, a challenge to fight again, this time with love as a weapon.

Susan had written to her mother. "I've met a boy. You won't like him one bit—not at first, anyway. He's a bit odd, but I do find him fascinating. He's terribly, terribly brilliant. Can you imagine someone like that paying attention to me? Do you remember when I was little a program called *The Whiz Kids*? He was one of them. I remember him from then. He was the one with the scientific mind. Why he's at Tufts I can't imagine. Anyway, he's been paying a lot of attention to me. He thinks that underneath my Peck and Peck exterior, as he calls it, there breathes a free spirit.

"I'm telling you all this because he may show up in Chicago over the holidays, and you ought to warn Father. You're so good at preparing him for things. I know you won't mind that he isn't Jewish and that he looks rather odd. He's terribly attractive, but Father will think he's a hippie. I mean he does have long hair and he does it up in a ponytail with a rubber band. But if he is a hippie, he's an awfully clean one. He has some kind of shower fetish. I told him that if he showed up in Chicago without a haircut and decent clothes instead of his torn jeans, I wouldn't let him in the apartment. But he won't do that. If he shows up at all, he'll be just the way he is and one way or another, we'll have to cope with it.

"All of this may be for nothing. He's such a kook and he's confusing my life right now, and maybe it will all be over before the holidays. But I'm warning you just in case . . ."

Crossley had been defeated by his own emotions. No matter how he rationalized it or fantasized the relationship, he was classically in love in the established pattern of love. To court her and to consummate that love, it had to be on her terms: marriage and a married life in her world. He went through the motions of compliance; he cut his hair, shaved every day, wore conventional clothes and moved to Chicago to live in the Stonehill tradition. But he never believed that Susan was only the Susan which surfaced. He tried in every way to free the spirit he believed trapped inside her, through love, by gently developing her startling eroticism, and finally, in desperation, by trying through drugs to break down the barricade of her consciousness.

From the beginning Crossley had blamed Stonehill for the wall around his wife and after the accident with heroin and his banishment he planned a vendetta against his father-in-law. In the last four years his revenge had been extended and abstracted into a war against all the Stonehills of the world, a cold war of emotional destruction. Stonehill had become all Jews, and the Palestinian Arabs were an extension of himself, robbed of their homes and birthright by Jewish money and influence.

The voice over the plane's intercom said, "Please fasten your seat belts. We are beginning our descent into the St. Louis airport." Crossley checked his watch; they were on time. In St. Louis, he was thinking, everything would dovetail again and fall back into place. In St. Louis, it would be time again for putting the machinery of action into high gear.

After he had picked up his luggage, Crossley went over to the Hertz desk. "Collier," he said. "Jason Collier."

The agent pulled out a boldly lettered portfolio, then looked up and smiled. "We weren't able to fill your request for a white Maverick. Would a red one do?"

"Is that what you have reserved for me?"

"Yes."

"Fine."

As he drove to the downtown Holiday Inn, Crossley reached under the floor mat of the Maverick and groped until he found the edge of a card. Pulling it out, he glanced at the string of numbers filling both sides of the card, put it in his pocket, checked his watch and smiled.

At the hotel there were two telephone messages for Jason Collier, each of them consisting only of a telephone number: 305-687-7065 and 414-171-6043. "Are you sure that there are no other messages?" The room clerk looked again and shook his head.

Quickly Crossley checked out the room, closed the draperies, and moved the chairs away from the window, leaving a clear floor space. He unpacked his toilet kit, lining up the contents on the bathroom sink with military precision, in the order in which he used them. He studied the bulge of his crotch reflected in the mirror and frowned at the tingling sensation beginning there. Back in the bedroom he took a small black case, opened it, took out an electric cord and plugged it into the wall under the window near the space he had cleared. As he flicked the switch on and off to make certain that the base plug was alive, the telephone rang. He looked at his watch. The call was eight minutes late. Inexcusable. He let the phone ring until the message operator answered and the room became quiet again. After a few minutes, the red light glowed on the phone. He took the card which had been concealed in the car and the two telephone messages, spread them out on the bed and studied the numbers. He had committed the complicated mathematical code to memory, but he took no chances and from his code book double-checked the information, then dialed the operator. "This is Mr. Collier in room 1204. I was in the shower and heard the phone ring. Is there a message for me?"

"Yes, sir. You are to call 614-543-2609, extension 403. That's a lot of numbers, Mr. Collier; do you want me to have the message sent up?"

"No, that's all right. I know the number. Thank you."

The information was now complete. All contacts had been made by the twenty-eight agents, except for one victim in Pittsburgh who had died of a coronary before contact could be established. Crossley had foreseen such a possibility; the agent of each web had alternate subjects, and they had been instructed to inform the center computer which would automatically make the necessary adjustments.

He tore up the index card and the two telephone messages

and put the shreds of paper in a glass ash tray. From his suitcase he took a box of incense and sprinkled some in it, lit the paper and made sure it was burning properly. Then he removed his boots, his Schlitz T-shirt and his jeans; he wore no socks or underwear. Running his hands over his body, he tried to massage the tension away. Damn Stonehill. Why had there been compassion, even a hint of forgiveness, in his eyes? Forgiveness for what? Suddenly the source of his anger became clear: Stonehill had made him feel guilty about what had happened to Susan. But it was Stonehill who should be feeling guilty, Stonehill who had built the wall of repression around Susan, Stonehill who had imprisoned her essence so that she could never soar to the heights of happiness. Damn Stonehill. Damn all the Stonehills.

From the bathroom he took two bath towels and spread them out in the cleared area in front of the window. The fire in the ash tray had subsided, and the strong aroma of the incense filled the room.

He sat naked on the carpet of towels, his legs crossed, his head dropped so that his eyes focused on his penis. Fingering the tiny silver spider at his neck, he began the mantra. *Quoththespidernevermorequoththespidernevermorequoththespidernevermorequoththespidernevermorequoththespidernevermore* . . .

But it would not happen; he could not transcend the gap between the reality of the hotel room and the void of Nirvana. Nor could he stop the flood of memories which he thought he had disciplined out of his consciousness, or erase the pictures of his past unreeling through a projector he could not disconnect. *Quoththespidernevermorequoththespidernevermorequoththe spidernevermorequoththespidernevermore* . . . *DamnStonehill damnStonehilldamnStonehilldamnStonehill.*

His penis remained limp. His rage was making him impotent, it had to be redirected to strike out.

Quoththespidernevermore . . . It was no use. He released the silver spider and raised his head to see the patterned draperies depicting a fox hunt. His legs still crossed, he rose straight up, stretched his arms above his head, then straight out in a Christ-like cruciform.

Taking out his code book, Crossley memorized four series of numbers, dialed 8 for long-distance, then 800-623-7600. The operator came on the line. "What is your room number?"

"I'm making a toll-free call. You don't need my room number."

"What number are you calling?"

"It doesn't matter. Let the call go through. It's an 800 number. That indicates it's a toll-free call."

"I don't know, sir."

"I do," he snapped. "Let the call through."

There was a silence for a moment, then the sound of ringing. "New Classic Record Company," a woman's smooth voice said. "This is a recorded message. Our operators are not on duty at this time. When you hear the tone signal, you may leave your name and phone number and the call will be returned tomorrow. Or if you have our catalog and wish to order by number, supply either your American Express or BankAmericard number. Please give your complete address, including zip code. Allow six weeks for delivery."

Crossley waited for the sound. "This is Elmer Brunridge, 706 18th Street, Omaha, Nebraska 70562. My BankAmericard number is 4674 100 376 428. I have your catalog and would like to order three albums. The numbers are 1127, 1165 and 756. I would also like to order the 8-track cassette number 4531." He hung up and lay back on the bed for a moment. Tomorrow in the Dallas papers there would be a story about the mysterious bombing of a Rolls-Royce Corniche drop-head convertible belonging to Sherman Weinstein. The Monday papers in San Francisco would carry a piece about ten-year-old Barry Plitzer, who disappeared on his way to school but was later discovered heavily drugged but otherwise unharmed, in a movie theater in Oakland. There would be an attack by vandals in Palm Beach on a large home being constructed by Milton Friedman of Passaic, New Jersey. The damage would be over fifty thousand dollars, and the police would theorize that it had been done by a cult of young people camping on the beach twenty miles east of Daytona. And in Chicago, unreported to the police or newspapers, there would be a beating and attempted rape of Myrna Gordon in the laundry room of her apartment building.

Crossley flexed his muscles, shook his hands to get his blood circulating, and smiled as again he sat cross-legged on the floor. His hand touched the spider and his eyes lowered to his penis. Already he sensed relief from his pent-up tensions. *Quoththespidernevermorequoththespidernevermorequoththespidernevermore* . . . Slowly, like a snake being charmed, his penis became tumescent, erecting to a straight, thin shaft with a purple-blue head. He maintained the erection and the chant of the mantra for almost an hour, until every thought was gone from his mind and he was suspended in Nirvana, the supreme serenity of nothingness, an endless, verdant desert bathed in sourceless sunlight. Then, from the small black case on the floor he took a long, clear plastic tube with a condomlike casing at one end. Taking out a tube of lubricant, he applied it to his penis, his eyes closing at the delight of his own touch, then slipped the condom over his penis, set the speed dial to slow, the timing dial to twenty minutes and flicked on the starting switch.

As the machine sucked at him, massaged him, his body stiffened, his entirety a massive erection. Each time he neared orgasm he shouted the words of his mantra and the sensation ebbed, only to build again, closer to orgasm each time. In eighteen minutes he ejaculated into the machine a surging rush of stored-up semen, his voice screaming, the machine sucking in the seminal fluid, storing it in a disposable plastic bag. He fell back on the floor, the machine still pumping. At twenty minutes exactly, it automatically shut off.

Exhausted, Whiz Crossley had at last achieved complete physical and spiritual alienation from the world as it existed by a calculated synthesis of onanism and asceticism.

Sunday, February 13
Seven p.m., Chicago

WHILE HIS WIFE talked, Stonehill looked out the window and thought about love. They were sitting opposite each other at the small table in the dining room. From the eighth-floor vantage, the lake was black darkness, with an occasional rippling shimmer of light on the surface as the clouds broke density and let the moonlight through. Traffic on Lake Shore Drive was heavy in both directions, an endless snaky necklace of headlights moving slowly north and slowly south. Maude Stonehill, a pad and pencil next to her plate, was reciting a monologue of household problems and pending social engagements, interspersed with gossip and direct questions.

Stonehill was thinking about love. Since he had first met Maude and decided he was in love with her, he had not thought about the subject again despite their years of marriage, a succession of mistresses and casual affairs. He was dissecting his feelings for Myrna Gordon, analyzing his emotions, wondering if it really was love. She had catapulted him out of his own generation, where a man's sex life was established and controlled, into a maelstrom of animal action. She had made him a young lion again living in an unstructured jungle with a kind of exhilaration. But when the feeling ebbed, it left an afterglow of guilt and fear which made him more vulnerable to the other fear —that of the man in his office, the mounting threats, the physical danger. To break this chain of thought and forestall the terror, he said sharply to his wife, "For God's sake, Maude, do we have to talk about the plumber? We haven't seen each other for five weeks, and all you can talk about is the damn plumber."

"There's no need to raise your voice, Livie. They can hear you in the kitchen." Her pencil was poised on the pad next to the note about the plumber. She had already crossed off a question about the Palm Springs pool service, written *no* beside a question about a party the Goldhursts from Seattle were giving at the Racquet Club, and *yes* beside a notation about tipping the greenskeeper at Tamarisk Country Club. "I'm concerned about you, darling. You don't seem to be yourself and you don't look well. Have you had a checkup lately?" She scribbled a note on the pad. "Which reminds me, I ought to call Eddie Krause tomorrow and see if he can squeeze me in for an examination before I go back."

His voice was softer. "What's the matter, haven't you been feeling well?"

"I've had some flare-ups of irregularity. You know that I'm usually like clockwork. I thought I ought to go to the doctor to check it out."

"Christ, Maude, we're getting like everyone else. We're getting so old that all we can talk to each other about is how our bowels move."

"Livie!" She looked toward the kitchen.

"We ought to be talking about . . ." His voice trailed off into silence.

"About what?"

"I don't know, exactly. Important things, I guess. What we're like, what we're thinking about."

"After all these years?" She smiled and put her hand over his. "That's the marvelous part of our time of life, darling. I know what you're like and what you're thinking."

"Do you, Maude? I wonder. I wonder if I know what you're like anymore, or what you think about."

"You *are* in a mood, aren't you? You really ought to come back to Palm Springs with me. A week in the sun, thirty-six holes of golf a day, and you'll be your old self again."

He decided not to answer.

"I do think we ought to let the plumber go ahead, don't

you? Three hundred and eighty-five dollars is an outlandish price, but it's impossible to get anyone else in midseason."

"Go ahead." His voice was weary. "Tell the plumber to go ahead."

She wrote y·s on her pad, and poised her pencil at the next question. "There's a problem with the planting on the east side of our property. The landscaping service said that the only way we are going to block out those terrible new people next door is to plant a mass of oleander there. It's the only thing that will grow quickly and be dense enough. It will take about twenty-three fifteen-gallon containers. He wants eighteen dollars apiece —planted, of course. Mr. Aguiar says that it's a must."

"Then do it."

Moving her pencil to the next item, she looked up at him. "There's a problem about the I.Magnin billing."

"There's a problem about China and détente with the Russians. There's a problem about the United Nations and Zionism."

"Of course there are, darling, but you and I aren't going to solve those problems, but we *can* solve the I.Magnin bill. I never received credit for two pair of golf shorts I returned in November. I've written to them twice and haven't paid the bill. Now they've written me a threatening letter saying that they'll close the account. I've talked to the manager and even called the credit office in San Francisco, but nothing seems to happen. They keep apologizing and saying something about a computer. I have the receipts, but the computer doesn't seem to pay any attention."

Slowly, measuring the words, he said, "Speaking of computers, I ran into Whiz today."

She looked up from her list with fear in her eyes. "Whiz?"

He nodded his head. "There's only one Whiz."

"Where? What was he doing? Was he with Susan?"

"No, Susan knows nothing. I ran into him at the airport. He was changing planes, coming up from South America on his way to California."

"Is he married again?"

"No, but he seems happy enough. He looks well, brown and

lean. He looks like a hippie again—not the hair or the beard,
but . . . I don't know, something about him reminded me of the
way he looked when we first met him. I guess he looks the way
he *should* look, not like the man we tried to make him be. He
looks younger . . . healthy and strong. He doesn't seem to be on
fire anymore—at least not in the same way."

"Really, Livie, you sound as if you were glad to see him.
How can you, after all that he did?"

"I was thinking about that coming home from the airport. In
a way, I was glad to see him. For some reason, now that it's too
late, I felt that if I had understood him better, that if it all was
happening now I could handle it more intelligently."

"What did you say to him?"

"Not much; we only spoke for a minute or two."

"Will he try to see Susan and Stoney?"

"I don't know."

"What do you mean, you don't know? Didn't you warn him?"

"I asked him if he wanted to know about them, and I tried to
show him a picture of Stoney. He wouldn't look at it. He said
that part of his life didn't exist for him anymore."

"Oh, God, Livie, what are we going to do?"

"You mean about I. Magnin?" He smiled, trying to ease her
fright.

"Are you going to tell Susan?"

"I don't know. I wanted to talk to you first. What do you
think?"

"Definitely not." She shook her head determinedly. "That
part of her life is over. She doesn't even talk about him anymore."

"Do you suppose she thinks about him? She did love him
very much."

"I wish she'd get married again. It's not natural for a girl like
Susan not to be married." She took a bite of her salad. "It's
such a cloud over our heads all the time. I'd like to see her
settled."

"Maybe she *is* settled," Stonehill said, thinking of Myrna
Gordon. "Maybe this is the way she wants her life to be. It's
different from ours, but maybe that's not so bad. After all, she

has enough money from the trusts, a glamorous job, a good kid and lots of friends."

"It isn't natural for a girl like Susan. A girl like Susan must have a husband so that she can be safe. I've never told you this, Livie, but I live in dread that Whiz will come back into her life. That's why I'm so frightened now. Susan has told me a few things—well, more than a few things, really. The attraction was mainly . . . physical. I never really think of Susan as being physical in that way."

"You mean sexual."

"All right, sexual." The word was difficult for her to say. "I don't know if she . . . What I mean is that if . . ." She nibbled at her salad. "I do know that if she were married she could face Whiz again without being tempted."

"Does she have a lover?"

"How would I know? We don't talk about it. I wouldn't think so. Susan really isn't that kind."

"That's a lot of shit. All women are that kind in one way or another."

"Livie, they can hear you in the kitchen."

He laughed. "I bet Carl and Helga have both heard the word 'shit' before."

"But not from us, not at the dinner table." She rang the little crystal bell, and they were both silent while the houseman removed the salad plates. When they were alone again, Maude asked, "What about the I.Magnin bill?"

"How much were the golf shorts?"

"Thirty-six dollars and change."

"Pay it. Give me the receipts and I'll write them a letter from the bank. They're like everyone else, bogged down by technology. The worst that can happen is that we're out thirty-six dollars."

"It isn't the money, darling, it's the principle of the thing."

Carl returned with coffee. "Helga said that she did not make dessert. Would you like cheese?"

"That would be lovely, Carl, and tell Helga the dinner was excellent. I do miss her cooking in California."

"Thank you, ma'am." Carl went back into the kitchen.

"Maude, I have a problem," Stonehill began. "Maybe I will be coming back to Palm Springs with you."

"Oh, darling, that would be marvelous, but don't come until after the tournament. I've invited a houseful of guests and you won't be able to get on the golf course and I'll be busy every minute with the visiting golfers. Come right afterwards."

"I might."

"Oh, darling, I forgot. You have the dinner for Dinky next Sunday. Come the week after."

"That's the problem, Maude. I may not go through with the dinner for Dinky."

"Not go through with it? What does that mean?"

"Just what I said."

"But why not? He needs this badly. It's terribly important for him politically, and you've made the commitment. You're going to raise so much money, and they need it badly in Israel, particularly now with the United Nations censure. And everyone is so excited about Mark Mendoza. The press coverage will be unbelievable. There's such a mystique about the man. Even Susan is excited. It all seems to be going so well. Why would you back out now?"

"What if I were sick? I mean, really sick?"

"Are you, Livie? What aren't you telling me? I want to know the truth. Are you really sick?"

"No, of course I'm not; I'm healthy as hell. But what if I *were* sick?"

"Swear to me, Livie, that you're telling me the truth."

"I'm not sick, Maude, I swear it. But what if I have to fake a sickness to get out of a tight spot?"

"What kind of a tight spot?"

"A lot of pressure has been put on the bank about Dinky's stand on the Middle East. He made that dumb mistake of flying in when Sadat was in Chicago and attending the dinner in his honor. We do a lot of business with hard-nosed guys who are so pro-Israel they can't understand political expediency. They'll never forgive Dinky for shooting off his mouth about Middle East détente or for making a fuss over Sadat. They've been putting pressure on me."

"It doesn't make sense. Since when are you subject to pressure? I've seen you stand up for some really big things, and I've never known you to compromise your beliefs or betray your friends. I don't understand you at all. How can you let a handful of Jewish fanatics make you turn your back on one of your oldest friends and everything you believe in?"

Stonehill rubbed his eyes as Carl brought in a platter of cheese and fruit.

"Maybe I'm just tired. Maybe I'm getting old and I'm not tough enough anymore."

"The house phone rang," Carl announced. "Miss Susan is on her way up from the lobby."

The doorbell rang and Stonehill jumped up. "I'll let her in. Bring some coffee in for Miss Susan."

Opening the door, he marveled again at his daughter's beauty. They hugged each other, and then Stonehill remembered Whiz and the hurt which Susan must still be feeling, and hugged her again hard.

"Daddy, it hasn't been that long."

"I've missed you." He helped her off with her coat and stood back to admire her. She was wearing a black-satin jumpsuit, unbuttoned almost to her waist, a mass of gold and diamond chains around her neck cascading between her breasts. "What are you all dolled up for? Not us, I'll bet."

"Peter Frankel," she explained. "I'm meeting him at Zorine's in about an hour."

"It must be braless Sunday at Zorine's."

"Oh, Daddy, stop. You're not supposed to notice."

"Honey, when you let it all hang out like that, a man would have to be blind or dead."

"But a girl's father—"

"A girl's father is still a man."

She kissed him lightly. "A very dirty old man. Where's Mom?"

"We're just having coffee." She started toward the dining room. "Why doesn't . . ." he fumbled for the name.

"Peter Frankel?"

"Why doesn't he pick you up here?"

"Oh, Daddy, people don't do that anymore—at least not liberated people. You *are* out of touch. You're getting to be a fuddy-duddy. It isn't the same polite world that it was when you were young."

Stonehill saw himself in bed with Myrna, his face buried between her legs, his penis ramrodded through a bagel. "Tell me what the new world is like, Susan."

"Don't tease, Daddy. It's just that you don't understand the way people behave today."

"Go see your mother. I have a couple of fast phone calls to make. And Susan . . ." She turned to him. "Maybe we'd better have lunch one day so you can explain the new facts of life to me, and when you have maybe I'll understand why what's-his-name can't pick you up here rather than meet you at Zorine's."

"His name is Peter Frankel, Daddy, and you know him."

"I do? Whose son is he?"

She shook her head, annoyed. "None of those Frankels. His family lives in Lincolnwood and they're very nice. I've met them."

"Don't tell your mother that his family lives in Lincolnwood."

"Anyway, he's with the U.S. Attorney's office here, and he's on your committee for the dinner for Uncle Dinky."

"Oh, *that* Peter Frankel."

"Yes, *that* Peter Frankel. And the real reason he wouldn't pick me up here is that he's petrified of you. He says that you remind him of the late George Apley."

"I never gave Peter Frankel any credit for literary awareness. As a matter of fact, after listening to him at meetings, I wasn't even certain that he knew how to read."

"He's bright, Daddy. He's a hothead, and he may be a little rough around the edges, but I . . ." She thought better of what she was going to say.

"But what, Susan?" She did not answer and looked perplexed. "You can smooth out the rough edges, is that what you mean?"

She nodded. "Yes, that's what I was going to say. Except that I tried doing that once before, to make a man conform to . . . You know what I'm trying to say."

"You're growing up, Susan."

"It's hell being without a husband. You feel like a piece of meat on the market."

He went over and held her close. "You have one consolation," he said soothingly. "It's prime meat, well packaged."

She put her hand over his mouth. "You *are* a dirty old man." She kissed him lightly. "But thank you for the compliment, chauvinistic though it was."

In his dressing room, Stonehill flopped in his chair, reached for the telephone, pushed the button to a recently installed private line and dialed Myrna's number. The line was busy, so he called Sheldon Cole.

"It's Livie Stonehill, Shellie. Can you talk?"

"Wait a minute." He came back on the line. "Go ahead. What's happened?"

"I think I've found another victim."

"Are you sure? I've been sitting around trying to bullshit myself into thinking that all this is some kind of hoax. Are you sure?"

"Almost positive. It fits your theory exactly." He described briefly his conversation with Irving Feldman.

"For Christ's sake, that Mandlebaum broad has got to be eighty years old."

"Have you seen her lately?"

"I've never met her."

"Actually she's probably not much more than sixty. Her husband was a lot older, and he kept her middle-aged from the time she was twenty-two. But you should see her now."

"Dynamite?"

"Something like that."

"How can a sixty-year-old broad be dynamite?"

"Look, what I really called about was Feldman. How well do you know him?"

"Fairly well. He handled an antitrust suit for me a year ago. Did a hell of a job. A shrewd cookie."

"Maybe he can help us. He has very good connections in Washington—a hot line to the FBI and CIA if we need it. And I trust his discretion."

"Fuck his discretion; you're the one with puss stashed away, not me."

"What do you think?"

"I don't know. Maybe. If there was a way to smoke these bastards out, we'd have something to fight. Maybe what we need is a detective agency."

"We might be smart to lay it out in front of Feldman and get advice from someone not involved."

"I don't know. Livie, I'm so fucking scared and pissed-off that I can't think straight. Let's mull it over. See what this Mandlebaum broad knows."

"Do you want me to call you after I've talked to her?"

"Wait until tomorrow. Diane will know something's wrong if you call that late. Call me first thing in the morning. I'll get to the office early."

"All right, but think about Feldman in the meantime. He could be very helpful."

"He knows how to charge," Cole said.

"Think about the alternative. I'll call you tomorrow."

This time Myrna's line was free, but the phone rang for a long time before she answered. "Hi."

"What are you doing?" He could not block out the doubts that Cole had raised about her.

"Nothing."

"You sound funny. Is anything wrong?"

"No."

"Are you alone?"

"No, I'm not alone. I'm laying the whole Park Ridge B'nai Brith, two at a time. Does that satisfy you?"

"Don't get angry."

She hesitated for a moment. "I'm not angry, I'm lonesome, and I'm angry that I'm lonesome. If I were really liberated, the way I should be, I wouldn't be."

His voice was tender. "If you were really liberated, what would you be?"

"I don't know, but not like this, not mooning around feeling like a piece of leftover meat."

He laughed. "What is it with you young girls and your meat

complex? My daughter was just telling me that she feels like a piece of meat on the market."

"I saw her picture in the *Trib* this morning modeling something. That's some classy-looking tomato you got there. I hate women like her. They make me feel fat and dumpy and covered with acne."

"Well?"

"You old bastard. If I had you in bed I'd give you a bite you know where, and I'd make it hurt."

"I'd love it."

She laughed. "You probably would. The way you're going, you'll probably be into the s-m scene within two weeks."

"I have a great teacher."

"I don't like an empty classroom. Maybe I'll go to Butch's and recruit a student body."

"Good luck."

"You know I won't, don't you?"

"Yes, I know you won't."

"I'm going to finish my feet, wash my hair, have a frozen TV dinner and go downstairs and do my laundry . . . and a bit of yours too, Mr. Stonehill. And speaking of your laundry, if you're going to continue this affair would you mind switching to drip-dry shirts and underwear? I iron lousy."

"Buy me a drip-dry trousseau. I'll pay you back."

"Even bikini briefs instead of boxer shorts?"

"If it turns you on."

"With you I'm like a light switch. Anything turns me on."

"Stay that way."

"At the moment I have no alternative . . . Look, Livie, I'm not real great at telephone chitchat, especially with your wife there."

"She's in the dining room."

"It doesn't matter what room she's in. I mean, I know she's there and that you'll go to bed with her tonight, and . . . I don't know how to act, exactly. I mean, should I be polite and ask you how she is?"

"She's fine."

"That's nice. Now what do we talk about?"

"We talk about how we love each other."

"No, we don't. That hurts too much. We'll save that kind of shmoos for when we're together and I'm so overcome by your manly beauty that I forget that basically this is a lousy relationship."

"I love you."

"I know you do. And I love you, which is what makes this whole thing such a pain in the ass."

"Go fix your hair and do my laundry. I'll talk to you tomorrow."

Back in the dining room Maude was saying to Susan, "Ask your father. Perhaps he'll know what to do."

Stonehill sat down. His coffee was cold. "About what?"

"I got a call today from Rico del Gracia in Barbados."

"How is the Jewish matador?"

"Don't be funny, Daddy, this is serious. We had a date for the ball at the Art Institute on Wednesday night, and then Rico found that he had to go on location to shoot some ads. He just got to Barbados on Friday. Now something has come up and he has to fly back to Chicago unexpectedly, so he wants me to go to the party with him."

"So far I don't recognize the problem."

"The problem is that I made a date with Peter Frankel after Rico canceled. I told Rico, but he won't take no for an answer. Women's Wear is covering the party, and Rico is involved with the promotion of a new product. He says that it's important that we be seen together there, that it would help both him and my career." She fingered the chains around her neck. "So what do I tell Peter?"

"I wouldn't try lying to him. Frankel has a reputation for getting the truth out of people more experienced at lying than you are."

"How should I handle him?"

"First I'd suggest that you button your blouse so he'll look into your innocent eyes, and then I'd tell him the truth."

Susan shook her head. "He wouldn't understand, Daddy. As tough as he is, he's insecure about a lot of things. He would be hurt and furious and probably never speak to me again."

"If he gets that irate, unbutton your blouse again."

"Livie," Maude said, "don't be flip. This is serious." Then to her daughter, "Perhaps your father is right. Tell Peter the truth. You might add that Rico's family does a lot of business with the bank, and that your father insists. You do insist, don't you, Livie?"

"I take it that you ladies have decided that young del Gracia is the more eligible catch of the two. In that case, on behalf of the bank I insist. As a matter of fact, del Gracia has done a hell of a job with that line of men's toiletries of his. Grunswald International stock has risen over twenty points since Rico started that division. You could have fooled me; I thought he was the playboy of the western world like his father, without a thought in his head, but evidently he has inherited his mother's brains."

"I could fix Peter up with one of the other models. He keeps eyeing Laurie Potter."

"Isn't she the black model?" Maude asked.

"Very smart maneuver, Susan," Stonehill broke in. "It could lead to a little hanky-panky, but not to marriage. You're more devious than I gave you credit for."

"Livie, what has gotten into you? You're behaving ridiculously."

"In my own inept way, I'm protesting the tyranny of women."

"We're not tyrannical, Daddy; we're practical."

"Semantics, Susan, semantics."

"Mom, it might just work. Peter thinks Daddy is an ogre anyway. I'll tell him that he insisted and that I'll get Laurie and we'll all go together. That's a marvy solution."

"I rather think you could handle it on that basis."

"It may work out exactly right," Susan said. "And now I'd better run to meet Peter." She kissed her mother. "Glad you're home, Mom. I'll bring Stoney around right after school tomorrow. He's dying to see you." She hugged her father. "Goodbye, Daddy, you've been a love and a help."

"But a traitor to my sex." As she opened the front door he called, "Susan?"

"Yes, Daddy?"

He decided not to say anything more. "Have fun at Zorine's."
"We always do." She stopped and turned back to her parents.
"I almost forgot to tell you. I had a funny call tonight just
before I left. It was a man from London with a Russian name—
something like Tatov. I wrote it down at home. I don't think
he's really Russian—he has a very proper British accent."
Stonehill asked, "What was so strange?"
"He said that he'd seen Whiz. He seems to know him. He
said he'd seen him in Damascus, of all places."
Maude Stonehill avoided looking at her husband, and her
voice was controlled. "What did he want?"
"A date, I guess. He asked what I was doing tonight. I
couldn't because of Peter Frankel. I'm having lunch with him
tomorrow."
"Do you think that's wise?" Maude asked.
"What harm? I'd like to hear about Whiz." She looked at
her father for approval. "Do you see anything wrong in having
lunch with him, Daddy?"
He shrugged his shoulders. "What will it accomplish?"
"Satisfy my curiosity, I guess. I'm not afraid. I mean, I'm not
afraid to hear about Whiz and I'm not afraid of this man. He
rattled off a whole bunch of names—people I know in London
and New York. I'm sure that he's harmless."
"Be careful," Stonehill warned.
"I've got to run, I'll be late. Good night, Mom—night,
Daddy."
When the front door closed, the Stonehills looked at each
other, not hiding their concern. Maude broke the silence. "For
so many years we've heard nothing about Whiz. Now suddenly
he seems to be everywhere. It's strange."
"I didn't understand about Damascus. Whiz told me he'd
been in South America. But that's Whiz, I guess. I never did
know when he was lying and when he was telling the truth."
"Your coffee is cold, Livie. Do you want some hot?"
"I'm fine."
"Rico del Gracia is the kind of boy Susan should have married in the first place. It would be quite a match, wouldn't it?
They make a stunning couple."

"A Jewish mother is a Jewish mother."

"Any mother wants to see her daughter well married."

"Don't be defensive. There's nothing wrong with being a Jewish mother. As a matter of fact, I find it refreshing."

"You *are* in a mood tonight, Livie. I'm afraid that I've left you alone too long." Turning back to the list, she picked up her pencil. "Helga tells me the laundress says we need a new washing machine. Do you think Sears is the best place to buy it, or should I go wholesale?"

Stonehill was looking out the window again, thinking about love.

Sunday, February 13 Nine p.m., Seawall Airport, Barbados, W.I.

Rico del gracia stood leaning against the fence, his head raised and moving like a beacon, monitoring the night for the sight or sound of the airplane which would bring Mike Nelson from New York. The blackmail threat had been made five hours before, too late to divert Nelson. By the time del Gracia's call got through to Kennedy the plane was already airborne. The decisions he had made, the plans he had formulated were tentative, depending on Nelson. So much depended on how Nelson would react. No matter how hard he fought to quell his doubts about Nelson, the shadow kept surfacing; the logic of two and two making four was undeniable. Rather than think about the threat and the consequences, he had made plane reservations back to Chicago, called Nicola Ursini, the photographer, to see if he had shooting time open, alerted his houseman that he was returning unexpectedly, called his mother to test her mood and to make sure that she was in the city, rang Susan Crossley to tell her that his schedule had changed and that they could go to the ball at the Art Institute together. Even with the delays of the primitive telephone service, there had been time left over to be frightened and enraged, introspective and retrospective.

The Barbados night was balmy, a soft warm wind wafting the tall grass which edged the runway. Del Gracia's body was burned bronze by the sun. He wore white shorts, a thin white shirt tied loosely at his waist, and three gold chains around his neck, their pendants buried in the thick mat of hair on his chest.

There was still neither sound nor sight of the plane, but he kept his vigil, phrasing and rephrasing the words he would say to Nelson.

Two American tourists, also waiting, stood a hundred yards away. The wife said to her husband, "Do you recognize Rico del Gracia?" The man didn't turn to look. "I thought he would be taller."

Rico del Gracia was encased in the macho shell of his Sephardic antecedents, proud Jews living in Spain as Spaniards, physically undifferentiated from other Spaniards. After the Inquisition these Sephardim wandered the world mixing with Jews of other heritages, diluting their Spanish blood, combining and changing their chromosomal structure and gradually diminishing their physical distinctiveness, assimilating into the Jewish mass, melding with them to face other inquisitions with other names in other places, only to be driven to wandering again.

At the age of thirty, through a genetic mystery, an accident in Africa and deliberate grooming, del Gracia was a pristine reincarnation of the Sephardic Jew. The genesis from American Jewish boy to charismatic conquistador was not an easy one, and it had left him with psychic scars. Until he was twenty, he had been a typical product of suburban Highland Park, Illinois: overindulged, his upbringing left to servants, too thin, Semitic-looking, large nose, diffident with his elders, shy with girls, cowed by his domineering mother, akin to but disappointed in his alcoholic father, who had brought only an ancient name and a decorative grace to a German family of hard-nosed merchant tailors.

The Grunswald fortune started with a tailor shop in Chicago, growing into the country's largest manufacturer of men's clothing and then into a nationwide chain of department stores. Although it was a public company, fiscal control of Grunswald International and its direct management was still tightly held by the family, Leo and Lester Grunwald actively and their sister Vera del Gracia in the background, her shrewd, moneymaking creativity masked by her husband, Isidro Federico del Gracia III, who represented her at board and stockholder meetings.

In the summer of his twentieth year, gangly and uncoordinated, Freddie del Gracia accompanied his father on an African safari. When he returned to Highland Park, Illinois, three months later, the music of the bull ring sounded silently as he walked, the pulse of the flamenco beat in his blood and he moved with the fearless grace of the matador. A Land Rover accident in a remote part of the Serengeti had taken care of the size of his nose. An inadequate African doctor had reset it ineptly, giving him the look of a fighter and making his deep-set, heavy-lashed black eyes his most dominant feature. The doctor had also neglected a short, deep cut on his cheek which healed with a noticeable scar, adding a swashbuckling dimension to what had become a handsome face. Two recuperative months in Rome, lazy days of sun and pasta, had begun to fill out the boy body into that of a man.

It was during these days in Rome that Rico became aware of his new attractiveness, seeing the change in himself through other eyes that suddenly looked at him differently. Sitting with his father one afternoon on the Via Veneto, conscious of the parade of women eyeing his son, his father asked, "Freddie, are you much of a cocksmith?"

"Sir?"

"I thought so. Tell me the truth, boy, have you ever been laid?" Young del Gracia shook his head. "This is between you and me, son. I'm afraid your mother wouldn't approve, but I have to tell you that I am a sensual man. I understand sensuality, and because I do, I know that every woman walking down this street has round heels for you. Do you understand what I mean?"

"I think so." He thought further. "Yes, sir, I do, but what do I do about it?"

His father shook his head sadly. "It's a damn shame, Freddie, that you and I haven't been closer. You could be one of the great cocksmiths of your generation—women by the carload, and enough left over for dear old dad. Do you know what I mean?" He laughed, testing his son. Rico looked shocked.

After sampling several of the local prostitutes, the junior del Gracia realized that for him sex was not much different from being tutored in trigonometry. He had finally mastered the subject, but he could not see what was so important about it or what he was going to do with it.

Still, the sessions with the prostitutes did give him courage to experiment on his own, without his father's sponsorship. As he sat at a sidewalk café in the Roman sunlight, a camera-slung American girl, clean and well-scrubbed, the kind he knew at home, approached him. "Look," she said, sitting beside him, "you probably don't speak English and I sure don't speak Italian, but I'm smiling hard and that means the same thing in any language. Right? You don't speak English, do you?"

He was so surprised that he said nothing.

"But you're Italian, and all Italian men want to make it with a blond American chick, right?" She nodded her own head in answer to her question, mistaking the bewilderment in del Gracia's eyes for smoldering passion. "So I'm leaving Rome tomorrow, and right now you're going to come up to my room and we're going to make it together." She reached across the table and took his hand. "And when I get back to Cleveland, I'll be able to tell all my friends about the most dynamite Italian in all of Italy, and how we had this little affair. Sound good? And I have my camera and flashbulbs so that my little show-and-tell bit will come with lurid illustrations. Do you get the drift?" Still del Gracia said nothing, thinking that this girl reminded him of Peggy Goldberg from Winnetka. "Okay, so you're a dumb wop, but you're beautiful and you're about to get laid. Have I made all this clear to you?"

He smiled finally, the way he would at Peggy Goldberg.

"Clear as hell, but you have one thing wrong. I'm not a dumb wop, I'm a dumb American, just like you."

"Son-of-a-bitch, you could have fooled me." She withdrew her hand. "I don't know whether to be embarrassed or to laugh." She decided to laugh, then stopped abruptly. "What about it; do you want to get laid anyway?"

The experience with the American girl had been a disaster; he had been unable to achieve a full erection capable of penetration. Humiliated by his performance, he fled frantically to one of the prostitutes. With her he was able to perform perfectly, though somewhat perfunctorily. The sexual pattern of the man was thus established.

At last there was the sound of a jet and a flurry of activity on the ground. Del Gracia felt a hollow of fear in his stomach. Red and green lights loomed larger as the plane made its approach and touched the runway softly, with a great backwash of air and dust as the pilot hit the brakes.

Del Gracia walked to the gate and stood behind a group waiting for arrivals. He saw Mike Nelson as he came through the door of the plane, hesitating, searching the people waiting at the gate. Rico smiled to himself, his doubts lessening. Mike was Madison Avenue even here on this tropical island. Nelson was wearing a gray plaid suit, a trench coat slung over his shoulder, a battered attaché case in his hand and his usual wing-tipped, laced-up shoes. He could have been getting off the commuter train in any United States suburb, looking for his station wagon among all the others, searching for his wife and children among all the other waiting wives and children.

Nelson was frowning, squinting through his heavy-framed glasses as he shouldered his way through the crowd. Then he saw del Gracia, stopped, smiled and seemed to come alive.

They shook hands. "I knew you had to be here. I got a hard-on during our final approach, and when I get a hard-on it means you're within a fifty-mile radius."

"I'm glad to see you, Mike."

"And, Christ, am I glad to see you. It's been almost two weeks, do you realize that? I'm so horny I think my balls are going to bust."

"Come on. They bring the luggage around the front." They walked together, brushing against each other lightly as they moved. "How's New York?"

"Yecchy. Cold and damp and frantic. Boy, I need this break. It's beautiful here. And I need you, Rico. Jesus, do I need you."

It was too soon to start telling him, so Rico asked, "Do you want a drink while they unload the luggage?"

"No, I'm high just seeing you. You look great, Rico, Jesus, I'm glad to be here." He dropped his coat and briefcase on a bench in front of the terminal, took off his suit jacket and loosened his tie. "Tomorrow I'm going to soak up all the sunshine there is. What's the cottage like?"

"Nice."

"Remote enough so we can make love bare-assed on the beach?"

"You really are horny."

"I'm a little upset that you're not as horny as I am."

"Who said?"

"You'll find out."

The two men grinned at each other.

There would be time later to tell him what had happened, Rico decided. He looked up at the sky, felt the warm night blowing through his thin shirt and grinned. "Did you bring your golf clubs?"

Nelson shook his head. "I can't handle you on the golf course —I can't afford it. How are the tennis courts here?"

"Good. I warn you, I'm improving. There's a great pro at Sandy Lane. You'll see the difference in my serve."

"Tomorrow," Nelson said, "we'll play first thing. The camera crew and models aren't due in until noon."

"How's the new baby?"

Nelson shrugged his shoulders. "How can you tell when they're only seven weeks old? She cries a lot. It's driving Sarah crazy; the baby keeps waking up the other kids. Our house is like an asylum. Believe me, I need this change."

"When's the christening?"

"I don't know yet, but remember that you promised Sarah you'd show. What's a christening without a godfather?"

When the luggage came, they piled it into the small convertible, del Gracia gunned the accelerator and they sped down the highway into the night. Nelson leaned back against the headrest, his long legs stretched out, and put his hand on del Gracia's bare leg. Feeling the communication of exhilaration, del Gracia accelerated the car even faster and put his hand on Nelson.

"Christ, Rico, I can't ever remember being this happy. It's like all my life before this has been nothing. It's like I wasn't alive before."

The two men had been lovers for over seven months. What had started as a casual business association developed into friendship, and what appeared to be an accidental experience thrust the friendship into an intensely physical, emotional relationship.

The line of men's toiletries and cosmetics bearing the Rico del Gracia label had been Rico's own concept. He had developed the idea, including the manufacture and merchandising, into a viable package before presenting it to his mother and her brothers. He had done extensive marketing research on the sales potential, and his presentation was complete, professional, undeniably documented and geared to the Grunswald financial mentality. The force of his personality, the symbiotic duality of playboy and hard-nosed businessman, caught the family off guard and captured their moneymaking imagination. His facts were indisputable. The brothers worried about the future of their sons and sons-in-law in the business competing with this sudden dynamo, and his mother felt her silent power growing over her brothers.

Del Gracia's plan used the umbrella of Grunswald International for a preliminary marketing test in selected retail outlets. Three months after the first products appeared on the counters, it was obvious that Rico's predictions had been right; the potential was even greater than his original projection. Rumors of the successful test bounced back to Wall Street, and the Grunswald stock jumped four points in a week of a down market. For the first time in a long time, there was excitement in the executive suite of Grunswald. There was pressure to move into high gear and market the products nationwide through conventional markets, instead of limiting the sale to Grunswald-owned stores. There was infighting between Rico and his uncles and cousins, but he held the high ground, proved himself a tough infighter and got his way: his own division of Grunswald International under his direct control. One of his first actions was to hire an advertising agency and give them the broad concepts of a campaign based on his personal identity with the product, his signature on the label.

The agency came up with a plan to use Rico as his own model, both in magazines and on television. There was Rico playing polo in India, playing roulette at Monte Carlo, at Anabel's, skiing at Zermatt, playing tennis at the Racquet Club, at Zorine's, racing at Le Mans. Rico became the symbol of the product, the Walter Mitty dream of the American male, sporting and playing around the world, a man's man of action, always with one or two beautiful women at his side.

Concurrent with the advertising, a public relations campaign was aimed at editorial coverage of del Gracia playing across the world, inside stories of the man behind the label, a beautiful-people celebrity to be created from the handsome cloth of the man from Chicago. Originally Charlie Webster had handled the public-relations blitz. A high-powered talker who knew everyone and went everywhere, he molded Rico's image quickly and well. *Playboy* did a piece called "Rico: The New Rubirosa?" But though the stories about Rubirosa were essentially true, the information on del Gracia, including the rumored size of his penis, was mostly the creation of Webster.

The combined penetration of the two campaigns lifted Rico into instant notoriety, and the skyrocketing sales of the products was reflected in the steady upward trend of Grunswald stock.

Mike Nelson was the replacement when Charlie Webster was stolen by another agency. He was much younger, about del Gracia's age, less high-powered and less flamboyant. The first time they met, Rico cased the gray flannel suit, oxford shoes, button-down shirt and regimental tie. "Yale?" he asked.

"1966," Nelson answered.

"Married, two and a half children . . . ?"

Nelson smiled. "Two and a third," he corrected. "You may be quoting statistics, but my wife is three months pregnant."

"Station wagon?"

"You bet."

"Volkswagen to leave at the station?"

"Datsun. I have a rich father-in-law."

"Mortgaged house in Westport?"

"Stamford."

Rico held out his hand. "What's a nice boy like you doing in a business like this?"

Nelson was less creative than Webster, but the promotion campaign was already well established and he did a good job of keeping it energized, running smoothly. He also paid more attention to detail, which made Rico's days and nights less frantic. Somehow Nelson quietly organized everything so that camera shootings were on schedule, the right personnel were on tap at the right time, and Rico's baggage was mysteriously packed and ready for instant departures. As he came to know Rico, Nelson could anticipate his needs and maintain him on his frenetic schedule with smiling calm.

One night in New York the two men had a long, winy dinner at "21" with an editor of a women's magazine and a feature writer. The editor started by asking Rico to pose for a centerfold, and he ducked the request as he always did. The feature writer asked him the same questions every other interviewer had ever asked, and he good-naturedly parroted the answers she could have read in any number of previously published interviews.

Finally Mike put the women in a cab and returned to the table. "I either need a glass of milk or a straight shot of booze." He fondled the wineglass. "This vintage stuff is too high-class for me."

"Mouton Rothschild 1956. Don't knock it."

Nelson looked at his watch. "Not only that, but I think I missed the last train home. Shit."

"Stay in town," Rico suggested. "We have an early shooting in the morning anyway. I'll loan you a shirt."

"Maybe I will."

"Call the Regency and talk to Jacques Camus; he'll get you a room."

"Good thought. I'll call Sarah and tell her not to wait up." He stood up. "Hey, Rico?"

"What?"

"I made a decision. Order me a glass of milk. If it embarrasses the waiter, tell him to bring it in a martini glass."

In the Regency lobby, Nelson briefed Rico on his morning schedule as they went up in the elevator together. Nelson got out on the third floor and Rico went up to his suite on sixteen, kicked off his shoes in the living room, put his jacket over a chair and walked into the bedroom. The king-sized bed was turned down, and propped up on the pillows, fast asleep, was a naked young woman, a big, pink bow covering her pubic hair, a card tied to the bow. Without waking her, del Gracia carefully picked up the card and returned to the living room to read it, closing the door softly.

> Rico—*This one is on me. I won't even*
> *put it on my expense account. Enjoy!*
>   *Mike*

Rico picked up the telephone and had the operator put him through to Nelson.

"You're a nut, Nelson."

"You got my present?"

"All tied up with a pussy pink ribbon."

"I figured you were due, Rico. I looked at your schedule and couldn't figure out when you ever had the time or energy for a little snatch."

"Beautiful present, Mike. I had only a quick scan, but I'd guess she was a least a two-hundred-dollar hooker."

"Two fifty with a blow job encore."

"I can't handle it tonight, Mike. I'm out of steam."

"You gotta be kidding. I paid in advance."

"Look, she's fast asleep. She won't know you from me. You fuck her and I'll put it on *my* expense account. Come on down. I'll hide in the shower or behind the couch."

"I don't know . . . I've had a lot of wine, and . . . Well, what the hell, it's immoral to piss away two hundred and fifty bucks, right?"

"Right."

"As long as you put it that way, and in view of the general economy . . ."

"You're a good sport, Nelson."

"You talked me into it. I'll be right up. What room number?"

"1604."

When he heard the light tap on the door, Rico let Nelson in. "You're sure about this, Rico? It's like giving somebody a box of candy and then eating it yourself."

"Rotten analogy. Go to it, tiger."

"Where are you going to be? It would make me nervous if I thought you were watching."

"Not one of my shticks, Mike. I'll take a shower in the bathroom off the living room. Do you come fast or do I have to take a long shower?"

"With a two-fifty price tag, it seems a shame to go wham-bam, thank you, ma'am."

"I'll hole up on the couch until you give me the all clear."

"Thanks, Rico." Nelson started for the door, loosening his tie. "I feel kind of funny about this. To tell you the truth, I've never laid a hooker before."

"Try it, you'll like it."

"It's not that . . . Shit, you'd think I never banged a broad before." In a surge of determination he flung open the bedroom door, slamming it loudly behind him, and Rico heard his muffled voice say, "Wake up, baby. It's party time." Rico laughed and went into the shower.

When he came out of the bathroom fifteen minutes later, the door to the bedroom was open, the light still on. Tying the towel around him, he looked cautiously into the room. Nelson was alone on the bed, smoking a cigarette, staring at the ceiling. "Where's the girl?" Mike started to get up, but Rico motioned for him to stay where he was.

"Gone. Two hundred and fifty bucks pissed away because I couldn't get it up. A beautiful broad, incidentally, and a real pro. She tried every trick in the book, but I still couldn't make it."

Rico sat on the bed, unwound the towel and leaned over to dry his feet. "It happens sometimes."

"Not to me. Usually I have trouble keeping my pecker down."

"Hand me a cigarette from over there, will you?" Nelson lit one and handed it to del Gracia, who lay on the other side of the bed. "I knew I couldn't get it up tonight either," he said, "not for anything. Maybe it was the wine. We can always blame it on the wine, Mike."

"I'll accept that. Stay away from Mouton Rothschild 1956."

Nelson propped himself up on one elbow and looked over at Rico, first at his face and then down to his penis. "I'll have to correct our file on you. We have the most vital of your vital statistics wrong."

"So I'm not as big as Rubirosa. Nobody's perfect." Looking down at himself, he saw his penis erecting, and for a moment was too startled to move. But when he tried to get up, Nelson's arm held him back and stayed on him.

"Hold it, Rico. Maybe our records are correct, after all. I thought you said you couldn't get a hard-on tonight for anything."

"I don't know. I don't understand it!"

Almost imperceptibly Nelson's voice was growing huskier. "Don't try to understand it. Just enjoy it."

"How? The broad is gone."

"Beat yourself off. Grown men have been known to do it— even I've been known to do it."

"You forget my Judeo upbringing. Beating yourself off gives you pimples and makes you insane. Besides, I've tried it and can't make it work."

"For Christ's sake, Rico, you can't be as hung up as all that." Releasing his hold on del Gracia's arm, Mike moved his hand quickly to encircle his penis. At first hard grasp, a shiver went through del Gracia's body, his eyes closed, and there was a depth of sensation he had never experienced before. "Don't, Mike," he said, but he did not move. Nelson's hand went up and down, a dry, hard rubbing at once painful and stimulating.

Then the hand withdrew for a moment, and when it grasped him again it was slippery with saliva. Nelson's hand moved fluidly now, the pleasure to del Gracia almost intolerable, too great to fight, with no ending possible except in orgasm. It came quickly, spurts of semen ejecting with a force and from a depth he had never felt before, and continuing longer than seemed possible.

When the orgasm had almost subsided, Nelson released his hand and substituted the fleshy warmth of the inside of his mouth. The diminuendo reversed and started to build again in intensity. Del Gracia opened his eyes and touched the top of Nelson's rhythmic moving head tentatively, then tenderly, but as he climaxed again, his hand tore at Nelson's hair with brutal force and he screamed out loud. The eruption had enough force to break down psychic dams and change the current of his life.

Now, on the beach in Barbados, they lay touching each other slightly, each man smoking and feeling a sense of release, looking up at the stars with sated eyes.

"Mike, something's happened which involves both of us."

"I knew something was wrong. Do we have to talk about it tonight?"

"I'm going back to Chicago first thing in the morning."

"What happened?"

"I was in the cottage after lunch when a maid and houseman came in to do some special cleaning. Both appeared to be natives, and I had no reason to be suspicious. When they were certain that I was alone, the woman pulled a gun and the man sat down as though he owned the place and started telling me things about you and me—things that I thought only you and I knew. He mentioned places we had been together, secret hideouts we've used. He knew everything, Mike—all of it."

Nelson sat up and turned to Rico, but did not speak.

"They had a cleaning cart with them. It was filled with evidence—infra-ray photographs, tapes of some of our conversations. Then the man pulled out the clincher. He had a copy of the *National Enquirer*—do you know the paper?" Nelson nodded. "There was our story, complete with pictures of us making it together. I didn't read the whole thing, but I saw enough to know that it was accurate. The date of the newspaper was March ninth, three weeks from next Thursday. Do you know what it must have cost to print that copy?"

"How much do they want?"

Rico shook his head. "I'm trying to keep calm while I'm telling you this. I still can't believe that it happened. It's like a bad porno movie. They didn't want any money; they aren't ordinary blackmailers. As far as I can tell, they're Palestinian terrorists, or some breed of radical kooks. These two black people, with English calypso accents, began talking to me about Jews, about Israel, about Zionism, about Israel kicking them out of their homes. You know the kind of talk. When they mentioned Jews and Israel they got all fired up. The woman with the gun scared me; she almost lost control."

"What do they want?"

"They want all my family's money that is pledged to Israel to be cut off, not a dime to be contributed to the Jewish United Fund or any other organizations that supply funds or aid to Israel. That's a lot of dough they're talking about—all the money contributed by Grunswald International, plus the personal contributions of my mother and her brothers. What I give is the least of it; the big money comes from the Grunswalds."

"Or they'll expose us? Is that it?"

"Yes."

"Fuck 'em. Blow the whistle on them. It's time somebody did. Call their bluff."

"It's no bluff, Mike."

"Rico, look at me." Del Gracia turned. "I've been doing a lot of thinking since we last saw each other. I've been thinking about my life, and what I want, and how I want to live the rest of it." He picked up a handful of sand and let it run through his fingers. "I want to come out of the closet, Rico. I don't want to live a lie anymore . . . Shit, I thought you and I could say anything in the world to each other, but this is tougher to say than I thought it would be."

"Don't say it, Mike. It wouldn't work. It wouldn't be any good."

"Why? Because of Sarah and the kids?"

"That's part of it."

"You mean more to me than Sarah and the kids. I know that's a lousy thing to say and a rotten way to feel, but I have to face up to it, Rico; it's the way I am. Why should I live the rest of my life being something that I'm not? Not only will it fuck up my life, in the long run it will fuck up Sarah and the kids. If I make the break now, they'll have a chance. Sarah's still pretty. She can meet a guy and put another life together for herself and the kids, the kind of life she wants to live with a guy who deserves her and will love her. Am I making sense?"

"If this hadn't happened, maybe. I don't know. I don't think ahead about you and me; it scares me. But now it doesn't make any sense at all. It's the wrong thing to do and the timing is terrible."

"You're wrong. The timing is perfect. I'm telling you, Rico, I'm willing to risk exposure. It's not going to be the end of our lives; it's going to be the beginning. Tell those terrorists to go fuck themselves. Let everyone know about us. So what? There are thousands of men in the world who—"

Rico interrupted him. "It's more complicated than that, Mike, much more. For one thing, your children will have to live with it for the rest of their lives. If I know Sarah, she'll fix it so that you'll never see your kids again."

"I've considered that. It's probably true. If I have to make that sacrifice, I will. They'll live with it and I'll live with it."

"There's more to it, Mike, than just you and me. You're going to think it's hard-nosed, but I have to be tough. This kind of scandal will ruin the del Gracia line. All that macho build-up, the masculine mystique, every image we've created of me will be turned around. We'll be laughed off every counter in every store. The Grunswald stock will drop like lead and we'll lose everything and more that we've gained since we've been in business. There'll be panic at Grunswald International, and I'll have to face my mother and uncles and cousins. It will destroy my mother and the power she's built up."

"I'm talking about our lives, Rico; you're talking about money. I don't understand that kind of thinking. I'm willing to give up my family, and all you're worried about is the price of Grunswald stock."

"Mike, there has to be a way that we can go on as we are."

"Not forever, Rico. Sooner or later we have to make a choice."

"Then later, when we can plan for it and cover all the bases. Not now. We have to find a way to keep going the way we are now."

"How?"

"I don't know. There's nothing to fight. They told me that I'd have no further warning and would never be contacted again. What do I do? Do I wait for the March ninth *National Enquirer* and hope that it was all a joke? I can't afford to take that chance. The PLO's credentials are too formidable for that. They've pulled off some pretty unreal things more daring than this. I have to believe them, Mike."

"How do you suppose they knew about us? Where did they get all their facts?"

"I've brainstormed that one around all afternoon and evening. It keeps going around in my head."

"And what do you come up with?" Suddenly Nelson's voice was hard and menacing.

"I have to ask the question, Mike. It's the only answer I come up with. I know it's not true, but I have to ask it. Maybe it will finish what there is between us, but if I don't ask, it will be finished anyway."

"You son-of-a-bitch. You've got that *dumb goy* attitude about me again. You're such a smart-ass Jew that you think I'm too dumb to know what's going on in your mind. That shrewd, devious Grunswald part of your brain is adding it all up. Except this time you came up with the wrong answer. The answer is *no*, Rico, I did not set you up for this. I'm not a Palestinian terrorist or a spy. You dirty son-of-a-bitch. I may be a lot of things, but I'm not low enough to do that." He stood up, his legs apart, straddled over del Gracia's supine body, and with brute-force strength broke the chain around his neck, throwing the sliver of gold far down the beach. "If I were any kind of man, I'd beat the shit out of you, beat you bloody, you lousy cocksucker."

Then Nelson turned and ran full speed to the water. He hit the first wave hard, and swam with angry, vengeful strokes until he was part of the ocean, part of the night.

Sunday, February 13
Eleven p.m., Chicago

THE DOORMAN said, "Mrs. Mandlebaum is expecting you, Mr. Stonehill. Go right up."

He rang the bell three times before the door was opened by a young, white-uniformed doctor, a stethoscope around his neck, who was smoothing his tousled hair. "Mr. Feldman?"

"No. I'm Livingston Stonehill. Mr. Feldman is not coming. What's wrong with Mrs. Mandlebaum?"

The young doctor smiled. "Not a thing. Mrs. Mandlebaum is in remarkably good physical condition." He stood back to let Stonehill enter. "Evidently she phoned the clinic in a state of near hysteria. They sent me over to administer a sedative, if necessary." He straightened his collar. "I suggested a cold shower instead."

Stonehill smiled, indicating that he understood. "This is the first time that you have treated Mrs. Mandlebaum?"

"I'm new at the clinic. Some of the other residents . . . well, they briefed me on her medical history and record. Some record —three interns and four residents in one night. That ought to go in Guinness'."

"I agree. Mrs. Mandlebaum is quite a character."

"I'm Sid Katz." The young doctor held out his hand and Stonehill shook it. "Mrs. Mandlebaum said to tell you that she's pulling herself together and to fix yourself a drink. She said you'd know where the bar is."

"No thanks."

"Do you mind if I do?"

"Go ahead. It's hidden behind those doors."

As he poured, Dr. Katz asked, "Are you a relative?"

"No, a friend. Her banker, really."

Katz swirled his drink. "Funny, ever since I was a kid and wanted to be a doctor, I had my eye on the Mandlebaum Clinic and working with Dr. Stetson. Every guy in the GI field dreams about a residency at the Mandlebaum Clinic. Your career is made if you've trained under Dr. Stetson and made it through the Mandlebaum Clinic." He sat down and sipped his drink. "It's the best gastrointestinal hospital in the world, both in research and therapy. The work that Stetson's done has saved thousands of lives all over the world." He swallowed the rest of his drink in one gulp. "That has to count for something. It gives that old girl up there"—he nodded toward the staircase of the duplex apartment—"a lot of Brownie points."

"You have the right attitude, Dr. Katz."

"Sid. I'm still not used to being Dr. Katz."

"How old are you?"

"Twenty-eight and unmarried." His eyes and face lit up. "Why? Do you have a girl for me?"

"I might."

"On second thought, forget it. Stetson works our asses off. No time for play. But it's worth it."

They heard Mousey Mandlebaum calling from upstairs, "Doctor, doctor!"

Slowly Katz walked to the staircase and looked up. "Yes, ma'am?"

"Are you sure that I don't need a shot of something or other?"

"Positive," Katz called back. "I left two tranquilizers beside your bed. Take them if you feel stress. Mr. Stonehill is here."

"Livie," she called, "is Feldman here yet?"

Stonehill walked over and stood beside Dr. Katz to watch Mousey Mandlebaum make her entrance. "Feldman may not come, Mousey. But I've spoken to him." Looking up at her, he decided that she didn't even look fifty, but she had to be in her sixties. "You look great, Mousey. Absolutely great."

She descended regally and offered her cheek to be kissed.

"Don't say that, Livie. I hate people who tell me I look absolutely great. There are three ages for a woman—young, middle-aged and you-look-absolutely-great. You're a dear to come over at this hour. How's Maude?"

Stonehill smiled. "Absolutely great."

"Did you fix yourself a drink? I think I need one. Fix it for me will you, Dr. . . ." She fumbled for his name.

"Katz, and I suggest that you don't drink tonight if you're going to take tranquilizers."

"Nonsense. Fix me a double vodka on the rocks, please."

Dr. Katz shrugged, looked at Stonehill for help, found only amusement, and poured a double vodka for Mrs. Mandlebaum. She held up the glass—"*L'chayim*"—and took a deep gulp. "Notice how I get *ch* in *l'chayim*. Not bad for an old Irish broad. That Jewish bastard I was married to didn't even know what *l'chayim* meant. It means 'To life.' I'll drink to that."

Mousey Mandlebaum had her first nonmasturbatory orgasm the morning of her husband's funeral. She had been married very young to Leo Mandlebaum, the heir of a mail-order fortune who was forty years older. He always referred to her as his little mouse, and he kept her that way: shabbily dressed, colorless and plain, speaking only when spoken to and then answering only monosyllabically. She was more of a servant in the vast, old Mandlebaum mansion than mistress of it. When Leo finally died, most people had forgotten that he had ever been alive and did not remember the wife listed in the obituary as his sole heir. The body lay in state for two days in the dining room of the bleak old house, the light from the crystal chandelier making the corpse look waxen, as though there never had been blood in the drained veins or a brain in the death-mask head. The night before the funeral, only three old friends came to pay their respects, and when they were gone the widow drank too much of her late husband's best brandy, looked at the corpse and said out loud, "Now it's my turn, you old fart."

The next morning when a young man from the undertaking establishment came to supervise the removal of the body to the funeral home and to conduct the bereaved Mrs. Mandlebaum to the funeral services, he found the widow upstairs fully dressed in traditional widow's garb, sprawled abandonedly across her bed, smiling radiantly, still drunk and unabashedly horny. He resisted politely, tried to show compassion and made several attempts to talk his way out of the bedroom, but in the end he had to protect himself physically from her attacks. In the course of this violent encounter, Mrs. Mandlebaum managed to strip herself naked except for black stockings and a complicated black veil. She had the body of a young girl, firm and flawless, with a luminous glow to her flesh and sassy, rosy-tipped breasts. The apprentice undertaker, a young man of several sexual persuasions, found himself looking at his watch, pressed for time and with an enormous erection. Hoping that they could climax quickly, he stripped himself as naked as she, down to his black stockings and shoes. When she saw the size and girth of the young man's penis, Mousey crossed herself twice, moved her lips in silent recitation of a Hail Mary and then looked up to heaven and said, "You old fart, this is what a real pecker looks like."

They both climaxed quickly and simultaneously, and exquisite cries echoed through the house for the first time since it had been built. It was a turning point in both their lives. The young man never touched another young man again, and Mousey Mandlebaum never again stopped touching young men.

Now, handing her glass back to Dr. Katz for a refill, she said, "Why don't you be a dear boy, fix me another drink and then wait for me upstairs in case I need a sedative or something. I want to talk to Mr. Stonehill."

"Mrs. Mandlebaum, my job is taking care of the sick. You're healthy as hell. I'm going back to the clinic. I'm on medical duty, not on stud call."

"You're being insolent. I could have you discharged." She poked an angry finger into the ice in her glass.

Katz smiled broadly. "I know you could, Mrs. Mandlebaum, and I also know that you won't. Now, don't drink any more vodka, and try to sleep without taking the tranquilizers." He shook hands with Stonehill and picked up his bag.

"How do you know that I won't?" She was more coquettish than angry.

"Because I'm a very good doctor and you're a very nice lady and you love your clinic more than anything in the world. You wouldn't do anything to hurt it."

"Get out of here." She motioned with her head toward the door. "Go on, get out." When he was gone she smiled at Stonehill. "I like that young man."

"So do I."

"Where the hell is Irving Feldman? I told him to be here at eleven o'clock."

"He's not coming."

"Why not? For what I pay his firm every year he should be here with bells on anytime I snap my fingers."

"I told him not to come, Mousey. I wanted to talk to you alone. I think I know what your problem is."

"Don't shilly-shally, Livie. Either you know it or you don't."

"I know it, Mousey. You've been threatened by the PLO or some kind of terrorists, haven't you?"

She poured herself another drink. "Those bastards think they're dealing with an aging Jewish princess. They forget that I was a tough Irish Catholic from the wrong side of the city and that I know how to fight. I'm more Jewish than you are, Livie, in many ways. When the good Lord saw fit to rid me of Leo, I knew I owed Him something. Leo Mandlebaum was the tightest old fart who ever lived; he never gave a nickel to anyone for any cause. I'm paying the good Lord back with all that Mandlebaum money, smart Jewish money. That's why I built the clinic, and that's why I give away millions every year to Jewish charities and Israel. I can't spend all the money, you know that, so I give it away, and no Arab bastards are going to stop me."

"What do they want?"

"They want me to cut off all funds to Israel. I have plans to build a Mandlebaum Clinic in Haifa, and they told me I'd have to forget it. No way, Livie. As long as I live, I'm not going to stop paying God back for Leo being such a miserable, dumb tightwad."

"What did they threaten you with?"

"Not with what you think. Look, Livie, I know all about what people say and how they smile at my face and laugh behind my back. My private life is no secret—I don't even try."

"Then what?"

"They're a bunch of hophead maniacs. They say that they have a plan to discredit the clinic and dear Dr. Stetson. An accident in administering an anesthetic, an overdose of medicine, a string of little catastrophes. The young man was very explicit, and medically sophisticated. He knew what he was talking about."

"Young man?"

"How else would you get to me?"

"Where did you meet him?"

"He was cutting the lawn in Palm Beach—rather well, I thought. I assumed he was part of my landscaping service, but he was bare-chested and handsome, dark and swarthy, and he kept eyeing me as I was taking a sunbath. I learned one thing from it: never trust an uncircumcised man."

"How much time did they give you?"

"Two weeks, and then the accidents would start. But that isn't the worst of it. If I don't do what they say, they'll kill Dr. Stetson and make it look like suicide over the discrediting of the clinic. Dear Dr. Stetson, who never did anything but good in his whole life."

Stonehill shook his head in disbelief. "It's unreal. I wonder what kind of misdirected genius dreamed all this up. It's frightening how well they know how to get to us, how much information they have about us."

"I was so mad that I didn't stop to think. I just started calling everyone on the telephone. Flying up here tonight I had time to figure it out. I realized that I couldn't be alone in this, that there must be others threatened. But you surprise me, Livie. Why you? What did they threaten you with? Maude? Your daughter? Your grandson?"

"It doesn't matter."

She stared into her glass. "You're an attractive man, Livie." She looked up and smiled. "A little old for me, but still very attractive." She waited a moment for him to speak. When he didn't, she went on. "Is she young and pretty? I hope she is, and that she's enjoying it."

"What are you going to do, Mousey?"

"I'm going to fight, that's what I'm going to do. For openers I'm going to hire an architectual firm first thing tomorrow morning, and they're going to draw a pretty picture of a lovely building. On Wednesday I'm going to announce to the press that I'm building another Mandlebaum Clinic in Haifa as a memorial to my late husband and as a statement of my faith in Israel, and you're going to get twelve million dollars out of the trust so I can start building. I'm going to Haifa myself to break ground."

"It won't work, Mousey. They mean what they say. They can make it happen—the accidents in the clinic, the death of Dr. Stetson."

"I don't believe it."

"You have to believe their past performances, Mousey. Remember Munich. They'll make it work."

"There must be a way to stop them. This is a big, strong country. We'll go to the police or the FBI. That's what they're for, to protect the United States citizens."

"What will we tell them? What leads can we give them? Each of us has seen only one person, and by now that person is probably back in the Middle East."

"Who else is in this?"

"Only one that I know for sure."

"Who?"

"Sheldon Cole."

"Never heard of him. Must be new money."

"New and a lot of it. He's a damn smart guy."

"What's he doing about it?"

"We've been talking, but we haven't figured anything out yet."

"Men are so damn helpless. You're talk and talk, and meanwhile everything we believe in is crumbling."

"We can't match their violence, Mousey. We have to do it with brains."

"You have to learn to fight bare-handed, Livie. You're too much of a gentleman to fight without gloves. I'm not."

"Who and what are you going to fight?"

"I don't know. Maybe you're right. Maybe I should wait until we figure something out. I'm not sure. My first instinct is to call their bluff. That's why I want to go ahead with the Haifa project now."

"There's no point in doing that if they succeed in discrediting the clinic here."

"There must be people at the clinic involved—someone on the staff. They can't know as much as they do about its operation without having a spy there. I'll start a security check first thing in the morning. I'll personally go over every personnel record."

"Don't, Mousey, not yet. Don't arouse suspicions. It's too dangerous at this point."

"I'm not going to sit on my ass and let it happen, and I'm not going to withdraw my support from Israel or give up building a clinic there."

"Please wait, Mousey. Wait until we all get together and have a plan."

"Three days, Livie. I'll wait three days, and then I'll do it my way."

"Fair enough, Mousey. Incidentally, Maude knows nothing of this, and neither does Cole's wife. It's important that we keep it secret for now. That's why I wanted to talk to you before you spoke to Irving."

"Why? Do you think Feldman is an Arab? He charges like a Jew."

"I think he may be the man to represent us. He has powerful connections in the State Department. I believe that we ought to work through the State Department or the CIA, and my hunch is that Feldman will know how to go about this."

"Call him and tell him to get his ass over here."

"I promised Cole that I would discuss it with him first."

"Well, call Cole. Tell him I agree we should go with Feldman."

"I can't call him tonight. He's afraid his wife will guess that something is up."

"You men are unreal. Your whole existence is being threatened and you're worried about waking someone up."

"Tomorrow, Mousey. I'll put it all together tomorrow." He stood up. "Meanwhile, I'm going home to sleep. Maybe all the pieces will fit together tomorrow. I'll call you right after I've spoken to Cole and Feldman." He walked over to her chair. "We'll figure it out, I promise. Will you be all right?"

"I'll be fine." She looked at him. "Three days, Livie, and then I do my own thing, is that clear?"

"I'll talk to you tomorrow morning, Mousey."

She walked him to the door. Her voice was soft now. "We have real trouble, don't we?"

"Yes."

"You can't believe it's really happening, can you?"

"No."

"Good night, Livie."

"Good night, Mousey."

Outside, the night air was cold, clear and invigorating. He thrust his hand in his pocket, felt the key to Myrna's apartment and looked up and down the street for a taxi. He couldn't be sure that Maude was asleep yet; she was still on Pacific time, after all, and it was two hours earlier in Palm Springs. On the other hand, perhaps she was worn out from the trip and had gone to bed early. Until he heard himself giving the cabdriver his own address, he wasn't sure whether he was going home or to Myrna's.

Maude was asleep when he got home. There was a message on his pillow that Dinky had called from Washington. Also Irv Kupcinet; could he please call him back at the *Sun-Times* in the morning? "Love you," Maude had scribbled at the bottom, "but I'm tired from the trip."

"In his dressing room Stonehill dialed Myrna, but there was no answer. He let it ring for a long time. Even if she was asleep, she would have heard; the phone was next to her bed. She'd probably gone to Butch's, after all. He couldn't blame her. Then he rang Feldman. "It's Livingston Stonehill, Irv. Were you asleep?"

"With a Gary Cooper Western on the Late Show? Never."

"Mousey can wait until tomorrow. I got her calmed down."

"I knew you could handle it better than I. I had so much confidence in you that I'm already in my pajamas."

"But it won't wait beyond tomorrow morning. I'll call you first thing to set up a meeting."

"Try to have it at my office, will you?"

"It may not be feasible. I'll talk to you in the morning."

He dialed Myrna again, but there still was no answer. He did not blame her, but . . . Stonehill knew then that he could not go on like this. He cared too much. He undressed quickly, brushed his teeth and slipped quietly into bed beside his wife, hoping that she would not awaken.

Sunday, February 13
Eleven p.m., Chicago

THEY WERE SITTING in the farthest corner of the bar at Zorine's, the peach-glow light reflecting in their solemn, silent faces. The music from the main room was a muted sound here, muffled by the padded walls and the body-to-body crowd jammed into the snake-shaped confines of the architecture. Even removed from the source of the sound, the disco beat penetrated, unceasing and persistent, the repetitive rhythms hypnotizing consciousness and releasing an adrenal flow of in-animate frenzy. In the other room, on the lighted dance floor, the frenzy could be released physically through movement; here, in the corner, it smoldered.

Peter Frankel hated Zorine's. He hated it actually and con-ceptually. Decadence was built into the structure and the design itself, surfacing in an atmosphere of permissiveness, a mirrored world of unreal light and savage sound. Windowless, shut off from the outside world, it had a kind of narcotic airlessness in which moral law could not exist, and Peter Frankel was a law man, committed professionally and by personal conviction.

Susan Crossley could live in this world and not be touched by it. Frankel understood this. Her kind could emerge into the daylight of reality untarnished. Old money and social status created a special kind of insulation against the unreality here and the reality outside. Frankel had neither money nor status. He had brains, education, an innate shrewdness, integrity and courage, but all of them were inadequate equipment for loving Susan. He rubbed his hand against the nap of his black-velvet leisure suit and looked at the garish pattern of his shirt cuffs turned up against the black velvet. Thinking of what he was and what he meant to be, he wondered why he was here, dressed like this.

"I don't see why you're angry, Peter. You *are* angry, aren't you?" Frankel stared into his drink. "It's only a dumb party, and it's only one night in our lives. We'll all still be going together," Susan explained. "You have to understand that I've known Rico all my life, and that he's asked me to do this as a special favor."

"You don't have to elaborate. I understand; my skull isn't that thick. He's one of your crowd, and that gives you a special dispensation from the manners expected from us more humble folk."

"That's a cruel thing to say."

"Meant to be."

Peter Frankel was different when he was alone with Susan Crossley, the sensitivity and insecurity of the private man contrasting with his public image. The newspapers portrayed him as a tough, fearless fighter against crime and corruption. Without consciously being aware of it, Susan understood this dichotomy, and handled their relationship by tenuously avoiding the pressures which could force an eruption of violence from him.

"You'll hate what I'm about to say, Peter. Should I say it anyway?" She put her hand on his to soften the blow.

He withdrew his hand. "You might as well. Give it to me all at once."

"In many ways you're like my father. Does that surprise you? You both still believe that there are boundaries separating different kinds of people."

"Aren't there? In your world isn't it important where people come from? I've listened to your father at meetings. In his world, La Salle Street is the western boundary of civilization. Except for the University of Chicago the South Side doesn't exist at all, and his world ends at North Avenue and doesn't begin again until Kenilworth."

"That may be true for my father, but it doesn't make it true for me."

"Not necessarily, but in fact it *is* true for you."

"Why are you so bitter tonight?"

He rubbed his eyes. "I'm tired, I guess. And I'm up to my ass and maybe over my head with a problem at the office." Then he looked at her, was turned on again to what he saw. "I'm lying, Susan. What I really am is angry. I'm not angry at you; you are the way you are, and that's that. I'm angry at myself because I'm so upset about this dance at the Art Institute. Isn't that stupid? I'm behaving like a sixteen-year-old boy. There's a whole world out there that needs me, people who need help, wrongs that need righting—things which I can do something about." He looked around the room. "And here I sit inside this glitzy douche bag, mooning over a beautiful girl and being jealous of a feather-brained glamour boy. I'm smarter than this, I'm tougher than this. I should know better." A smile began inside him. His face lost its black look, and the square set of his jaw softened. "Why am I sitting here, Susan?" He took her chin in his hand and moved her face so that she had to look at him. "What gives between us? What's that beautiful face of yours hiding?"

His words triggered other memories. These were Whiz's words and eyes measuring her. She felt a shiver of cold despite the body heat of the crowd. Would Whiz ever be out of her system? Would there ever be a time again when she could think of him and not feel a mixture of terror and sensuality?

"What's the matter, Susan? You look funny."

"I'll be all right." She took his hand for strength.

For the last three months Susan had known that a showdown

with Peter Frankel was inevitable. He had come into her life just when she had finally put it together again: single, a career, being a mother, living without sex. Men had entered her life easily, but departed quickly when confronted with her anachronistic standard of sexual behavior. They dismissed her as frigid or homosexual and went on to easier relationships. Except for Peter Frankel. Somehow he understood and did not feel his masculinity threatened. On their third date he had made the expected sexual pitch. Susan had refused him and waited for him to disappear from her life as the others had done. But Frankel had not flinched, and did not retreat or become more aggressive. "It's all right," he had said. "I don't mind. I can get laid any time. How about dinner Tuesday?"

"I ought to explain," she told him.

"You don't have to."

She thought for a moment. "I'd like to."

"Okay, explain."

They had been at her apartment having a nightcap. She walked to the window so that she would not have to face him, and looked out over the dark city. "I was brought up in a certain way. Old-fashioned, perhaps. You haven't met my mother and father yet. They're dear people, and I'm not faulting them for what they taught me. It's the way they were raised. I'm not saying that it's right or wrong, I'm just saying that it exists." She turned to him quickly. "Am I making any sense?"

"Some. You forget that I'm a nice Jewish boy. We're all brought up a certain way."

"Is that the reason? I never really think about being Jewish. I suppose there is an inherent Judaic code of ethics. I wonder. My father is the most unreligious man I know, and yet he has the most stringent standards. I don't think he's a cold fish, but I know he could never look at another woman other than my mother. It just isn't in his make-up."

Walking over to her, Frankel gently touched her shoulders with both hands and smiled at her. "All you're trying to tell me, Susan, is that you're a nice girl who wants to get married first and fucked later."

She laughed in spite of herself and shook loose from his

touch. "You have such an earthy way of putting it, Peter."

"I'm an earthy guy."

"Are you? I suppose part of you is, but not the part of you that understands how I feel."

He kissed her lightly on the lips. "Dinner on Tuesday?"

"You still want to?"

He smiled again. "Besides survival, a man has two basic biological needs. He needs to eat and to get laid. It's very simple. I'll eat with you and lay somebody else."

She walked him to the door. "I'm not sure that it's so simple. I don't know if I can accept a double standard."

"Would you be jealous?"

"Maybe."

"If you get jealous enough, maybe your Judaic code of ethics will change. Maybe I'm fighting fire with fire."

"And if it doesn't happen, what then?"

Frankel shrugged. "Depends. Could be that the time will come when I'm fulfilling one biological need and wishing I was fulfilling the other."

"Meaning?"

"You can't be that naïve, or can you?"

"I'm not asking you to marry me, Peter."

"That's good, because I had no intention of asking you."

"What are you asking, then?"

He kissed her again lightly and opened the door. "Tuesday," he said. "We'll have dinner Tuesday."

Since that night there had been no conversations between them that further defined or probed their relationship. They continued to see each other one or two nights a week and talked on the phone almost daily about her job and his, or about young Stoney. Frankel had made no effort to be a surrogate father; his attitude toward the boy was casual and cordial, but he kept a distance between them.

Still, their temporary emotional truce was crumbling the dike which kept them apart while keeping them together. All because Rico del Gracia was returning unexpectedly and because she was remembering what Whiz had tried to find in her.

"Don't make me anything I'm not, Peter. I am exactly what you see, nothing more. Don't try to find any hidden qualities in me. There aren't any."

"I won't accept that."

She began buttoning her blouse higher. "I'd like to go home."

"Not yet, Susan. This is showdown time. You knew that it would have to come. Don't cop out—you've been doing it all your life." She stood up, but Frankel grabbed her arm and pulled her down roughly. "Don't run away."

With her cocktail napkin, she dabbed at her tears. "I'd like to go home," she repeated, but this time she did not move.

They sat in silence in the noisy room, the silence of other voices saying other words as the disco beat pounded on relentlessly. When he was in control again, Frankel said, "I'm sorry."

"I wonder if we should go on seeing each other. It all seems so pointless."

"Are you in love with Rico del Gracia?"

She shrugged and said nothing.

"I have to assume that you're not in love with me."

She hesitated. "I'm afraid of you, Peter."

"Of me, or of falling in love and getting hurt again?"

"I don't know. Don't make me think about it."

"You never talk about your husband. Do you think about him a lot?"

"Sometimes. Not very often. It's as if it all happened to somebody else ages ago."

"Do you have any sex life at all?" She shook her head. "That isn't natural. You need it. We all do."

"You know how I feel about it; we discussed it before. I had a rough time, Peter, when I was married to Whiz. Perhaps our marriage was more physical than I could handle. I was hurt physically and emotionally, and it took me a long time to restructure my life."

"You're back in your father's world, insulated and safe with your own kind. It's not the real world, Susan. Your world is shrinking, and it can't exist forever."

"We talk in circles, and always come back to the same thing: my world, your world. Is your world real?"

"Dirty and dangerous and frantic though it is, I live where it's happening. I couldn't live in your world, Susan. Your kind look back to the way things were thirty years ago and try to make today like that. But today isn't like that, and I don't want it to be. Besides everything else, there's a basic philosophical difference between us."

She nodded. "And where does that leave us, Peter?"

"I don't know. I suppose I'll back off, lick my wounds, plow into my work until it isn't enough anymore, and then, if you're still around, come back and try again."

Slowly, testing the words, she asked, "Are you in love with me?"

He stretched his neck to look at his reflection in the mirrored ceiling. "Appears that way." He looked at her. "This is the first time I've even admitted it to myself."

While she was wondering what to say, the owner of Zorine's appeared at their table and put his hand on Frankel's velvet shoulder. "Peter, you're a blockbuster. Did you see tomorrow's paper? Sensational article about you. Six indictments. You really nailed those bums. You're something this town has needed for a long time."

"Thank you. You know each other, don't you?"

They nodded.

"Peter, your boss called about ten minutes ago. Dynamite Dan never turns it off, does he? I tried to bring a phone to your table but there was no way to get it through this zoo tonight. I told him that I'd find you and have you call him. He's still at the office, believe it or not."

Frankel stood up quickly. "Excuse me, Susan, I'll be right back. Thank you."

He slid into the banquette beside Susan. "You look stunning tonight."

"Let's not start that again."

Dan Moynihan answered on the first ring. "Peter?"

"What's happening, Dan?"

"Suppose you tell me, O fearless crime fighter."

"You've seen the morning paper?"

"You bet your Jewish ass I've seen the morning paper. Who's handling your PR?"

"I told you it was going to happen. John Farrow got wind of it and zeroed the whole staff in on me."

"It's like telling a guy you're going to shaft him. It still hurts when you do it."

"I'm sorry, Dan."

"Don't cloak your chutzpah in humility, Frankel, it doesn't become you."

"Lay off, Dan. I've got enough trouble tonight."

"I haven't even begun. What kind of hanky-panky are you playing with the Big Man in Washington? Are you bucking for my job?"

"What are you talking about?"

"Washington has been on the horn all night trying to locate you. The Attorney General himself, plus the FBI. You're playing in the big time, Frankel, and they can't find the fearless crime fighter because he's making out with the jet set, playing cutesy with the beautiful people. So they have to get *this* Irish ass out of a poker game—while I'm losing, mind you—to play supersleuth and find you."

"What's it about?"

"Suppose you tell me. Let me in on your little secret. They want you in Washington first thing in the morning. Now, would it be asking too much if I wanted to know what the hell this is all about? I realize that you and the Big Man wear the same school colors, and maybe you go to church together, but this Irish boy from the back-of-the-yards is still running this office and I want to know what's going on."

Frankel followed his instant instinct and lied. "I don't have the foggiest idea, Dan. Honest."

"Would it be too much trouble to fill me in when you do find out?"

"As soon as I know."

"The orders are that your ass is to be in Washington at eight o'clock tomorrow morning."

Frankel looked at his watch. "How the hell do I do that? The earliest flight won't get me in till ten."

"Are you ready for a little cloak-and-dagger? Listen carefully. You're to drive to the airport now. Do you read me? Now. Leave your car in the parking lot, go into the terminal, rent a car and drive to the Milwaukee airport. There'll be a private plane there waiting to take you to Washington. Go to the desk at Butler Aviation, where there's a special section for private aircraft. Give them *my name*, not yours. Is that clear? *My name*, not yours."

"Clear," Frankel answered, "but I don't understand it."

"Boychick, I don't understand it either, but when the Big Man and the FBI say move, we move. So move."

"I'll call you from Washington tomorrow."

"That would be lovely, Peter. Do call if you can spare a minute." The falsetto turned back into a growl. "Get your ass in gear."

Moynihan hung up.

Frankel shouldered his way back through the crowd to the table. His gut reaction had been right. When his father's friend, Sam Weiskopf, had called him on Friday, he sensed something bigger than was surfacing. He routed Weiskopf deviously to the Attorney General, circumventing the district office, where the report would get bogged down in petty paper work.

A fashion model and a man he didn't know were standing at the table. Susan said, "You know Melanie, don't you, Peter?" He forced himself to smile at the girl. "And this is a friend of hers from London . . ." She fumbled for the name.

The Englishman held out his hand and Frankel took it firmly, assessing the man quickly. In contrast to the clear white skin, ruddy cheeks, traditional blazer and careless scarf around the Englishman's neck, Frankel felt grubby, dark and coarse in his black velvet leisure suit. "Tatov," the Englishman said brightly, smiling easily. "Leonid Tatov. You Americans always expect someone from the Russian ballet when you hear my name. Or a spy. Bolshoi or Bolshevik!"

Peter Frankel smiled back. "Frankel," he said, "Peter Frankel, and I *am* from the Russian ballet."

Tatov laughed. "Good show. I'm going to like Chicago." Taking Melanie's hand, he looked down the front of Susan's dress. "Love Zorine's. It's better than Anabel's, don't you think, Frankel?"

"Never been there." He turned to Susan. "There's an emergency at the office. I'll have to take you home."

As Susan started to rise, Tatov said, "Nonsense. It's early yet. Melanie and I will take charge of Susan and see that she gets home safely."

"I'd better go with Peter." She pecked at Melanie's cheek and held out her hand to Tatov. "See you."

Tatov held her hand longer than was necessary.

Driving to Susan's apartment, Frankel was thinking about Sam Weiskopf and the fear in his eyes when he had told him about the threats to his son. He had already pigeonholed Tatov to be dealt with later. Weiskopf was now.

"What about Wednesday, Peter?"

"Wednesday?"

"The dance at the Art Institute. Are you coming or not?"

"Christ, Susan, there must be something more important in the world than that damned party."

"I'm sorry, but I have to know whether you're coming. If you are, I'll call Laurie and see if she's available."

"I can't think about it now. Can't you realize that all hell is breaking loose?"

"All you have to say is yes or no."

"I don't know. I don't even know if I'll be in town."

Susan slid down in her seat, sulking. "Why does my life have to get so screwed up?"

"You don't even begin to know what screwed up is, Susan."

Monday, February 14
One a.m., Lake Forest

SHELDON COLE woke up screaming, his body covered with perspiration, the nightmare of the distorted faces and bloodied, blond hair of his mangled children still vivid.

Diane had awakened with the screams. "Shellie, are you all right?"

He looked around, focusing on the familiar objects in his bedroom, and realized that it had been a dream. He felt the wetness on his skin and the tremor of chills beginning.

"Are you all right, Shellie?"

He looked at his wife, reacted to her nakedness, needing to act out his own fear. "Do you want to fuck?"

Monday, February 14
Two a.m., Barbados, W.I.

RICO DEL GRACIA lay in the darkness, alert for the sound of Mike Nelson. It had been four hours since he'd disappeared into the black water. Once again del Gracia told himself that there had been no way to avoid the confrontation, and that neither of them could continue together with suspicions unspoken. Yet he could not have predicted the violence of Mike's reactions; there was nothing about the man which could have predicted such behavior.

Nelson swam well and was in top physical shape, del Gracia reassured himself. But the ocean could turn unexpectedly treacherous, and there could be sharks; warnings were posted from time to time. There was no place he could have gone without returning to the bungalow. Where could a naked man go?

There was time now to assess the importance of Nelson in his life. If the situation were reversed, how violent would his own reaction have been? Enough to be self-destructive? Gnawing at the edge of his awareness was the realization that Nelson could have deliberately destroyed himself. Not Mike, he was thinking. Mike loves life too much. Yet in many ways they *were* each other's lives.

Del Gracia had no religious structure in his life. He tried to remember the few times he had been to a synagogue, and the words which had been said there, but it was all a blur. Silently he said words to himself which became a singsong internal chant, a narcotic to his consciousness. Now he knew that he loved Nelson as a man loves a woman or a woman a man.

There was a sound in the room. At first he did not open his eyes, and he heard it again. Every part of his body came alive. Then there was a slight pressure at the foot of the bed, and he saw the silhouette of Nelson standing there, a few drops of water glistening on his skin.

Nelson tore off the sheet covering del Gracia. His voice was deliberately controlled. "Turn over," he ordered.

Del Gracia tried to see the other man's eyes. They were glass, revealing nothing. Obediently he turned on his stomach. Instantly Nelson was on top of him with a hard impact, penetrating him for the first time ruthlessly and painfully. Del Gracia screamed with the tearing pain, then bit his lip as Nelson humped with furious thrusts. At last the organic fluids of love turned pain into pleasure, summitting another plateau.

Monday, February 14
Three a.m., Chicago

Wʜᴇɴ sᴛᴏɴᴇʜɪʟʟ ᴀᴡᴏᴋᴇ, he made certain that Maude was sleeping deeply, went to his study and phoned Myrna. The phone rang a long time. He hung up, put on his reading glasses and called again, this time dialing carefully to make sure there was no mistake. There was still no answer.

Returning to bed and trying to fall asleep again, he went through the old dialogue with himself. There's no fool like an old fool, it began. She doesn't love me; she loves the *idea* of me. She needs a young stud; a man my age can't keep her satisfied. Then the replies. If she's only after your money, why won't she accept any? And damn it, you've been satisfying her; she couldn't fake orgasms like that.

The dialogue went on. Sleep would not come. If only Myrna had not gone to Butch's.

Monday, February 14
Four a.m., Milwaukee Airport

Tʜᴇ ᴅᴏᴏʀ to the cabin of the small private jet was closed. The anonymous man who had escorted Frankel from the terminal to the waiting plane hoisted himself on a rung, knocked three times and jumped back to wait. As the door opened, Frankel caught a glimpse of a uniformed man. Steps came down automatically, but as he started toward the plane the other man held him back. From the cabin, rubbing his eyes and yawning, a man in shirt sleeves appeared, shuddered against the night cold, came halfway down the stairs, looked up at the cloudy sky, and then nodded. The hand was released from Frankel's arm and pushed him toward the plane.

The man on the steps said, "May I see your identification?"

Because of the bulge his wallet made in his black velvet leisure suit, Frankel had only carried his driver's license and Zorine's credit card. The man on the steps scrutinized them and frowned. "Don't you have official identification?"

"My instructions were to report directly here. I didn't have time to go home to change or get my papers."

The man studied the credit card, turning it over. "What is Zorine's?"

"It's a disco."

The man on the steps studied Frankel. "Cha cha cha." He handed the cards back. "Don't you want to see *my* identification?"

"I didn't know I was supposed to."

"I may be from *Star Trek*." He rubbed the stubble on his face. "A very old rerun of *Star Trek*." He handed Frankel his own wallet, flipped open to an identification card: Garrett Randall Taylor, the Federal Bureau of Investigation. Frankel looked from the small photograph to the face of the yawning man. "I guess it's okay," he said, and held out his hand. "Glad to meet you."

Garrett Randall Taylor did not bother to shake Frankel's hand. "I'm freezing my balls off. We can play Rotary Club inside."

Except for the narrow beams of reading lights, the interior of the jet was dark. Frankel saw that another man was seated in darkness in the rear of the small cabin. Taylor ordered, "Sit across from me, strap yourself in and let's get this show on the road."

The co-pilot appeared from the cockpit and looked at Frankel, then at Taylor. "All clear?"

"All clear."

The stairs were retracted, the door closed, the co-pilot returned to the cockpit, locking the door behind him, and within seconds there was the whooshing sound of the engines igniting. As soon as they were airborne, the no-smoking sign went off. Taylor lit a cigarette, and then perfunctorily offered one to Frankel. "I don't smoke."

"Bully for you." He turned away.

"Did you fly in just to pick me up?"

"Wasn't that nice of me? I got out of a nice warm bed, drove twenty miles half asleep and flew a thousand miles in this automated sardine can all for you, Mr. Frankel. Just for you."

"Do you have any idea what this is all about?"

"You *are* naïve, aren't you?"

"I didn't think so until tonight. Maybe I am."

"Don't let me be the one to tarnish your ingenuousness. I've been at this a long time—too long, maybe. But you must understand that unnecessary knowledge makes for security leaks. Like robots, each of us does his part, never knowing what the exercise is unless we happen to read it in the newspaper the next day or empty the Director's wastebasket. My job is to get you from here to there"—he made a vague gesture—"and that's all I know and all I need to know."

"I know where I came from. Where am I going?"

"To never-never land and into the hands of someone called Waldo Dirksmith."

"Who's that?"

"Haven't the vaguest idea."

"One of yours?"

"Could be. He sounds like a Russian spy to me, but then I've been around since the old days, and everyone sounds like a Russian spy to us old-timers."

Frankel fidgeted. "Is there a place to pee on this plane?"

"Barely, if your pecker isn't too long. Try the door on your right."

When Frankel returned to his seat Taylor had moved to the

rear of the cabin and the man back there had moved up. He was much younger, with horn-rimmed glasses, a square haircut and clutching a too-new briefcase. Frankel waited for him to speak first.

"I represent the Attorney General," the man began in a soft Southern accent. "I understand that you are a personal friend of the Attorney General." It was not a question. Frankel was flattered. Their relationship had been that of teacher-student, but it had endured beyond law school. Frankel was beholden to the man for many things, including his present job.

In his last year at law school, when the Attorney General was still president of the university, Frankel had been assigned as the prosecuting attorney in the moot-court exercise of the senior class. It was the period of student unrest all over the country, and the law school's charge was against the president, the indictment claiming that he had violated the Bill of Rights and the Constitution in suppressing civil disobedience on campus.

Frankel had worked hard on the case, using all his skill, education and cunning. He had resorted to deceit and deviousness to acquire evidence: bribes, telephone taps, the burglary of files, some of it inadmissible but effective nonetheless. His courtroom questioning of the defendant had been unceasing, ruthless and brilliant. He had watched the president at the beginning of the trial, smiling and faintly amused at the fervor of the law students, remembering his own student years. But after Frankel had finished his relentless examination, producing actual evidence which made his witness gasp and turn silent, twisting the president's published words into a self-indictment, the benign figure on the stand had turned into a frightened, angry man. Through Frankel the president came to see the narrow line between law and lawlessness in quelling civil disobedience, and another interpretation of his own words and actions. The president had fought back as if for his life, but Frankel, countering blow with blow, had won the case. He also gained the respect and friendship of the man he had mootly destroyed.

"The Attorney General sends you his best personal regards."

"Am I going to see him?"

"There won't be time for that, I'm afraid. You must understand that my information is limited. My instructions were given to me by the A.G. himself, but I know nothing about the case. First off, he told me to make it quite clear that you are his personal—'Underline personal,' he said—representative at this meeting."

"What meeting?"

"I don't know. Mr. Taylor's instructions are to conduct you to a meeting. I was not informed of its nature, only that you are representing the A.G."

"My boss in Chicago is going to blow his county cork."

"At the moment you are on special assignment; the only boss you have is the Attorney General himself. That was made quite clear to me."

"Okay, I'll handle Dynamite Dan later. Are you going to be at this meeting?"

"No. As you must know, there's a new look in the administration now. We all interrelate—the Attorney General's office, the FBI, the CIA and the NSC." The Southern softness was gone from his voice. "It says we are all to pool information, be helpful to each other and be noncompetitive." He took off his glasses and rubbed the bridge of his nose. "In your ass," he snorted.

Frankel smiled. "Am I allowed to know your name?"

"Jeff."

"Look, Jeff, if I'm going to be the A.G.'s official representative, you ought to wise me up on the ground rules."

"A dog fight. Polite, mannered, structured, but still a dog fight. You'll find that no matter how many directives are issued, infighting takes precedence over fighting a common enemy." He looked across the aisle. "Balloon-bursting time, Frankel?"

"I get the pitch."

"The briefing that I received indicated that you're a fighter. If you are, I strongly suggest that you start training right now."

"Who is Dirksmith?"

"The Attorney General has chosen him to head this investigation. I have no idea who he is or what agency he represents."

"Do you know what will go on at the meeting?"

"Very little, except the general format. You have a piece of information. There will be others with other pieces of information. I suspect that it will be a little like show-and-tell. Then the combined brains will figure out what to do next."

"To whom do I report after the meeting?"

Jeff slumped in his seat and closed his eyes. "One thing will lead to another. It may even eventually all become clear to you."

Frankel looked back in the darkness toward Taylor, who appeared to be sleeping. Frankel methodically began to compose in his mind the words that he would speak at the meeting, the story he would tell about Sam Weiskopf and his son's bar mitzvah.

Monday, February 14
Seven a.m., Chicago

THE PRIVATE PHONE rang in Stonehill's dressing room while he was shaving. He dropped his razor, looked toward the bedroom where his wife was still asleep and answered before the second ring.

"Livie?"

Her voice was weak, hardly audible.

"Where are you?"

"I'm all right, I'm all right." And then the tears turned into gasps for breath amplified through the receiver.

"Where are you?"

Her words were staggered between sobs as she struggled for breath. "I'm all right. Don't worry. Give me time."

"Where are you?" He heard her trying to regain control. "Where are you?"

"I'm all right. There was an accident, but I'm all right. I'm in the hospital, but I'm not hurt."

"What hospital?"

"You can't come here, Livie. My mother is here."

"What hospital?"

"Darling, I love you. Don't make it worse than it is."

"I'll find you anyway. Tell me what hospital."

She hesitated. "Michael Reese, but please don't come. My mother is here and everyone will recognize you. I swear that I'm all right. Please don't come." She began to cry again.

In the taxi he felt the terror again and a hot stab of anger at himself for not having anticipated danger this quickly. He should have expected trouble. Instead he had been immobilized by jealousy, by his doubts of her, and by his feelings for her. There was no doubt anymore. Block by block through the heavy morning traffic, he cursed himself for his insensitivity.

It took ten minutes for Stonehill to thread his way from the main building through tunnels and corridors to Myrna's room. He was on the board of directors of the hospital, and six years ago had been chairman of the board. Consequently he knew most of the administrative staff, as well as many of the doctors, some of whom were his personal friends. But though he heard his name called several times as he charged through the tunnels, he only grunted acknowledgment and never looked left or right. He was thinking about Susan; this was like the time he rushed through the halls to her bedside. The scene with Whiz in the waiting room became vivid again.

The door to Myrna's room was blocked by a woman smoking a cigarette. She was a bleached blonde and wore heavy eye make-up, a black turtleneck sweater and black pants molded over a trim, corseted body. Stonehill tried to step by her. "Not so fast." She held out her hand. "Who are you?"

"I'm going to see Myrna Gordon."

"I know who you're going to see, but that doesn't answer my question. Who are you?"

"Livingston Stonehill."

"That tells me nothing. Are you a doctor?"

"No, a friend."

"That's what I thought." She sized him carefully without yielding her position. "I knew there was 'a friend.' I'm Myrna's mother. We ought to talk first."

He tried to slip past her.

"Don't get excited. Calm down. Myrna's all right. Trust a mother to know." She looked at Stonehill. "We ought to talk first."

"What happened?"

"What happened?" She shrugged her shoulders. "Plenty happened, but thank God nothing happened, if you know what I mean." She touched his arm and led him a few steps down the corridor. "Somebody tried to rape her in the laundry of her building. That's all. A nice girl goes quietly to do her laundry in a nice neighborhood and almost gets raped. Almost. That's a very important word, almost. You know what I mean?"

"Is she all right?"

The mother shook her head wearily. "A mass of bruises. Black-and-blue like you wouldn't believe. She fought. My daughter fought. My daughter is a fighter, Mr. Stonehill. Did you know that? Thank God, nothing is broken, no internal injuries. But psychological injuries? Who knows?"

"I'd like to see her now."

"She's fixing her hair. She'll wait. We ought to talk first."

"Not here."

"Where, then? Maybe in her room, so that she should hear? That's all she needs is more tsuris. She's had enough tsuris. You know what tsuris means, Mr. Stonehill?" He nodded. "I wouldn't have thought so. You're Jewish, Mr. Stonehill?"

"Yes."

"My late husband used to say in every bad thing there is a little good. In this case, you could have been a goy, Mr. Stonehill." She dropped her cigarette on the floor and stamped it out with her heavily wedged, open-toed shoe. "For a long time I've known that there is a Mr. Somebody in Myrna's life. Trust a mother's instinct. She didn't say a word. That daughter of mine, close-mouthed like you wouldn't believe. Since she was a little girl, close-mouthed. But believe me, a mother knows. Are you a married man, Mr. Stonehill?"

There had to be a way out of this, Stonehill thought, but he was trying to avert a scene.

She pressed her question. "Currently are you married, Mr. Stonehill?"

"Yes."

As she shook her head sadly, not a strand of blond hair moved. "It had to be. Otherwise why wouldn't a daughter tell her mother about a Mr. Somebody? Listen, these days with daughters, who knows what goes on? Do you have a daughter, Mr. Stonehill?" He nodded. "Then you know that with daughters, you never know." She sighed again, her bolstered breasts rising and falling. "I knew there was somebody . . . but not you. In a million years I wouldn't have thought it was somebody like you." She studied his face again. "You look like a nice man, Mr. Stonehill, a very nice man. But for my Myrna?" She touched his shoulder. "Come on, Mr. Stonehill, let's face facts. No offense, but you're a little old even for me. The difference in our ages could be understandable, but not with my Myrna. Now, why don't you be a nice gentleman and go away? Leave. Get out of my daughter's life once and for all."

"You don't understand."

"Oh, I understand, Mr. Stonehill. I understand plenty." She bobbed her head. "I understand that when an older man is shtupping a young girl, there can only come trouble. That I understand very well."

"I think we ought to talk to Myrna. You don't understand that we love each other."

"Love!" she pointed a finger at herself. "You think I don't understand love, Mr. Stonehill?" Her voice lowered. "Do you have grandchildren?" He nodded. "I also. A darling boy and a beautiful baby girl by my older daughter. You know what I feel for them, Mr. Stonehill? I feel love. For people our age, that's love." She nodded her head toward the closed door. "The other isn't love, Mr. Stonehill, it's hanky-panky. So why don't you be a nice gentleman and get out of here before I lose my temper?"

Stonehill shoved past her.

Myrna was sitting up in bed, her face pale but unmarked, her lips tight, holding back tears. But when she held out her arms to him, her face twisted with pain. He went to her, and they held each other tenderly at first, then violently. He buried the tears in his eyes in the softness of her hair.

"Let go of my daughter. You'll hurt her." When they both ignored her, she ran to the bed and grabbed Stonehill's coat, trying to pull him away and screaming, "Nurse, doctor, help, help."

Reacting quickly, Stonehill jumped up and put his hand over the woman's mouth. He felt the impact of her teeth as she tried to bite him, and the force of her body trying to break his hold.

"Mama, it's all right. Mama, stop it. Please, Mama, stop it."

She stopped struggling and backed off as Stonehill released his grip, slowly taking his hand away from her mouth. Gasping for air, she held her hand over her heart.

"Are you all right, Mama?" Mrs. Gordon nodded, smoothed her lacquered hair. "He wouldn't hurt me, Mama. Livie wouldn't hurt me."

"You lied to me, Myrna. There was no man in the laundry." She pointed at Stonehill. "He did it. You're trying to protect him."

"No!"

"The truth, Myrna. Tell me the truth." She shook her. "No, don't tell me the truth; I know it already. The truth is that this monster beat you. You lied to protect him."

"No, Mama. I told you the truth. There was a man in the laundry. That's the truth."

"Swear it. Swear it on your father's grave."

"I swear it, I swear it, Mama."

"On your father's grave."

"On Papa's grave I swear it."

"I don't believe you. You're lying. God forgive you." She turned to Stonehill. "You may think I'm a nothing, but I know men, and I know a brute when I see one. It's in his eyes, Myrna. Look at his eyes."

Myrna had started sobbing again. "Stop it, Mama, stop it."

Stonehill's voice was suddenly menacing. "Both of you stop it at once." He moved toward Myrna's mother and she moved away, cowed. "Sit down, Mrs. Gordon, and keep your head on your shoulders. Getting emotional will solve nothing."

"Emotional! Look who's calling who emotional. Let me tell you, Mr. Stonehill, that in my—"

He cut her off. "I said to sit down and be quiet." She wavered. "I said to sit down, Mrs. Gordon, and be quiet." She perched on the edge of a chair, but as he moved toward Myrna she began to get up again. Stonehill turned back toward her, threatening with his eyes and the set of his jaw, and she sank back.

"Myrna, listen to me carefully. It is important that I know exactly what happened last night. Start from the beginning."

Mrs. Gordon broke in, "The beginning is that she should have been out with a man her own age. Then none of this would have happened."

"If you cannot be quiet, I am going to see that you are removed from this room. Is that quite clear, Mrs. Gordon?"

"Her own mother and he's going to have me removed from the room."

"Please, Mama."

"Start from the beginning," Stonehill repeated.

"It happened so quickly," Myrna said shakily. "I took the elevator down to the laundry room on the mezzanine. Before I even began to load the machine this man came into the room. At first I didn't pay any attention. Lots of men do their own laundry. But I had never seen him before, and he didn't have a basket or any detergent. He just looked at me. He looked funny, as if he was dazed or doped or something."

"What did he look like?"

"I don't remember exactly. He was white, maybe in his middle twenties. Dark hair and dark eyes. Small. He could have been Mexican or Puerto Rican—dark like that. Glassy eyes. A smirk around his mouth. I get chills all over again just remembering it."

"What did he say?"

"He didn't say anything; he just looked at me. I don't remember what I said—something funny, maybe, like what I would say to one of the guys in the building who comes down to do his laundry. He never answered, just kept looking. I tried to get past him. I just left the laundry where it was. I got almost to the door, and then he grabbed my arm and threw me back across the room, against one of the machines. He threw me hard, and he began to laugh when he saw that I was hurt. He kept laughing as he took off his belt, a big wide leather one with a heavy metal buckle. I guess I tried to scream, but I don't think any sound came out. It was like a dream, trying to scream and no sound coming out. Then he whipped the belt at me and the buckle hit me in the arm." She lifted up the sleeve of her hospital gown; almost her entire upper arm had turned purple from the impact. Stonehill's hand touched his own biceps, feeling pain there. "Then he did it again, and this time I tried to turn away and it caught me on the hip. He was still laughing. Then he started unzipping his pants. I tried to make a run for it again, but he caught me and slammed me against the dryer. When I looked up, his pants were down around his shoes. He didn't wear any underwear and he had this ugly . . ." She fumbled for a word, looking at her mother, then dropped her head and whispered, "He had an erection. I didn't turn away. I wanted to look someplace else, but I remember thinking I had never seen an uncircumsized penis before. I just stared at it; I couldn't move my eyes away. Then he started hitting me with his belt again, swinging wildly, hitting me no matter which way I ran. Somehow I fell down or he pushed me. It was such a nightmare I really don't remember. He stood over me and kept beating me with that big buckle faster and faster. I tried to protect my face. Then it stopped suddenly. Just stopped. I heard the buckle hit the cement floor, and when I looked up he was just standing there. His eyes were closed and stuff was spurting out of his cock and his body was rocking and he was making strange sounds.

"I don't know where I got the strength, but I crawled past him and ran and crawled and dragged myself up the five flights to my apartment. I didn't know if he was following me or not. I didn't even know if he knew that I'd run away. I didn't think, I just kept moving. I don't remember opening my door or locking myself in the apartment, but I did. I was like a wounded animal."

Stonehill could no longer keep control of himself, and he tenderly took her in his arms. At his touch she cried again, a crescendo of tears beginning, her body racked with the terror she was reliving. He held her close, letting his body absorb her shock, his lips skimming the surface of her face. Finally her body began to relax, and the tears diminished until she was able to speak again. "I'll never forget it. Not as long as I live."

"Did you call the police?"

"No. I should have, I know, but I felt so humiliated. He made me feel so dirty. I know it doesn't make any sense now, but all I could think of was how dirty I was. I felt the blood through my clothes seeping out."

"What did you do?"

"I cried. I just lay on the floor and cried. I saw the blood on my hands and the blood on the carpet and I kept crying and crying. It was as if I was two people. I knew that I should call the police, but I couldn't move. I didn't want to look at myself in the mirror. I heard the phone ringing and ringing. I knew I should try to answer it, but I couldn't move."

"Was it about midnight?" She nodded. "I was calling you. I just wanted to say good night and tell you that I love you."

"I didn't have any more strength. I must have passed out. The last thing I remember was the phone ringing, and then there's a void until I regained consciousness. I was all right then; I knew that I was still alive. I got my clothes off without looking at my body. I ran hot water in the tub and somehow got into it with my eyes closed, not daring to see what my body looked like. I don't remember any pain until then; all I remember is feeling dirty. But when I got in the bathtub the pain was excruciating. I called the doctor and told him what happened. He came right over and called an ambulance, then Mama . . . That's it, Livie. That's the whole, horrible thing."

"Didn't the doctor call the police?"

"No."

"Doesn't he or the hospital have to make some kind of report to the police?"

"No. He made up some kind of story for the hospital. I couldn't have handled the police and the reporters. Maybe I could now, but it's too late, isn't it?"

"It wouldn't do any good now, and you've had enough anguish. You have to start forgetting."

"Never."

"Yes, you will. I'll make you forget it. I promise."

"You know the first thing I thought about when I woke up this morning? They knocked me out with a shot as soon as I arrived at the hospital. The first thing I thought when I came to was what you would say when you saw me. Would you still love me, still want me."

"You knew the answer, didn't you?"

For the first time Myrna was able to smile. "You know what else I thought? It shows you how petty women are. I wondered how I'd ever be able to go to the party at the Art Institute. Dumb, isn't it? I didn't tell you yesterday that I wanted to go so bad I could taste it. Even though it meant going with that shmuck from the Commodities Exchange. I wanted to be ravishing for all your swell friends. I wanted you to be proud of me and jealous of every man who danced with me. It shows you how stupid women can be, worrying about all the wrong things."

Mrs. Gordon walked over to the bed and sat beside her daughter, opposite Stonehill. She smiled at both of them and touched her daughter's hair, smoothing it gently. "What party at the Art Institute?"

"Nothing, Mama. It's not important."

"No? It sounds like it's important to you. Listen, a terrible thing happened to you, a terrible thing, but, thank God, you were only hurt, not killed. It could have been worse." She shook her head. "It could have been a lot worse. Listen, you read it every day in the papers. It was a terrible experience, but you'll forget. Like Mr. Stonehill says, you'll forget."

"Never."

"You say that now, darling, but you'll get over it. When your father, *alav ha-sholom*, died, I said to myself, I said, never. But time heals. You'll see, my darling. You'll go back to work, you'll go out with your friends again." She leaned over and kissed her daughter's cheek. "Who's the schmuck from the Commodities Exchange? Do I know him?"

Myrna laughed; the laughter hurt. "You're incorrigible, Mama."

"What's so terrible if I want to know who your friends are? I'm only asking because I was playing mah-jong two days ago with a lady who also has a son who is a commodity trader. Such a fortune he's made and so quick. A year ago he was a bum; today's he's a millionaire." She looked at Stonehill. "Tell me, Mr. Stonehill, what do you do for a living?"

He looked for help to Myrna, who was amused. "Mr. Stonehill is in the banking business, Mama."

"Banking? It's a nice business, banking. Would you happen to know a Mr. Rapapport who happens to be second vice president of the Rogers Park Trust and Savings?"

"Offhand, I don't think so." He held Myrna's hand tightly. "There are many banks in Chicago."

"Also a very nice man," she said. "Refined. In my experience bankers are very refined. Isn't that your experience, Mr. Stonehill?"

Before he could answer, Myrna broke in. "Livie, I'm all right now. Go back to your office. Really, I'm fine. I need sleep, that's all. I'll talk to you later."

He leaned over and kissed her lightly. "I'll call you this afternoon. Forget what happened and don't discuss it with anyone." He stood up, nodded at Mrs. Gordon and started for the door.

"Mr. Stonehill."

"Yes?"

"You have to understand how a mother feels." She was stroking Myrna's hair again. "This is my baby, my poor, fatherless baby. You have to understand how a mother feels."

"I understand."

"I maybe said some things that I shouldn't have, but you must understand how a mother feels."

"I do understand."

"I'm glad, Mr. Stonehill."

"Go on, Livie. I'll talk to you later."

After he blew a kiss and left, Mrs. Gordon said, "Funny about men. In the hall when I was talking to him, he looked so old. But here in the daylight, he looked different, not really so old at all."

"Mama, you must promise me that you'll forget that he even exists. Promise me, Mama."

"The party at the Art Institute is when? Wednesday? Listen, you'll get your hair done, and you can wear a long dress with long sleeves so that no one will know. It will do you good; it will take your mind off your misfortune. I'll call my beauty parlor today."

"Mama, promise you'll never mention his name."

"All right, I promise." She fondled Myrna's hair. "They give a rinse at my beauty parlor. Not a bleach, just a rinse is all. It gives nice highlights to the hair. A little blond comes out in everybody."

Monday, February 14 Eight a.m., Somewhere near Washington

THE ROOM was windowless and mechanically ventilated by a malfunctioning machine. Exposed fluorescent tubes of light cast a blue-white pallor over the eight men sitting silently, waiting, at the large oval table. At one side of the room was a folding table with plastic containers of coffee, cardboard cups, jars of powdered dairy substitute and packaged sugar. The walls of the room had been painted a meaningless green, marred by scratches and chips, black with soot around the ventilating grills.

Peter Frankel was the last man to be escorted into the room. No introductions had been made, only stiff, unsmiling acknowledgments of his presence by the other men already seated. He felt grubby, rubbing his hand over his emergent beard, and was conscious of how he must appear to these others who'd had time to shower and shave. His velvet suit was wrinkled, the synthetic fabric of his patterned shirt absorbed no perspiration, and he was aware of the rank smell of his unwashed body. Most of all, his mouth felt unclean; he had not brushed his teeth since Sunday morning. He glanced at the folding table, thinking that perhaps coffee would help, but it was obvious that no one had touched the pots and cups yet. There was a ritual here which he did not understand.

The eight men sat, not looking directly at each other but surreptitiously casing each other. They appeared to be strangers, and unidentifiable as to profession or function. It reminded Frankel of the first meeting of two families after his sister's engagement, a confrontation of strangers about to become related.

At precisely eight o'clock, a tall, gaunt man burst into the room, his step indicating military precision and his straight-ahead eyes indicating military discipline. Except for Frankel, the men around the table fidgeted to attention, sitting erect on the hard chairs. The man mounted the chair at the head of the table, and with a machine-gun action of his head assessed in turn the faces of the eight men who had been waiting for him. Frankel began to smile when the angular face targeted on him but thought better of it. Neither the leader nor any of the men carried a briefcase or papers, and no pencils or notepads were on the table. Obviously what they were to learn here was to be committed to memory.

"Gentlemen, my name is Waldo Dirksmith." His voice was higher-pitched than his size and stature indicated. "In the last three days there have been isolated reports of incidents which could indicate a calculated plot against certain citizens of the United States and, as such, a threat to our national security. It is our province here only to assess the information we each possess. Upon examination, it is conceivable that we will find that these incidents are unrelated, local threats of no national consequence. It is our purpose in this room to trade information, pool our expertise and arrive at a decision as to whether these incidents are of national significance or are only local problems. The resultant course of action will be determined by others. Are there any questions?" He looked from face to face. Nobody spoke. "It is my understanding that five of you here have a report on an incident in your area. I will call on each of you in turn. There will be no need to identify yourselves nor to identify the agency which you represent. It would also be prudent to avoid mentioning geographical locations. If this is all clearly understood, we will proceed." He waited a moment, then cocked his head at the man immediately to his left.

This man was stout and affluent-looking; Frankel guessed him to be in his early fifties. When he spoke, his words were coated in a heavy Southwestern drawl. Twirling a diamond ring on his chubby finger, he adjusted the knot on his heavily patterned Countess Mara tie. "There is an elderly lady in our area," he began, "a widow of great wealth and prestige in the Jewish community. I should have said that there *was* a lady in our area. Unfortunately, she is now deceased. On Friday afternoon two young men came to her house and were granted admittance by the maid, a black woman. From the testimony of the maid, it was ascertained that these men identified themselves as rabbinical students connected with the Hillel Foundation, a Jewish youth group which has received considerable financial support from the lady and her family. The information we have pieced together is from the testimony of the maid, who is quite unfamiliar with the Hebrew faith, and from a conversation with the lady's eldest daughter. Our information indicates that during the encounter with these two alleged rabbinical students, the lady suffered a coronary thrombosis. The maid found her prostrate on the floor approximately one half hour after the two men had gained entrance. The lady was in great physical pain but still conscious. Before she lost consciousness, she instructed the maid to call the police and told her that she had been threatened. Even after repeated interrogation of the maid, the police could not discover the exact nature of the threat.

"On a routine check of the area, the police found no one answering to the description of the young men; nor did they find any other witness to their presence. Under pressure from the lady's daughter, the three Hillel Foundation chapters in the area were questioned. No one had seen anyone answering to the description, nor had anyone been directed to the lady's house."

Dirksmith interjected, "Are you saying that the men could have been a figment of the maid's imagination?"

"Possibly, sir. There is no corroborating evidence. Unfortunately, the lady died in the intensive-care unit at a local hospital and could give no further evidence. Whoever these men were—if indeed they existed at all—there is no trace of them now. Whatever threat they made—if a threat was made—will never be known, since there are no witnesses. The local police feel that because of her age the lady may have imagined a threat, that the coronary thrombosis occurred during the visit of the two men, and that they became panic-stricken and fled. As far as the police are concerned, this closes the case. But in our opinion there are many unanswered questions. In the opinion of the local rabbinate, if the two young men were indeed rabbinical students they would not have fled, but would have assisted the lady and called for help. Being somewhat familiar with Hebrew culture, we are inclined to agree."

Frankel was thinking, Hebrew culture, my ass.

The soft Southern voice droned on. "We might have dismissed the case, as the police did, if there had not been another occurrence in our area. The other case involves the bombing last evening of a Rolls-Royce drop-head Corniche convertible belonging to a young Jewish gentleman who lives in—" He caught himself in time. "—who lives in an exclusive suburban area populated primarily by people of the Hebrew faith but considered exclusive nonetheless. The automobile was parked in the driveway of the home when it exploded. Fortunately, no one was injured, but the automobile was totaled. When questioned by the police, and in spite of incontrovertible evidence that the bomb was the work of a professional, the owner dismissed the incident as youthful vandalism, and could give no other explanation of the bombing. He spoke at great length about the prevalence of drugs being used by the young people of the area, and cited several incidences of other vandalism, but none of it was as serious as this or as professionally executed.

"On subsequent questioning by two of our own representatives, we found this man reluctant to discuss the episode. He seemed highly distraught, in contrast to the police report that he had been cool and seemingly unshaken by the incident. Our representatives also found evidence that the family was packing, evidently preparing to leave the city, although the man tried to conceal this. The airport and the main roads are currently staked out, and the house itself is continuously under surveillance."

"Is it your opinion that between the time this man was questioned by the police," Dirksmith asked, "and the time your representatives talked to him, he received a threat of some kind?"

"Yes, sir."

"Is that the end of your report?"

"Yes, sir."

Dirksmith nodded at the next man. "Our cursory information," he began, "shows a marked increase in the number of known foreign agents entering the United States during the last four or five days. There is not sufficient evidence at this time to indicate a pattern. The same report has been coming in from all points of entry—I repeat, *all* points of entry. This could indicate that all the operatives are not coming from the same area or continent, but this in itself is nonconclusive, since it may be a highly sophisticated operation and some entries could be diversionary. It is interesting to note that by the time we were alerted to a possible situation, we found that many of the known agents had already left the country. Most curious. We have begun strict surveillance of the known agents remaining here, and will have further information at a later time."

As he spoke, each man added another fragment to the puzzle, each of them inconclusive in itself but all together accumulating into an awesome mosaic. Each report was presented succinctly, the language formalized, the delivery deadpan and unemotional. Obviously these reports had been prepared in advance, phrased in the language the men had been trained to use, and rehearsed to be factual and without human emphasis.

"Do you fellows know what a bar mitzvah is?" Frankel asked after Dirksmith had nodded to him. He was slouched in his hard seat, smiling, at ease in an element which he intuitively understood. He was stimulated, and aware of a presage of further excitement. He forgot that his suit was wrinkled, that his teeth needed brushing. He was also angry at the emotionless recita-

tions of Jewish misery. His smile widened, and he looked from
face to face.

Dirksmith checked his watch and did not bother to conceal
his annoyance. "Suppose you tell us what a bar mitzvah is."

Frankel leaned forward, his elbows on the table. "A bar
mitzvah is a very special time in a Jew's life, a very important
occasion in the Hebrew faith. It's the time when a boy becomes
a man in the eyes of God. He stands in the sanctum as a peer
with other men and reads from the Torah and the Talmud. On
the day of his bar mitzvah he stands as a man among men, no
longer a boy. But it's a hell of a lot more than that. It's an
important event to the entire Jewish family, a celebration as
well as a religious ceremony. It's a time for dancing and eating
and laughing, for the Jewish family to restate its Jewishness to
themselves and to the entire world. There is a Yiddish word
calling *kvelling*. The word is untranslatable, really, but its most
simplistic meaning is . . . swelling with pride, coming alive with
pride."

Frankel saw Dirksmith check his watch again, and regarded
the other impassive faces. "A bar mitzvah is a time for kvelling.
I'm telling you all this because there is a man in my area, a very
nice man of the Hebrew faith who feels that God has been good
to him. Although he was married for many years, the union was
never blessed with a child. The couple had great riches and the
respect of the community, but never a child. After twenty-two
years, as if by some miracle, a son was born to them. The son is
a fine boy, steeped in Jewish tradition. God has also seen fit—"

Dirksmith could not contain his impatience. "Please condense the incident."

"This is no incident; this has all the ingredients of a great
tragedy. How do you condense human anguish?"

"Try," Dirksmith coaxed.

"Several years ago, on Mount Masada in Israel the remains
of the first temple were uncovered, an historic, sacred shrine.
This man is taking his son and his whole family—aunts, uncles,
cousins, everyone—to Israel for the bar mitzvah at Masada. And
for the privilege of doing this, and because the man loves Israel
and its people, he is donating three million dollars to the Israeli

nation now and five hundred thousand dollars a year for the next ten years. It is his way of saying thank you to God for all the blessings on his house." Frankel sat straighter and folded his hands on the table. "You want a condensation. This is it: two fucking Arabs come to this man and tell him that if he goes to Masada for his son's bar mitzvah and gives this money to Israel, they're going to blow up everything—the son, the father, the whole bar mitzvah, chopped liver and all." Frankel leaned back. "End of report."

Dirksmith didn't blink, but simply pointed his needle nose at the next man. The details of each report were of no consequence now; every man at the table realized that these were no isolated incidences but a massive plot of some kind, still undefined in scope or organization. A thousand questions nagged at Frankel's mind, and his body, keyed now for action, lost its weariness. But Dirksmith forestalled the building momentum by rising when the last report was finished. "We will take a ten-minute coffee break. The smoking lamp is lit."

Chairs scraped noisily against the wooden floor as the men formed a line at the coffee station. Frankel was the last in line. When he had poured a cup for himself he looked around, but the other men had formed small groups, their backs to him, their positions excluding him. Their clannishness both amused and enraged him.

"Tell me," the high-pitched voice asked, "about your own bar mitzvah."

Frankel turned to the stern face of Waldo Dirksmith. "Sir?"

"Don't tell me that you missed one of the great joys of Jewish life."

Frankel smiled. "Guilty as charged. No bar mitzvah."

"The Attorney General said that I'd like you." Dirksmith finally smiled. "I do."

"I suppose I should apologize for being a pompous windbag, but I was pissed. These guys were reciting statistics, not considering people's anguish."

"You'll come to understand that human anguish is germane to our profession, a Euclidean constant that one learns to accept, and to function in spite of."

Frankel said nothing.

"I think we all understood your feeling," Dirksmith continued. "You made your point. You also made a mistake: you underestimated the men in this room. We are professionals, and good ones. The impression you made was of a rowdy puppy, full of untrained, unharnessed power. These men now believe that you will bite the hand that feeds you and defecate on the living-room floor." He looked at Frankel carefully. "Perhaps you will, but I have to trust the Attorney General, whose judgment is usually impeccable. Meanwhile, we will have to do some face-saving so that these men will work with you willingly. The fact that I am here talking to you will make them wonder. They probably figure that right now I'm quietly eating your ass out—at least they hope that's what I'm doing. In a minute, I'm going to laugh out loud at something you say. I rarely laugh out loud. Then I'm going to pat you on the shoulder. I don't feel like laughing and I don't like touching other men, but you need official endorsement. Thereafter, for all your eccentricities, they'll accept you as a necessary evil. Do the same for them, will you? I have a feeling that before this is over we'll all need each other. Try, will you?"

"I will."

Dirksmith laughed loudly. "Good boy," he said so that the others could hear him, then patted Frankel on the shoulder, did a neat about-face, strode back to the center table and remounted his chair.

When they were all seated again, Dirksmith recapped the first part of the meeting, picking out salient points from each report, reconstructing them into a plausible whole. "I believe that we're all agreed that this is a cohesive plot being carried out nationwide by persons and/or organizations at the moment unknown." He looked at the eight men. "Is there any dissent?"

One of the men said, "No dissent, sir, but it seems obvious that we are dealing with some faction of the PLO. I think for the record, sir, that we should agree that this exercise is being conducted by and for the benefit of Arabs unknown against the Israeli nation."

Another man said, "It could be a diversion."

Dirksmith took charge again. "On the basis of the information supplied here this morning, I believe my original summation is correct and should stand for the record: persons and/or organizations at the moment unknown. Is there any further dissent?" No one dared. "In that case," he went on, "the next step is to recommend actions to be taken by the various agencies involved. In that case, only you, you and you will be required to stay." He had aimed his nose at three of the men at the table, and at Frankel. "The other gentlemen may leave, and we thank you for your cooperation. There will be a guard outside who will escort you to other locations for further interrogation."

Dirksmith relaxed as soon as the other men left, loosened his tie, yawned and rubbed his eyes. "We have a problem," he said, yawning. "I don't like it, not one bit of it."

"Who is he?" The youngest of the men remaining motioned toward Frankel.

"His name is Peter Frankel."

"Whom does he represent? What's his function?"

Dirksmith yawned again. "He's on special assignment to the Attorney General. What is his function?" He looked at Frankel closely. "His function is chutzpah. Did I pronounce that correctly, Frankel?"

"Perfectly, sir."

"I don't understand," the man persisted. "I know what chutzpah is, but why do we need him?"

"Because," Dirksmith explained, "we don't have any chutzpah. We have intelligence, elaborate networks of agents, computers, skill, experience . . . every human and mechanical device known to man . . . but in the final analysis I think we're going to need a little chutzpah. Do you agree, Frankel?"

"It's like chicken soup," Frankel replied. "It couldn't hurt."

Another of the men said, "I don't like amateurs doing a professional's job. They bungle."

"Would you prefer an Israeli agent?" Distaste came automatically to the faces of the other two men. "I thought not, though we may need them eventually, God help us."

The fourth man, who had not spoken yet, said, "Technically, this is straight Bureau jurisdiction."

The youngest answered, "Not if these are foreign agents in-volved; not if they're going to assassinate Americans on foreign soil."

"You gentlemen are not reading your mail. The directives say that we are all supposed to interrelate, to put all our input into one basket. None of us may like it, but I work according to the book and the book says to interrelate, so why don't we start?"

Dirksmith had been up most of the night studying the frag-ments of information which had been collated by his staff in the short time since the Attorney General had called him. He had made his own appraisal of the incidents and had already de-cided on a course of action, but it was necessary to go through the motions of a joint meeting of the agencies involved, and now he had to lead these men by deductive reasoning to a course of action which he had already plotted in his mind. The meeting had produced a plus which he had not anticipated: Peter Frankel. Actually, the idea of using Frankel had been put in his mind by the Attorney General's description of him and of his qualities. Frankel had all the characteristics which Dirk-smith distrusted in his profession: a hothead personality, over-confident bravado, a wise-ass posture, a deliberately dramatic and bathetic presentation of ideas. Yet the Attorney General had been right on two counts: Frankel was smart as hell, and he had a Jewish dimension which Dirksmith now saw how to use effectively.

In Dirksmith's mind, this plot, whatever it was, seemed a minor exercise in terrorism compared to other Arab operations he was familiar with. So far there were mostly threats of terror rather than, barring the Rolls-Royce, overt acts of terrorism. But what intrigued him was the seemingly low-key climate of the operation, the sights set at nickel-and-dime targets rather than a world-shaking blast. These goals were curiously non-Arab in concept, and his research and experience could find no previous examples of such thinking and planning. But because of these characteristics, this plan could be effective where other large-scale plots had failed. The factor which could make it work, in Dirksmith's estimation, was the nature of the Jew, the historical evidence of Jewish reaction to other acts against them. Rather than turn to outside authority for help, they turned to each other, secreting their terror incestuously, huddling together to accept the inevitable, knowing that somehow they would survive as their ancestors had. Intellectually, Dirksmith could understand why in the past they had not turned to authority; authority had been the enemy, after all. But this was the United States, not Hitler, or the Inquisition or a Russian or Polish pogrom. Why can't these idiot Jews understand that, Dirksmith asked himself? But Peter Frankel would fight; he was like an Israeli in that sense, not like those other American Jews whose organizations and leagues were ineffectual in protecting them in this situation. Properly provoked and motivated, Frankel could be militant.

The idea of using Frankel as bait had developed in Dirksmith's mind as the other agents droned their reports filled with details he already knew. But Frankel was smart, and he had to be hooked like a big-game fish, played tenderly before setting the hook. Their brief conversation during the coffee break had been the beginning; his sudden decision to keep Frankel on at this high-level meeting was part of the plan, and what would happen next would be further bait. The other men would continue to resent Frankel, which perfectly suited Dirksmith's plan. There would be time later to give them the rationale behind his using Frankel as a lure, an expendable decoy.

Dirksmith leaned over the table, folded his hands in front of him and said wearily, "What are we going to do, gentlemen?" The three professionals remained impassive, but Frankel was clearly bursting to speak out. Nodding at him, Dirksmith thought, Come on, my little Jewish shark, rise to the bait.

Monday, February 14
Eleven a.m., Chicago

IRVING FELDMAN'S owl eyes were wide with shock. He sat behind his massive desk, his small stature overwhelmed by the brown-leather swivel chair while Stonehill sat opposite, waiting for an answer. Sheldon Cole stood looking out the window down sixty-three stories to the busy streets. On the sofa in the far corner, Molly Mandlebaum sat drinking coffee, touching her hair. Each of them had just told Feldman his or her individual experience, and Stonehill's report of the assault on Myrna Gordon had eliminated any possibility that these were only the threats of a crank.

"Not to be believed," Feldman repeated, "not to be believed. In this day and age . . . in this country . . ."

Stonehill pressed him again. "What do we do?"

"For the moment," Feldman counseled, "nothing."

Sheldon Cole turned to face Feldman, his body contracted, a boxer waiting for the starting bell. "Not this Jewish boy. I'm not sitting on my ass and let them mutilate my kids." He strode to the desk. "You know what I do, Feldman? I give up." He slammed a clenched fist on the blotter. "I don't play against those odds. I'm not gambling with my kids' lives. I let them win, I let them beat me." As he turned around and lowered his head, his body seemed to shrink. "I let those mother-fuckers beat me." The fight was out of his voice. He looked across the room to Molly Mandlebaum. "Excuse me, Mrs. Mandlebaum, I forgot you were here. Pardon me."

Molly Mandlebaum fingered the choker of pearls around her

neck. "Pardon you for what, Mr. Cole? For calling those mother-fuckers mother-fuckers?" She walked toward him, smoothing her dress, holding her head erect. "I was beginning to think, Mr. Cole, that you were like these others—all talk, no action."

Stonehill objected, "That isn't fair, Molly."

"I know what you're all thinking. You're all tycoons, and I'm an old Irish broad who inherited a lot of Jewish money and who only thinks with her cunt." She looked at the startled faces. "It's true, isn't it? Isn't that what you're thinking?"

Irving Feldman stood up. "Mrs. Mandlebaum—" he began.

She cut off his words. "Sit down, Feldman. You look better sitting there with your hands folded telling us not to do anything. I've seen a lot of lawyers in my day, and I know how they work. You're about to tell us that we should contemplate the alternatives and explore the options, aren't you? All the while the time clock keeps running and the cash register keeps ringing."

Feldman tried to calm her. "You're distraught, Mrs. Mandlebaum. I understand your anguish."

"Anguish my ass, Mr. Feldman. I'm too old and tough to be anguished. I know exactly what I'm going to do and how I'm going to do it, and you and this fancy law firm are going to help me."

"Molly," Stonehill interjected, "Feldman is right. We have to explore all the avenues open. There must be some authority we can turn to."

She touched Stonehill's shoulder and let her fingers stroke his hair. "Poor Livie. You've lived such a polite life. Everything has been so structured and smooth. How old are you, Livie, fifty?"

"Fifty-two."

"You don't look it. Fifty-two. You're the one who has the anguish, Livie. After living fifty-two years according to the book, you've finally found a piece of ass that turns you on. You're lucky, actually; most of your kind never find it."

Sheldon Cole was smiling. "You're quite a broad, aren't you?"

"You bet I am, Mr. Cole." Sizing him up, she touched the hard muscles of his arm. "If you were a little younger, Mr. Cole, I might be tempted to let you find out just how much of a broad I really am."

Feldman interrupted. "This is getting us nowhere."

"Wrong, Mr. Feldman." Reluctantly she released her contact with Cole. "In the final analysis, we're all going to do what we're destined to do; we're either going to fight or fold up our tent. In my opinion, Mr. Cole has made the right decision. The stakes are too high for him, and it takes a lot of courage for him to admit that. He's smart; I don't blame him for not gambling with his children."

"I could make a case," Feldman said, "for the outcome of civilization if mankind had backed off from each threat, if sacrifices had never been made."

"I'm sure that you could. You're a brilliant man, I know that. I holler about your bills, but I wouldn't be here if I didn't respect your ability."

"Thank you."

"But it's not *your* children who are being threatened. A good lawyer can make a case for or against anything, but it's his babies who are targets, Mr. Feldman. Do you see my point?"

"I see your point, Mrs. Mandlebaum. On the other side of the coin, it's his children *now*, but if everyone backs down it could be my children *tomorrow*. Somewhere along the line, someone must take a stand."

"Precisely. I agree one hundred percent. Someone must take a stand. Mr. Cole cannot, but I can. Not only can I, but I will. I have no relative of any kind." Her voice lowered. "There is no one I love or who loves me. It is hard for me to face that, but it's true. If I lose my life, no other life will be destroyed." She looked at the men's faces. "Don't feel sorry for me. It gives me a strength which none of you can afford to have." She looked at Stonehill. "Think about the consequences to you, Livie. They beat up your girl and suddenly you're a tiger ready to charge— to announce to the world that you're in love and are laying everything on the line for that love. That isn't your style, Livie; it isn't what you were born to do. You'd hurt your wife and daughter and grandson—and yourself. They'd be cut out of your life, and I don't think you could survive that. It would mean giving up your position in the community and at the bank. You couldn't handle that either."

"Don't underestimate me, Molly. You don't really know what I'm like inside." He rubbed his eyes. "Until this happened, perhaps I didn't know myself either. Sometimes it takes an external force to make a boy into a man. I hope to God that it isn't too late, that I'm not too old."

Feldman's chair creaked back and forth, his body racking to the traditional rhythm of Hasidic prayer. "Not to be believed," he chanted, "not to be believed. It's as though we're all being manipulated, as though someone above us is pulling strings. Now that I think about it, this is what it's all about. Not to be believed, not to be believed." He continued rocking, looking at no one.

Cole asked, "What does that mean?"

"In each person's mind," Feldman began, "to a greater or lesser degree, there exists a dichotomy: the person who lives in the real world and the one who exists in the fantasy world. Occasionally it's reversed; some people hide the real person and expose only the one in the fantasy. But either way it's the same; they live their whole lives in desperation, fearing the dream and enduring the drudgery of life, or living the dream and fearing life. Almost always it takes an external force from the outside to bring it into focus and force a decision. The fairy godmother for Cinderella. The wounded lion confronting Francis Macomber."

"Who the hell is Francis Macomber?" Cole asked.

"Well, I'm Molly Mandlebaum and I'm also Cinderella, and my fairy godmother was that old fart who died without leaving a last will and testament. And this Cinderella isn't going to sit on her ass while you grown men pontificate and do nothing."

Feldman continued as though there had been no interruption. "I was born to immigrant parents. I lived behind a tailor shop on Division Street. My mother, God rest her soul, used to say that to every—"

"Knock it off, Feldman." Molly squinted at the clock behind Feldman's desk. "I have an appointment at the architect's office. We're going to design a new Mandlebaum Clinic to be built in Haifa. They should have a rendering by Friday. On that day I'm calling a press conference to announce to the world that I'm building the clinic—and also that there has been pressure to stop me. I'll spell out the threats to the Mandlebaum Clinic, and Dr. Stetson will be at my side. We'll crack this thing wide open. Once I expose the plan, they won't dare carry out the threats."

"You can't take that chance," Feldman warned.

"You call the FBI," she directed Feldman. "I want them at that press conference, too. That will put some teeth into this. Not only that; I'm hiring private investigators to investigate every son-of-a-bitch on the payroll at the clinic to find out who's been feeding them information." She threw her mink coat over her shoulders and picked up her purse. "Also, Feldman, you'd better figure out a way to break part of the Mandlebaum trust and get me the money I need right away."

"Mrs. Mandlebaum, I beseech you to wait. What you're doing is brave, but in my opinion foolish . . . too dangerous to yourself and others."

"Yeah," Cole agreed. "How do I know they won't retaliate against you by mutilating my kids?"

"Hide, Mr. Cole. Take your beautiful wife and beautiful children and hide."

Feldman shook his head. "If this is as big as I think it is, there's no place in the world to hide." He walked to the door, blocking Molly Mandlebaum. "I beseech you, Mrs. Mandlebaum, wait. Give us time to establish a prudent course of action."

"I can get another law firm, Mr. Feldman."

"If you persist in this, you'll have to. This firm will not have blood on its hands."

"Even for money?"

"Not even for money, Mrs. Mandlebaum."

"You have until Friday, Feldman. Come up with an alternative before Friday and I'll consider it." She brushed past the little man and slammed the door.

"We must stop her." Feldman looked from Cole to Stonehill.

"How?" Stonehill asked. "Who do we call?"

Cole spoke up. "I know who I call. I call the airlines. That old broad makes more sense than any of us. I'm getting out of the country."

"How long can you hide?" Feldman asked.

"I have enough dough. Forever, if necessary." He stood over Stonehill and held out his hand. Instead of shaking it, Stonehill put both hands over Cole's and clutched it. "Don't give it all up for cunt, Livie. It's not worth it. You have too much going for you. Don't destroy it." He withdrew his hand. "If you destroy it, you'll be destroying an idol of mine. Don't do that. Let the bastards win this round; it's going to be a long fight." He turned to Feldman. "Send the bill to my office . . ." He tried to continue, but couldn't. He left.

When the door had shut, Feldman asked, "Are we the only civilized men left in the world?"

"Is that what we are?"

Back behind his desk, Feldman took out a yellow legal pad and poised a felt-tipped pen over it, ready to write. "We ought to list the priorities." He wrote "1" on the empty sheet, circled it, then wrote "Senator" after it. "The first deadline they gave you was the dinner for your friend Dinky, as you call him."

"That one's easy. A few days before, I'll get sick and check into a hospital for observation."

"Not so easy. There's more to this dinner than meets the eye." Under "Senator" he wrote, "A. Fund Raising." "First of all, and think clearly, what were the exact words of the warning?"

Stonehill thought for a moment until the picture was back in his mind: the face of the ordinary-looking man, his extraordinary words. "Withdraw support . . . I think those were the words. Withdraw support."

"You see, it's not so easy. Being sick and not showing up is not, technically, withdrawing support. It's a halfway measure. I wonder if it's enough. There's so much at stake."

"Look, Irving, why can't we just call the police or the FBI? What do we have law-enforcement agencies for?"

"In a minute, Livie, in a minute. First we have to examine all the options; then we will know how to proceed." He looked at what he had written: 'A. Fund Raising.' "It's one thing to say you withdraw support from the dinner; that means you discredit your friend, the Senator. Then you are saying that the Senator isn't a friend of the Jews, that he shouldn't have supported détente in the Mideast, and that he shouldn't have made a tsimmis over Sadat when he was in Chicago. You're a symbol to the conservative faction of the Jewish community. Ideologically and intellectually you should understand détente and sanction it. When you do this, two things happen: big conservative money goes to Israel, and your friend Dinky gets reelected. But if you withdraw your support, for sure your kind of money doesn't go to Israel and maybe Dinky doesn't get reelected."

On the third line Feldman wrote "B. Mark Mendoza" and underlined it. "Now," he continued, "if you withdraw your support, we have problem number three, Mark Mendoza. Can you discredit the great Israeli folk hero? For the first time since the Yom Kippur war, Mendoza consents to leave Israel to tell the people of this country how valiant his country is and how much they need American dollars. It wasn't easy to get Mark Mendoza. For all his qualities as a lion on the battlefield, he's a very shy young man. He is important because not only does he play on the heartstrings of the older people, but he captures the imagination of the young. It's a young people's world, Livie. It's important to involve the young people of this country in Israel. Soon it will be their dollars. They must be made to care. It's the future for Israel."

"I didn't realize everything involved. Dinky called me to ask a favor, and I said yes without thinking. How could it get so complicated?"

"It's a complicated world. Like a house of cards."

"Now what?"

Feldman studied the yellow pad. "Three things I have written down, just three things, and already it's impossible."

"What's impossible?"

"Withdrawing your support. You can't. There's too much at stake." He shook his head sadly. "It's not enough for you to take sick. Look at it from the standpoint of the people who planned this. Because you're sick and don't make an appearance at the dinner means nothing. It only means that you're sick, not that you're withdrawing support. They want you to discredit Dinky and to make Mark Mendoza seem a radical fanatic." He thought for a moment. "Tell me again what the man said. Remember carefully exactly the words he used."

"I don't have to. I can't forget them. 'Withdraw support.' "

"Or what? That's important. Or what?"

Stonehill relived the scene again. "Reprisal. If I didn't withdraw my support he said I would experience the first reprisal. Then he said that as horrible as the first reprisal would be, it would be nothing compared to the ones to follow."

"Let me get this clear. The ultimate reprisal was exposure of your affair with this girl, is that correct?"

Stonehill shook his head. "More than that. They're going to kill her and make it look as if I did it."

"Not to be believed," Feldman said again. "But I believe that it could happen."

"Not if I stand up to them. Not if I come right out and say that I love her. I'll expose myself before they have a chance to expose me. Then what can they do? Kill me? It's better than living in terror."

"Always the same. The options for Jews are always the same. You must understand, Livie, that life means nothing to these people. They *still* might kill the girl. Or your grandson. Could you live with that?"

"There'd be nothing left to live for."

"Yet you'd have to live with it. You'd have to live with all the lives you destroyed, everything you stand for in the community. What would be left?"

Stonehill thought for a moment. "Vengeance," he said and then repeated it. "Vengeance."

"Vengeance is for young people, Livie, for dreamers and fanatics. You'd turn vengeance inside out and direct it against yourself. Vengeance isn't enough."

"I've made one decision, Irving: no matter what happens, I'm going to marry Myrna and start a new life."

"Not yet. Later there'll be time to make that decision." He held up the yellow pad. "Look, I haven't even written it on the list yet. It's way down in the list of priorities. Later, when the hurt is over and you can see clearly again you can make that decision, and if you still feel the same way I'll come to the wedding. I'll even be the best man. But not yet, Livie. We must examine the priorities."

"I don't see any hope. If only we can find who's behind this, we can destroy them before they destroy us."

"Exactly." Feldman picked up the phone. "Stella, get me on a plane to Washington as soon as I can make it. Cancel all appointments. Call Harvey Fazio and tell him I'm on my way. If for any reason he's not available, get Herb Johnson or his assistant."

"What do I do in the meantime?" Stonehill asked.

"Nothing. *Nothing*. Live your life as though none of this happened."

Stonehill stood up. "No way."

"You'll find the way, Livie."

When Stonehill had gone, Feldman squinted at his watch, wrote down the hours of the meeting on his time sheet and smiled.

His secretary came into the office, closing the door behind her. "What kind of a game are you playing now? There's no Harvey Fazio or Herb Johnson in my Washington file or in the black book."

Feldman was still smiling. "A temporary deceit, Stella, justifiable for a long-term gain. Did you make the plane reservation?"

"No. I wasn't sure. When you begin to play your little games I'm never sure what to do."

"Get me on the plane to Washington. And get me Seymour Danzig on my private wire. He should be in his Washington office."

"Should I scramble it?"

Feldman shook his head. "Not necessary. If he has a problem at his end, he'll call me back."

She came closer to his desk. "Listen, Irv, I've been trying to tell you since you got back this morning, but you've been so damn busy . . ."

Feldman had begun to arrange the documents on his desk in neat piles. "What is it?"

"I've missed my period again. It's the second month."

Monday, February 14
One p.m., Chicago

Sᴜsᴀɴ ᴄʀᴏssʟᴇʏ had lunch with Leonid Tatov.

Monday, February 14
Three p.m.,
Highland Park, Illinois

Iᴛ ᴡᴀs ᴀʟᴡᴀʏs called Vera's house, as though Fred del Gracia had never lived there. David Adler had designed it in 1945, one of the last he had built, and it was always cited as the most mature work of the famous architect, foreshadowing a blend of traditional and modern design. This house stood high on a bluff overlooking Lake Michigan, a perfectly proportioned brick and stone structure, with large bays of mullioned glass and a long series of glass doors to let the sunlight in and to look out at the endless expanse of lake.

Adler had simplified the Georgian design of the pine paneling in the living room, bleaching the wood to a pale gray-white color. Lighted glass vitrines built into the paneling were filled with blue-and-white Chinese porcelain. A Monet water lily painting of superb quality hung over the fireplace, and a "rose period" Picasso of a mother and child over the sofa. Most of the furniture was upholstered in the same blue-and-white quilted chintz, with fat, down-filled cushions puffed to plump softness.

Vera del Gracia sat rigid in a Queen Anne chair, her Wagnerian proportions overpowering its frail design, her gray hair almost the color of the walls, her tweed suit a slightly darker shade of gray. Her son sat opposite her, collapsing the cushions under his weight. Physically they seemed two different species, unalike in every way. Mike Nelson stood at the fireplace, studying the Monet, seeing nothing.

"It seems impossible that any of this is happening." Her voice was restrained, trained to show no emotion. "There must be a way we can hide the truth."

Nelson turned toward her. "I know that I've agreed to it, but I still don't see how Rico's marrying Susan Crossley is going to solve anything."

"It doesn't, of course, but it gives us some protection; at least there will an appearance of normalcy. I can't remember anything like this ever happening before to people like us. There have been scandals, of course, and divorces and remarriages, but those are normal. People always expect that kind of thing, no matter who you are. I could handle that, but this is impossible." She looked at her son. "What about money? Is there no way to buy them off?"

"Buy *who* off, Mother? I don't know who *they* are. They said that I'd never hear from them again. There's no one to buy off."

"I can't go to my brothers with this. It would be humiliating. They must never know."

"Face it, Mother, one way or another they'll have to know. If you tell them now, they'll understand the business problem and will withdraw their support of Israel, at least temporarily. Exposure will knock the Grunswald stock down twenty points in a day. Your brothers understand that, and they won't let it happen. They lose their high-and-mighty attitude when dollars are involved. When I've been married to Susan Crossley for two or three years, the exposure will be less effective, and in any case by then the threat may be over. Then you can all start contributing to Israel again."

"The tax structure is so crazy these days that not giving to Israel causes problems, but I suppose we could find other legitimate deductions." She shook her head. "It's facing my brothers. I don't think I can do it. They've just been waiting for something like this. You don't know how jealous they are of you and your success."

"Lie to them," Rico suggested. "Tell them the truth, but tell them that the evidence is faked, that none of it is true but that there's no way to prove it, and for business reasons it's not worth the risk. Maybe that, together with the announcement that I'm going to marry Susan, will make the whole thing credible. No matter what they think, they won't come out and say it. It's really the only way. You save face, the stock doesn't tumble, and I'll have a chance to keep building the business. We can gradually change the advertising so that there's no direct identification with me." He looked over at Nelson. "We ought to start on that right away, Mike."

"It's too late for the spring schedule. Ursini is shooting tomorrow. We're having deadline problems as it is. But after that we can think about a new campaign."

"Let me ask a question, Freddie. After you and Susan marry will you and Mr. Nelson continue to see each other?"

Nelson turned to look at Rico and waited for his answer.

"Yes, Mother. Mike and I will continue as we are."

"What a horrible thing to do to poor Susan."

"She won't know, I promise you."

"She's a lovely girl, and her parents are such dear friends. I wouldn't want to see her hurt, or for there to be any bad blood between us and the Stonehills."

"There won't be, Mother. I promise."

"I cannot condone this, Freddie. I blame myself. All afternoon I've been asking myself what I did wrong to make you the way you are. What did I do?" She looked to her son for an answer, but he was silent. "It's really a father's job, isn't it, to make men out of their sons? Your father's always had so many other interests."

"Whatever it was, Mother, it's done and it's too late to change anything."

"It's never too late, Freddie. My father lived by that saying: It's never too late. Perhaps if you had psychiatric help—"

Mike interrupted. "Explain to your mother, Rico, that we don't want to change, that we're happy the way we are. Explain that this is the way we were meant to be. Tell her that you're happy this way."

"What Mike says is true, Mother. I'm happy this way."

"And I must live with this?"

"Other mothers have, and have survived."

"I suppose that being married to Susan will help keep up appearances. When are you going to be married?"

"As soon as possible."

"There'll be so much to do. Does Susan want a big wedding?"

Rico smiled. "As a matter of fact, Mother, I haven't proposed yet. She knows nothing about this. I'll ask her tomorrow."

"I suppose her mother will want her to wait until spring for the wedding. Maude spends the winter in Palm Springs."

"Maybe we'll just run off and be married quietly without any fuss."

"That won't accomplish what we're trying to do, Freddie. It must be a big wedding with formal announcements. It's important that everyone know—even people we don't know or care about."

Not once during the anguished afternoon had either Rico or his mother considered confiding in or consulting the elder del Gracia, and neither of them had any doubts that Susan Crossley would agree to the marriage. Mike Nelson was aware of this, and conscious of the limited vision of mother and son. For the first time he saw specks of weaknesses in del Gracia, areas in which he felt a compensating strength in himself.

"Am I going to be best man at the wedding?"

Monday, February 14
Four p.m., Chicago

CHILDREN WERE PLAYING in the small park on Astor Street. Strong, late-afternoon sunlight, segmented by the tall apartment buildings to the west, formed two separate areas of warmth. Whiz Crossley sat on a bench, his body huddled against the cold, camouflaging his long, lean dimensions. He still wore the same denim jacket, buttoned high, a long orange scarf wound around his neck. His eyes were protected from the sun by huge ski glasses, darkly tinted, covering much of his face and obscuring his identity.

Most of the children were supervised by domestics, but a few mothers sat at the far end of the playground talking to each other, one eye on the running, climbing and swinging boys and girls. Crossley had come here often with Stoney, the only oasis of light and air in the concentration of high-rise apartment buildings, the only escape from the concrete and steel of the prison where he worked and the prison where he lived. He had sat on this bench, his hand on the handle of the buggy, rocking the infant, talking silently, telling Stoney of shattered dreams and soothing him with fantasies about the future. Then the infant had become a toddler crawling on the grass, attempting to stand up and walk, his little arms reaching toward the swings and slides. A few faltering steps, falling down, another try. Then all communication between father and son, the continuity of unspoken words and unconditional love, had ended abruptly.

Now Crossley searched the faces of the little boys who would be about Stoney's age, looking for a physical characteristic, some feature of his or of Susan's which would be unmistakable. But his son could be almost any one of these little boys, or none of them. If only he hadn't been stubborn and had looked at that photograph when Stonehill had offered to show it at the airport. That's when it had all started, at the airport; that was when the first slight chink appeared in the armor he had built up against his former life. It had been easy in the other world, where there was space and sunlight and palm trees and he was Lawrence of Arabia. There had been children in that world, little figures darting in and out of the narrow streets of the medinas, but there had been no identification with the blue eyes and light hair of Stoney.

The building where he and Susan had lived, and where she still lived, was directly across the street. Crossley counted fourteen floors about the entrance. The last eight windows on the north side had been where he had lived his life with Susan; the good times and bad had happened there. He was remembering too much, his discipline was breaking down, but he wondered if it mattered now. Couldn't he indulge himself in love again? He wondered if now he could begin to feel it again. His plan was in operation, committed to the computer, the machine programmed and not completely dependent on him anymore. Of course, there were adjustments to make to human reactions, and he was dealing with these on an hour-by-hour basis, but they only honed the plan to a finer point. Even without him, the programmed plan would proceed. He could be destroyed, and even then, like a decapitated chicken, the computer would still function, still carry out the mission.

If he kidnapped Stoney now and returned to the world where the sun was strong and the air clear and he was a blue-eyed prophet . . . if he kidnapped Stoney now . . . In time, the boy would grow to love him, and to love the other world where civilization did not imprison the body and spirit. The kidnapping would be construed as another retaliative incident, another piece of the puzzle. Tomorrow a plane would crash in the mountains, killing five of the Bronson family en route from Seattle to their condominium in Sun Valley. Tomorrow it would also be revealed that half the collection of Post-Impressionists belonging to Walter Schlender had been mutilated by vandals in his Washington home while Schlender was wintering in San Diego. Crossley smiled to himself. The remaining half was the real bait. And if tomorrow Stoney was kidnapped from a park in Chicago . . . Considering the idea, Crossley became aware that this plan had always been deep-rooted in his mind. It was a logical conclusion to these years of planning and working. When he escaped, he would take his son with him. But today was too soon, he decided. There was still work to be done, and he had developed an Arab patience, a calm which knew that the inevitable could happen next week as well as today.

Across the street, in front of the apartment's entrance, a taxi was pulling away. Crossley saw Susan then, as she was now, not the picture of the pathetic figure in the hospital bed which haunted him. She stood straight, her head high, the sunlight catching highlights of her long hair. She laughed and smiled, responding to the hatless man talking to her, touching the arm of his dark Chesterfield coat.

One of the little boys broke from the pack, ran to the chain-link fence, clutching at it with his little hands, and called across the street. His voice couldn't be heard above the sound of traffic, but a sixth sense made the mother turn. She smiled and waved to the child, said something to the man with her, took his hand, and together they walked across the street into the park.

Crossley's reactions were mercurial, zigzagging charges of emotion working simultaneously. His son. His wife. A stranger. He sat immobilized, looking into the sun. He saw the mother kiss the child; he saw the stranger squat in front of him to shake the little hand and tousle the sandy-colored hair. Eyes directly into the sun, corneal refractions into sunspots and the words to himself: *Quoththespidernevermorequoththespidernevermore-quoththespiderquoth . . .*

But the stranger was not a stranger. He had seen that face before in some other part of his life. Looking again at the stranger standing with his wife and talking to his son, he flicked through the roll of pictures in his mind. He blotted out the Chicago architecture behind the man, stripped the body of its black, velvet-collared coat. *Recently.* He had seen the face recently. It came into focus then. Damascus. Karim Hasad. The bright sunlight in the courtyard, the two figures on the balcony. Karim and the stranger.

Now that man was here, for some reason. An uncalculated factor, not programmed to be here.

When Susan and the man left and disappeared behind the lobby doors, Crossley stood up and walked slowly toward the gate. To the little boy who was his son, he said, "You wait."

The little boy looked up the long length of denim to the stern face staring down at him. He did not understand. Frightened, he ran off and plunged into the protective pack of other boys. Once he looked back at the tall figure walking slowly away, then forgot him.

Driving northwest on the tollway, the low sun in his eyes, Whiz Crossley made two basic decisions. The idea of kidnapping Stoney had been implanted unconsciously two years before, and only now was he aware of it. It would be easy. Obviously, Stonehill was taking no precautions to protect his family. Crossley had counted on this, foreseeing that the greatest threat to the man was to attack his stature as a nonsectarian pillar of the community, and that this defense would be shored up first.

The second decision was to red-alert Hasad in Damascus. He had to know the identity of the face on the balcony, the man who was seducing his wife and play-acting father to his child. There were two possibilities: the man could be an Israeli agent who had somehow penetrated Hasad's palace, or he could be Hasad's own agent. Crossley had no illusions about Hasad, either about the deviousness of his mind or about the strategical and tactical brilliance of the guerrilla fighter. Hasad would protect himself on every flank, even from his own generals. Still, either way Crossley would have to know. If the stranger was an Israeli agent, he would have to be assassinated quickly. If he was Hasad's own agent, there would be time for the assassination when nothing else was endangered.

Hasad did not know that there were two assassins on alert. He was unaware that Crossley had hedged the odds by secretly hiring his own man in addition to the one supplied by Hasad. The Arab assassin, Hasad's man, waited nervously in a hotel room in St. Louis, checking telephone messages four times a day, anxious for the first signal to act. The other, an American, was on a firing range now, waiting for Crossley, practicing against moving targets, keeping his perfection honed. Crossley had looked a long time for this American. The first requisite had been a physical similarity to the Arab's dark coloring and compact, thick body. To keep Hasad deceived the two men had to be interchangeable. Secondly he had to be accurate, with a proven ability to perform under stress and without fear of his own destruction—with an underlying suicidal tendency.

The war in Vietnam had been a fertile spawning ground for this kind of man. Crossley finally found one, retained him, and controlled him by drugs, music and kinky sex. He nurtured the man in order to implement the plot, but also for his own protection against Hasad. From the beginning Crossley had been aware of the one basic flaw in this operation: his own survival. Hasad could never allow his own connection with this operation to be revealed, and Crossley was the single direct link back to him. In spite of the Arab's promises and Oxford-enameled words of brotherhood, Crossley knew that under no circumstances could Hasad gamble on his remaining alive to tell the truth, so there were two assassins, alike in appearance, each loyal to a different master.

Crossley looked at the clock on the dashboard of the nondescript Buick. The rush-hour traffic was already heavy, slowing him down, throwing him off his timetable. The expressway was a long line of barely moving metal bugs enclosing trapped spirits on their way to suburbia, where they would docilely exchange one cage for another. *Quoththespidernevermorequoththespidernevermore* . . .

Monday, February 14
Six p.m., Washington

SEYMOUR DANZIG had no official designation. On the surface he was a self-made millionaire originally from the Detroit ghetto, who had retired at sixty to dedicate himself to the funding of Israel with American dollars. Actually, he served as a lobbyist for the Israeli government, handling all unofficial negotiations, troubleshooting, pre-testing Israeli plans with politicians and statesmen. Much of his time was spent taking care of friends in Washington, Detroit and Florida, arranging decent hotel accommodations, lunch with Moshe Dayan and cocktails with Rabin when they made their luxury pilgrimages to Israel.

A six-room suite on the top floor of the Georgetown Inn was Danzig's unofficial headquarters. Its six-minute distance from the Capitol gave him a kind of perspective. The main-floor restaurants were dark, the food was good, and he had used his lobbying expertise on the hotel manager to put in a new bar with a dance floor so that he could show off the results of the dancing lessons his wife forced him to take in Miami when he visited her on weekends.

While Irving Feldman was talking, Danzig's mind raced in many directions toward his own goal. If only it wasn't Feldman who was initiating this. Danzig did not like Feldman, and resented his prestige. There had been too many times when he'd contacted a high figure in the administration, only to be rebuffed with the suggestion that the matter ought to be taken up with Irving Feldman, that it was his jurisdiction.

"What you're saying, Irv, is that when you have a lemon, make lemonade out of it."

"That's one side of the coin, Seymour, and eventually it may prove to be the right side. But there's time for that. The immediate concern is to thwart the plot before it has a chance to be successful."

"Would it be so terrible if there was a little trouble? It would serve some of those German Jews right, and it would get the rest of them off their goyish asses to support Israel openly. The way I see it, properly channeled, this could be the biggest fund raiser since the Six-Day War."

Aware of Danzig's single-mindedness and obliviousness to any gradations of black or white, Feldman had foreseen this reaction, and he had not come unarmed. "You must understand, Seymour, that I am here as an attorney protecting my clients. My first responsibility is to protect them from harm or exposure. Later there'll be a way to make this raise dollars, but not yet. We must consider priorities. First things first."

"There is only one first thing," Danzig insisted.

It was time for Feldman to use his ammunition. "Maybe the real first thing is something neither of us has talked about. Maybe the real first thing is airplanes—fighter jets." Feldman hunched forward as though there was a tallis around his shoulders and a yarmulke on his head. "As a matter of fact, I'm here accidentally. I had to come tomorrow anyway for an informal policy meeting—some people from the Defense Department, God knows who else. A little input, a little output, show-and-tell—you know how those meetings are. I wouldn't be surprised if we talked about airplanes. There's a rumor that Cruikshank from the House committee will be there. But in Washington, that's all there is, rumors, but maybe he'll be there."

Danzig stood up. "That's blackmail, Feldman."

"Everything is blackmail, Seymour. Usually we call it trading. One hand washes the other. Be pragmatic, Seymour. You didn't get to where you are today without being pragmatic. How many dollars do you have to raise to buy one fighter?"

Silently, Danzig cursed Feldman. Damn that pompous Yid, that little kike with his rabbinical ways. But Feldman had the ability to touch Danzig's nerve center. He had used two words like a stiletto: *pragmatic* and *airplane*. Danzig knew that his own success had been based on pragmatism, and that what Israel wanted most was the new jet fighter. Pragmatically he said, "For the moment we will look at your side of the coin, but in the long run it's the other side of the coin which is more important."

"Understood, Seymour, understood. But first things first." Feldman settled back in his chair. "You know that Mark Mendoza is coming to Chicago to speak at a dinner. Between him and the Senator, it should be one of the biggest fund raisers in the last three years."

Danzig knew very well that Mendoza was coming to Chicago, and he also knew that Feldman had arranged this with a single phone call. Danzig had tried to do the same thing five times, each time unsuccessfully; no amount of political pressure had been able to get the reluctant hero out of Israel. Feldman had accomplished the impossible with one phone call to Mendoza's mother.

"I would assume," Feldman continued, "that the Israeli Secret Service will be coming to Chicago to check the security for Mendoza. Maybe they've already been there." He waited for Danzig to volunteer information, but Danzig said nothing. "Either way, it makes no difference; what's important is that the Israeli Secret Service in Chicago will cause no suspicions. Everyone will expect them to take elaborate measures to protect Mendoza, so as long as they are in Chicago, they can send a few extra men to work on this problem. You understand?"

"They'd be working with the FBI and the U.S. Secret Service. It would be a perfect cover."

"Exactly. You understand why it is important that the FBI or the State Department know nothing about this. I must protect my clients. The FBI could lead to the IRS and then who knows what could happen?"

"I'm like you," Danzig answered. "I'd rather let our own handle it. It's essentially a Jewish problem."

Feldman shook his head. "That's not the point. As you know, I'm very close to the FBI, but there are some internal-policy problems. In the long run, it's important that none of this information be in any official government files. Do you understand? Secrets aren't secrets anymore. It's the climate of the country. Even when it's for our own good there aren't secrets. All this honesty and openness can be dangerous. You and I understand this."

"I'll get on the horn tonight. You'll have your Israeli intelligence."

"Masquerading as Secret Service. That's very important, Seymour."

"I'm not an idiot, Irv."

Feldman held up his hands, then turned them into a position of prayer. "I didn't mean to imply that, Seymour. Would I have come to you for help if I thought you were an idiot?"

"Give me the names of the people in Chicago. I'll check on Detroit and see if similar things are happening there."

Feldman shook his head. "No names, Seymour. Send the agents to me."

"Look here, Feldman, this is a cops-and-robbers business. You're an attorney. Stick to what you know. Let me handle this. It won't be the first time."

"You're right, Seymour. I know nothing about business like this. That's why I came to you. You're the professional and I'm just a lawyer. On the other hand, it's the responsibility of the lawyer to protect his clients. There are some very personal matters and lives at stake here."

Danzig was relentless. "No deal, Feldman. I do it my way or not at all."

"Consider, Seymour, all the things involved. The final goal is what is vital. How it's accomplished may not be so important. Let's be practical."

"What makes you think you can swing the jet fighters?"

The owl eyes opened in deliberate surprise. "I didn't say that I could swing them. Did I say that I guarantee them?" Feldman answered his own question by shaking his head violently. "I only said that we were going to talk about it, that's all. Maybe they'll ask my opinion; maybe they won't ask my opinion. In these crazy meetings, who knows what will happen?"

"No deal, Feldman. It's my way or not at all."

"Listen, I could have gone to the Israeli embassy. The Ambassador and I are very close, you know that. But this kind of trouble is better handled by men like us, to manipulate in our way. When the time comes, you'll be able to turn it around and use it as a fund-raising device. You're a pro at that, nobody better."

Danzig understood that Feldman had won this round, and like a professional fighter he returned to his own corner. It was the fifteen-round decision which finally counted. "The code word will be . . ." He considered for a minute. "No, no code word. Israeli intelligence will find you." He picked up a book of matches and looked at the name of the plumbing firm advertised on the cover. "Locker and Green. The men will call themselves Locker and Green."

Feldman smiled brightly. "Wonderful. I knew I could count on you." When he stood up, his back went out, producing a sharp pain in his lower spine. He stood hunched over, his mouth twisted.

"You all right?"

Feldman nodded. "If I'd known I was going to live this long, I'd have taken better care of myself."

Monday, February 14
Five p.m. to six p.m.,
Chicago and Miami

SUSAN CROSSLEY was soaking in the bathtub when she heard the telephone. She let it ring for some time before answering, forgetting that the maid had taken Stoney to her mother's and that she was alone in the apartment.

"Susan?"

"Peter! Where are you?"

"Florida."

"Whatever for?"

"Business. Listen, I'm sorry about last night, leaving you like that at the last minute. But all hell is breaking loose and a job is a job."

"You sound tired. Are you all right?"

"I'm fine. Listen, about last night . . . Well, I've been on a lot of airplanes and I've had time to think. Nothing is any different, Susan. I mean, what I said still goes. Do you know what I mean?"

"Not now, Peter. Not over the phone."

"You were so upset. I wanted to make certain that you understood what I was trying to say."

Susan slid lower in the bathtub. Underwater she soaped her pubic hair, lost the soap and let her fingers creep lower, gently touching herself, closing her eyes against the sensation. There had been those times with Whiz, when they were separated, each one lying alone in a bed, talking erotic words of love over a telephone and manipulating themselves to orgasm. "Say it, Peter." Her breathing was heavier. "Say it, Peter."

"Are you all right? You sound funny."

"Say it, Peter."

"I love you."

Gently she put the phone back on the receiver and with both hands stroking herself, slipping lower in the water, not caring that her hair was getting wet. The phone rang again persistently, adding urgency to her movements that exploded in an insufficient orgasm.

The phone was still ringing. "Peter?"

"What happened? What's going on there?"

"We were cut off, that's all. When will you be back?"

"I hope tonight. It all depends. There's a ten-twenty flight, and another one at one A.M. If I were smart I'd wait until tomorrow. I've had enough red-eye expresses in the last twelve hours."

"Why don't you wait until morning so you won't be too tired for the party?"

"That's the problem. I have to rent a tux. There won't be

time if I take the morning flight. I have a lot to do when I get back, and they usually need a day to get it ready."

"So you'll definitely be at the party?"

"Unseen catastrophes aside, I'll be there. Do I have a date?"

"It's such a mess, Peter. You just wouldn't believe all the complications. First of all, Rico is back, and he brought a business associate from New York—Mike something or other—so I have to get a date for him. Then there's a man in from London. You met him at Zorine's last night."

"The Russian?"

"He's not Russian. I mean he *was*; his grandfather was related to Czar Nicholas or something, but he's more British than anyone I know. But I have to get a date for him. All I need is one more girl."

"I've got a steady in Lincolnwood named Linda Schwartz."

"Be serious."

He laughed. "I used to be about Linda Schwartz."

"What happened?"

"I met you."

"Forget Linda Schwartz. Rico is determined to collect a bunch of beautiful people. I told you that *Women's Wear* was covering it for a story they're doing about him."

"I'm not so beautiful."

"You would be if you let your hair grow a little in the back, Peter."

"*Gar nicht helfen.*"

"What does that mean?"

"It means nothing will help. I'll never make it in your world, Susan."

"Will you try?"

He laughed. "I'm trying. I'll tell you one thing, I'm getting used to the fact that I love you."

"How's the weather in Florida?"

"Muggy. How is it there?"

"Cold but sunny. Not bad."

"Are you going out tonight?"

She paused before answering. "Well, I'm working tomorrow. Rico is using me as a model in the shots he's doing. It was all supposed to happen in Barbados, but at the last minute they decided to come back here and shoot. Ursini is doing it and Rico wants to use me. It's really quite a break. Meanwhile, we're all having dinner at Zorine's tonight with Nic and Rico's friend from New York. But it will be an early night. I have to look my best in the morning—no bags under the eyes. I'll be home early."

"Behave yourself."

"Peter?"

"What?"

"When you go to Gingiss tomorrow to rent a tux, do me a favor, will you?"

"What?"

"Get a plain one, and get a white shirt without ruffles or colored trimming."

"You can take the boy out of Lincolnwood—" Frankel began.

"For my sake. Please?"

"You don't think it really matters to me how I look, do you?"

"For my sake. Please."

"Given my face, I'll look as goyish as possible under the circumstances. Good night, Susan."

"Good night, Peter."

Monday, February 14 Five-thirty p.m., Rolling Meadows, Illinois

THE LARGE one-story building visible from the tollway was an unlighted hulk of concrete block isolated from any other structure. The façade of the building faced a large parking lot. In daylight, the outline of letters over the stone lintel was still legible: WORKERS AMALGAMATED INSURANCE COMPANY. Specializing in mail-order health and accident policies, the insurance company had outgrown the quarters two years before, and their old building had been sold for the asking price to a real-estate syndicate from New Jersey. It had been a turnkey purchase, all equipment and furnishings included. The purchasers had given the building only a cursory inspection, concentrating mainly on the large computer area, the nerve center of the business, and the auxiliary equipment.

There was no direct access from the tollway. Crossley drove a mile beyond to an eastbound exit, threw coins into the toll hopper, drove east to the first road and turned right to approach the building. The driveway had been blocked off with a large wooden sign:

110,000 sq. feet
FOR SALE
or
LONG TERM
LEASE
by appointment only
(609)   784-6705

The few individuals and real estate brokers who called this number were connected to an answering service in New Jersey, but never received an answer to their inquiries.

Crossley drove beyond the sign to a service road, approached the building from the south side, where a large garage had been built for the key executives of the insurance firm, and activated one of the doors with the remote-control device in the glove compartment of the Buick. A single bulb hanging from the ceiling dimly illuminated the area. Three other cars and a large motorcycle were parked there. At the far end, a door in the unpainted block wall led into the main building. The tiny red light of the alarm system glowed from a box at the side of the door. When Crossley inserted a key and turned it, the red light changed to white. Unlocking the door, he stepped inside, re-locked it and reset the alarm so that it glowed red again.

The interior of the building was exactly as the Amalgamated

Workers Insurance Company had vacated it, area after area of huge secretarial arenas surrounded by windowless cubicle offices. The secretarial desks were aligned in neat formations, identical typewriters covered with identical gray plastic covers and empty wastebaskets in line at the same interval from each desk. Even the telephones remained, squared exactly in the right-hand corner of the desks. Long rows of filing cabinets formed corridors and directed traffic flow. All of this was now coated with two years' accumulation of dust, unbroken labyrinths of cobwebs linking walls to ceilings, furniture to walls, floors to furniture. The thermostat was set at sixty-two and Crossley felt the chill, more penetrating than the cold outside, as he breathed through his mouth so that the building's dank, musty odor would not nauseate him.

The computer area had been built in the exact center of the building, accessible to all departments. It was, in effect, an eighty-foot-square building within the building, with eight-inch-thick steel walls, heavily insulated against sound and air, with a separate and independent heating, air-conditioning and ventilating system to keep the room dustproof. Another red light glowed at the side of its steel entrance door. Using a different key, Crossley deactivated this alarm, unlocked the door and entered blinding brightness. Quickly he locked the door behind him and reset the alarm.

A middle-aged woman wearing a white laboratory coat over her sweater and skirt and immaculate white shoes looked up from a desk. Everything here was spotlessly clean, the entire compound meticulously maintained. Behind her, a huge glass room enclosed the machines, the muffled hum of their mechanism audible in spite of acoustical engineering and the rubber gaskets between the sheets of glass. The machines were two-toned, IBM blue and yellow, a tableau of robots, spinning tapes, blinking lights, ejecting cards and ribbons of white paper, performing their mysterious rites under the glare of a luminous ceiling reflecting harshly on the white, nonstatic floor. A narrow corridor surrounded four sides of the glass enclosure, and offices abutted it. Some of these rooms had been converted into makeshift sleeping quarters. The kitchen and cafeteria had been left intact, but on the south side walls between five of the offices had been knocked down and the far end of the space lined, floor to ceiling, with bales of shredded paper, in front of which a crude mechanical target had been erected. The practice range was empty, and Crossley glanced toward the closed door of the room where the marksman slept.

Crossley went directly to the largest office, closed the door, unwound the long orange scarf from his neck, folded it carefully and stood on his toes, stretching his body and his arms upward, almost touching the ceiling. Taking deep mouthfuls of the mechanically freshened air, he expanded his chest, contracting the hard cortex of muscles in his lower torso. As he silently recited the words of his mantra, he saw Susan's and Stoney's faces, and the nameless face of the man who was lover to his wife and wanted to be father to his son.

When he removed the ski glasses, they left deep marks on his face, and he rubbed the lines to erase them. He checked his watch against the digital clock on the wall. That damn traffic, he thought. Quickly he undressed, wadding his clothes in a bundle, stripped off his boots, and stood naked and barefoot. He repeated the stretching exercise, up and down in rhythm. Touching his limp penis, he felt no reaction. He took a long, white caftan from the closet, put it on, thrust his feet into white-leather Moroccan slippers, returned to the main area and walked to the woman sitting behind the desk.

"Red alert," he said. "Route it through Bogotá, Rio, Cape-town, Kinshasa and Hawaii. Call me when it's ready. I'll transmit the message myself."

"How do you spell Kinshasa?"

"Look in the damn manual. What do you think I wrote it for?" He walked past her around the corner and into the computer room. Inside the noise was at a deafening decibel; in spite of the cushioning under the floor, the vibrations produced a sharp staccato under his feet.

One of the machines had been altered, a panel of twenty-eight buttons affixed crudely to its side. Crossley pushed the first one. A blue light indicated no information. When he pressed the next, there was a loud clatter of clicking sounds and three sheets of paper appeared in the receptacle of the machine. He pushed each of the twenty-eight buttons in turn, waiting for either the blue light or the clatter, and letting the stack of papers accumulate in the receptacle. Most of the lights glowed blue in response to his touch, and he was pleased. No communication indicated that everything was proceeding on schedule, without problems. This particular machine was programmed to respond to telephone activation, recording voices which enunciated words and numbers; the machine then decoded words and numbers into its memory bank, quickly producing the actual communication.

The woman had come into the room while he worked and was making adjustments on a machine next to the teletype, consulting the manual from time to time.

In the last six months, mainly in Europe, Crossley had handpicked computer experts, technicians, programmers and processors to form his staff. He carefully chose displaced persons without a visa or a permit to work in a foreign country. In the United States he paid them meager wages in their own currency, retaining their perfectly forged visas and work permits which would be their final payoff when the operation was over. They worked glumly but efficiently, unaware of the scope of the operation or any of the other personnel involved.

On the way back to his office, the sheaf of papers in hand, Crossley opened the door to the assassin's room. Instantly a loud stereo blast of acid rock filled the corridor. The assassin was supine on a small cot, smoking a sloppily rolled joint, staring up at the ceiling, not turning toward the sudden light. On the floor, propped up on one elbow, was a young black man, naked except for black leather pants, a barbed silver-chain dog collar around his neck and handcuffs around his ankles holding his legs painfully together. He, too, was staring into space, unaware of the light. Crossley closed the door.

At the desk in his office Crossley read the communications from the reporting webs. Some of the information he already knew; when he was in the field, he could activate the information from any telephone, but had to decode it himself. After reading each message he made notes on a legal pad. When he was through, he pulled out the messages from webs seven, sev-

enteen and twenty-six and turned to the giant map on the wall, a
scaled-down replica of the original which had been projected on
the screen in Zurich. The tracery of lines between the intertwin-
ing webs were indelible on this map. Crossley stood up and with
his finger touched the vortex of the twenty-sixth web, Dallas,
then followed the intricate path of membranes to the seventeenth web, Miami, and from there to the seventh web, Washington, D.C. It didn't make sense. He could understand the
Dallas-to-Miami part; Weinstein in Dallas had agreed to the
terms, but then had fled to Miami with his family, probably only
a jumping-off point to a more remote hiding place. Sherman
Weinstein had certainly not called the FBI—Crossley documented this again, rereading the message from Dallas—but
somehow the agency had become involved. That was documented from Miami, where FBI surveillance of the Weinstein
family had begun when they landed at the airport and was
continuing now at the hotel where the family was staying.
Crossley knew that Weinstein was too fearful to tell the FBI
anything; he would conform. But who was the man who had
flown from Washington, spent an hour secreted with Weinstein
and was now in the same hotel? The man had registered under
the name Peter Frankel, with a Chicago address.

Crossley pushed a button on the intercom on his desk.

"Yah?" A man's voice responded.

"Track down subject Peter Frankel, Two West Oak Street,
Chicago. Try the big machine first. I don't think you'll find him
there. If not, try operator twenty-three. Have him do a rundown
and report back at once." He turned off the intercom, then
switched it on again and pressed the buzzer.

"Yah."

"After that, alert number nineteen. Message: 605-376-
4976." Crossley did not need the code book; he had committed
these numbers to memory. They put the assassin in St. Louis on
stand-by. "Are you still there?"

"Yah."

"If anything else comes through, I'll be in the computer
room." He switched off the intercom and returned to the glass-
enclosed room. When he looked at the woman operating one

teletype, she shook her head, mouthing the words, *Not yet.*

Crossley sat at another machine checking his notes against the original communiqués and typed messages with two fingers, hitting the keyboard rapidly. In the next fifteen minutes, he activated the vandalism in Washington, the plane crash in Utah, a burglary in Des Moines, a mysterious disappearance in Los Angeles, a boating disaster off the Florida Keys and a kidnapping in St. Paul. Then he studied the report from the twenty-third web. Livingston Stonehill had not yet withdrawn his support for the Man of the Year dinner, but there would be time to think about him tomorrow. He flicked the switch and the machine stopped, his messages already routed to the other machines, coded and sent out across the network. Taking his messages and notes across the room, he inserted them into the paper shredder and waited until the machine had done its work.

Now the woman tapped him on the shoulder and nodded toward the Telex. Gesturing for her to leave the room, he sat at the keyboard and typed out the message to Hasad:

URGENT REQUEST IDENTIFICATION MAN ON BALCONY PAL-
ACE LAST MONDAY ABOUT TWENTY SEVEN TALL SANDY
HAIR PRESENT NOW CORE TWENTY THIRD WEB SUSPECT
ISRAELI AGENT

Crossley waited while the message was coded and transmitted through the circuitous route he had specified. Five minutes and forty seconds elapsed before the machine typed out an answer from six thousand miles away.

SUBJECT SECURITY CLEARED NOT ISRAELI AGENT HAS NO
KNOWLEDGE DO NOT ESTABLISH CONTACT REPEAT UNDER
NO CIRCUMSTANCES ESTABLISH CONTACT HASAD

Crossley reread the message. It eliminated the possibility of the man being an Israeli agent, but increased the probability that he was Hasad's special agent.

And who the hell was Peter Frankel?

Monday, February 14
Six-thirty p.m., Chicago

THEY HAD just sat down to dinner at the small table by the window and Maude Stonehill was beginning to narrate the odyssey of her day, beginning at the dentist, then the appliance department of Sears and on to the fitting rooms of Stanley Korshak, when the butler interrupted.

"Mr. Stonehill, Mr. Kupcinet is on the phone. I explained that you were at dinner, but he insisted."

"Tell Mr. Kupcinet that I—"

"Talk to him, Livie. He called yesterday. Why didn't you call him back today? Carl, tell Helga to hold dinner for a minute."

Reluctantly Stonehill stood up. "I'll take it in the library, Carl."

In the library he picked up the telephone. "Hello, Irv."

"Livie, old boy, you're harder to get to than Elton John. How goes it all?" The columnist's voice was deep and booming.

"Busy, Irv. It's been a rat race the last few days. I'm sorry I didn't get a chance to call you back."

"How's Mrs. Stonehill?"

"She's fine, just back from Palm Springs for a few days."

"Did she come in for the Man of the Year dinner?"

"No, that's Sunday. She'll be back in California by then."

"Too bad. We're all excited about that dinner. I want to run an item in the column tomorrow. How did you ever entice Mark Mendoza out of Israel? The kids on the paper have been doing a little research for me. Quite a man, that Mendoza, but almost a hermit."

"I have to be honest with you, Kup. It wasn't my doing. You know Irving Feldman, don't you?"

"A dear friend."

"Well, Feldman did it. Ask him."

"He's out of town. Do you know where?"

"Probably Washington. He always seems to be in Washington."

"I figured the same thing, and our Washington bureau is trying to run him down, but so far no luck."

"Sorry that I can't help you, Irv."

"The other thing is that I want to build my television show around Mendoza. I've spoken to the Senator, he'll make himself available at Mendoza's convenience. You know that we tape the show in advance. But no one seems to know Mendoza's schedule or how to get to him. I'd like to build the whole show around him. I think I can get Kissinger, but I have to deliver Mendoza and give the Secretary a definite time and date."

"I can't help you, Kup. I haven't been briefed on any of the details. Maybe Feldman will know."

"I called the JUF office and they told me that your daughter was going to escort him around town and act as hostess at a cocktail party before the dinner."

"My daughter?"

"You sound so surprised, Livie; didn't you know she was Jewish?" Kupcinet laughed at his own joke.

"She didn't tell me. Did you talk to her?"

"I tried just before I called you, but she's not home. The maid said that she went to Zorine's, so I may stop in there on the way home. She's a beautiful woman, Livie."

"Thank you. If you see her, send her my love. If I can get any details for you about Mendoza's schedule, I'll call you back."

"Livie, I'd like you to be on the show too."

"Not my cup of tea, Irv. You must realize that I'm only a front for this whole affair. I don't have many convictions one way or the other. I'm doing this only because Dinky asked me as a personal favor. We were roommates in college. I don't see how I would add to the discussion."

"You'd add a touch of class, Livie." Kupcinet laughed again. "Just your being there would give the show a certain stature. Besides, it'll turn my wife on. She rates you right after Cary Grant. Think about it, Livie; it's important. The Mendoza show will be dynamite coast to coast. Once we get the commitment from him we'll probably have full network coverage."

"All right, Irv. I'll think about it."

As soon as Stonehill returned to the dining table, the odyssey segued from Stanley Korshak to the Drake Hotel drugstore and lunch with Florence Thompson and Blanche Levy.

"Maude, did Susan say anything to you about Mark Mendoza?"

"I can't keep track of the men in Susan's life. Who's Mark Mendoza?"

"He's the main speaker at the Israel dinner. He's a famous Israeli fighter, a hero of the Yom Kippur war."

"Why would Susan have anything to do with someone like that?"

"I just wondered if she'd mentioned anything."

"I've hardly had a chance to see her. She's busy today and tomorrow shooting some photographs with Rico del Gracia. Stoney was over this afternoon; the nanny brought him. He's grown so, Livie, just in a few months. He's such a little gentleman, so well-behaved."

Stonehill pushed back his chair. "Excuse me, I have to make a phone call."

"Your brisket will get cold."

"It doesn't matter." He started toward the library again.

"Livie?"

"What is it?"

Maude stood up and came over to him. "There's something wrong, isn't there? I've felt it ever since I came home. I saw Eddie Krause this afternoon. He said he saw you at the hospital this morning, and that you walked right by him without seeing him."

Stonehill fumbled. "I was late for a meeting. You know how I hate to be late. It's true; I didn't see Eddie."

"What did Kupcinet want?"

"Something about the dinner for Dinky. Nothing important."

"Are you sure that everything's all right?"

He kissed her lightly on the forehead. "You worry too much, Maude."

"Perhaps I do. But Eddie said that my blood pressure was an absolute joy for a woman my age."

"I'll be back in a minute, dear. Eat your brisket while it's still hot."

The background music was louder than the voice which answered, "Zorine's."

"Is Mrs. Stonehill Crossley there?"

"Could you talk a little louder, please?"

"Mrs. Stonehill Crossley," he shouted. "Susan Crossley."

"Oh, Susan. Yes, she's here. She's having a drink at the bar. I'll get her."

Stonehill was forced to listen to the music and the high-pitched clatter of dishes and voices while he waited what seemed an interminable time.

"Hello."

"Susan."

"Daddy? Is everything all right?"

"Everything's fine."

"My heart's going a mile a minute. Every time I get a call when I'm out, I think something has happened to Stoney. What is it?"

"Can you get to a quieter phone? I can hardly hear you."

He heard her say, "Kenny, is there another phone?" Then into the receiver again, "I'll call you right back, Daddy. Kenny is taking me to his office. Are you home?"

"Yes."

There was time until the telephone rang again to think about how Susan had become involved in the dinner for Dinky. First Myrna, now Susan; he was putting the women he loved on the firing line. In his mind the impotent syllogistic reasoning had begun again: the words he had said in Feldman's office and the rebuttals the lawyer had made.

When it rang, he picked up the phone instantly. "Daddy, is everything all right?"

He could hear now. "Everything's fine. Your mother was impressed with Stoney, how much he's grown and what a gentleman he is."

Susan was slow in answering. "I see him every day and it's hard to tell. He has a funny, withdrawn way about him sometimes. Like Whiz. It scares me."

Stonehill reassured her, "He'll outgrow it."

"You didn't call me to talk about Stoney. It must be something important."

"Not really. You're so damn busy all the time that I can never get hold of you. I called your house and the maid said you were at Zorine's, so I figured you could stop being Queen of the May long enough to talk to your old man for a minute."

"What about?"

"Who spoke to you about escorting Mark Mendoza and being the hostess at a cocktail party for him?"

"There's been so much going on that I'd forgotten all about it. I don't remember who called. Someone from Israel Bonds or the JUF. They said you were chairman of the dinner and that I didn't have to do anything, really." Her voice was hesitant. "Didn't you know about it? I assumed that they'd set it up with you. I didn't pay much attention. They even had to explain to me who Mark Mendoza is." She laughed a little. "I figured that it was Mother's idea after I found out that he's unmarried and is a nice Jewish boy. Evidently the ultimate nice Jewish boy. Is anything wrong?"

"No, but I didn't know anything about it. Those pushy bastards never know when to stop. Once you say yes to them they milk you all the way."

"It *is* a good cause, isn't it, Daddy?"

"The cause is all right; I just object to the methods."

"Don't you want me to do it?"

"I don't think that there's any way out of it at this point. I resent them exploiting you. They know damn well that you're good press and will get them more coverage."

"I don't mind as long as it's a good cause. Besides, it helps my career."

"Look, Susan, I think Irv Kupcinet is on his way to Zorine's to ask you some questions about the dinner and Mendoza. If he shows up, tell him as little as possible. Say that you were asked to do this, but that you're not certain of your schedule. Tell him that you may have to be out of the country on a modeling assignment."

"I don't understand, Daddy."

"Trust me. I'm teed off that they've involved you. I hate being used by anyone. Trust me, and don't tell Kup that you've spoken to me. He knows that I didn't know anything about this until he told me. Say that you didn't mention it to me because you weren't certain that you'd even be in the country on Sunday."

"Whatever you say, Daddy."

"I'll explain all the ramifications later. It's not very important, but I am angry." He softened his voice. "Are you having fun?"

"We just got here. I'm here with Rico and a friend of his from New York. Nic Ursini and Bruce are meeting us. It's kind of a business meeting. They're using me as a model tomorrow for some of Rico's ads."

"Have fun and just give Kup the lines I told you. See what kind of actress you are."

Monday, February 14 Eight p.m., Miami to Washington

THE FIRST telephone number did not answer. Peter Frankel hoped that he had memorized it correctly; Dirksmith had been adamant about not writing anything down. When he dialed it again, it still did not answer, so he tried the second number. After three rings he heard Dirksmith's voice.

"It's Peter Frankel."

"Where are you calling from?"

"A damn hot phone booth, just as you said."

"Give me the number and stay there. I'll call back."

"305-742-3477." Frankel hung up, opened the door and waited. It hadn't been easy finding a phone booth. The Doral Hotel, isolated from the Miami Beach hubbub, had some telephone cubicles, but they didn't seem private enough, so he had walked over to the clubhouse and found an enclosed booth outside the pro shop.

When the phone rang, Frankel picked it up and started talking. "I don't understand this one-sided security shit. You let me fly around and register in hotels under my own name, but you protect yourself all over the lot."

To himself Dirksmith said, *Not yet, my little shark. Don't wise up quite yet.* To Frankel he answered, "It has nothing to do with security. I was on the toilet."

"You're a fucking liar, Dirksmith."

"What do you have?"

"Very little. Sherman Weinstein is scared shitless. He's chartered a boat under another name, and is taking the whole family to cruise the Caribbean for an undetermined length of time to undetermined places. Is there a way I can help him?"

"What do you mean?"

"I have to be honest with you, Dirksmith. I traded him protection for information—a lot of protection and very little information."

"Give me the information. We'll discuss the protection later."

"It's not much, Dirksmith. I'm apologizing in advance."

"Anything is more than we have."

"White Caucasian male."

Dirksmith interrupted. "White Caucasian is a redundancy."

"Forgive me. I'm only a poor night-school lawyer."

"Go ahead."

"Age about thirty, give or take. Hair sandy. Eyes undetermined. American, probably Midwest. Weinstein said his accent was funny, which probably only means that the guy's not a Texan. No outstanding physical characteristics. Weinstein kept referring to him as average, whatever that means. In every description 'average' was used adjectivally."

"That doesn't sound like a night-school lawyer."

"Cum laude, you son-of-a-bitch. Anyway, I at least got Weinstein to admit that he'd been threatened. The same as Weiskopf. Cut off funds to Israel and you'll live happily ever after. No cut-off, disaster. His wife and kids were threatened. That wife of his is something else, one dynamite tomato."

"I checked out the description you gave me of the two men who threatened Weiskopf. There's nothing to go on."

"There may be one break," Frankel continued. "This man saw Weinstein in his office at the department store, using some syndicated buying story to get to him. Weinstein said that the man was a cold, controlled character. The only nervousness he showed was in playing with a silver pen on Weinstein's desk. He kept taking it out of the holder, playing with it and putting it back. There may be fingerprints on the pen. I have the name of the chief of security for the department store. I tried to get Weinstein to call him directly to clear the way for one of your men to check the prints on the pen, but he's too scared to call anybody. The security chief's name is Vernon Hepwaite." Frankel spelled it.

"You're not bad at this."

"I called back Weiskopf, figuring, as I said, that maybe the character who called on him could have left some prints, but the guy was wearing gloves. Did you find out anything else at your end?"

"We thought we had a break in Seattle. The FBI received a call there from a woman named Bronson. It seems her husband had been threatened. She wouldn't give any details over the phone—only that her husband had been threatened and was very frightened. He forbade her to go to the authorities, and she was doing it behind his back. But when the FBI checked the residence, the family was gone without a trace. They'd just packed up and left. The Bureau is still on it trying to locate them. But that seems to be the only direct lead we've had. Everyone else is too frightened to talk."

"There's got to be a hundred, maybe two hundred guys in this country who were fingered this way, and they're all sitting on their asses not doing anything. If only a few of them had the balls to call the authorities we could bust this wide open fast."

"In a case like this one has to pray a lot and hope for luck."

"I've been thinking, Dirksmith. What if we planted a fictitious case—made up a victim and a plot against him. You with me so far?"

"Go ahead."

"Then we release this phony story to the newspapers and say we caught the guys. Don't you think that then all the real victims might be encouraged to come out of hiding and tell their stories?"

"Possibly, but too many people would get killed before we could get enough information to stop them. It's too dangerous."

"As a last resort?"

"Maybe. Let's play it by the book for a moment."

"What do I do now?"

"Go back to Chicago. You'll be contacted tomorrow."

"What about my boss? Has anyone explained anything to him? If I walk in that office tomorrow, he's going to have my ass unless someone has spoken to him."

"That's another department, not mine." Dirksmith sounded impatient.

"I'm not up to the Irish wrath of Dynamite Dan. Oh, well, I'll live through it." The telephone booth had become unbearably hot, so he opened the door and looked around. "Listen, how do I get Sherman Weinstein on that boat without anyone knowing about it?"

"That's your problem."

"Son-of-a-bitch, I promised the guy."

"Look, Frankel, if I figure this out for you I'm duty-bound to inform the FBI. If the FBI knows, it's conceivable that other people will know. If you do it all by your little self, only you will know."

"You're a tough bastard, Dirksmith."

"By profession, Frankel. By profession."

While he was walking back to the hotel, Frankel was trying to formulate a plan to get the Weinsteins on their chartered boat without the FBI or anyone else knowing about it.

While Dirksmith was walking back to the bathroom, he was plotting how to involve Frankel further tomorrow, what ruse he would use to expose him more openly.

Monday, February 14
Twelve a.m., Chicago

As MIKE NELSON went down on Rico del Gracia, he was seeing the face of the young Englishman who had joined them at Zorine's. He wondered if the man swung both ways.

Tuesday, February 15
Twelve-thirty a.m., Chicago

THE MESSAGE read: TELEPHONE OFFICE TEN A.M. LONDON TIME G. TATOV.

Leonid Tatov stuffed the pink slip into his overcoat pocket and took the elevator up to his hotel room. There was a six-hour time difference between London and Chicago, leaving three and a half hours to kill before he could return his father's call. He was sorry now that he had turned down Barbara Moore's offer of bed and breakfast. He thought about calling her back, but the Chicago night had turned bitterly cold and she lived a half-hour away. Not worth it, he decided. Better to use the time to get his head together, and sort out loose ends before he spoke to his father.

He felt frustrated because he was nowhere with the assignment his father had given him. After bird-dogging Whiz Crossley halfway around the world, he had lost him. In one split second of turning his eyes away, Crossley had disappeared in the Chicago airport. He knew that Hasad's plan was in operation all around him, but he had no clue of what was happening or how, or of the cast of the characters. What would he report to his father?

Angola had been easy compared to this—the battle lines clearly defined, the enemies identified, the course of action distinctly plotted and defined. There had not been the Ritz Hotel, Zorine's and beautiful models to boogey and sleep with, but that mission was delineated rather than vague like this, not based on his father's gut instinct or a priori estimate of Hasad's motivations.

Tatov was feeling guilt. His original objective in seeing Susan Crossley was to use her as bait to find her ex-husband. After having lunch with her, he was convinced that she did not know where Crossley was, did not even know that he'd been in Chicago recently. He kept his inquiries about Crossley low-key and offhand, never pressing her. She answered tersely, never condemning Crossley or offering a reason for the break-up of their marriage. Only when she talked about Crossley's devotion to their son had she revealed any emotion. But somewhere after the second martini and before the salad course, Tatov lost the purpose of this mission, the tactical reason for the lunch. Hasad and his father were thousands of miles away and a beautiful woman was sitting next to him, touching his arm sometimes, a litmus reaction in her mood to his own. The name of the game became the game itself. Running into her at Zorine's earlier that night had been deliberate. The same interchange of excitement had continued in spite of other people sitting between them.

Now, without turning on the lights in the hotel room, Tatov threw his overcoat on a chair, loosened his tie and flopped fully clothed on the bed. Looking up at the darkness of the ceiling, he examined his unseen reflection there. The message button on the telephone glowed red in the darkness.

He was feeling guilt because he liked Chicago, the excitement and the people he had met. He was fascinated by Ursini, the photographer, the lens he used to look at the world with which he could see beauty in ugliness. He and Rico del Gracia had met briefly twice before, at Le Mans and at Gstaad, and were able to talk about mutual acquaintances. The other man, Mike Nelson, had been more typically American, open-faced and smiling, square and pleasant.

He had to flush Whiz Crossley out of hiding. There had to be a way, something that would make him surface.

He could not remember having seen gray eyes like Susan's before, framed with lashes like that.

If the Crossley child was kidnapped, he thought, the father would come out into the open.

Susan would like London, and it would take to her instantly. He saw the two of them at his parents' country place in Essex, living in the small cottage near the trout stream. He saw them together at Anabel's. Everywhere he could imagine himself, he could imagine himself with Susan.

Tatov picked up the phone and left a call for 3 A.M., allowing a half-hour for the transatlantic call to get through to London. As he lay on the bed, he tried to concentrate on what explanation he was going to give his father, but he kept seeing himself with Susan Crossley, imagining her beside him now.

Tuesday, February 15
Two a.m., Lake Forest,
Illinois

DIANE COLE sat naked on a chair in the bedroom, which was a shamble of half-packed suitcases, open drawers, and clothes draped on the bed and chairs. The lights were on and the heavy draperies drawn. Sheldon Cole lay asleep in a fetal position on one side of the huge bed. The ash tray next to her was filled with barely smoked cigarettes. The television stand had been turned so that she could watch it, but the screen was blank. She stared at the nothingness there and saw what was happening to her life.

On the ottoman in front of the chair all her jewelry was spread out on a large monogrammed bath towel. On Cole's instructions, she had gone to the Lake Forest Bank earlier that day and emptied her safety-deposit vault. He had given her no reason and would answer none of her questions, but he was adamant. There were two diamond necklaces, an emerald, ruby and sapphire necklace from David Webb, three diamond bracelets, an emerald and ruby bracelet, a 17-carat emerald, a 21-carat pear-shaped diamond from Harry Winston, and earrings and brooches of various stones.

She turned from the blank screen to the dazzling spread of jewels she rarely wore. The fiction which she had read was not fiction any longer; she was living it now. In her fantasies she was the heroine escaping the Nazi pogrom, dressed in rags, clutching a bag of diamonds, her children disguised as urchins as they moved through the night toward the shelter of a Swiss bank account.

At first, when Cole had finally told her the truth and outlined the threats to their children, documenting the danger with what he learned from other victims, Diane Cole had reacted with the same horror, fear and panic of persecution that Cole himself was feeling. She was caught up in the secret plans, a private plane leaving at dawn with the children, a bag of jewels, a suitcase full of cash and a few clothes. She sped through the preparations without analyzing the problem, moving with urgency as though the Nazi army was bivouacked in Winnetka, twelve miles away.

Now, at zero minus four hours, she had time to think about who she was, where she had come from and where she was going. The difference in hereditary and cultural lineage between her husband and herself had never before been as clearly delineated. Her ancestors had fled the oppression of a tyrannical landed gentry once, never to flee again. When the tyranny followed them, they stood their ground and fought.

She was Diane Tugwell, the descendant of a family who had arrived twenty years after the *Mayflower*. Her mother was a Wheelwright, a family traceable in United States history almost as far as the Tugwells. She was Diane Wheelwright Tugwell, not a Jewish peasant with a babushka on her head escaping at dawn.

She lit another cigarette, leaned over and put the emerald on her right hand, the large pear-shaped diamond on her left. She fastened one diamond bracelet on each side of the wide emerald and ruby bracelet, put the David Webb necklace around her neck, and selected a pair of earrings, clipping them carefully on each lobe. On her way to the bed, she stopped before the mirror and smiled at the glitter of the jewels against her naked body. Sitting softly on the edge of the bed, she touched her husband's shoulder gently and whispered his name tenderly.

Like an animal, Sheldon Cole uncoiled from his sleeping position, bolting up, his eyes squinting at the bright light, ready to strike. "Is it time to go?"

"We're not going," she said.

Tuesday, February 15
Four a.m. to ten a.m.,
Chicago and London

THE TRANSATLANTIC CALL came through almost exactly on schedule.

"How is Mother?"

"She's quite well, as a matter of fact." The elder Tatov cleared his throat. "How are conditions in America?"

"Can we talk freely?"

"Yes, of course."

"I'm afraid that I'm not doing well here, Father. I picked up the contact in Damascus . . . Are you terribly angry with me about Damascus?"

"Not angry, disappointed. It was dangerous, headstrong. A mistake, Leonid, is forgivable if it teaches a lesson."

"I learned a lesson, Father. But, I rather liked Hasad. Right out of a book, isn't he?"

"That's why I called, Leonid. It's about Hasad. It seems he responded well to you, liked your . . . I don't remember quite how he phrased it, but he meant bravado. As a matter of fact, he might have used that very word."

"It was chancy, I know, Father, but I really had nothing to go on. As it happened, I was able to get a look at his young American mathematician and followed him as far as Chicago."

"Way out there? It's rather dangerous in Chicago, isn't it? Gangsters, that sort of thing?"

"Surprisingly, quite civilized, Father. The gangster days seem to be over."

"You've seen no evidences of Hasad's plan in operation?"

"None at all. Moreover, Hasad's American came a rather devious way, and I'm afraid you'll be rather upset at my expense account. We went from Dakar to Rio to Bogotá and to Miami before landing here."

"Do you suspect that Chicago is central to the operation?"

Tatov lay back on the bed, more relaxed now. He had expected anger from his father. "The American has some roots here. He lived in this city for a time, and still has a former wife and a child here. My guess is that if I continue to stake them out, I'll eventually pick up his trail again."

"Eventually may not be soon enough, Leonid. The premonition I had about Hasad is becoming stronger every day. Particularly after what happened yesterday."

"What happened?"

"You knew about Hasad's son. When he called from Damascus that day, he spoke about you and about his own son. He talked about my great fortune in having such a fine specimen, and then about his own misfortune."

"I saw his son, Father, in a wheelchair in the courtyard of the palace. It must be shattering to have only three fourths of a body, to be immobilized when one is bred for action. I didn't talk to the son, but certainly Hasad was shattered."

"Hasad is more shattered now. Yesterday his son killed himself."

"Killed himself?"

"Quite."

"How?"

"A mutual associate telephoned me from Beirut yesterday. It seems the young man bribed an attendant for a length of rope, somehow managed to lasso it over a tree in the courtyard, tied the other end around his neck and released the brake on his invalid's chair. The chair rolled toward the fountain, leaving the body hanging from the tree. Our mutual associate was rather more explicit than necessary, I thought."

"What a dreadful picture, three-quarters of a man hanging from an olive tree. Are you going to Damascus for the funeral?"

"I think not. I'm not even certain that Arabs go in for that sort of thing. In any case, it wouldn't do for me to be seen with

Hasad at this moment. He'll understand that. I will indicate my condolences in another way."

Tatov could not shake the picture from his mind of that powerful fragment of a body swinging from the tree in bright sunlight. "What's your premonition, Father? Retaliation?"

"I explained to you before about Hasad. He's very petty in many ways—or, rather, traditional according to Arabic custom. I told you that he cuts off the hands of thieves and tongues of liars. My premonition was strong before this death, and now this can only add fuel to the fire."

"Can you make an educated guess about what Hasad might do?"

"Unfortunately, Leonid, my intelligence sources are not good enough—or perhaps Hasad's security is too good. I was hoping you had come upon something which might give us a clue."

"Nothing, Father."

"Well, stay alert. If anything surfaces at this end I will be in touch. And be careful, Leonid. Your mother would never forgive me if anything happened to you while you were working for me."

"What about you?" Leonid laughed audibly to disguise the concern behind the question.

"We might turn out to be a good team, mightn't we? I would not want anything to spoil that. And don't start looking for me to retire yet; I have a good fourteen years before the legal retirement age."

"And even then you're above the law, aren't you, Father?"

Tuesday, February 15
Three twenty-six a.m.,
Chicago

As soon as Delta Flight 8 had arrived at the gate and the door was opened, an announcement came over the address system. "Would passenger Peter Frankel please contact the Delta representative at the end of the jetway for a message?" Still groggy from his few hours' sleep, Frankel asked the man in front of him if he had heard the message. The man seemed not to understand English. Frankel checked again with the stewardess on his way out. "Did I hear them paging Peter Frankel?"

"I don't remember," the weary girl said. "Check with the agent at the end of the jetway."

The red-eyed passengers filed slowly off the plane. Frankel was still wearing the same velvet leisure suit, by now completely shapeless. He had bought another synthetic shirt at the airport in Miami, this one even more garish than the one he had been wearing at Zorine's last night. Now even this one smelled of stale perspiration. He rifled his pockets for his parking ticket. Was it only last night? He wondered if he had enough strength to walk to the parking lot and search for his car. In forty minutes he would be home. A shower, the hottest shower he could subject his body to, clean sheets, and tomorrow clean clothes.

"Were you paging Peter Frankel?"

"Are you Mr. Frankel?"

"Yes, what is it?"

"There's a photographer from the *Chicago Tribune* over there." He indicated a tall man in the center corridor leaning against a telephone stand.

Frankel thought he knew most of the photographers from the

Tribune. He did not recognize this one. "You looking for me?" he asked as he approached.

"Peter Frankel?" He said the name in a loud voice, and people turned around.

"Yes."

"Metcalfe . . . *Chicago Tribune.* Want to get a shot of you."

Before Frankel could say anything, the man pulled out his wallet and opened it. "Here's my press pass."

Looking at the identification, Frankel shook his head in disbelief. Now what did the FBI want? The flashbulb exploded while he still held the wallet in his hand. Taking it back, the photographer whispered without moving his mouth, "Call Dirksmith at once, from the airport." A small group had clustered around, wondering who Frankel was, so he took off quickly, trying to lose himself in the trickle of people in the airport late at night.

Dirksmith answered the first telephone number on the third ring. "I only have one consolation," Frankel began without identifying himself. "At least you have to stay up all night figuring out ways to keep me up all night."

"There's an eight-five A.M. flight on Northwest Airlines to Seattle."

"Fascinating."

"Be on it."

"That I already figured. What happened? Did you get another lead on Bronson?"

"Part of the Bronson family were on a small charter on their way to Sun Valley. The plane hit the side of a mountain. Clear sky, good visibility. It doesn't figure."

"It figures very well, Dirksmith, and you know it. No survivors?"

"Not on the plane. Mrs. Bronson stayed home with a three-year-old child. Bronson and the rest of the kids were on the plane. You remember, she was the one who tipped us."

"What am I supposed to do? The woman must be hysterical, a basket case. How am I going to talk to her? How am I even going to get in to see her?"

"There'll be a photographer waiting at the Seattle airport. He'll give you further instructions."

"Isn't there a less obtrusive way of passing information to me? I keep being the center of attention. Right outside this booth there are three kids waiting for my autograph. They think I'm a rock star or something."

"Probably Russian spies," Dirksmith grunted. "Incidentally, the Miami agents are frantic. They can't find the Sherman Weinstein family. It seems they just disappeared into thin air."

"No shit. I wonder where they went."

Tuesday, February 15
Eight-thirty a.m., Chicago

THE TELEPHONE rang and the room-service waiter knocked simultaneously. Jumping out of bed, Leonid Tatov moved toward the door while his hand reached for the phone. "This is Tatov. Hang on whoever you are."

"It's Susan."

"Then particularly hang on. One minute, Susan."

In a minute he was back under the covers talking to Susan. "I rather like waking up to your voice."

"Do you have someone with you?"

"Jealous? I like that about a woman; it makes a man feel wanted."

"Is there someone?"

"Yes, as a matter of fact." He held out his hand for the breakfast check and signed his name. "There is someone here. Five feet eight, perhaps. One hundred and eighty pounds, not much hair, what there is gray. Nice eyes, though. A gentle blue-green." He handed the check back to the waiter and smiled. "Still jealous?"

"A waiter?"

"You've got it."

"Did you have fun last night? Barbara Moore's very pretty, isn't she?"

"Is she? I'm afraid I didn't notice."

"A woman likes that about a man, when he lies to make her feel good."

"I never lie—well, almost never, and not this time."

"I'll remember that about you."

"How about lunch today? Or breakfast? I've ordered enough for two. Come right over."

She laughed. "You wouldn't like me at this minute. I'm all greasy and my hair's in curlers."

"I'll uncurl your hair and wash your face. How about it?"

"You're crazy. Besides, I'm working today. It's for a series of ads with Rico del Gracia. Did you know him before?"

"I've met him before, but don't really know him. We see a lot of the same action on the Continent." Hugging the phone to his ear, Tatov got out of bed, snatched the glass of orange juice from the table and maneuvered himself back under the covers. "Are you involved with him?"

"We're old friends. Our families have known each other for three generations, maybe more."

"He could have fooled me. I'd never have thought he was from Chicago. I assumed he was Spanish or Portuguese. I couldn't tell last night whether he was looking at you with smoldering passion or whether he has new contact lenses."

"You're awful. Now who's jealous?"

"I am—unabashedly. But you haven't answered my question."

"I'm not really involved with him."

"In that case hope springs eternal. How about dinner?"

"I don't think we'll be through shooting until late, and even if we are I'll be too tired. I do mostly runway modeling, and photographic modeling is a lot harder. But we'll all be together at the Art Institute party tomorrow night. I've got you a terrific date. You'll like her."

"Your date will be old Flamenco Eyes?"

"Yes."

"Then how about breakfast tomorrow morning?"

"You're incorrigible. Tomorrow morning I have to get my hair done, and then there's a meeting for a charity thing my father got me involved in. Incidentally, will you still be here on Sunday?"

"Make it worth my while and I'll be here forever. Well, maybe not quite forever. I'll be here as long as it takes for me to entice you to come back to London with me for a week of fun and games."

"You're crazy."

"I don't think I'm at all crazy. I'm making eminent good sense."

"Your name is in the paper this morning. Did you see it?"

Instinctively his body stiffened. "What for?"

"Do you remember meeting Irv Kupcinet last night? He stopped by the table at Zorine's."

"Vaguely."

"He's a columnist with the *Sun-Times*. Do you have the morning paper?"

"Room service seems to have brought one with breakfast." Cradling the telephone again, he leaped out of bed, took the newspaper off the cart and a piece of toast which made a loud crunching sound through the telephone receiver. "Got it," he said, fumbling through the thick tabloid. When he came across the column, he saw Rico del Gracia's name first.

> Beautiful People Department: Dining at *Zorine's*, *Rico del Gracia*, international playboy and men's toiletry tycoon, *Nic Ursini*, the famous photographer, *Leonid Tatov*, here from London and squiring still another Chicago lovely and *Susan Stonehill Crossley*, the very social model, who will be official escort and hostess when *Mark Mendoza*, the Israeli war hero, comes here as main speaker at the Man of the Year dinner honoring Senator *Hart Caldwell* on Sunday . . . Birthdaying: *Ginger Rogers*, the Cub's . . ."

Tatov stopped reading. "Is this your work?"

"He asked me who you were. It's all right, isn't it? You're not trying to hide or anything, are you?"

"Since I am here on business, I don't think my father would be overjoyed, but then there's very little likelihood of his seeing this. His communication with America is limited to the *Wall Street Journal*, the *New York Times* and reruns of *Bonanza*."

"That's why I asked you if you'd still be here on Sunday. It might be fun to meet Mark Mendoza."

"I'll be here, and I'd like to meet him."

"I'll arrange it with Father. You don't have to pledge any money or anything. The dinner will be dull, but the cocktail party first might be fun. That's the meeting I have tomorrow. We're going to finalize all the plans. You'll know some of the people."

"You're giving me a complex, Susan. I keep being with you and yet not being with you. Tomorrow night you'll be with del Gracia, Sunday night with Mendoza. Incidentally, have you met him before?"

"Never. Father's chairman of the dinner; that's how I got roped into it. We're Jewish. I never thought to tell you. I hope you don't mind."

He laughed. "It seems inconsequential at the moment."

"You'll come?"

"Yes. But on Thursday, Friday and Saturday, you will be mine and mine alone. Understood?"

"I can't. Thursday is okay, but Friday and Saturday I can't. Maybe I can juggle Friday." There was a pause. "Oh, my God, I just looked at the time. I'm going to be late. Talk to you later." She hung up.

Tatov reread the column, sat at the table, poured his coffee and removed the cover from his fried eggs. Directly in front of him was the television set; he turned it on and began eating his breakfast as he turned to the financial section of the newspaper and tried to find the London exchange quotations. His eggs were cold and the coffee tasted rancid.

The newscaster behind the desk began, "An unusual reprisal raid six miles inside the Israeli border killed four children, three adults and wounded twenty others yesterday. Here is an on-the-spot filmed report from NBC's John Powers in Israel."

Tatov looked up. The camera was on the face of a sun-burned, khaki-clad American newsman. "We are at a small Israeli settlement six miles from the Syrian border." The camera moved back to show the full figure of the man, the village square and some anguished, weeping adults and children. The camera panned back again, revealing a dead, bloodied lion in the foreground. "Early this morning, a half-starved, wounded lion was let loose here while the people of the settlement still were asleep. He marauded the area looking for food, killing four children from one family all asleep in the same shelter. This is an agricultural settlement unprotected by the Israeli army, with only a few weapons in the hands of some of the men. Before the crazed animal was killed, three adults, trying to capture the animal with no weapons, were also killed and a score more mauled by the lion." There was a close-up of the lion. "There is much divergent conjecture here and in the Israeli capital on the source and meaning of this attack. It appears that the lion was deliberately starved and wounded, then brought across the Syrian border to attack this settlement, but by whom or for what symbolic reason is not yet known. This is John Powers reporting from Israel, six miles from the Syrian border."

The camera switched back to the unruffled face of the newscaster in the studio.

Tatov turned off the set. It was all clear now. Why didn't the NBC newsman see the symbolism?

Tuesday, February 15
Nine a.m., Chicago

Sᴛᴏɴᴇʜɪʟʟ returned Sheldon Cole's call immediately.

"That fucking shiksa is out of her fucking mind," Cole began without saying hello. "She won't go."

Stonehill was puzzled. "She won't go where?"

"Anywhere. I had the whole thing set up. We could have slipped out of the country without anyone knowing it or being able to follow us, but this stupid cunt I'm married to won't leave. She keeps giving me this Bicentennial shit about fighting for freedom. All I've heard from her this morning is about the Tugwells, the Wheelwrights and a lot of American history crap."

"You know, she's right, Shellie."

"Maybe. And maybe we'll all wind up dead because of it." His voice lost its toughness. "All I know is that she's the most dynamite broad I've ever met. I've never been more turned on than I am at this very minute—more in love."

"What are you going to do now?"

"Nothing. Play ball with you and Feldman for the moment and see what happens. Is there anything new?"

"Feldman went to Washington. I've been trying to reach him, but he's en route to Chicago. He has some kind of an idea, but I don't know what it is. I'll talk to him this afternoon and keep you posted."

"All right. I'll play it your way for the moment."

"Tell Diane that I agree with you that she's a dynamite broad."

Stonehill sat in his office looking at his private phone, wanting to call Myrna but not daring to. She had been released from the hospital late yesterday and gone to her mother's apartment. "A little chicken soup," she'd explained to him, "and a little tender, loving care. Besides, I'm not ready yet to go back to my own place. When I feel well enough to make love again, I'll move back."

His Tuesday schedule was jammed. Somehow he would get through another day.

Tuesday, February 15 Nine-thirty a.m., Rolling Meadows, Illinois

I<small>T WAS</small> a difficult decision. The Northwest flight was due to arrive in Seattle at 10:02 A.M. Pacific time, which was two hours earlier than Chicago. It was a question of how long Peter Frankel stayed in Seattle. There wasn't time to get the assassin from St. Louis to Seattle before Frankel talked to Mrs. Bronson. But his talking to her wasn't important; what was essential was to exterminate Frankel before he could relay any information back to Washington or Chicago. Crossley still was not clear on Frankel's function—how he was operating or under whose direction—but at this point deductive reasoning was a waste of time. Frankel had to be eliminated. He was too close to Weinstein in Florida and Bronson in Seattle, and it had probably started in Chicago with either Stonehill or Weiskopf, each of whom had access to Frankel. Frankel was an X factor, not programmed into the computer, and he had to be stopped.

Crossley made two decisions. First, he would activate the assassin from St. Louis, taking the risk that Frankel might be gone before his man arrived in Seattle and chancing his being four hours away from the core of the action. In an emergency the other assassin could be used as a back-up. Secondly he decided to instruct Seattle, the twenty-eighth web, to delay Frankel at all costs, to risk relying on the tactical judgment of the web's leader to keep Frankel there and out of touch with a telephone until the assassin arrived from St. Louis.

In the communication center, Crossley punched out the instructions to Seattle and St. Louis. Even as he was doing this, his mind was on the next problem, Leonid Tatov. In reading a report from the twenty-third web which quoted a newspaper item on Rico del Gracia, Crossley had seen Tatov's name and put the name with the face on the balcony in Damascus and the same face play-acting father to his child. When he had run the name through his own computer, he'd drawn a blank. The newspaper item had said Tatov was from London, and through another network Crossley was having the man's identity checked there, but the report had not come back. In any case, Tatov's specific identification was not important; obviously he was Hasad's man, and probably he was another professional assassin. If so, Crossley had no illusions about the target. Hasad's instruction had been not to contact the subject under any circumstances. Self-preservation, Crossley decided, transcended all circumstances.

After an hour and twenty minutes at the machine, sending out directives all over the country, Crossley went into the firing range, flicked the switch which activated the mechanical moving targets, picked up a revolver and began firing. Each bullet hit the target with deadly accuracy. He started to reload, changed his mind, felt the hardness which had begun in his genitals, returned to his office, closed the door, connected his machine and masturbated into it.

Tuesday, February 15
Ten-thirty a.m., Chicago

MYRNA GORDON and her mother were in a fitting room at Saks Fifth Avenue. When Myrna undressed, the saleswoman recoiled at the sight of the mass of bruises and lacerations. Myrna's mother explained, "An automobile accident. A terrible thing. It's a miracle she's alive."

Now Myrna stood in front of the mirror sheathed in silver sequins, the high neck and long sleeves covering the marks.

"Like a vision."

"It's too tight across the ass."

"What kind of a word is that for a nice girl? It cups a little over the tuchis, so they'll let it out maybe a half inch." She examined her daughter's reflection in the three-way mirror. "Ravishing."

Myrna looked at the price tag. Even the slightest movement pained her. "There's no way I'm going to spend this kind of money on a dress, Mom. I'll wear it maybe once. It's ridiculous."

"Don't get excited, don't get excited." Mrs. Gordon touched the dress where it was too tight. "Sometimes a dress can be a very good investment. Your friend from the Commodity Exchange will understand that."

Myrna started to unzip the side. "No way, Mom."

"You could possibly rob a bank or maybe a banker?" She winked.

"Stop that, Mom. I won't take a dime from him."

"A joke, Myrna. Your mother was making a little joke."

Then to the saleswoman. "We'll take it. Call the fitter. We need it by tomorrow."

"Mother—" Myrna began.

"It's my present to you, darling. If a mother wants to be extravagant with her daughter, why not?"

"You can't afford it, either."

"I've got a little pushke that will take care of this very nicely. You know, a few dividends, a little mah jong money, a little here and a little there."

Myrna kissed her. "You're something else, Mom. I love you."

"I think of it as an investment."

Myrna shook her head. "Forget it, Mom. No way am I going to marry that schmuck from the Commodity Exchange."

"Who knows, darling?" She looked up through Saks' ceiling toward Heaven. "Who knows what's written up there?"

Tuesday, February 15
Eleven a.m., Chicago

THE YOUNG ARCHITECT from Skidmore, Owens and Merrill spread the three rough sketches out on the dining-room table. All of them were rehashes of recently completed buildings around the country but each had large lettering with the words THE MAN- DLEBAUM CLINIC over the entrance. Mousey, still in a long, light-blue dressing gown, a ruff of marabou covering the wrinkles of her neck, moved her head from side to side as she examined the the drawings and stepped back and forth to gain perspective, occasionally brushing the body of the young architect.

"It's hard to decide," she said sweetly. "They all look shitty."

"Mrs. Mandlebaum!" The young man's nostrils flared and his

eyes widened. "These are based on some of our prize-winning buildings."

"I was just teasing." Her voice was coy. "I was testing your loyalty to the firm. Bruce is a very good friend of mine. He said that I'd like working with you. What's your name again?"

"Denby. But call me Roger."

She touched his arm. "Very well, Roger it shall be. Now, Roger, if you were me, which one would you choose?"

"It's hard to say. The site hasn't even been chosen yet. My understanding is that this rendering is just for publicity purposes."

"Something like that, Roger, something like that." She backed up, her body against the young man. "But just for sheer beauty, Roger, which would you pick?"

"It's hard. Form has to follow function . . ."

"You're so right, Roger."

"I've never been to Israel. I looked at many pictures of Haifa and the terrain around it. Terrain has a lot to do with it. There's something young and vital about Israel." He pointed at the sketch based on the Baxter Laboratory Building in Deerfield, Illinois, a complex whose low roof was broken by a huge column extending fifty feet into the air, supported by exposed wire struts. "But all other things being equal, I think I'd pick this one. Somehow it has the most integrity, and yet there's a romantic aspect to it, a vitality."

"Roger?"

"Yes, ma'am."

"Answer a question for me?" He nodded. "Are you gay?"

"Ma'am?"

"Are you gay?"

His nostrils flared again, and his eyes looked disbelieving. Finally he said, "Yes, ma'am."

"That son-of-a-bitch."

"Who?"

"Bruce. Your boss."

"Why?"

"Because you're gay. He did it on purpose."

"I don't understand."

"You like that one because that looks like a big prick." She pointed to the center column. "And all those wires aren't holding up the roof; they're restraining that big prick." She picked up the drawing and tore it up. "Develop that one." She pointed to a simpler design. "The rendering has to be completed by tomorrow afternoon, in time to have prints made for the press kit. Is that clear?"

Tuesday, February 15
Two p.m., Chicago

AT FIRST, Susan refused. Ursini's studio was a mob scene of agency executives, photographers, assistants, prop men, hairdressers, wardrobe people and make-up artists. Cups of half-drunk coffee littered every surface. Sets for the ads had to be improvised from what was available at the studio or what could be quickly borrowed. In the morning they had done a shot of del Gracia stretched out on a voluptuous sofa, his shoes off, his black tie undone and his head in Susan's lap. She was wearing a Halston halter-top gown and one Tiffany earring, and was propped against a mélange of puffy, patterned pillows. What seemed like a simple shot took hours to do. Ursini kept fussing with the lighting, the number of opened buttons on del Gracia's shirt and the way Susan's hair fell as she inclined her head over his face.

The second shot had been taken in the kitchen of Ursini's slick apartment above the studio. It had been Mike Nelson's idea to use the kitchen and to photograph Rico in jeans, T-shirt and sneakers sitting at the kitchen table, his arms folded to emphasize his muscles, one leg up on the table to accentuate his crotch. Susan was in the background, back to the camera, preparing a large wicker picnic basket. They had raided Ursini's wine cellar and refrigerator for the props arrayed on the kitchen counter: wine, caviar, fruit, a loaf of French bread, a wheel of ripe Brie.

Ursini had the idea for the third shot, using his own brown-marble and stainless-steel bathroom as the setting. He wanted to pose Rico naked, his back to the camera, shaving at the sink, his face and upper torso reflected in the mirror. Susan, also nude, was to huddle on the toilet seat, watching Rico shave. Ursini had published two books of nude photographs, and had a Michelangelo kind of fascination for anatomy, flesh and bone structure. The agency people jumped at the idea; thought it would make a great ad, cause a stir in the media. Del Gracia was uncertain and looked to Mike Nelson for an opinion. Nelson shrugged his shoulders noncommittally.

Susan refused. Ursini had asked her to pose for him twice before, photographs to be included in each of his books. She had refused then, and had no intention of changing her mind now. Ursini, turned on by the concept of the shot, pleaded with her, imitating the position of the pose and demonstrating that neither her breasts nor pubic area would be exposed. "All I want," he explained, "is the long line of your shoulder and arms, and the way it flows to your hip and down your leg. I won't even show your face if that makes it any easier."

"It's not that. I just couldn't stand around here naked, not with all these people and in front of you and Rico."

"You get undressed in front of your doctor, don't you? Can't you see that I'm looking at beauty? This isn't porno, you know me better than that."

She shook her head defiantly and looked up at Rico. "I don't want you to do anything you don't want to do, Susan. I'm going to be bare-assed to the world, and I'm not all that comfortable about it either. But I think it will make a great shot and project the kind of image the product needs."

"I don't think I can, Rico."

"What if we cleared everybody out, so that there'll be just

you and me and Nic? You can stay dressed while they set up the shot, and at the last minute everyone else will leave. Would that make you more comfortable?"

"Maybe. I don't know." She turned to Ursini. "Could you do it so that my face doesn't show?"

"If you insist." He took her head, tilting it, and let her hair fall over the side of her face. With his fingers he fluffed her hair, arranging it so that only a part of her nose and chin were exposed, then stood back and narrowed his eyes. "That should do it. Your own mother wouldn't know it was you."

"I hate to be a rotten sport about this, Nic, but I've told you before how I feel . . . I'm sorry, Rico. I guess I'm just too hung up to do it."

"I don't want to force you, Susan."

"Can't you get another model for this shot? I think it would be a great shot and I hate to louse it up."

"Not at the last minute," Ursini said. "The only other model I know with the body for this shot is Marisa Berenson or Daphne Nelson, and neither one is in town."

Susan looked away from both del Gracia and Ursini. The entire crew was motionless, looking at her and wanting her to say yes. "Okay, I'll try it. But I'm not promising that I won't chicken out at the last minute."

Ursini kissed her and the studio became a tumult again as they began preparing for the shot.

It took almost two hours to set up for the photograph. Susan spent almost an hour in the dressing room while the make-up girls dusted her body with powder. Ursini's instructions had been, "I want her white and dry-looking." Then she put on one of Ursini's silk robes and went upstairs. She hesitated when she saw del Gracia in position, and drew the silk robe tighter around herself. She moved forward slowly, suddenly fascinated by del Gracia's round, white buttocks in voluptuous contrast to the bronze of his torso and legs. His back and legs were hairless, smoothly muscled, and the heavy mat of black on his chest was reflected in the mirror. The make-up people had heavily oiled his body so that the ligaments under the skin were patterned by the lights. Most of the shaving cream had been removed from his face, and he held a straight razor in position. In his shirt-sleeves, Mike Nelson was huddled on the toilet seat approximating Susan's pose. The two men were talking to each other, and Rico said something which made Mike laugh. Then from behind the camera Ursini called, "Hold still, Mike," and Nelson refroze in position. Susan realized that from the position of the pose, there was no way she could avoid seeing del Gracia's penis. The picture of Whiz naked flooded instantly into her mind—the long thin shaft, the tight sac—and she saw herself touching him, mouthing him, burying him in the web of her hair. It all came alive again: the sensory expectancy, the chemistry of juices and fluids in a gradually ascending motion. She knew that she was blushing and looked around to see if anyone was watching her. No one was.

Ursini called, "More powder on Rico's ass." A young man rushed forward with a spray can and a pastry brush and repaired the areas where perspiration had seeped through. Seeing Susan, Ursini gave her a reassuring smile. "Stay bundled up; it will be a minute or two."

When he was completely satisfied with the lighting and composition, he turned off the hot lights. "Rico," he shouted, "relax for a minute. Are you all right?"

"This damn marble sink is cold against my cock."

"You want a robe for a minute?"

Del Gracia shook his head. "I'll survive."

Ursini walked over and touched Nelson on the shoulder. "Thanks, Mike." He smiled. "Your career as a stand-in is over. Susan, come on over. Keep your robe on."

Susan walked over, clutching the robe even tighter, and sat on the toilet seat, trying not to look at Rico. "You remember the position?" Susan nodded. "Try it. Keep your robe on for a minute. I want to get the angle of your head and hair right."

It was awkward adjusting her body under the cover of the robe, but she sat quietly while the photographer manipulated her head and body. When he was satisfied with the general contour, he called back, "Try the lights," and they came on brightly. Susan kept her eyes closed to avoid staring directly at del Gracia. He was standing away from the sink, out of contact with the cold marble, while Ursini was back at the camera, again examining the composition. "Head up a little, Susan. Open your eyes; it's doing funny things to your nose."

Del Gracia's penis was much thicker than Whiz's, and the head of it bludgeoned out, with a faint circle of purplish flesh at the base. When he saw her staring at him, he moved closer to the sink to cover himself.

"Okay," Ursini called, "everybody out except Gloria." He waited. "Close the door." Then he walked over to Susan, motioning for Gloria to follow. "It's all clear, Susan. You ready?" She nodded without lifting her head. "I'm going back to the camera. Gloria will take off your robe and touch up your make-up. There's no one else here. Okay?" Susan nodded again, felt the silk of the robe being pulled off her body, tightened and then relaxed.

"I guess if we were both pros," Rico spoke softly, "we'd take this in our stride."

"I feel so silly," she said, talking so that her lips barely moved. "I don't mean to be so damn prissy."

"I kind of like this. I could get used to it."

"Used to what?"

"To having you sitting there watching me shave and being naked together. It all seems kind of natural."

"Relax a minute," Ursini called. "The damn light blew."

Rico turned to Susan, purposely exposing himself. "I don't feel any excitement. I thought I would with you, but I don't. You seem to be relaxing a little, too. Are you?" She looked up and smiled back at him. From his position, he could see parts of her body which were hidden from the camera. "You're beautiful, Susan. I wish they weren't all here, that it was just you and me. It seems right."

"Does it? I feel as though my father is going to walk in here and catch me. Silly, isn't it, for a grown woman to still have those hang-ups?"

"You know, I think our families always thought that someday you and I would be married. Maybe we should have been by now. Funny things happen. But maybe it isn't too late. We've both had our flings. Maybe now is the time."

"I don't believe you, Rico. Are you really proposing now while we're in this position in Nic's bathroom?"

He laughed a little. "Dumb place, huh? But it all seems as if it's meant to be."

"You can't be serious?"

"I'm dead serious, Susan. I think we ought to get married." Just then the burned-out light went on, and Rico resumed his pose, the razor poised, while Susan adjusted her body.

"Tighten your ass, Rico. I want to see those dimples. Susan, think fluid."

Silently they held their poses while Ursini photographed, moving the camera to various angles, adjusting the lights himself, working quickly and expertly for the next twenty minutes. "That's it, kids. All done. Gloria, give Susan her robe."

Susan stayed huddled until the robe was around her. Rico wrapped a bath towel around himself and walked over to her as she stood up. "I'm dead serious, Susan. What do you think?"

"You are, aren't you?" She could smell the man beneath the perfume of his product, and had never felt more aware of herself and her body. "It's not fair to propose to a girl when she doesn't have any clothes on."

"What do you think, Susan?"

"I don't know, Rico. I feel so awkward."

"What would you say if it was eight years ago and we were out on the golf course at the club, hiding behind the pine trees in the moonlight?"

She turned away. "But it isn't then, Rico; it's now and I'm confused as hell."

Firmly he turned her so that she faced him again. "Admit that it feels right."

"You haven't said that you love me."

He reached over her shoulder and shut the bathroom door so that they were alone. "Do I have to say it? Don't you know it?"

"There have been so many times when . . ." She decided not to say any more.

"When what? When I could have said that I loved you?"

She shook her head and felt the tears on her cheeks. "No. When I wanted this, when I wanted you to . . ."

Rico kissed her gently at first, then hard. Her eyes closed to the impact of his body and the probing of his tongue. With her eyes closed all she could see was the Rico del Gracia of the television commercials, kissing other girls against exotic backdrops. There was none of the surrender to emotion that she had hoped to feel, no blocking out of consciousness or plunge into ecstatic physical experience.

Rico went through the mechanics of the kiss waiting for a sensation which he knew would not occur.

"Hey, what goes on in there?" There was a pounding on the door.

Rico drew away and called through the door, "We'll be right out, Mike." He started back to Susan, but she held him off. He whispered, "We'll talk later tonight. When we're alone."

Mike Nelson was blocking the door when Rico opened it, and his shirt was as wet as if he had been the one under the lights.

Tuesday, February 15
Two p.m., Seattle

PETER FRANKEL hung up the phone. His trip to Seattle had accomplished nothing. He had just finished reporting this by phone to Waldo Dirksmith, and now he sat at Sanford Bronson's desk, looking at pictures of the Bronson children. He picked up the picture of Bronson's wife and examined it more closely. The woman was upstairs under heavy sedation, and her doctor had told him that he intended to keep her that way for several days. Under no conditions would he permit his patient to be questioned. The family lawyer was also there, backing up the medical decision with legal teeth.

Dirksmith had been able to contribute nothing. He told

Frankel that there were no new developments, and that the
rundown on the fingerprints from Weinstein's office had not
been completed. He instructed Frankel to return to Chicago and
await further orders.

Frankel dialed his office in Chicago. The switchboard girl
answered. "Carrie, this is Peter. Could—"

"Everybody's looking for you. I have nine thousand telephone messages. Mr. Moynihan said that if I heard from you I
was to—"

He cut her off. "Put me through to the big man." He waited,
fumbling with the objects on the desk.

The low, calm voice said, "Moynihan."

"It's Peter, Dan."

The voice turned sweet, the thick syrup of venom. "Peter
Whom?"

"Come on, Dan."

"Not Peter Frankel, lately of the United States Attorney's
office. Not that Peter Frankel."

"Dan, don't get your ass in an uproar. I'll explain it all
tomorrow."

"Tomorrow? Don't tell me that the Jewish Steve McQueen is
going to show up for work tomorrow? How nice." Moynihan's
voice returned to normal. "Where the hell are you?"

"In Seattle."

"What the hell are you doing in Seattle?"

"I can't explain it now. I'm on my way back. I'm catching the
five-ten out of here. What I really called for was to see if you
can do me a favor."

Moynihan exploded. "Favor? What makes you think I'd do
you a favor?"

"Because you're sweet and lovable, as well as being even-
tempered and soft-spoken."

"As long as you understand my real nature, Frankel, I'll
make a sincere attempt. What the hell do you want?"

"Do you know anybody at Gingiss, the tuxedo rental place?"

"A tuxedo? What the hell do you want a tuxedo for? Come
to think of it, you're going to need a tuxedo. After I kill you
tomorrow they can lay you out in it."

"Do you know anybody there?"

"Sure, I know Ben Gingiss. Why?"

"I need a tux for tomorrow night. I know damn well that if I go in tomorrow, and get a shnook salesman, he won't even talk to me. They need at least twenty-four hours for delivery. I thought maybe you could exert some clout."

"Do you want a pink one or a blue one?"

"Tell Gingiss I'll be in his downtown store first thing in the morning."

"First thing in the morning you're going to be in *my* store, Frankel, talking your little heart out, trying to get back in my good graces."

"Right after Gingiss, Dan, right after Gingiss."

"Is there any other little thing I can do for you?"

"I don't suppose you'd like to call the barber shop for me, would you?"

"You have terminal chutzpah, Frankel." Moynihan hung up.

The Bronson attorney, who was standing in the entrance hall, called to Frankel as he came out of the study, "There's a car here for you."

"I didn't order a car."

"It's the FBI." He walked toward the door with him. "I don't understand what's going on here. First you and then the FBI. Is there something funny about the accident?"

"I'm not sure. Is there?"

Bronson's lawyer looked puzzled. "I don't know. Bronson was acting strange. He got me out of bed in the middle of the night to come over here and talk about an emergency. But when I got here he wouldn't talk and sent me home. The next morning he said he was coming to my office. He never showed. It wasn't like Bronson; he was a very meticulous man. Something must be wrong or you wouldn't be here. How does the FBI figure?"

"I can't tell you anything—mostly because I don't know anything. But I'll give you a tip. Keep Mrs. Bronson guarded." The lawyer started to ask a question, but Frankel shook him off. "I can't answer any questions. Just trust me."

A nondescript gray four-door Chevrolet was waiting in the

long U-shaped driveway directly in front of the entrance. One of the back doors opened and a man leaned out. "Hop in, Frankel, we'll give you a ride to the airport."

Frankel started toward the car. "Are you from the FBI?" He had one hand on the door and was about to get in when his attention was diverted by another car, its tires screeching, driving fifty miles an hour up the driveway. The man inside the Chevrolet tried to pull him in as the Chevrolet lurched forward, and Frankel was knocked down by the impact, hit by the opened car door and thrown to the driveway. The approaching car rammed the Chevrolet but it kept going, picking up speed. There was the screeching of rubber again as each car made the sharp turn from the driveway onto the road, leaving behind a fog of dust. Frankel·raised his head just in time to see the last car turn the corner. He would not be able to identify it.

The sleeve of his jacket was shredded from the abrasion against the gravel, and there was a bloody gash on his forehead where the edge of the door had struck him. Slowly, in pain, he raised himself on all fours and caught his breath. It took tremendous effort to stand up. He looked at his scraped hands and the dust covering his clothes, touched the gash on his head and saw the blood on his hand. Turning back to the large carved doors of the Bronson house, he managed to find the tiny circle of the door buzzer, and with great effort pushed it.

The Bronson lawyer opened the door and could not believe what he saw.

Frankel asked, "You got a Band-Aid or something?" then collapsed on the front stoop.

Tuesday, February 15
Six p.m., Chicago

IRVING FELDMAN's plane had been delayed at National Airport by a mechanical problem and he arrived two hours late at O'Hare. He dialed his private line as soon as he disembarked. Stella was still at the office. "Those men," she said when he called, "the ones you told me might come at any time, have showed up. Locker and Green."

"What did you tell them?"

"Not a thing. They're waiting in your office, watching television. Who are they?"

Feldman wiped the perspiration from his forehead. "Maybe new clients."

"They don't look like client material to me."

"What *do* they look like?"

"The young one is dynamite, kind of a post-hippie type. He's Locker. The other one looks like he should be behind the counter at the Bagel and Bialy Store; he even smells of corned beef. I told them your plane was delayed and that I didn't know whether you'd come into the office or go right home. They insisted on waiting. What are you going to do?"

"Do I have a dinner date?"

"You're supposed to be at the Standard Club at eight—dinner with the Katzes and the Harrises. Your wife has been calling every ten minutes, as have Livingston Stonehill, Graham Marshall, Mrs. Mandlebaum, Seymour Danzig, Morry Bruce—and I could go on and on."

"Call my wife and tell her I'll meet her at the Standard Club. Say I may be a little late. Let me think for a minute . . ." He considered whether to face the Israeli agents now or wait until Wednesday morning. He had bought both the *Washington Post* and the *New York Times* and had time to read them thoroughly during the delay, clipping out three articles which changed his mind about the approach he would take with the agents. "Tell those men that I've just phoned and that I'm on my way in from the airport. Explain that the traffic will be heavy."

"Do I have to stay?"

"Yes, you'd better wait. Then call Livingston Stonehill and stall him. Tell him there's nothing new and that I'll talk to him tomorrow." About to hang up, he thought of something. "Stella?"

"Yes, Irv."

"What's lying on top of my desk that those men might see? Anything important?"

"I don't think so. Harrington just brought in a brief on the Garand case. Nothing else except your telephone messages—all thirty of them."

"I'll be there as soon as I can."

It took fifty minutes before Feldman was behind his desk facing the agents. The lines of telephone messages next to the blotter were not in the precise order in which Stella usually placed them. The older man, Green, sat directly opposite, while the younger, dressed in jeans, an open shirt and sweater, lounged on the sofa at the far end of the room.

"Such a tumult at the airport," Feldman explained. "The traffic was unreal." Casually he stacked the telephone messages in a pile. "As a matter of form, I'd like to see your identification."

"I am Green," the older man answered, "and that's Locker. That is our identification."

"You're American. That surprises me. It's a long way from Israel, and I didn't expect you this soon."

"We were in the area. Is your secretary still out there?" ·

"I think she's left. Can I get you something?"

"No, just checking. Incidentally, you can talk freely. We've checked your office. No bugs." He stood up and squinted at the intercom on Feldman's desk to make sure it was off.

"I've had a little experience with intelligence," Feldman said, managing a smile. "With our own CIA. Allen Dulles was a very close friend of mine, very close. Really a marvelous man."

From the background, soft-spoken, the younger man said, "Suppose you outline the nature of your problem." There was no question that he was the leader of the team.

Feldman had decided to stall. The piece he had read about the wounded lion and the raid of the Israeli settlement had changed his thinking. He couldn't be the only one who saw the symbolism of the lion and Mark Mendoza. It was likely that Mendoza would cancel his appearance here and remain protected in Israel. If so, he had time. If Mendoza canceled, the bond dinner could be delayed or called off, the immediate pressure on Stonehill would be lifted and there would be time to maneuver. Feldman knew that once the Israeli agents were turned on there would be no stopping them, and that their job was to protect Israel, not his clients. Looking at the older man, he kept the volume of his voice low, trying to draw the younger man out of the shadows at the back of the office. "First we must have an understanding. I hold some very privileged information, both personal and political. I must have assurances that this information will remain confidential."

"We do not make deals, Mr. Feldman," Green said. "We are not allowed to make deals. You either need our help or you do not. Tell us what you know and what your problem is, and we will make the judgments."

"I must have assurances." Feldman took off his glasses, placed them in a holder on his desk, removed another pair from a drawer and put them on.

Green restated his position. "There are too many of them and too few of us," he explained. "Deals waste a lot of time—time we don't have."

"I understand the problem of not having enough personnel. But as I told you, I have had a little experience with our own CIA. I know that in the intelligence game everything is not always definitely black or white. Even in your business, deals are made, one hand washes the other."

"The United States is very rich and very powerful. Your

country is not constantly under the gun as we are. You have the luxury of making deals; we do not."

"You must understand that an attorney has obligations to his client."

From the back of the room Locker sauntered forward, sat on the edge of Feldman's desk, took the letter opener lying there and played with it, running his index finger over the sharp edge. The power of his young body was outlined under the tight-fitting clothes. Both Feldman and Green waited for him to speak, but he said nothing.

"Our only obligation," Green persisted, "is to our country, and we do whatever is necessary and expedient to protect it. Those are our rules, and it's why Israel has survived while everyone has been trying to eliminate it."

"You don't have to tell me about Israel." Feldman smiled. "Golda Meir is a dear personal friend of mine, very dear. It couldn't be more than two or three weeks ago that she called me about a legal problem. Did you know that there is going to be a Broadway show based on her life? Imagine a Broadway musical about Golda Meir! Only in America. Did you know that the producers are talking about Ethel Merman for the lead?"

Though Green may have looked as if he belonged behind a delicatessen counter, his mind was disciplined and unyielding. "Time is running out, Feldman. Suppose you tell us the nature of your problem."

Feldman looked directly at Green, but he knew that Locker was ready to take over. "First the assurances."

"I told you before that—"

Locker interrupted. "What's your deal, Feldman?"

Feldman tilted back in his chair and looked at the ceiling. "The first condition is that you not directly contact any of my clients if I give you their names." He looked at Locker. "Agreed?"

"Let's hear it all."

"Secondly, no information is routed through Danzig unless it is first cleared with me. Agreed?"

"Keep talking."

"The third and most important condition is that under no

circumstances you relay any information to the FBI, the U.S. Secret Service or the CIA."

"Is that all?" Locker was holding the letter opener as though he were about to throw it, feigning practice shots at an imaginary target behind Feldman's desk.

"That's all."

Locker laughed and stood up. "What's your real game plan, Feldman?"

"What do you mean?"

A careful ear could pick up a trace of foreign pronunciation when Locker spoke. "You know that we cannot officially agree to any of those terms. You also know that if we made an off-the-record deal we'd have no intention of living up to it. We do what we have to do, and in our way. You know all that, Feldman; Allen Dulles and Golda Meir must have explained it to you. What is your game plan?"

Feldman smiled in mock defeat. "Time," he said. "I need time."

"There is no time. We've been briefed on what's happening. There is no time; you must understand that."

"Danzig?" Feldman asked. Neither man answered. "Danzig knows nothing, only the broad outline. I only told him enough to get you two here."

"We're here."

"Wait until tomorrow. I need one vital piece of information." He looked at his calendar. "I can see you again at ten-thirty tomorrow morning. Come back then."

Locker said harshly, "You pushed the panic button, Feldman, and you can't switch it off now. We're on assignment now, and we can't turn back. You could make our work go faster by telling us what you know right now. If you don't, we'll go ahead anyway, working with what we have and finding out the rest. Either way, it's too late to stop us. The exercise is in progress. Are you going to make it easy or are you going to play cute?"

Feldman pleaded, "Tomorrow. I can make it even a little earlier—say, ten o'clock."

Locker shook his head. "It may be over by then."

"You haven't done your homework on me." Feldman was

tough now, his veneer of humility discarded. "If you had, you'd know that I call the shots. I initiated this action, and I'm damn well going to control it. Don't try to threaten me with what you're going to or not going to do. At this moment the most you can have is guesswork. Wait until tomorrow."

Locker signaled to Green, who stood up. "Goodbye, Feldman."

"Let me remind you, gentlemen, that you are in this country by the grace of the United States government. I have some official status here. When I come to Israel, you can push *me* around. Rabin won't like it, but you can try. Did I mention that Rabin is a very close personal friend of mine? We work very closely together in areas of mutual interest." He came around his desk, tugging at his gray broadcloth vest. "I think when you have considered all the possibilities and had a chance to talk to some of your superiors, you'll come to the conclusion that my way is the best way." He opened the door to his office. "See you in the morning." It was a statement, not a question.

When they were gone, Feldman unlocked the cabinet behind his desk, took out the phone that was concealed there, dialed the numbers that activated a special overseas call system that operated through the Defense Department in Washington, and dialed. Looking at his watch, he tried to figure out what time it was in Israel.

Tuesday, February 15
Ten p.m., Chicago

Susan was on a new kind of high, a giddy exhilaration generated by the excitement of the day and a little too much wine at dinner. After the shooting at Ursini's studio, eight of them had gone to Gene and Georgetti's for spaghetti and steak. Rico and she had been squeezed together in the far corner of the downstairs booth and there had been none of the embarrassment she thought she might feel. Rather, being next to him produced a physical excitement. It was the first break in the dam of the reserve she had so carefully constructed after the break-up with Whiz. Toward the end of dinner she put her hand on his leg, and uncontrollably it inched up toward his crotch. He put his hand over hers lovingly, but stopped the movement.

They were the quiet ones. The agency people, Ursini and Mike Nelson were all turned on by the success of the day, building new ideas from the base of today's photographs, all talking at once, each topping the other with plans for a new advertising campaign. They all looked to Mike Nelson for approval and direction, and Susan admired the way he handled the confusion of creativity, sorting out the concepts, combining words and pictures, marshaling the brainstorming into a workable campaign.

There was no talk of going on after dinner; everyone was feeling the exhaustion, the letdown, after the high. Del Gracia took Susan home and came upstairs with her.

"Do you want a drink?" He shook his head. "I'm going to check Stoney," she said softly. "Go into the living room. Turn on some music, but not too loud. I don't want to wake the maid."

Stoney was sleeping diagonally across the bed, his head not touching the pillows, his legs uncovered, the small night light on beside the table. Susan leaned over, holding back her hair so that it would not brush his face, touched her lips lightly against his forehead, and rearranged the blanket to cover his legs. She took off her shoes and went into the kitchen. The door to the maid's room was open so that she would be able to hear if Stoney called, and Susan closed it carefully. Next to the telephone in the kitchen the maid had scribbled messages. Mr. Frankel had called from Seattle. He would be home in the morning and would call her then. Mr. Tatov had phoned, and would she please call him as soon as she came in—943-1111, ask for the Backgammon Club. Susan started to leave the kitchen, then turned back and dialed.

She waited a long time before Tatov came to the phone. "I'm across the street at Maxim's, killing time until you came home. May I come over?"

"I'm exhausted."

"You're also not alone."

"How do you know?"

"An elaborate spy system and two ten-dollar bills—one to the doorman at Maxim's and one to the doorman in your building. They work wonders."

She laughed. "You're incorrigible."

"How long will he stay?"

"I don't know. Not long. I really *am* exhausted. Call me in the morning."

"I'd rather jostle a very passionate elbow into a very beautiful rib in the morning."

"Call me early. I have to be at the hair-house by nine-thirty."

"You can't get rid of me that easily. I must get back to my chouette. I'm destroying them. See you later, darling." He hung up, and Susan returned to the living room.

Del Gracia had taken off his jacket, loosened his tie and lay on the sofa in the same pose they'd used for the ad. "Is Stoney all right?"

"Fast asleep." She sat down opposite him on a small chair.

He raised his head and motioned for her to come over to him, then resumed the pose. "You know what I did when we took a break today?" He did not wait for an answer. "I called Harry Winston in New York. I told them that I wanted a diamond for a beautiful woman with gray eyes." She touched his forehead with her fingertips. "We'll have to meet at noon tomorrow. They're flying in a man with a case full of rings. I want you to have it to wear tomorrow night."

"Rico, it's too fast."

"Do you think I should ask your father for your hand? I keep forgetting that he's from the old school."

"It's not Daddy that I'm worried about; it's me. I'm not sure of what I want anymore."

"It will be a marvelous life, Susan—all over the world, all the time. You and me, everywhere."

"And Stoney."

"Of course."

"I'm so mixed up. Why does it have to be so quick?"

"What's the use of waiting? We're right for each other, Susan; we always have been. Your marriage was a mistake but that's all over. We'll start fresh, the way we should have in the beginning."

Wiggling free of him, she walked to the window and looked out to the entrance of Maxim's across the street. The doorman was just inside the door. Del Gracia sat up, watched her and then went over to her. When he touched her, she turned and they kissed. Again the dam burst inside her, and this time she matched his urgency, clutching him, pulling his body toward her, thrusting her pelvis against his groin, rubbing against him.

Del Gracia was praying for the miracle to happen, but he could not will a hardness. Closing his eyes, he saw Mike's face and felt his own instant response to that touch. He saw the anonymous faces of all the prostitutes and recalled all their ways of arousing him. Nothing—not even now, when everything depended upon it. Breaking the kiss, he moved his mouth against Susan's hair. Her hand slid down his back and clutched his buttocks. She turned her face and this time initiated the kiss, plunging into his mouth fiercely, seeing him naked as he had been that afternoon, imagining his penis penetrate her with the same ferocity.

"I'm tired," he whispered. "There will be other times."

But the dam had burst. She took his head in her hands and jammed his lips against hers. He pulled away. "Sorry, baby. Sometimes a guy just isn't up to it." Feeling herself shaking, Susan folded her arms, bit her lip and turned away. "You understand, don't you?"

She nodded without saying anything.

"I'll meet you tomorrow about noon, okay?"

"You must think I'm terrible."

"Why would I?"

"There was never a man before Whiz, and there hasn't been one since." She walked toward the darkness at the far end of the room. "Is that hard for you to believe?"

"No. I know you, Susan, and it's not hard to believe. You're that kind of woman."

"Am I? I wonder." She breathed deeply and spoke so softly that he had to strain to hear. "Why did I want you so much just then? Why did I let myself go like that?"

He followed her into the darkness. "We love each other."

"Do we? Is that what love is?"

"It's part of it."

"In the end I was like that with Whiz. I wanted it as much as he did—more, sometimes." She shook her head. "But it wasn't enough for him. It was for me, but not for him. He was always looking for something deeper. When he left, when it all turned off, I wondered if I could ever be like that again." She faced him now in the half-light. "Go home, Rico. I've never felt so tired in my whole life."

He walked to the entrance hall and took his overcoat from the bench. "Susan," he called, "come here."

Hesitatingly, walking into the bright light of the hall, she smiled at him. He kissed her lightly on the lips. "It will all work out, Susan, I promise you. I'll see you tomorrow." She nodded and stood at the open door as they waited for the elevator in the tiny vestibule. They heard the sound of the door closing in the lobby, and of the machinery turning as the elevator started up, and finally the door opened. Del Gracia stood back as the attendant held the door open, kissed Susan lightly again and stepped inside.

From under the jacket of his uniform, the elevator man handed Susan an envelope and winked at her. "Good night, Mrs. Crossley."

She did not open the letter until she was in her bedroom. The bed had been turned down, and the pink, yellow and green flowered linen was fresh and crisp. Sitting on the edge of the bed, she held the note under the light.

> *Darling—*
> *I have charmed your lift operator with*
> *my sincerity and bribed him shamefully.*
> *I want desperately to see you tonight. If*

> *you want to see me, leave your door on*
> *the latch. I have made all other necessary*
> *arrangements. If the door isn't on the*
> *latch, I will understand, but both the*
> *lift operator and I will be terribly*
> *disappointed.*
>
> L.

In spite of her depression, she smiled, crumpled the note and threw it in the wastebasket, went into the bathroom and let the hot water run in the tub. While she waited for it to fill, she returned to the bedroom and began to undress, then retrieved the note, spread it out, reread it and laughed again. When she was undressed, she put on a terrycloth robe, turned off the tap, sprayed some perfume on the water and watched its oily drops settle. Taking off her robe, she tested the water with her foot. It was too hot. Putting on the robe again, she returned to the living room, turned on all the lights, went to the front door and put it on the latch. Then she went back into her bedroom, closing the door behind her.

Immersing her body in the hot water began to relieve the tension. She closed her eyes and slid forward in the tub. There was so much to think about: today and all the things which had happened, and tomorrow. She wondered about tomorrow. Would she accept the ring? If it had happened a week ago, before she knew that Peter Frankel loved her, before Tatov had appeared from nowhere, there would have been no question. She would be on the phone this minute, telling her mother, planning a wedding, feeling content about her destiny with Rico. But it was not a week ago.

Her eyes still closed, her body relaxed into a kind of half-sleep, she reviewed the day, the gown she had worn, their naked pose in the bathroom. Every day with Rico would be like that, doing things together that they were accustomed to doing. It was all a logical extension of the life she had been bred for. Not like Whiz—not everything different and unfamiliar.

When she opened her eyes and saw Leonid Tatov standing beside the tub, she was too startled to cover herself or to make a sound. He was in his stocking feet, wearing gray slacks and a turtleneck sweater, clutching a silver wine cooler filled with ice, a magnum and two wineglasses protruding from it. Finally she sat up, pulling up her knees, leaning forward, covering herself, still too startled to speak.

Tatov placed the wine cooler on the edge of the tub. "You are a wondrous sight to behold, Mrs. Crossley."

"Please get out of here."

Ignoring her, he sat cross-legged on the floor, twirling the wine in the bucket. "It's a rather good estate but a rather mediocre year. Still, it was the best Maxim's had to offer. Frightfully expensive, but then I won quite a bit of money." He took the bottle out of the ice and began to open the seal. "Are you the kind of girl who is frightened at the sound of a cork popping?" A faint smile began at the corners of her mouth. "I'm sure you'll stand up to it like a good soldier." Expertly he worked the cork loose and it popped from the bottle into the bathtub. A little foam from the wine oozed onto Tatov's hand. He dipped his hand in the water, retrieving the cork at the same time, and smelled it. "Chanel?" he asked. Susan did not answer. "It doesn't matter. Any kind of perfume goes with Dom Perignon." Ceremoniously he poured the wine into the tulip-shaped glasses and handed one to Susan. She did not move to take it. "I'm a clod. It's more romantic if I hold the glass and let you sip from it." He held the glass to her lips with his left hand, and his own glass to his mouth with the other. "Shall we drink to love?" He forced the edge of the glass between her lips and tasted from his own at the same time. "Not bad. A little acidic, but on the whole rather pleasant. What do you think?"

"I think that you're crazy."

"Of course I am. Would you have me another way?"

She shook her head, no longer able to control her smile, and took the glass from his hand, partially exposing one breast. "It's lucky the wine is good or I'd scream for help."

"Thank God I did the right thing. I almost took a less expensive Tattinger."

"Do you always act this crazy?"

"Only when I'm hopelessly attracted. Otherwise, I'm quite

sane. Dull, as a matter of fact." He refilled both glasses, set the bottle back in the cooler, then removed his socks. "What sign are you?"

"What do you mean?"

Standing up, he pulled off the turtleneck sweater and folded it neatly. "I'm Taurus, but you probably guessed that. I assume that you're a Virgo."

"What are you doing, Leonid?"

"Are you?"

"No, I'm Pisces."

"You see; you never can tell about people." He unbuckled his belt and unzipped his fly. "On your birthday I shall buy you a jeweled fish. Not diamonds—nothing that gaudy. Perhaps sapphires with emerald eyes. When is your birthday? It must be soon." He turned as he took off his slacks, folded them carefully and placed them over the turtleneck. He wore no underwear. Susan looked away and then back again. He was built more like Whiz—lean, not fleshy.

When he turned around he was smiling and his penis was fully erect. "Are you going to be a good girl and make room for me? I could catch my death standing here."

Later they were in the kitchen and Tatov was wolfing a bowl of cereal and drinking a glass of milk. "You're not really going to kick me out when you have that nice warm bed with those lovely pink sheets."

"Ssh. The maid is a very light sleeper."

"Which is her door, that one?"

"No, that's the back door. Her door is there." She pointed.

"How does she hear Stoney at night when you're out?"

"She leaves his door and hers open."

"Was Stoney's room the closed door in the hall?"

"Yes."

"We'll look in on him on the way back to your room. It's been a long time since I've seen a child sleeping. It may awaken a domestic side of my nature."

"You can't spend the night. You can't be here when Stoney and the maid wake up."

"I promise I'll be gone before then." He crossed his heart. "I have a very strong code of ethics—that is, if you have a very loud alarm clock." He put down his spoon, touched her hand. "You do want me to stay, don't you?"

Taking the empty cereal bowl, she rinsed it and put it in the dishwasher. "God help me, I want you to stay."

He finished his milk, carried the glass to the sink, put it under the water to wash it out, handed it to Susan who put it in the machine. "Do you want to talk about love?"

Susan shook her head. "No."

"Too soon?"

"Too late at night, and too soon."

He started for the door. "Not that one, that's the broom closet." Taking his hand, she led him out of the kitchen. On the way back to her room, they looked in on Stoney. His legs were uncovered. Susan pulled up the blanket and then, their arms around each other, she and Tatov went into her bedroom.

Wednesday, February 16
Seven p.m., Chicago

THREE CLASSIC Rolls-Royce limousines pulled up in front of the steps of the Art Institute. A red-and-white striped awning had been erected from Michigan Boulevard up the stairs to the entrance of the museum, a wide red carpet had been laid over the sidewalk, and the two landmark bronze lions that guarded the building had been specially lit for the gala. A handful of passers-by clustered on each side of the carpet gaping at the guests, searching for a recognizable celebrity.

Mike Nelson had arrived earlier and was waiting inside the

building with the reporter and a photographer from *Women's Wear*. They started out into the cold night as soon as the limousines arrived. Through some of del Gracia's friends, Nelson had arranged to borrow the three cars. Del Gracia and Susan Crossley were in the Phantom V with Marcy Cunningham, Nelson's date for the evening, and Leonid Tatov and Peter Frankel, each squiring several models, were in the other two.

Shuffling between the reporters and models, Nelson was setting up shots: a group getting out of the 1926 Rolls, Rico and Susan in front of one of the bronze lions. As the flashbulbs stabbed the dark night, Nelson was careful to see that del Gracia was the focus of most of the shots and that Susan Crossley was at his side.

The crowd on the street was larger now, attracted by the flashing lights and the classic cars waiting at the curb. Peter Frankel examined the faces of the gapers on the sidewalk. Alert to danger, he looked for the anonymous faces of Dirksmith's men who were supposed to be protecting him. His wound had been reduced to a small Band-Aid cutting slightly into his hairline, and a red scrape mark on his cheekbone. Alone, exposed, thinking about Susan, he wondered why he was here.

Arriving limousines stacked up behind the Rolls-Royces were becoming impatient. One chauffeur in the line, goaded by his employer, sounded his horn; the other drivers picked up the cue and began a steady, staccato tooting. Nelson ignored the noise and continued doing his job.

Inside the Art Institute, the center hall was already alive with the excitement of the crowd. The balcony was lined with glass-in-hand spectators watching the other guests as they arrived and walked up the grand staircase, pausing at the first landing where Livingston and Maude Stonehill and the other sponsors were grouped in an informal receiving line.

A special exhibition of contemporary art had been mounted for the gala. Few people glanced at the paintings. They were looking at each other, crowding the bars, one eye out for the waitresses elbowing through the crowd with platters of canapés.

Between greetings, Stonehill and another trustee talked Art Institute business, low-voiced comments on contributions for the new fund-raising campaign, and the possible addition of some new millionaires to the board of trustees. The other man's comments reflected his assumption that Stonehill would be the next chairman of the board. A week ago that position was something Stonehill had wished for more than anything else, a culmination of his years of devotion, a reward for the hundreds of thousands of dollars he had contributed.

Myrna Gordon had arrived early. Stonehill had seen her as soon as she entered, walking beside a deeply sunburned young man with bright white teeth, shiny black hair and built like a linebacker. He watched them start up the stairs, Myrna moving slowly, each step painful, the burly man beside her, gently guiding her, slowing his pace to hers. Stonehill realized that he seldom saw Myrna dressed, and when she was it was usually in jeans and T-shirt or a shapeless quilted wrapper. She was different now, sheathed in sequins, her eyes heavily made up, her hair done in a new way, with reddish blond highlights which had not been there before. She seemed to be an electric sign flashing sexuality. He closed his eyes to see her the way he knew her: the soft, round body, the scrubbed face.

"Livie." He felt a light touch on his arm, opened his eyes, turned, and saw his wife. "Darling, did you remember to tell Carl what time we have to leave for the airport tomorrow?" He nodded, and Maude turned back to continue her conversation with a friend. Could he stand here next year with Myrna, the obvious second wife, at his side broadcasting that kind of sexuality? And what would she talk about to the wives of other trustees?

Myrna and her escort half smiled and nodded at the Stonehills and others in the receiving line, but stopped to talk to Jim Speyer, the curator of contemporary art. Stonehill envied the ease with which the two younger men fell into conversation, obviously reestablishing a prior rapport. He heard them mention Pearlman and Cottingham. Myrna laughed at something Speyer said, throwing her head back as she did so. Not a strand of her hair moved.

Stonehill was distracted by the photographers' flashing lights down at the main door where Rico del Gracia and his party

were making an entrance. A fashion reporter stopped Susan and
posed her with her arm through del Gracia's, her mink coat,
held in her right hand, carelessly being dragged on the Art
Institute floor. Susan and Myrna were almost the same age, and
they each radiated a kind of sensuality, but Susan's was easy, an
endemic part of her, not teased and constructed to be provoca-
tive. Even her hair moved naturally, in cadence with the way
her body moved, not lacquered to rigid perfection.

When the photographers were finished, del Gracia took Susan's coat to the checkroom and she stood alone for a moment.
Looking up, she saw her parents and waved to them. Then
Harley Grunswald came up to her. "Congratulations, Susan. I
think it's super."

"What are you talking about, Harley?"

"You and Rico. We had kind of a family board meeting
today and Rico told us. I know it's a secret, but I think it's
super. He also told us about the ads you shot yesterday. They
sound super."

Before Susan could answer, Rico was back. Shaking hands
with his cousin, he led Susan away toward the stairs where the
photographers were stationed halfway up, cameras ready. Del
Gracia and Susan were up three steps when the *Women's Wear*
reporter motioned for them to start over again, said something
to her photographer, who backed up another step.

Susan had moved through her morning schedule exactly on
time, but it was another woman following her calendar, going to
her beauty shop and to meetings, shopping. The real Susan was
back in bed with Leonid Tatov, loving and laughing, being
wanton and passionate, experiencing summits of physical sensation she had never known before. And easily. She still could not
believe how easily it had all happened and how each progression of the act of love had come so naturally, without delibera-
tion or fear. Now she knew what joy was. With Tatov all the
unfamiliar had become instantly right; nothing scraped against
the grain of her upbringing; no hang-up existed. She had met his
inventiveness with her own inventiveness, instinctive devices
which she had not known existed in her. And no recriminations
in the morning, no secret blushes of shame. Instead, she felt

alive all over, catapulted into a new awareness of her own body. Each time that she looked at Tatov now, the signals started again.

It had been difficult with Rico. At first she had refused to see the salesman from Harry Winston, but when Rico threatened a scene, she reluctantly looked at the three black velvet trays of diamond rings of every imaginable shape and size. First Rico selected a large pear-shaped stone. Susan studied it on her finger, feeling its weight and pressure where she used to wear the plain gold band Whiz Crossley had given her. To save face for Rico, she had tried to be light-hearted. "It's too big. I'm not Liz Taylor and I'm not sure that I like the shape." She put her finger on a much smaller stone, square-cut, rectangularly shaped, but Rico pulled her hand away, selected another ring, much larger but the same shape, and slipped it on her finger. She walked across the room and stood at the window, staring at the brilliance of the diamond in the sunlight, seeing the refracted sparks of light and its prismatic rainbow of colors. Rico stood behind her, and she felt the warmth of his breath against her ear.

"It isn't fair, Rico. They're all so beautiful and I'm not sure. Let's wait until we're certain that we love each other and belong together."

"I'm certain," he whispered.

"How can you be? How can you be so certain this suddenly?" She turned to him, keeping her voice low. "We've known each other all our lives, and yet we don't know each other at all. We've never even touched each other . . . made love to each other." She lowered her head.

"That doesn't sound like Susan," Rico said.

"I don't know who Susan is, Rico. You have to give me time. I don't understand the urgency. We're not kids rushing into something. We have time to be sure."

"I want you to wear the ring tonight. It's a perfect night to tell the world."

"You can force me to look at rings but you can't force me to wear one. I wish I'd never heard of tonight. I don't even want to go anymore. It's just another dumb party. I don't know why everyone is in such an uproar about it." Peter Frankel had said that; he had berated himself for getting caught up in the hysteria of going to a dance. Peter had said he was better than that, tougher. Maybe, after all, Susan was thinking, she was more like him—tougher and smarter than this, too smart and too tough to be dazzled by diamonds and turned on by the male scent of Rico del Gracia. She took off the ring and handed it back to him. "I'm going to lie down. Make some excuse about not buying the ring right now. Say anything—blame it on me. I need time to think." Without looking back she went into her bedroom and closed the door.

Later, on her way to the kitchen, she saw the opened box and the huge diamond like a headlight on the table in the hall. There was a note beside it:

Pick you up at six-thirty
I love you
R.

She put on the ring, wore it into the kitchen and watched it flash as she opened the refrigerator and while she poured herself a glass of milk.

It took a few seconds for their eyes to adjust after the barrage of photographers' flashbulbs. Rico put his arm around her waist as they reached the first landing and held her possessively as they approached her parents. As Stonehill kissed his daughter, he whispered to her, "Are you aware that you look like a woman in love?"

She stood on her toes, her mouth against her father's ear. "I didn't know it showed."

Laughing, Stonehill looked up and saw Myrna watching him from the balcony. He shook hands with del Gracia, appraised him as a son-in-law and saw the logical progression of this man in Stonehill's own ascending pattern.

While del Gracia kissed Maude Stonehill and talked to her, Susan caught Tatov's hand as he passed by and pulled him away from Marcy Cunningham. "Daddy, this is Leonid Tatov from

London." As they shook hands, Stonehill realized that he had misjudged the source of the excitement in Susan's eyes.

"Hello, sir. I'm very glad to be here."

"Evidently we're delighted to have you here. Are you in Chicago on business, Mr. Tatov?"

"More or less, sir. I am enjoying the less a great deal more than the more, if you know what I mean." He took Susan's hand. "I would like you and Mrs. Stonehill to have dinner with Susan and me one night before I leave."

Stonehill smiled at the young man; he liked his open approach. "Mrs. Stonehill leaves for California tomorrow."

"What about lunch, sir?" He glanced at Susan. "I don't mean to seem pushy, but I do think it would be a good idea if we got to know each other a bit. Are you free tomorrow?"

Susan interrupted. "I have a luncheon meeting tomorrow on that Mark Mendoza thing."

"What about just the two of us, sir?"

"Why don't you phone me at the office tomorrow morning? No, that won't work. I'm taking my wife to the airport. Her plane leaves about nine."

"Why don't we just say twelve o'clock at the Racquet Club? If for any reason you can't make it, just leave word. But I hope you can join me; it could be rather important."

Stonehill looked at his daughter. "Could it, Susan?"

"I don't think that it has to be tomorrow." She began guiding Tatov toward her mother. "We'll talk later."

When Stonehill looked up, Myrna was still leaning over the balcony rail watching him. Then Laurie Potter, Susan's friend, was kissing him on the cheek. "Do you know Peter Frankel, Mr. Stonehill?"

They shook hands. "What happened to you, Frankel?" Stonehill indicated the Band-Aid. "You have a reputation for being invincible."

"But vulnerable," Frankel said. "As long as I keep getting hit on the head, I'll be all right. That's the thickest part of me."

"Are you still active on the committee for the dinner Sunday night?"

"I've sloughed off. It's been bananas at the office. Been traveling a lot. I know it's sold out, but I'll be there, that's for sure. Going with your daughter."

"I thought she was going with Mark Mendoza."

"That's for show," Frankel said without smiling. "I'm for real." He nodded and moved down the reception line.

A few minutes later one of the Institute guards broke through the receiving line. "Mr. Stonehill, there's a telephone call for you in the office downstairs. It's a man named Dennis Lepawski calling from the bank."

"Thank you, I'll be right down." He turned to his wife. "Keep smiling; it'll be over soon. I have to disappear for a minute. My kidneys aren't what they used to be."

Dennis Lepawski was the chief of security at the bank. Stonehill was alarmed; if Lepawski called him directly, particularly after hours and at a party, it must be a major catastrophe. He was led through a library into a small office. The guard pointed to the phone and left the room, closing the glass door behind him.

"Yes, Dennis? What's happened?"

"It isn't Dennis, Mr. Steinberg, but a great deal has happened."

Recognizing the voice instantly, Stonehill saw again the ordinary face, the gun pointed at him, and terror zigzagged through him. He looked frantically through the glass door, but no one was in sight. There was a pad and a pencil on the desk, and as he talked he printed in bold letters TRACE THIS CALL. Into the phone he said, "I thought you'd gone back to the Mideast."

"What are you thinking, Steinberg? Do you still believe, even now, that it cannot happen to you? We thought that when your Jew girlfriend was beaten up, sexually assaulted, if you will, we thought you might finally be convinced. But you German Jews are hard-headed, aren't you?" Stonehill looked again through the glass door. His hand holding up the message, but the library was empty. "What does it take to convince you? By now you should have made a public statement withdrawing your support from the dinner honoring the Senator. This is Wednesday and the dinner is Sunday. What does it take to convince you?" A man had come into the library and was scanning the shelves, not looking in Stonehill's direction. He waved the slip of paper in an arc, but the man did not look over. The ordinary-sounding voice continued. "We asked ourselves, What will it take to convince you and we think we found the answer."

There was a small metal paperweight on the desk. Stonehill threw it at the glass panel of the door, but it fell short. He looked for another object to throw. There was nothing heavy enough. He stood up to try to reach the paperweight without releasing the phone, but the cord was not long enough. Putting his hand over the mouthpiece, he shouted, "Hey!" When the man in the library looked over, Stonehill waved the paper and motioned for him to come into the office.

"Do you know what the answer is, Steinberg? Can you guess?"

The man in the library moved slowly, uncertain of the meaning of the gestures. Stonehill's answer was slow and deliberate. "I can't guess."

"We've kidnapped your grandson. Does that surprise you?"

"You've what?"

"You see, Steinberg, it can happen to you, and right here."

"I don't believe you."

"That's your trouble. If you had believed us in the beginning, none of this would have happened. But it happened to your Jew girlfriend, and now it's happened to your grandson."

"Where is he? Is he with you? Let me talk to him."

"Now, now, don't panic. At the moment he's quite all right. We don't like violence, Steinberg—that isn't our way. Only when we are forced. But now that you have forced us to violence, rest assured that we are skilled at it, quite capable of killing when necessary."

By now the man in the library was standing outside the glass door, looking puzzled. Stonehill crumpled the message in his hand and motioned him away. If they did have Stoney, he could take no risks. The man opened the door, and again Stonehill waved him away.

"How much?" Stonehill asked.

"You still have that Jew mentality. How much? Everything is how much. We aren't interested in money—I told you that before. We have more money than your whole bank."

"What do you want me to do?"

"I needn't warn you about calling any authority. If you did, your grandson would be killed instantly."

"I understand. I'll call no one. But what do I have to do?"

"Actually, this kidnapping is only a warning. We just wanted to show you how easy it is."

"For God's sake, tell me what I have to do."

"Patience, Steinberg, patience. We were patient with you. We thought that by now you would have issued a press release withdrawing your support for the dinner, denouncing your friend the Senator and stating that you believed Mark Mendoza to be a fanatic. Those were the instructions, weren't they?" Stonehill did not answer. "Of course they were, and that was only phase one. Phase two is withdrawing all your pledges to Israel. You do remember, don't you, Steinberg?"

The man in the library had taken a book off the shelf and sat at a table skimming through it. "I remember," Stonehill answered. "Tell me exactly what you want me to do."

"You are to tell no one—do you understand, no one—that your grandson has been kidnapped."

"My daughter will know."

"She doesn't have to. We would much rather she did not, actually. Everything will be much less complicated if she doesn't know. Your grandson could be home safe in his bed two hours from now, and his mother would never know. It all depends on you, Steinberg."

"What did you do with the maid?"

The man laughed. "We were quite clever about the maid. We made quite sure that she slept soundly this one time. She doesn't even know that your grandson is missing. In the morning she'll have a rather heavy head, a kind of hangover, if you will, but she will not know that your grandson was kidnapped and returned. Of course all of this depends on your following our instructions precisely."

"I'll make the statement tomorrow."

"Of course you will. We have anticipated that. In the mail at your office tomorrow, in an envelope marked 'personal,' you will find a statement we have already prepared for you. We suggest that you read it to the press exactly as we have written it. I also suggest that you forewarn your secretary—it wouldn't do for her to open the letter first."

"I'm taking my wife to the airport in the morning. She'll be suspicious if I don't."

"You'll find a way to instruct your secretary, Steinberg."

"How do I get Stoney back?"

"You are convinced by now, aren't you, that this is not a practical joke? Because from now on you must follow instructions precisely and promptly. Remember phase two, Steinberg, or Myrna Gordon will be dead and you will be disgraced. You do remember that part, don't you?"

"How do I get Stoney back?"

"I want to hear you say that you remember."

"I remember." Stonehill's voice was just above a whisper. "Tell me what to do."

"Check your watch. What time do you have?"

"Seven fifty-one."

"You're a bit fast, but never mind. At exactly five after eight, be out in front of the Art Institute. A Yellow taxi will be going by. Hail it. Check the number on the door. The number will be eight twenty-two—repeat, eight twenty-two. Get into the cab. The driver will take it from there. Is that clear?"

"Yes."

"Do you have a key to the rear door of your daughter's apartment?"

"No."

"I suggest that you borrow your daughter's keys without her knowing it. I'm sure that you'll find a way. It is important that no one see you enter your daughter's building with the child. We will leave that to your discretion."

"I'll manage."

"One other thing. You know Peter Frankel, don't you?"

"What does he have to do with this?"

"It's not important. Use whatever pretext you like, but get Peter Frankel to accompany you. I've made it easier for you by pretending to be the chief of security at your bank making an emergency call. Elaborate on that—Frankel loves playing cops and robbers—but tell him nothing about your grandson. Have I made it perfectly clear that one deviation from our instructions means that your grandson will be killed instantly and his body never found?"

"Yes."

"Let's check the time again. Do you have seven fifty-three?"

"Yes."

"Five after eight. Taxi number eight twenty-two." The line went dead.

Without hesitating, Stonehill dialed Susan's number and waited while it rang and rang. There was no answer. As he hurried from the office the man in the library stood up, blocked the door and stood firm as Stonehill tried to pass. He held out a wallet, opened to an identification card. "Benjamin Cardiff, Israeli Secret Service. I'd like to talk to you."

"Not now. There's been a break-in at the bank."

"I'll go with you."

"I can't permit that."

"I know about everything, Mr. Stonehill. You must trust me."

"You know nothing. Stay here. Don't try to follow me. A life is at stake. Stay here." He grabbed the younger man and shook him violently. "Don't you follow me. If you fuck this up, I'll kill you, so help me God." He pushed the man aside and went back into the confusion of five hundred people talking over cocktails and the music of Peter Duchin struggling to be heard over the high decibel of voices.

The receiving line had broken up, but he found Maude standing near one of the bars on the second floor talking to a man he did not know. He drew her aside, excusing himself to the stranger. "There's a security problem at the bank. Lepawski called me. I have to run over there for a little while. Don't worry. I'll get back as soon as I can. Where's Susan?"

"What's happened?"

"I'm not sure. Have you seen Susan?"

"Not for about ten minutes, but just head toward the flash-bulbs. It's disgraceful the way Rico is making a public spectacle of himself and Susan."

As Stonehill started through the crowd, checking his watch,

he saw Peter Frankel standing alone. "Don't ask any questions. Follow me. Have you seen Susan?" Frankel nodded toward a large sculpture composition and a series of flashing strobe lights. Stonehill walked rapidly, Frankel directly behind him, grim-faced. Del Gracia was the center of the pose in front of a huge, garish Wesselman construction, a still life of a twenty-foot toothbrush, a twelve-foot ruby ring and a set of house keys. Susan and two other models were grouped around del Gracia. Seeing that his daughter was clutching a small handbag, Stonehill spoiled a shot by walking in front of the camera and taking it from her. "Here, honey, I'll hold this for you." Before she could answer he had backed out of the picture, held the purse behind him and in a low voice directed Frankel, "Get her keys." As he felt Frankel take the bag, he looked at his watch. One minute after eight. He had four minutes. As Frankel placed the bag back in his hand, the posed group dispersed and he returned Susan's purse to her, kissing her quickly and waving as he walked off.

Ignoring the people who called to him or tried to talk to him, Stonehill moved quickly through the crowd, down the grand staircase and out into the cold night. At 8:04 he was at the curb, Frankel at his side. "I can't explain, Frankel. You'll have to trust me."

"I think I know what's happening. What are we waiting for?"

"A taxi—a Yellow cab, number eight twenty-two."

"I have a gun."

"For Christ's sake, don't use it. Don't spoil anything."

"I'll be careful."

Then they saw the cab cruising slowly down the street. Stonehill hailed it, checked the number, opened the door and let Frankel enter first. The face of the driver did not match the photograph on the license registration. It was a nondescript, middle-aged face, shadowed by a peaked baseball cap. Turning the handle on the meter, he started north on Michigan Avenue, turned east and headed to the Outer Drive.

"Do you have instructions?" Stonehill leaned forward, talking through the clouded plastic division between himself and the driver. "What are they?"

"You stay in the cab," the driver answered. "He gets out and picks up the kid."

"Who?"

"The guy with you."

Looking at Frankel, Stonehill felt reassured by the set of his jaw, the tense ready-set of his body. "Then what?"

"The kid'll be sleeping." The driver looked at a piece of paper clipped to the sunvisor. "They gave him Pentothal. It's harmless. He'll sleep through the night and never know what hit him. Don't call a doctor, understand? He'll be okay."

On the Outer Drive, the cab turned south and drove at a moderate speed toward the Field Museum. The driver was looking at them through the rear-view mirror. "The other guy gets the kid and brings him back to the cab. I take over after that, understand?"

They both nodded. Stonehill felt Frankel's hand fumbling beside him, then the contact of cold steel as Frankel shoved the gun between the seat and the back of the upholstery. Frankel's eyes never flinched, his stare fixed on the rear-view mirror. Stonehill felt for the gun and turned it so that he could pick it up quickly. As he touched the trigger, he wondered if something had to be released before it could be fired. And he wondered, too, if he would have the courage to fire it.

At this hour traffic on the Outer Drive was light, and the taxi driver maintained the maximum speed limit, driving carefully, not changing lanes. At the rear of the Field Museum he swung left, turning east on the deserted road leading back to the northbound lanes of the Outer Drive. There was a stoplight at this entrance to the northbound traffic, and while they waited for it to change, the driver instructed, "Don't get out of the cab until you see the kid on the ground and the other car has taken off. Understand?" He was looking into the rear-view mirror and waited until both men nodded. "And no funny business," he warned. "I've got a gun, and if anything goes wrong the kid gets it first."

When the light changed, the driver turned partially north but drove across the lanes to an access road leading to the Adler Planetarium and beyond that to Meigs Field, a municipal airport for small aircraft which was seldom used after dark during winter. The entire road was only a half-mile long, and the east- and west-bound lanes were divided by a landscaped median strip. There was no traffic on it or parked cars. Cutting off his headlights, the driver proceeded east slowly. Stonehill looked at the meter still running: two dollars and forty cents. The driver had even pushed the button ringing up an extra twenty cents for the additional passenger.

Almost at the end of the drive, in the center of the median, was a large monument to Copernicus, a marble plinth topped by a bronze of the seated astronomer holding celestial symbols. The cab stopped thirty feet in front of the monument. As Frankel reached for the door handle, the driver shouted, "Wait!"

There was a split second of light as a car door opened across the median, and in that instant they could make out the form of a man carrying an orange bundle. The man appeared more clearly as he approached the base of the monument; he was tall and slender, but his features were obscured by the darkness and distance. Putting the bundled figure on a bench, he returned quickly to the car. Again there was the instant of light, then darkness as the door closed and the car lurched forward, west-bound.

The driver got out of the cab, opened the rear door and motioned for Frankel to get out. "Go get the kid." Frankel moved quickly. As Stonehill slid over to where Frankel had been sitting, the driver warned him, "Stay there."

Stonehill could not believe what was happening. As Frankel trotted toward the monument, the driver took out his gun and aimed it at Frankel. Stonehill groped behind him and grasped Frankel's gun, but before he could aim it, a shot sounded. The figure of the driver crumbled to the ground just as Stonehill fired into the emptiness where he had stood.

Frankel turned at the sound of the two shots that were so close they might have been one. He saw Stonehill getting out of the cab, gun in hand, then began running again to retrieve the orange bundle.

Two men stood near Stonehill, beside a car which had pulled up behind them, the trunk lid open, the engine still running.

They walked forward, not looking at Stonehill, keeping their faces in shadow. Before picking up the dead driver, one of the men took the baseball cap off the corpse and tossed it into the front seat of the cab; then together they picked up the body, threw it in the trunk and slammed the lid.

Now Frankel was running back toward them, hugging the orange bundle. The two men waited, and as he handed the child to Stonehill, one of them asked, "Is the boy all right?"

Frankel nodded, out of breath. "He seems to be."

The other man said, "I'm getting tired of saving your ass, Frankel."

Frankel wasn't certain. "Dirksmith?"

Neither man answered. They both turned and got into their car, drove to the end of the road, followed the U-turn leading to the westbound lanes and headed toward the Outer Drive.

Stonehill got into the back seat of the taxi with his grandson and unwound the oversized orange muffler which had protected Stoney from the cold. "Is he all right?" Frankel asked.

"His breathing sounds normal." He ran his hands over the small body. "He seems to be in one piece."

"What do we do now?"

"Back to Susan's apartment. Go through the alley. We have to go in the back way."

Frankel got into the driver's seat, put on the driver's baseball cap and started the cab with a lurch, which threw Stonehill and Stoney forward. "Sorry," Frankel said. "I'm used to driving a Mustang." He turned on the headlights and drove toward the turnabout in front of the planetarium. "Toss the gun up front, will you?" He waited until he heard the thud on the driver's seat beside him, touched the still hot barrel and slipped it into his pocket. "Who got the driver, you or the other guys?"

"They did. I was too slow. Who are they?"

"The other guys? I guess they're friends of mine. They're the good guys."

"Who are the bad guys?"

"We don't know. We're trying to find out. I didn't know you were involved. You want to talk?"

"Later." Stonehill kept hugging the sleeping child, alert for a change in the rhythm of his breathing. "I don't know how to say thank you."

"Goes both ways. If they hadn't nailed the driver, you would have."

"Would I? I don't know. Would you believe that I've never fired a gun before?"

"No reason to."

"Would I have killed him before he killed you?" Frankel did not answer. "We'll never know, will we? I'll never know about myself."

"You had the balls to pull the trigger. That's a start." Waiting at the long light to turn onto the Outer Drive, Frankel started to turn off the meter, then changed his mind. "Christ," he said, "cabs are expensive."

"Who are you really, Frankel? Are you with the FBI?"

"I'm a nice Jewish boy who somehow got in over his head. I'm not with the FBI. Those guys who helped us, they're probably FBI. Whatever's happening to you, Mr. Stonehill, is happening all over the country to other people just like you." The light changed and he turned right. "We know what's happening, but we don't know who's making it happen, or how."

"You were deliberately set up tonight, weren't you? Do you know too much?"

Frankel shook his head. "They must think I do, but I don't."

"I'm wondering about myself." Stonehill held his grandson closer. "If I'd known I was leading you into a trap, would I have done it anyway, sacrificed you for Stoney?"

"It didn't happen, so forget about it."

"I never had doubts about myself until all this started. I never thought about courage, about being able to function under pressure. I never had to make life-and-death choices before. You do it all the time, don't you?"

Frankel shrugged his shoulders. "One man's shtick is another man's poison. You can't fault yourself for belonging to another culture and another generation. You were brought up insulated from terror and violence. Old money does that. You can't expect to suddenly become a fearless hunter."

"Like Robert Wilson?"

"Who's that?"

"A fearless hunter." Restlessly, Stoney mumbled garbled words in his sleep. "He was in a Hemingway short story I read many years ago. There were two men in the story, one without fear and the other a coward."

"Nobody is just one thing and not the other," Frankel said.

"When you heard the shots, were you scared?"

"Shitless."

"But you kept doing your job. I've underestimated you, Frankel. I thought you were just a . . ." Stonehill's voice trailed off.

"Another what, Mr. Stonehill? Another loud-mouthed Jew boy? Is that what you meant?"

"I'm sorry."

"For Christ's sake, don't be sorry. You are what you are. Don't be sorry. Sorry is passive. Try to understand. Understanding is aggressive. I used my wise-ass and loud-mouth the way you use your money and social position. Can you understand that?"

"I'm beginning to."

Frankel swung the cab around the sharp S-curve of the Outer Drive, zigzagging lanes. "You fired the gun, Mr. Stonehill. You and I may be the only ones who will ever know that, and I don't count, but you know that you had the balls to fire the gun. You passed the test. That ought to wipe out any doubts you ever had about yourself."

"What are your doubts, Frankel?"

He thought for a moment. "Am I better off exiting at Ohio or going down to Chicago Avenue?"

"Get off at Chicago Avenue. What are your doubts?"

"Can I live in your world? I doubt it. Do I want to? I don't know if I don't want to because I'm afraid of it or because I *really* don't want to."

"Are you in love with Susan?"

Frankel studied Stonehill's face reflected in the rear-view mirror. "God help me," he answered.

They drove in silence, waited for the green arrow at Chicago Avenue and turned off onto the Inner Drive. Stonehill looked at his watch. It was not quite eight-thirty, he had lived a lifetime in under twenty-five minutes. Stoney became restless again, flailing his legs and arms against the confining orange muffler. Stonehill loosened it at the bottom so that his grandson's legs could move. A label was sewn on the bottom of the scarf. Stonehill held it toward the streetlight so that he could read it. "Frankel."

"Yes?"

"There's a label in the scarf. Turnbull and Asser, Limited, London. Are you thinking what I'm thinking?"

"How much do you know about Tatov?"

"Nothing. I met him tonight for the first time." He covered his grandson's feet with the scarf again. "What do you know about him?"

"I've never paid any attention to him until tonight. I met him once before, and Susan's mentioned him a couple of times. I never had any reason to connect him with this."

"Do you think that Susan's in love with him?"

"Appears that way. I've been in and out of town all week, so tonight was the first time I've seen her since Sunday. She's changed. She seems . . . well, more fluid, if you know what I mean. She moves freer, like she's not so hung up anymore. Could be love. Could be sex. Mostly it looks like trouble."

"You think Tatov may be involved?"

"Must be. The timing is just too accidental. I should have thought of it before. Frankly, I was so pissed off by Susan making a fuss over that Latin lover-boy that—"

"Rico del Gracia?"

"Yah. I was busy being jealous of him and didn't pay enough attention to the London entry."

"He was at the party, but I suppose he could have set it up."

"I'm damn well going to find out," Frankel said. "Meanwhile, I think you and I ought to do what we can to keep Susan from being alone with him."

"I don't have much control. I'll do what I can."

"Listen, I've been thinking about something." Frankel changed lanes to turn at Walton Street. "Those guys who engineered this think that I'm dead. The cab driver was obviously a trained assassin, and they'd expect him to be successful." He stopped the taxi and turned around to face Stonehill. "Tell me the exact instructions you were given."

"Just to get into the taxi. He said the driver would take over from there. The only other instructions were to return Stoney to Susan's apartment by the back way, and to make sure that no one saw me. He also said that Susan mustn't know, and that I wasn't to call a doctor or anybody in authority."

"They probably have the alley behind the building staked out. If they see me alive, it might screw up the whole thing. How do you feel, Mr. Stonehill?"

"Well enough to do what has to be done. What do you want me to do?"

Frankel fumbled in his pocket and handed Susan's keys to Stonehill. "I turned off here because there's usually a line of cabs at the Drake Hotel. I'm going to let you out in front of the hotel. Make sure that you get into a Yellow cab. It will be dark in the alley, too dark to read the number of the cab. Pay the driver in advance and tell him that the minute you get out of the cab he should get out of the alley fast. Got it?"

"What are you going to do?"

Frankel took off the cap, ran his fingers through his hair, and looked for a label inside, but there was nothing. He folded the cap and put it in his pocket. "I am going back to the party," he said, "and pretend nothing has happened."

"You'll watch Tatov?"

"You bet."

"What should I do?"

"Get Stoney settled. Check out the apartment and make sure that no one's inside it or hanging around outside. Then get back to the party. It shouldn't take more than a half-hour. If you're not back in thirty-five minutes, I'll know there's trouble and act accordingly, okay?"

"Let's go." Stonehill arranged the sleeping child so that he could carry him easily while Frankel drove the taxi to the end of the street and stopped in front of the Drake. There were two Yellow cabs. Stonehill carried Stoney out of the rear seat and was talking to the doorman under the bright heat lights of the hotel marquee as Frankel pulled away.

Frankel drove around the block and parked the car in front

of 199 East Lake Shore Drive. He started to wipe the steering wheel, realized he would be destroying other fingerprints as well as his own, turned off the lights, stopped the meter and turned off the ignition, leaving the key in it.

The wind chill was always strongest on this stretch of the Drive. Frankel turned up his collar, scrunched up his shoulders, thrust his hands into his pockets and trotted to the rear entrance of the Drake Hotel. Finding a pay phone, he dialed Dirksmith directly. When the operator came on, he gave her his credit card number. The phone rang for a long time, and interruptions in the rhythm of the ringing indicated that a relay was being used.

When a voice answered, he said, "Frankel."

"You ass hole." It was Dirksmith, all right. "Don't you have more brains than to say your name out loud?"

"I'm a fucking lawyer, not a spy. Anyway, thanks for saving my ass again."

"Where are you?"

"In the Drake Hotel. The cab is parked next door at 199 East Lake Shore. Get it out of there fast. Hide it."

"Who was the man? Who was the child?"

"I'd better tell you later. I've got to get back to that party. I may have a strong lead."

"You'd better tell me what you know right now," Dirksmith commanded.

Frankel would not endanger Susan's child at this point even if it meant defying Dirksmith. "Sit tight. Don't leave that phone. I'll call you later." He hung up before Dirksmith could protest and walked through the lower level of the hotel to the Walton Street entrance, where he had let off Stonehill. Signaling the first taxi in line, he told the driver to take him to the Art Institute.

Stonehill checked the apartment thoroughly. The usually light-sleeping maid was snoring loudly, but nothing seemed even slightly out of order. He wondered about the ring on the table in the hall, the huge diamond sparkling against the black-velvet-lined box. After checking his grandson again to make sure that his breathing was easy, he kissed Stoney's forehead and rear-ranged the blanket which he had kicked off. Then he left the apartment the same way he had come in, by the back door, down the service elevator, and through the rear entrance into the alley. It wasn't until he was alone and exposed in the alley that a sudden explosion of fear in him surfaced. Sweat poured off his face, the cold night chilled his body, and he could not seem to move. He looked both ways; the alley seemed empty, but he felt eyes watching him. Susan's keys were cold and his hand was hot. The orange scarf. He had forgotten the orange muffler. He had put it on a chair in Stoney's room. He looked at his watch to see if there was still time to retrieve it, but decided he could not take a chance on being later than the thirty-five minutes Frankel had allotted him. With enormous effort he made his legs move down the alley out into the street. It was three minutes before he saw the lights of a taxi approaching and flagged it down.

The main floor and center staircase of the Art Institute were almost empty now. The sound of voices and of the orchestra floated down from the second-floor galleries. Stonehill checked his watch again. It was ten after nine, and dinner was to be served at nine. He had only been gone an hour, a lifetime.

Nodding to a guard, he walked up the stairs slowly, willing his strength and calm back. He knew that nothing about him could arouse suspicion in his wife or in Susan. Or in Tatov, either. Particularly Tatov.

His wife was talking to Marilyn Alsdorf. He sat in the empty chair beside her. "Livie, is everything all right? I was worried."

"It was a false alarm. Everything's fine. The party seems to be going great. Where is Susan sitting?"

"Back with the younger people near the orchestra, somewhere beyond the Gauguins. Did you meet that English friend of hers? Awfully attractive, isn't he? She seems quite smitten. It's not like her to show emotion like that. Did you notice?"

"What do you know about him?"

"Nothing. Susan mentioned him the night I came back from Palm Springs. I think they have mutual friends in London. She did say that he'd known Whiz in Africa or somewhere. Do you remember?"

"Damascus. He met Whiz in Damascus. I remember now."

"Don't look so worried, Livie. Susan isn't the kind to rush into anything." She touched his arm. "I'm still worried about you, darling. You haven't been yourself since I've been home."

He tried to shake off her concern. "Just a lot of damn petty annoyances. I'm really fine." He pushed back his chair. "What about a dance? We ought to get out on the floor while Duchin is still playing something we can understand."

Maude stood up and took his arm. "Susan says that they're giving bus-stop lessons at Zorine's. Perhaps we ought to learn some of the new dances. We don't want to be old fogies, do we?"

"I'm too old to learn new tricks," Stonehill said.

Myrna was dancing with the man from the Commodity Exchange, her eyes closed, her face resting against his shoulder. This last hour had been the first conscious sixty minutes in the past month when he had not thought about Myrna. In this crisis she had been completely out of his thoughts; yet the ultimate danger was to her. The terror and the love flooded back again, as well as the jealousy . . . the way her head lay against the man's shoulder and her fingers moved against the nape of his neck.

Dancing with Frankel, Susan blew a kiss over his shoulder and steered him toward them. "What kind of a sport are you, Daddy?"

"What do you mean?"

"This will break up early, and we're all going to Zorine's. Why don't you come? You've never been there."

Frankel interrupted. "Wait a minute, Susan. I may not be up to it."

"Of course you will be, Peter. How about it, Daddy? I know Mother wants to go."

"If your father isn't too tired," Maude said.

Stonehill looked at Frankel, who nodded, almost imperceptibly. "I'll try it," Stonehill agreed. "Are you sure you're game for it, Maude? You know you're leaving in the morning."

"I'd love to see it." She turned to Susan. "We'll go. Let us know when you're ready."

Suddenly Tatov was tapping Frankel's shoulder. "Do they still cut in in America?"

Frankel snarled, "No."

Susan slid out of Frankel's arms. "Of course they do. Don't be a boor, Peter."

"You won't forget about tomorrow, will you, sir?" Tatov called back to Stonehill.

"Mom and Daddy are coming to Zorine's with us," Susan said to Tatov. "You men can make your plans there."

They danced away, leaving Frankel without a partner. He shrugged his shoulders. "See you at Zorine's, I guess."

Wednesday, February 16 Eleven p.m., Rolling Meadows, Illinois

THE FEW MINUTES he had spent with his son shattered Whiz Crossley. He saw himself in the boy's features, felt his blood in the boy's body. Now, in the computer room sending out messages, he wondered why the assassin from St. Louis had not been at the rendezvous point after the kidnapping. He had seen the cab let Stonehill off in the alley and drive away on schedule, then had waited ten minutes beyond the allotted time at the North Avenue entrance to the expressway. The dumb bastard, he thought, couldn't even follow simple instructions. He should have checked him out more thoroughly. Hasad had promised him that the man would perform perfectly. The dumb bastard, he thought. He should have known better than to trust Hasad's evaluation of the man.

If he had stuck it out, if he had not tried to find the real Susan beneath the veneer, if he had really tried to be the things

Stonehill wanted, he would be at the Art Institute tonight dancing with a beautiful wife, returning home to a beautiful apartment, with a beautiful son safely asleep in his bed, unthreatened
and secure.

He looked at the monster machine, calculating, communicat-
ing, spinning wheels of destruction. Was it too late to turn it all
off, to smash the IBM brain? Perhaps he could make it up to
Susan now, say the words that used to turn her on, touch the
places that used to make her shiver with delight under his fingers.

He shook himself. There was no going back. Yet as he sat
there activating death and destruction, he kept picturing himself
with Susan and Stoney, with the way his life could have been.

Thursday, February 17
One a.m., Chicago

FRANKEL FOLLOWED STONEHILL into the men's room at Zorine's,
gave the attendant two dollars and sent him out for a cigar.

"Look, Mr. Stonehill, we'd better talk, and it ought to be
tonight." They stood side by side at the urinals.

"I think we ought to drop the Mr. Stonehill, don't you,
Peter?"

"What do you want me to call you?"

"My friends call me Livie."

"I'll try."

"Where do you want to meet?"

"I'm not sure. I know we're both being watched by a lot of
people. It could be dangerous."

"What about my apartment? Could you get in without anyone seeing you?"

Frankel shook his head. "It's too risky."

"Tatov wants me to have lunch with him tomorrow. Should I?"

"You might as well. Play him cool until we have something to work on."

"Have you found out anything about him yet?"

"I'm working on it." He zipped up his pants, walked over to the sink and began washing his hands.

Beside him, Stonehill looked at him in the mirror. "Susan's going to get hurt if our suspicions about Tatov are true."

Frankel nodded. "Can't be helped." He looked directly at Stonehill. "We'll be there to pick up the pieces. I don't want to see her hurt any more than you do—you know that."

"Where do we meet?"

Frankel dried his hands. "Let me think. I'll figure it out before we leave this joint."

"Does Susan ever talk about Whiz, her first husband?"

"No. I didn't even know his name until this moment."

"A funny thing happened," Stonehill said. "Susan says that Tatov told her that he had met Whiz in Damascus."

"Damascus?"

"The funny thing is that I saw Whiz last Sunday, just by accident. I met him at the airport when I was picking up my wife. I wonder if it *was* an accident? Whiz told me he'd just flown in from South America."

The attendant returned with the cigar, and Frankel shook off the change. "We'll set up a meeting later"—he hesitated—"Livie."

Thursday, February 17 One-thirty to seven-thirty a.m., Chicago-London

"FATHER? Leonid here. Sorry to wake you, but there's a bit of an emergency here."

"Are you all right?"

"First-class, Father. But I think I've found out what Hasad is up to here—I mean besides the obvious ploy with the American computer fellow."

"What is it?"

"Do you know who Mark Mendoza is, Father?"

"Vaguely. An Israeli soldier, some kind of hero during the Yom Kippur war. Why?"

"Well, the way I see it, Hasad is taking advantage of this plot as a cover for his real purpose. Mendoza is scheduled to arrive in Chicago in a day or two. He's speaking at an Israel bond dinner on Sunday. I think that Hasad plans to have Mendoza murdered here."

"Whatever for? It would be stupid of Hasad to kill Mendoza. In a way, it would defeat the other plan. If he's assassinated, every Jew will pour money into Israel. The whole world will join the Jewish United Fund. Hasad wouldn't be stupid enough to try it."

"With all respect, sir, I think he would. It was you who gave me the clue. You explained the traditional Arab way of cutting off the hands of a thief or the tongue of a liar. Do you remember?"

"Of course."

"Well, in some way Hasad thinks he can avenge his son by

killing Mendoza. Did you hear about the raid made on an Israeli settlement from behind the Syrian border two days ago? A
wounded lion was let loose in a farming village and killed a lot
of people. Did you happen to read about it?"

"There are so many of those things that it's hard to keep
score."

"Except that this one, Father, had Hasad's special touch. It
happened directly after Hasad's son hanged himself. Mendoza is
known as the Lion of the Desert. The symbolism is obvious
when one looks at it."

"Who else knows about this?"

"No one yet. For one thing, no one knows Hasad besides you
and me. My question is, Will killing Mark Mendoza affect your
plans here?"

"Very much."

"I suspected that."

"We are about to underwrite a substantial series of real estate
ventures in the States. If someone scratched the surface a bit, he
could easily discover that Arab money was behind us, and it
wouldn't do for America to be up in arms against the Arabs at
this point. It would make negotiations rather sticky; in fact, it
just might queer the whole endeavor. It wouldn't do at all if this
Mendoza chap were knocked off in Chicago—that is the expression there, isn't it?"

"I think they say 'bumped off.' Either way, I can see your
point."

"Do you have the vaguest idea of who the assassin is or when
and where it will happen?"

"Not the vaguest. I haven't even been able to find this Crossley chap, but I'm certain that he will be the key figure in the
attempt. I've thought about this a great deal. I realize it's pre-
sumptuous of me to try to pit my mind against Hasad's, but I
have studied this from his standpoint, tried to use his rationale.
If I were he, I would have the American kill Mendoza. Don't
you agree that Hasad might think like that?"

"Very likely. But as far as I am aware, the American is the
only direct link back to Hasad. Would he risk that?"

"Exactly the point, Father. He definitely would not. For

Hasad to make it work, it would have to be like the assassination of their President Kennedy—that is, the assassin must be killed before he can talk to the authorities. I was thinking that if I were Hasad, I would arrange for Crossley to pull the trigger, but I would also arrange to have someone close by kill Crossley in a matter of seconds."

The elder Tatov was quiet for a moment. "You are probably right, Leonid, but how do we stop it?"

"By stopping Crossley. The trouble is that I can't find him. I told you that I've been staying a bit too close to his ex-wife, hoping that my attentions to her might smoke him out, but no luck." He waited a moment, carefully phrasing his next sentence. "Since I cannot seem to find him, perhaps if I were a danger to Hasad, a potential saboteur of both his plans, then Crossley might seek me out and try to eliminate me."

"It's too dangerous, Leonid. Your mother wouldn't permit it."

"How is Mother?"

"Your mother is well, but your plan is out of the question."

"I am quite prepared to protect myself, Father. I thought that there might be a way for you to let something slip to Hasad, to plant the seed in his mind that I've gone off on my own crusade against your orders. If Hasad had the idea that for some reason or other I was about to expose the Crossley plot—he mustn't know that we suspect about Mendoza—to the authorities, he would have Crossley try to get rid of me. I'd leave the details to you, Father. I know that you're awfully good at that kind of intrigue."

"Don't be impudent, Leonid."

"Realistic, Father, not impudent. I trust you, more than anyone, to create a scenario which would accomplish our purposes without sacrificing my life."

"It is out of the question, Leonid. I would not consider endangering you for any reason whatsoever. Do you understand?"

"Think about it, Father. I'll call you at the office in three hours. I know you'll come up with a first-rate scheme."

"Save your breath. It is out of the question."

"I'll talk to you in a few hours, Father." Leonid hung up.

Thursday, February 17
One-thirty a.m., Chicago

Mike Nelson and Rico del Gracia were in the large marble shower stall together, the steam in the immense bathroom fogging the mirror, leaving a wet film on the marble. Nelson was aroused, but del Gracia remained flaccid, and when Nelson soaped his hands and put them on del Gracia's penis, Rico moved away and turned off the water.

Out of the shower stall, Nelson took his eyeglasses from the countertop, wiped the wetness off with a tissue, then began to dry himself with a heavy towel. "This thing's getting you down, Rico. Forget it, it isn't worth it."

"I just don't understand Susan."

"If you ask me, that crazy Russian Englishman is after her ass and she's about to give it to him—if she hasn't already."

"You don't understand, Mike. Susan isn't like that."

"For the right guy, I don't care who the broad is, she'll give out, no matter what." He turned around and handed Rico the towel. "Do my back, will you?"

"You should have seen the ring. Sixteen perfect blue-white carats and she didn't want it." He turned around so that Nelson could dry his back. "Do you think that she's in love with Tatov?"

"I hope so. It would put a stop to all this shit. We are who we are, Rico. The hell with the business."

Del Gracia shook his head. "There's still a little time. Maybe it will work out."

"I'm going home tomorrow to tell Sarah. I've made my decision."

"Don't Mike. Give us some time."

"Aren't you sure about us, Rico?"

"I'm sure, Mike, but there's so much more at stake . . . there are other lives which will be affected." He moved away. "Do what you want, but I think you should wait."

"What are you going to do if Susan won't marry you?"

"I'm not sure. Keep stalling the Grunswalds, for one thing. They've agreed to cut off some of their contributions to Israel temporarily, and I hope that will do the trick. We won't know for sure until we read the *National Enquirer*."

"Do you think your uncles and cousins believed the story that the exposé is a phony?"

He shook his head. "They don't believe it. My cousin Harley took me aside and did a man-to-man number on me. Evidently he's A.C.–D.C., and he told me more about himself than I wanted to know. They don't really believe me, but they're all saving face. That's why my marriage to Susan is so important."

"Let's go to bed."

"I don't think I'm up to it tonight."

"You underestimate me, del Gracia."

Thursday, February 17 Two a.m., Chicago

THEN THE ELEVATOR stopped on Susan's floor, Tatov slipped a folded hundred-dollar bill into the operator's hand, smiled and winked. Before he entered the apartment he took off his black patent dancing pumps, undid his black tie and opened the top buttons of his shirt. Susan had left the door on the latch, and he closed it quietly. The diamond ring was still in the box on the table. He picked it up and held it under the lamp, admiring the size and the brilliance of the stone. He noticed that one of the buttons of the telephone on the table was lit; Susan must be talking to someone. Deftly, with the silky fingers of a safe-cracker, he picked up the receiver and heard Susan's anguished voice. "Stop it, Whiz, stop it."

Then a man's voice. "Do you remember, Susan, all the ways we used to do it? Like this, over the telephone. I would tell you to touch yourself and imagine it was just the tip of my tongue, just a little lick. Now touch yourself. Not all the way in, just touch yourself, close your eyes and feel my tongue. Just the tip of it, wet and hot. Just a lick."

"Stop it, Whiz. I won't listen. Where are you?"

"Then a little more. I'd put it in a little more now. I can taste you now. Can you feel my tongue and my whole mouth covering you? Can you feel it, Susan. Can you?" His voice was becoming thicker. "I can taste you, I can smell you. Oh, God, Susan, it feels so wonderful. Feel it, can you feel it?"

"Don't, Whiz, don't. Please don't."

"It will never be like this with anyone else, you know that. You know how we are with each other. Now I'm all the way inside you. Do you feel it, Susan? I feel you. I feel you enveloping me. Don't stop, Susan. Don't stop. Keep moving. Oh, God, Susan. Don't stop."

Tatov returned the phone gently to its cradle, took the ring out of the box, put it on his little finger, examined it again under the light and then made his decision.

Susan did not hear him come into the room. She was on her bed, the telephone on her pillow, her body gyrating, her hand working against the rhythm of her body. She was crying. When she saw Tatov at the foot of the bed, her eyes opened in fear, but her body did not stop its movement; the pelvic thrusts were automated by an uncontrollable sensory mechanism. Tatov took off his jacket, ripped off his pants and threw himself on top of her, his body moving in counterpoint. He felt Susan's fingernails dig through his shirt into his back. Whiz's voice still sounded through the phone, but almost inaudibly through his heavy breathing. "I'm coming, Susan, I'm coming. Oh, God. Oh, God." Crossley's scream of release touched off a simultaneous orgasm in Susan and Tatov, and their own sounds obliterating all other sounds. When the intensity subsided and the room came back into focus, they were aware of a persistent buzzing through the telephone receiver. Without moving off Susan, Tatov reached over and hung it up.

She sobbed softly, and Tatov kissed the tears as they came out of her eyes, rocking her body soothingly with his, a father with a wounded child. Then the rhythmic rocking became sexual as well as protective, and this time their passion was not triggered by another voice in another place.

Tatov had showered, and now lay beside Susan, cradling her head in the pocket of his shoulder. "We ought to talk, Susan."

She snuggled closer. "I'm so tired."

"We can't put it off forever. Tell me about Whiz. Do you still love him?"

He felt her head shake. "No. I'm not sure that I ever loved him. He was always so different from anyone I'd ever known. I was hypnotized by him, fascinated. He was such a mysterious . . . I don't know how to say it. Whiz was the one person who undid me . . . undid everything I am. I was uncontrolled, someone else. It was as if I lost control of my own actions. He pulled the strings and made me move the way he wanted me to. Can you understand?"

"Does he phone you like this often?"

"This is the first time I've even heard his voice since he left me. I didn't even know whether he was dead or alive until that day you told me you'd seen him in Cairo."

"Damascus."

"Wherever." She sat up and turned so that she could face Tatov directly. "You might as well know some things about me. Since Whiz . . . until you, last night, I haven't slept with anyone. I haven't wanted to, really, or perhaps I was afraid. Whatever, it doesn't matter now. You see, my parents were dead set against my marrying Whiz. They had brought me up in a certain

way and they have old-fashioned moral codes—particularly
Daddy. They were right about Whiz; I should never have married him. I almost died because of him, and it taught me that
maybe the old-fashioned moral code is better. Look at my parents, how long they've been happily married. When Whiz left
and I recovered, I decided to live by my parent's ethics. Then
you came along." She bent over and kissed him, the tips of her
breasts brushing his chest. "I'm not being Daddy's good little
girl, and I don't feel the slightest bit of guilt. That surprises me.
This morning when I woke up, I thought I'd feel terrible, overcome with guilt. But I felt just wonderful."

"Do you want to know if my intentions are honorable?"

She smiled. "I don't even care." She cocked her head. "That
doesn't sound like Susan Stonehill, does it?"

"What happened to Susan Crossley?"

"I guess you've made me a maiden again. At least suddenly
I'm using my maiden name."

Tatov's eyes moved toward the telephone. "Tell me about
Whiz."

Susan lay down again and found the protective pocket for her
head. "When Whiz worked for Daddy at the bank, he used to
travel a little. When we were separated at night, he would call
me and . . . well, it was what he was doing tonight."

"Masturbation does not cause insanity, acne or one's fingers
to fall off."

"It seems so dirty now."

"Susan, how grown-up are you?"

"At this moment?"

"At this very moment."

She considered the question. "I feel grown-up right now, but
your arm is around me and your body is warm and strong. I
don't know. Why?"

Tatov moved his shoulder from under her head, got out of
bed and walked across the room. "You can't keep moving from
one daddy to another. I'm not a daddy, Susan, I'm your lover.
Like all lovers, I give a bit and I need a bit."

"I don't understand."

"I need you to be grown-up, Susan. I need your strength and your help."

She pulled the sheets around her, covering her nakedness. "You say that you are my lover. Do you love me?"

"Equivocally."

"What's that supposed to mean?"

"It means that we don't really know each other, though we do know some marvelous things *about* each other. In bed, for example. Absolutely marvelous, a marvelous fit, don't you agree?" Looking away, Susan did not answer. "And you are smashing to look at. You don't have to agree; everyone else does. You're beautiful and a joy for me to be with. Your eyes react exactly right when I talk, as though all the dribble I'm uttering is the most important conversation in the world. A man likes that about a woman. And I hang on every word you say and think you're marvelous. But all of this is froth on the trifle, isn't it? We don't know much about the substance of each other, do we?"

"I have no substance," Susan said. "I am what you see. Don't try to make me anything I'm not. I am exactly what you see, nothing more."

"That's perfect rot, darling. We're all much more than surfaces, though it may take a bit of scratching, and it does depend on who does the scratching." He sat down beside her and gently ran his fingernails across her shoulder. "I'm scratching the surface, darling."

She took his hand and held it. "Under that surface is another surface, and under that another. It's all surface, Leonid; there's nothing else underneath."

"I don't believe that. You don't either, not really."

"I don't understand the game you're playing with me. Please don't play it anymore. Maybe you'd better get out of my life while I can still piece it back together."

"With diamonds from Harry Winston?" He lay beside her. "That's an awfully good stone—a bit vulgar, but beautiful nonetheless. It will take a lot of diamonds to bind you to del Gracia, but then he's filthy rich, isn't he? I am, too, as a matter of fact, but you're well enough off so that you don't need either of us."

She started to get out of bed, but he caught her arm and eased her back. "Susan, everyone spares you unpleasantness. Everyone protects you from the hard facts of life. Your father, your friends, your money, your beauty—all of them insulate you from what is really happening. I'm not going to do that. I'm going to share my burden with you, make you responsible for some of it. Maybe that's what love is."

"What burden?"

"I must see to it that Whiz Crossley is killed before he does irreparable harm to a great many people. If necessary, I must kill him myself."

It took a long time before she answered. Looking at the ceiling, Tatov did not see the change in her expression from astonishment to terror to calm again. "What do you want me to do?"

He sat up quickly and looked at her. "No questions, Susan? I mean to kill your former husband, your son's father, and you have no questions?"

"I'm not sounding like Susan Stonehill, am I? Something about you makes me different too. I'm not afraid of doing anything wrong; I don't think you'd make me. I trust you—perhaps it's that simple. I do have questions, but you'll answer them in your own time. And I'm not surprised about Whiz. There was always a destructive quality in him. He tried to destroy me and my family and everything we symbolized. You didn't know that, did you?"

"He means to assassinate Mark Mendoza, and I mean to stop him."

"Are you an Israeli agent?"

He laughed. "You don't know my father, darling. If anyone mistook me for an Israeli, it would destroy his image of himself and of me."

"I don't understand."

"You will, darling, when you meet him. The old boy can be a charmer. He's a bit like your father; he still has the charisma—and uses it, I might add. He's still active on various mattresses. He doesn't know that I know, but it does give me hope for my own dotage."

"Are you an Israeli agent?"

"Unequivocally no. I'm a businessman with international interests. I protect those interests, and at this moment Crossley and the people behind him are a threat to them. I mean to destroy the threat, and to save Mendoza's life in the process."

"Are you a friend of Mendoza?"

"Never met the lad. Never even heard of him until four days ago."

"What do you want me to do?"

"To stop Crossley, I first have to find him. That's why I'm in Chicago, really. I think he's here. You couldn't tell when you were talking to him, could you? Did he say where he was?"

"Is that why you made love to me, to find Whiz?"

"You know better than that."

"Do I?"

His answer was to kiss her. What started as a token meeting of their mouths developed into a shivering, clutching, probing urgency of mutual need and hunger. When it was over, Tatov said, "I love you unequivocally. I lied before. It's the baser part of my nature. I do lie, sometimes—very little white lies." He held his thumb and index finger almost together. "I knew instantly that I loved you unequivocally." He kissed her again.

This time Susan broke away. "How do I help?"

"I think Crossley will call you again, perhaps tonight or tomorrow. When you were married, did he ever call again after doing it once?"

"Often. Even when we were together and had sex, he would sleep for an hour and then want to do it again, and sometimes he would do the same thing over the telephone."

"I hope to God he does tonight. If he does, tell him you must see him. Plead with him, tell him that you can't go on without seeing him. Tell him you need him physically—anything to draw him out of hiding so that he'll suggest meeting."

"Do I have to meet him? Must I go through with it?"

"It depends, darling. I wish I could promise you that you wouldn't have to go to bed with him, but it may be necessary. It would only be one more time. It wouldn't mean anything."

"I don't think I could. I'd freeze up. He'd know there was something wrong."

"Did he ever beat you or threaten you physically?"

"Never. You don't understand. Whiz loved me, and he may still. He was angry at the world and violent about many things, but never with me or Stoney. He can be very gentle."

"Whatever, I'll be close to protect you. But it's important that I flush him out before he can cause real destruction."

"I'll try, Leonid."

They were asleep, their bodies entwined, when the telephone rang. Daylight was just beginning. Susan clutched Tatov's hand, holding it tightly, and with her other hand picked up the telephone.

Thursday, February 17
Nine-thirty a.m., Chicago

THE NEWS of the murder had been on television and radio all morning, and the later editions of the *Tribune* and *Sun-Times* both carried the story on page one. The newspapers were spread out on Irving Feldman's desk, and the tiny Sony behind his desk was turned to the news. Stella set a cup of coffee in front of him. "That guy Green, the one who was here the other day, is waiting outside foaming at the mouth."

"In a minute." He was reading the story over his glasses, which had slipped to the end of his nose. "Not to be believed."

"It seems impossible," Stella said. "She was just here, when was it . . . Monday? Yeah, Monday. You could have fooled me. She looked like such a classy old dame. Who would have thought she got her jollies off with young men and handcuffs and whips. Appearances can fool you. You never know about people." She walked behind the desk and put her hand on Feld-man's shoulder, bending to read the article. "They still haven't identified the guy they found dead in her bedroom, have they?"

Feldman shook his head. "Not yet."

"What do you suppose happened?"

"The paper says that she must have picked up a couple of young men somewhere. They're investigating a massage parlor on Wells Street that specializes in that kind of action. Maybe the men came from there. They found her naked, with both her feet and her hands handcuffed, and bruises around the face. The man was horsewhipped bloody, and then shot like her. Who knows the kind of craziness that goes on in the world today."

They turned to the television as they heard her name. The newscaster was saying, "Mrs. Mandlebaum was a wealthy philanthropist who founded the famous Mandlebaum Clinic in Chicago as a memorial to her late husband, a hospital specializ-ing in gastrointestinal diseases. Mrs. Mandlebaum had sched-uled a press conference for this afternoon in the offices of Skid-more, Owens and Merrill, an architectural firm. It is believed that she planned to announce the building of another Mandle-baum Clinic in Haifa . . ."

"Not to be believed."

"Sooner or later," Stella said, "some reporter is going to learn that we're her legal counsel. What do I tell them when they call?"

"What is there to say? A lovely lady, tell them. We know nothing about the murder, or about a new Mandlebaum Clinic in Haifa. You can always transfer the call to somebody in the trust division."

"You want to see Green?"

"Is he the young one?"

Stella shook her head. "It's the corned-beef guy."

"Send him in."

"You want to call back Seymour Danzig first?"

"He'll wait."

"What about Kupcinet?"

"Call him back and tell him Mendoza will be here in time for the taping of the television show tomorrow. Tell him it's defi-

nite. Mendoza will be in Chicago tomorrow morning, I promise."

The Israeli agent rushed into the room as soon as Stella
opened the door and stood over Feldman's desk, breathing
heavily, his eyes seething anger. Stella waited at the door. Green
said, "Get her out of here."

"It's all right, Stella."

"Buzz if you need me." She closed the door.

"You're cute, Feldman. You play a real cute little game,
don't you?" Everything about the man was different; there was
no question that he was a ferocious fighter. The way he stood,
the set of his body, the way his hands clenched, was terrifying,
and Feldman felt fear. "You tried to make a deal. You know
what your deal cost, Feldman? It cost the life of a tough, dedicated soldier. He's dead, and it's all because you wanted to
maneuver for an advantage."

"Who's dead?"

"The man you called Locker. My boss. That kid was my boss
because he was smarter and stronger than I am, and because the
survival of his country was the most important thing in his life.
You played your lawyer's game—negotiated strategy—you're
famous for that. You negotiate and maneuver and play chess
with men's lives, and you never get off your fat ass."

"Locker?" Green pointed to the newspaper and the picture of
the body on the floor of Mousey Mandlebaum's bedroom. "Oh,
my God." Feldman's tears were real.

"You could have helped us, Feldman. Instead, you decided
to play it cute, and we had to pick up scraps and threads and
move into this mess unprepared, with no facts. You had the
facts."

"How did it happen?"

"We saw her name on your desk. There were other names,
and we did routine checks on all of them. The man you called
Locker drew Mrs. Mandlebaum. God knows what happened,
but he was set up and now he's dead. There's a man named
Stonehill who's so scared that he can't talk. There's a man
named Sheldon Cole who took off this morning in a private jet
for God knows where. Who else, Feldman? This time you're

going to tell me everything. And no deals. You're going to tell me everything you know or I'll beat it out of you. I can beat the truth out of you, Feldman. Do you believe me?"

"I believe you."

"Then start talking."

Feldman put on his glasses, instantly reviewed everything that had happened, and selected the truths he would choose to tell this man. Just because a soldier dies, he reasoned with himself, is no reason to change the strategy of the war or the tactics of the battle. He had read Clausewitz, after all, and by definition, a soldier is expendable. "Sit down, sit down." He motioned Green to the chair opposite him. "There isn't much to tell," he began.

Thursday, February 17 Nine-forty a.m., Chicago and Lake Forest

STONEHILL WAITED five minutes after his wife boarded the plane to Palm Springs, then walked back to the main terminal, not certain if he was being followed. Frankel had warned him that he was probably under constant surveillance, and to follow his usual routine as closely as possible. His car and driver were waiting at the American Airlines entrance on the upper level. "Carl," he said as he got in, "instead of returning to the bank, I'm going to Lake Forest. Take the toll road. How's your gas?"

"It's not that far, Mr. Stonehill. We have plenty."

"Stop at the Standard station at the Lake Forest Oasis anyway. I am going to get out there, Carl. Pay no attention to what I do. Buy some gas and drive on to Gurnee, turn around and go home. If anyone stops you for any reason and asks about me, tell them the truth—that I asked to be let off at the service station." He leaned forward and touched the driver's shoulder. "Do you understand?"

"Yes, sir. Is everything all right?"

"Boys will be boys, Carl. I'm going to meet a lady. You've driven me to meet ladies before."

"I understand." He looked back at Stonehill through the rearview mirror and allowed the trace of a smile to appear on his mouth.

Stonehill used the car telephone to call his private number at the bank. When his secretary answered, he asked, "Did that envelope marked 'personal' arrive yet?"

"The mail isn't in yet, but I've alerted the mail room. Do you want me to check again?"

"Yes. I'll call back in about twenty minutes. Any other messages?"

"Irv Kupcinet called again. He wants you tomorrow at one o'clock to tape his show with Mark Mendoza. Mr. Mendoza is arriving in Chicago tomorrow morning. He said to tell you that the Senator will be there too, and that the program will be televised on Sunday, right after the dinner. He's going to call back any minute. What should I tell him?"

"Tell him yes, for the moment. If I change my mind, I'll get in touch with him later, but don't tell him that. Anything else?"

"Nothing important. The rest can wait until you get here. What time will you be in?"

"I'm not sure. I have a noon lunch date at the Racquet Club, and then some personal business on the North Side. I'll stay in touch. Meanwhile, hassle the mail room and get that letter."

It was a thirty-five minute drive to the Lake Forest oasis. When the car stopped at the pumps, Stonehill got out, walked casually toward the men's room at the side of the station, went inside, urinated, washed his hands, walked around the building, crossed the parking lot and went into the restaurant straddling the tollroad and servicing both southbound and northbound traffic.

Once inside the restaurant, Stonehill strode quickly through the building and out the other side to the duplicate filling station servicing southbound traffic. Frankel was waiting at the designated spot in the parking lot. Stonehill got into the car quickly, and Frankel pulled out immediately onto the ramp to the southbound tollway. "Were you followed?"

"I don't know. I didn't look around."

"We don't have much time." Frankel checked his watch. "You're meeting Tatov at noon?"

"Yes, at the Racquet Club."

"Where is it?"

"On Dearborn, 1400 North. Get off the expressway at Division." Stonehill groped at the side of the seat. "Is there a way to push this seat back?"

"There's a lever in the front. The only one who ever sits in that seat is Susan."

"Did you talk to Susan this morning?"

"I called her early. She was making breakfast. She said that the maid had a bad headache, so she was fixing Stoney's breakfast herself. She didn't say anything about Stoney being sick, so he must be okay."

"What did you find out about Tatov?"

"Nothing yet. I've put the wheels in motion and he's being investigated, but it may take some time and I don't think that we have time. In the meanwhile we have to play it the way we see it and assume that Tatov and Crossley are in this together. I'd guess that Tatov is the brains of the plan, and that Crossley is the technical genius. What's happening to you is happening all over the country, so there must be a communication center. Crossley would be good at that kind of thing, wouldn't he?"

"He's a mathematical genius. He designed the computer operation at the bank, and it's extraordinary. Say what you want about him, he is a genius."

"I don't think he's really the dangerous one. The guy that worries me is Tatov. That baby face and those beautiful English manners camouflage a killer. At least that's the way I see it, and I've told my people to play it that way."

"What should I do at lunch?"

"Live by your wits. I don't know what he's up to. Don't give him any information."

"I think he wants to ask my permission to marry Susan."

"Play the irate father. Pretend it's me, and that I'm taking you to lunch at the Covenant Club. Instead of the Racquet Club menu you'd have your choice of knishes or boiled beef with matzo balls. That ought to make you irate enough."

"You're wrong about me, Peter. If you and Susan loved each other I wouldn't object."

"Be honest with yourself. You would have objected a week ago."

"I'm not sure. So much has happened. Things that used to be important don't seem important anymore. I honestly don't know."

"I know," Frankel persisted. "You would have objected. You would have talked about differences in background, about Crossley and the mistake Susan made in marrying out of her crowd. You would have told me that you didn't want her to make the same mistake twice." As he drove he kept glancing into the rear-view mirror, shifting lanes in the light traffic to see if a trailing car revealed itself. "Be honest. Moment of truth, Mr. Stonehill."

"I honestly don't know. All I can tell you is that if I were on my way to the Covenant Club now, I'd order the boiled beef with matzo balls and say that I'd be proud to have you as a son-in-law."

"After the fact," Frankel said. "Too late. I've thought about it. When Susan gets over the hurt of loving Tatov, she's going to rebound right into the muscular arms of Rico del Gracia. When all is said and done, maybe that's where she really belongs. It won't be any adjustment for her. She can go right on being Susan Stonehill, who just happens to be married to Rico del Gracia."

"I think Susan is better than that."

"So do I. Evidently so did Crossley. Only Susan doesn't think so."

"Listen, Frankel, I have to stop at a highway telephone and call my office. I told you that one of the conditions last night was that I release a statement to the press today. I've called twice but my mail hadn't come upstairs yet."

"I'll stop at the one right after the Deerfield exit. Are you going to release the statement?"

"I have no choice. The alternatives are unacceptable."

"Try to stall until I talk to my people."

"I've stalled all week. That's why they kidnapped Stoney. I can't take that risk again."

"I have Stoney covered," Frankel said. "My people are staked out. Nothing will happen to him."

"What about Tatov? I'm sure he goes to the apartment."

"Tatov wouldn't get his own hands dirty. I know his type. He's going to remain clean and smiling until I nail the bastard. His kind uses other people for their dirty work."

"I don't know how I'm going to get through lunch."

"Is the food that bad at the Racquet Club? I can still take you to the Covenant Club."

Stonehill had to laugh. "I wish it was going to be that way, Peter, I honestly do. I'd live the rest of my life easier knowing that you were taking care of Susan and Stoney."

At the Deerfield toll plaza Stonehill phoned his office, then got back into the car.

"The letter arrived. My secretary read it to me over the phone. She was shocked. I told her to type it up on my own letterhead and send it by messenger to John Farrow."

"Who's he?"

"A friend of mine. He's the editorial director of the *Daily News* and the *Sun-Times*. I dictated a note asking him to place the statement in tonight's newspaper."

"Listen. So far I've been able to keep your name out of this. I didn't tell the people in Washington the whole truth. I'm trying to protect you and Susan, but when this story breaks all hell will be breaking loose. I have to tip off my people before that happens. You'd better start from the beginning and tell me everything. Give it to me straight, Mr. Stonehill. I need every fact, no matter how unimportant it may seem to you."

Stonehill looked at his watch. He had forty minutes to describe six days of terror. "I thought you were going to call me Livie," he started.

Thursday, February 17
Eleven a.m., Rolling
Meadows, Illinois

IT HAD BEEN almost an hour since the red alert had gone on, and still there was no message from Hasad. Everyone was on stand-by in the computer room. Crossley waited in his office, lying on a narrow cot. He had abandoned the words of his mantra. Pieces of the smashed Accujac machine lay in a shattered heap on the floor.

When the horn signal finally went off, echoing against the concrete walls, Crossley jumped up, ran into the computer room, waved everyone out, sat down at the machine and watched Hasad's words clicking out from thousands of miles away, coded and decoded in split seconds.

MARK MENDOZA ARRIVES CHICAGO FRIDAY MORNING BY PRIVATE JET. HAS INFORMATION WHICH WILL DESTROY SPIDER OPERATION. MUST BE ELIMINATED AT ONCE. REPEAT. MUST BE ELIMINATED AT ONCE. AT ALL COSTS. REPEAT. AT ALL COSTS.

                                    HASAD

Thursday, February 17
Twelve p.m., Chicago

IT TOOK all of Stonehill's concentration not to be disarmed by Leonid Tatov. During the small talk over cocktails, he found himself laughing with the young Englishman, admiring the way he used the language, respectful of his perception as he made offhand comments on the world economy. In his years as a loan officer at the bank, every known device had been used to flatter Stonehill and establish a rapport, but never quite as well as Tatov was doing it, never with as much casual grace and subtlety. Tatov used his charm and diffidence to screen a steel-trap mind. A week ago Stonehill would have been delighted with his daughter's choice. Tatov had qualities that could make him a major figure in international finance. But now he was looking at these attributes in another way, as confirmation of Frankel's theory that these same qualities could be used to mastermind this plot against the Jews.

"I mean to run off with your daughter and your grandson, Mr. Stonehill. I thought it might be a good idea to give you fair warning so that you'd have a chance to get used to the idea."

"You don't give me much choice."

"I'm afraid, sir, that given the way Susan and I feel about each other, there are no choices, not even for us."

"You're both sure?"

"It won't be so bad, really. With the SST, London is only three and a half hours away. We would hope you and Mrs. Stonehill would come to see us often."

"I don't know anything about you, Mr. Tatov."

"Leonid, sir. It's a frightful name to get used to saying, but once you've mastered it, you'll find it easy enough."

"I repeat: I don't know anything about you."

"That's why we are having lunch, isn't it? Ask me anything."

"I wonder what kind of questions a father asks these days."

"I've never been married. I am straight sexually. Public schools. Both Oxford and Cambridge. Rather overeducated, but it hardly slows me up at all."

"Are your parents alive?"

"Quite well, thank you, sir."

"What does your father do?"

"I suppose you would call it dabbling. He has interests in various ventures around the world. I might as well explain that we are frightfully rich. I don't mean to brag about it or to be ashamed of it; I simply state it as a fact. It does make life easier for overseas telephone calls and for flying across the Atlantic. I'm trying to say that though I mean to run off with Susan and Stoney, they will not be gone from your life."

"Do you work for your father?"

"I'm not quite certain that I work at all. It's so stimulating that I don't really think of it as working. I help him manage things here and there. I jump about quite a bit for him. He's getting a little crusty about leaving home too often. He won't leave our summer place in Ireland at all. It's a marvelous place, really. It rains too much, but even then it's marvelous. Stoney will love the horses. Father dabbles in horses, too. Susan and I will live in London at first, but there's a cottage at the country place in Essex where we'd spend the weekends."

"It sounds like a wonderful life."

"I mean it to be, sir. I want it to be a wonderful life for all of us."

"There's really nothing for me to say, is there?"

"You could say that you wish us well. We'd like to know that you and Mrs. Stonehill wish us well."

"I can't say that yet. I need time to think and to talk to Susan."

"I understand, sir. In your position I'd be cautious, too." He picked up the menu and studied it. "What the devil is 'fin n' haddie'?"

Thursday, February 17
Three p.m., Chicago

I t was the first time he had not brought Myrna to an orgasm. He had tried to hold back his own as long as possible but she had coaxed him to ejaculate quickly. "Psychic scars," she said, touching the bruises still visible on her arm. "I've done a little reading on the subject. It's not unusual to be frigid after a rape attempt."

"I'm sorry. You'll get over it."

"I have every intention of doing so. Part of it may be that I still have a lot of pain." She got out of bed and put on her robe. "Can I get you anything?"

Stonehill shook his head. "It will never be quite the same again for us, will it?"

"I don't know, Livie. I really don't know. I have two kinds of psychic scars—the ones you see and the beating I took last night."

"At the Art Institute? What happened?"

"I saw you as you were meant to be, standing there proud and tall and something beautiful. Everybody loves you, Livie; they all respect you. You're a real somebody. It almost made me afraid of you. If I had known who you were and what you stood for in the community . . . if I had known that first day you came into the gallery everything I now know about you . . . I wonder if I would have fucked you."

"We have more than sex, Myrna."

"Do we? You busted in here today as if I was a bitch in heat. You couldn't wait to get your pants off. Fuck first, talk later. I don't know if I like that."

"Last week you did. You were as anxious as I was."

"That was last week, before I saw you standing in that receiving line next to your wife. She's a good-looking woman, Livie. I mean she still looks good. She doesn't look as old as I thought she would. And your daughter, she scares the hell out of me too. She's like a movie star. You should have heard that schmuck I was with on the subject of your daughter—admiring her from a distance like she was Faye Dunaway or something. I'm outclassed, Livie. I couldn't hack it with all those people. I don't think I'd even want to. I couldn't see myself at your side, talking bullshit with all those people. It's not who I am."

"You could make it."

"What for? Why would I want to? Just so I can fuck an old fart like you?"

"You love me, Myrna."

"Do I? You ought to hear my mother on that subject. Along with the chicken soup and the tender, loving care came a lot of conversation from my mother. For the first time in her life she put human dignity ahead of money. She surprised me. You know the shit that mothers usually give their daughters—it's as easy to love a rich man as a poor man? Well, my mother's improved on the saying. As long as you're going to love a rich man, she says, it's as easy to love a young one as an old one."

"The schmuck from the Commodities Exchange?"

"He's not so terrible. I keep looking at him through my mother's eyes. Except that he goes to his mother's house every Friday night for dinner, he's not so terrible. He bought a gorgeous de Kooning drawing this week. He wants me to go to New York with him on Tuesday to look at a new Dubuffet."

"Are you going?"

"I don't know. I have a lot of decisions to make."

"Have you already made the one about me?"

"I think it was made a long time ago, Livie. I don't think either of us made it. It was baschert. Do you know what that means? Predestined, written in the Jewish galaxy, fated to happen."

"It doesn't have to be."

"The minute you get your rocks off, Livie, you get honorable. Do you know that about yourself? As soon as you stop feeling horny, your Judaic sense of moral obligation takes over." She wrapped the robe tighter. "You didn't do me wrong, Livie, you didn't take advantage of me. I wanted it as much as you did."

"Next time you get rid of a lover, wait until he has his clothes on. I feel so damn vulnerable like this."

"But beautiful." She sat beside him, held his penis, leaned over and kissed it. "If it means anything there'll never be a time I see you or your picture in the newspaper that I won't get turned on." As she leaned over to kiss him again, her breasts seemed flabbier as they flopped out of her robe.

Thursday, February 17
Four p.m., Chicago

Frankel saw the orange muffler folded neatly on the table in the entrance hall the instant he entered Susan's apartment. The ring and box were also there, along with three messages from del Gracia. In the living room Stoney was sitting cross-legged on the floor watching television. He stood up quickly and extended his hand to Frankel. "My mother says that she will be out in a little while and if you want a drink I am to tell Bertha, or you know where it is."

"Thank you. What are you watching?"

"Some dumb show. My mother also said that as soon as she comes in, I'm to go to my room. Can I go now?"

"Don't you want to stay and talk?"

"I'd rather go to my room."

"Okay, take off."

"Should I tell Bertha you want a drink?"

"Forget it." He touched the top of Stoney's head. "You don't like me much, do you?"

The child looked up at him. "I never thought about it." He ran off to his room.

In a robe, her hair tied up and with no make-up, obviously just out of the bathtub, Susan entered the room talking. "I'm sorry I'm late, Peter. I thought I'd never get out of there. I was at that meeting for the JUF dinner Sunday night. I'm to be Mark Mendoza's escort—I guess because Daddy is chairman of the thing. What a mess. Didn't Stoney ask you whether you wanted a drink?"

"He asked me. I don't."

"Mendoza is arriving early so that he can tape the Kup show tomorrow. His plane from Tel Aviv is landing in New York, and a private jet will be standing by to bring him to Chicago."

"Is he landing at O'Hare or at Meigs?"

"I don't remember. Maybe Meigs." She thought for a moment. "No, I guess it's O'Hare. It doesn't matter; they're sending a car to take me out to the airport, whichever one it is."

"What time?"

"Eight-thirty. He's supposed to land at ten, but they want me out there early for some photographs. We can't figure out what to do about Friday. Nobody's bothered to find out if he observes the Sabbath. I don't know whether to take him to a synagogue or to Zorine's. And what about the dietary laws? There's a cocktail party before the dinner, but we don't know what to serve. He's such a mystery man that no one seems to be able to get any information on him."

"Have you tried the local Israeli consul?"

"Dreadful man. He was at the meeting fouling up everything. The whole purpose of having Mendoza here is to attract young people, but the consul is trying to cram in a bunch of geriatrics just because they give a lot of money. The social politics is worse than the Cotillion."

"You'll survive."

"Did you have fun last night?"

"Sort of. Not my glass of borscht, but I managed. Now, suppose you tell me why you wanted me to come here."

"To be honest with you, it wasn't my idea. Leonid Tatov asked me to do it. He wants to talk to you."

"It appears that you're in love with him."

Susan's face reddened and she turned away. "What do you think of him?"

"Not fair. Not fair to ask me that. First of all, I'm jealous. Secondly, you forget my profession. I'm trained to be suspicious of everyone."

"You don't like him."

"I'm not a girl. I have a different set of gonads working for me—and thank God for that." He went over and turned her so that she faced him. "I don't want to see you hurt, Susan. I care very much what happens to you."

"What makes you think that Leonid wants to hurt me?"

"Gut reaction. You know so little about him. No one else does, either."

She looked angry. "Have you been investigating him?"

"I warned you that by profession I'm a law man. I'm over-trained, maybe, but I did check him out."

"I don't want to hear. I wouldn't believe it anyway."

"There's nothing to hear. I can't find out anything. Tatov's like Mendoza, a mystery man. I'm still working on it, Susan, and if I do find out anything, I'm going to tell you whether you listen or not."

"Trust him, Peter. It's important. I do."

"Love disqualifies judgment."

"Don't be pompous, Peter. Listen to what he says. It's important for all of us."

As Frankel looked at his watch, the doorbell sounded. Susan touched her hair and went to the front door. There was a moment of silence before Frankel heard their voices. "How was lunch?" Susan asked.

"It went well enough. Is Frankel here?"

"In the living room. Leonid, I meant to ask you, is this your scarf?"

"That? Who do you think I am, Hans Brinker? Whatever gave you that idea?"

"I found it in Stoney's room this morning. It has a London label on it and I thought you might have left it here."

"I wouldn't be caught dead in it, darling. Not my color."

In the living room Tatov and Frankel shook hands quickly. "There isn't time to beat around the bush," Tatov said. "I need some help and I need it quickly. Susan tells me that you are with the United States Attorney's office. As I understand the structure in America, your office is directly connected with your Federal Bureau of Investigation. Is that correct?"

"Yes."

"I need to make immediate contact with a person there, someone in authority."

"Try me first, Tatov. See what kind of a snow job you can do on me."

"This is not what you refer to as a snow job. Look here, Frankel, the reason you don't like me is subjective, isn't it?" Frankel did not answer. "Of course it is, and I don't blame you, but try to be objective for a minute. We can do the swashbuckling bit later—swords at dawn, fighting for the lady and all that nonsense—but right now I need someone who can get me to the proper man at the FBI fast."

"Try me, Tatov."

He looked at Susan and then back to Frankel. "I'm going to make an assumption, and I suggest you make the same one. I'm going to trust you because Susan says you're a good guy, and her judgment is enough for me. Is it enough for you?"

"Try me."

"I have strong evidence, which I am not at liberty to document, that an attempt will be made on the life of Mark Mendoza when he arrives in Chicago."

Susan interrupted. "He's coming tomorrow morning, Leonid. I didn't have time to tell you."

"Then there's less time than I thought." He moved closer to Frankel. "Now will you take me to someone at the FBI?"

"Tatov, I don't know your game or how you figure in any of this. You have me confused, I'll tell you that, but you're looking at the right man. Whatever's happening, I'm up to my ass in it.

Five minutes ago, I would have bet that ass that you were masterminding the whole thing, but if that's true, why would you want me to call in the FBI? It doesn't figure, unless you're even smarter than I give you credit for. God help me, you've got me, Tatov. Start talking."

Tatov was cautious. "You are a member of the Federal Bureau of Investigation?"

"I'm on special assignment. I know as much as anyone about what's going on. If there's a time problem, start talking."

"The ostensible mastermind, as you call him, is Susan's ex-husband, Whiz Crossley."

"I knew he was a part of it. I thought you two were in it together."

"Crossley or one of his operators will try to kill Mendoza. They'll probably make the attempt as soon as he gets in. It must be stopped. It's no good trying to head off Mendoza; Crossley and his group will just go underground, and we'll never get a shot at them."

"Are you Israeli intelligence?"

"No. I am exactly what I seem: a British subject here on business. You mustn't ask me how I know what I know; I'll never tell you. You'll just have to trust me."

"What do we do?"

"First, we must find Crossley."

"Where is he?"

"That's the game, isn't it, Frankel? He's in Chicago, we all know that much. Exactly where we're not sure, but you're going to find out."

"How?"

"I'm afraid that I've set up our friend here as a decoy." He moved to Susan and put a protective arm around her shoulder. "She has a rendezvous with Crossley tonight, though we don't know exactly where. She's to drive to the corner of Glenview and Harms Road. Crossley will either be there himself, or will send someone to meet her. We don't know what will happen after that, but we must follow her to find Crossley."

"Susan will be in danger."

"Your job, Peter, will be to find out where Crossley is hiding out. There's more to this than I've explained. There's another whole plot operating, and I believe that it's being directed out of some kind of communications center in this area. But that can be handled later; the important thing now is to protect Mendoza."

Frankel looked at his watch. "Susan, call your father at his office and get him on the line for me. There may still be time."

"Time for what? What does Daddy have to do with all this?"

"Hurry, Susan." He turned to Tatov. "Who else is in this with Crossley?"

"I don't know. I've been trying to smoke him out ever since I arrived in Chicago. He called Susan last night. It was the first break. Is Susan's father one of those being threatened?" Frankel nodded. "It was stupid of me not to have guessed that; I was so close that I didn't see it. Of course he would be; he's probably the prime target. What are you going to tell him?"

"I'm going to try to stop him from making a mistake."

Susan called from the telephone in the hall and waited anxiously beside Frankel as he spoke. "Livie, call your friend at the *Daily News* and kill the story. Don't ask questions; just do it. I'll explain later."

"They won't print it anyway without a personal interview. John Farrow thought I'd gone out of my mind, and he won't print the story without a confirmation from one of his own people. There's a reporter on the way to my office now."

"Call Farrow back and kill the story. Tell him you'll explain later." He hung up. "I don't know what to say, Susan." He cocked his head toward Tatov in the other room. "If we're wrong about him, we're all dead pigeons."

"Trust him, Peter."

"My ass is committed." He took her arm and led her back into the living room.

"I've had a minute to think," Tatov said. "I have some ground rules."

"Go ahead."

"It's your show, Frankel, beginning this minute, and my name must be kept out of it. You must never reveal your source. Do you agree?"

"I agree."

"Susan and her father are to be protected at all costs, both physically and as far as any connection they may have with any of this."

"I can't promise that, but I want to protect them as much as you do. Is that good enough?"

"Good enough." He smiled at Frankel. "We might even become friends. Wouldn't that be a surprise ending?"

"What else?"

"Try to keep Crossley alive until you've found his headquarters and destroyed his computer. I have a feeling that once he surfaces, there will be snipers coming at him from all directions. If you can find his base of operation and destroy it, I think you will have sabotaged the plot completely. Crossley is directing it all through a computer somewhere. If you have patience, Crossley will lead you to it. Take your man, but not before the computer is destroyed."

"Got it. Everything seems to be fitting together."

"I have one other condition." As he looked at Susan, the expression on his face did not change. "When you finally close in on Crossley after his computer is destroyed, take him dead, *not* alive. Is that clear?"

"Yes, but I can't agree. We want him alive so that he can talk. We want to find out who he works for so that we can clean out the whole bunch of them."

"*You* want that, Frankel. *I* don't. Take him dead."

"I can't agree to that. Besides, you've lost control. Even if I did agree, there's nothing that requires me to follow through."

"Except your own conscience. You have a sense of honor, and I have put all this in your hands. You owe it to me."

"Not to commit murder. If I can take him alive, I'm going to. Otherwise it's murder, and I'm not going to be a part of it."

"I understand. I shouldn't have asked."

"Why do you want him dead, Leonid?"

"I can't tell you that, Susan. You must trust me."

"Listen, Tatov, our job is to take prisoners alive, and we are going to shoot any son-of-a-bitch who tries to interfere with that—including you. The law is the law. Is that straight in your mind?"

"Understood," Tatov said, distracted. His mind was already beyond the immediate—probing alternatives.

Thursday, February 17 Ten p.m., Glenview, Illinois

Susan pulled over to the side of Glenview Road, stopping east of the junction with Harms. She was four minutes early. Traffic was light on Glenview and there seemed to be no cars going through the intersection. There was time now to be afraid. Both Peter and Leonid had assured her that she would be watched every minute, protected at all times, but she was afraid of everything except Whiz. She had never been afraid of him; she had always been certain of his love for her. But she was terrified of the night, of being alone in the car, of the unknown persons who would be taking her to Whiz, of all the uncertainties of the next few hours.

Two cars appeared simultaneously. One swung directly in front of her and the other pulled up behind. It was too dark to see faces or even to distinguish clearly the color of the cars. The headlights behind blinked bright and then back to low beam. The car ahead turned on its directional signal and pulled out onto Glenview Road. Susan turned on her signal and followed, the car behind her tailgating. She tried to see through the rearview mirror into the other car. She could not tell who was driving. The driver in front drove cautiously, timing the lights so that all three cars went through on the same signal. They were driving through a suburban part of Chicago unfamiliar to her.

After half an hour they approached a strip of brightly lit restaurants and bars. Just before a motel sign, the lead car flashed a right-turn signal and drove into its parking lot. Susan followed, pulled into a demarcated space when the lead car stopped; turned off her lights, ignition and put the car keys in her purse. Now the trailing car backed up so that its headlights illuminated a long row of motel doors. When the headlights blinked the door of the end room opened, a pinkish glow coming from the interior. The headlights of both cars went off, so that only the glow from the open door remained. Susan got out of her own car and walked across the rough gravel to the open door, looking straight ahead through the darkness which surrounded her.

Inside the room, the pinkish glow came from a small lamp next to a double bed. The remainder of the room was in darkness.

"Close the door."

She closed it behind her and started taking off her gloves. Another light went on. Whiz was sitting in a chair in front of the closed draperies, his hand on the pull chain of the lamp. He was the Whiz she had first known, barefoot and wearing jeans and a T-shirt with a Schlitz emblem. His hair was shorter but he looked as young as ever. There was a light chain around his neck with a shiny object suspended from it.

"I didn't think you'd come."

"It's been a long time, Whiz. You look well." She put her gloves on the dresser, slipped off her coat and threw it across the foot of the bed. "Why didn't you think I'd come? I told you I would. We never lied to each other, did we, Whiz? No matter what, we never lied to each other."

"I can't believe that I'm looking at you, that you're close enough to touch. I used to keep pictures of you, Susan. I never wanted to forget how you looked. It was important to me to remember how beautiful you are." She sat on the edge of the bed opposite him, crossed her legs and smoothed her skirt. "After a while, when I became myself again, I tore the pictures into shreds and burned them to erase every memory of you. But I couldn't. Every time I closed my eyes I saw a picture of you.

Now I've started again. I kept the pictures of you that were in the papers this morning. I've taped them up beside my bed." He shifted his body in the chair. "Are you happy, Susan?"

"I'm not sure what that is. I thought we were happy. I guess we were at first. But I'm older now, and I'm not sure anymore. I exist very well. I have fun sometimes. I'm lonely a lot. But I have Stoney."

"Are you in love again?"

She hesitated. "I think so. I hope so."

"Rico del Gracia?"

"No. It's no one you know. It's someone I've just met."

"The Englishman?"

She nodded.

Crossley's voice was steady and showed no emotion. "He'll never be your husband. He'll never be father to my child."

"You can't still be spiteful, Whiz, not after all this time. Don't you want Stoney and me to be happy? Don't you want your son to grow up leading a normal life in a normal household? I know how deeply you love Stoney. You must want him to grow up happy."

"There is no happiness here. Not in this city, not in this civilization. There's only suffocation. There's no room to be free here. You don't know what it's like to breathe clean air and feel your body soar into unpolluted space. You have to rid yourself of the shackles of what you call civilization."

"We tried that, Whiz, and it didn't work."

"Because of your father. That's what will happen to Stoney. He'll become another Sir Stonehill. I won't let it happen."

"Give him a chance, Whiz, let him grow up like a normal little boy."

"That's shit and you know it."

Susan smiled. "In five minutes we're back where we were five years ago—the same argument, the same immovable forces."

"You still love me, Susan."

"Do I? I probably do, in a way. You were the first, Whiz, and I'll never forget that. You'll always be a part of me."

"We could try again, Susan, you and Stoney and me. It would work this time. Now I have the money it takes to make men free. Your father's money is a ball and chain, but not mine, Susan. We can soar with it, live where the sun always shines and the wind blows clean against your body."

"Dreams, Whiz. You always were a dreamer."

"Not anymore. Now I make my dreams happen. I live them in a whole other world."

"Why are you here?"

"I've come back for you and Stoney."

"It's too late. I am still the person I always was, and so are you. No matter what you imagine, you're exactly the same."

"There was a time when you didn't think that my being the way I am was bad."

"I've grown up."

"No one will ever make love to you the way I did, Susan. No one will ever find all the secret places of your body and make you come alive in that kind of ecstasy."

"That's not true. You always tried to make me believe that, but it isn't true."

"The Englishman?"

"Yes."

"I'll kill him." His voice was still without emotion.

Susan laughed. "You won't kill him, Whiz. I know you too well. I know you better this minute than I ever have before."

His jaw tightened and the muscles in his arms tensed. "You don't know me at all. You never did. You tried to make me something I never could be."

"You did the same to me."

"But you're not what you seem, Susan. You have more soul than that."

She shook her head. "Not again. I won't believe that again." She rose, walked to the dresser and picked up her gloves. "It's no use, Whiz."

"Where are you going?"

"Home, where I belong."

"Why did you come here if you didn't want me to make love to you?"

"I wanted to see you again. Is that so strange? I haven't seen you in five years. I wanted to see how you are. I care about you. Is that so strange?"

He stood up for the first time and walked past her to the door. "You still love me," he said.

She stood almost touching him, looking up. "Of course I do—I've told you that. But it's different. I love you for the wonderful times we had, but that part of our lives is over. Let's not spoil the wonderful memories we have left."

"I can make it happen again."

"What for? What would be the point of it?"

Still barring the door, he leaned forward and kissed her. Susan did not back away. The touch of his mouth was no more than one strange hand meeting another. Crossley grabbed her then, engulfing her, pressing his lips against hers, forcing her mouth open, probing with his tongue, but she remained rigid. His hand covered her breast, his fingers seeking the nipple. With all her force she pushed him back against the door. "Not like this, Whiz. You're not going to spoil the good memories like this." She walked over to the sagging bed, pulled off the cheap bedspread, propped up the thin pillows, pulled the sweater over her head and started to unbutton her blouse. Crossley stood transfixed, watching her as she hung her blouse over the desk chair and unfastened her bra. She turned to him. "This is what you wanted, isn't it?"

"Christ, Susan, what are you doing to me?"

She sat on the edge of the bed, kicked off her shoes and stood up again. "Don't you want to make love to me?"

"Not this way, not as an act of pity. I want you to crave me the way you used to. I want you to want me, to scream for me to be inside you."

"You can't make that happen again." She unzipped the side of her skirt. "If you need to make love to me—"

"Not like this. Want me, Susan, oh, Christ, want me."

She did not answer as she stepped out of her skirt, folded it and placed it over the chair, then turned off the light near the window.

"Don't you know what this is doing to me?"

Taking off her pantyhose, she turned back the blanket and got into bed.

Where before his body had barricaded the way, he was limp now, using the door as a support. "I won't buy you like a whore, I won't use you as a machine. Beg me, Susan, plead with me. Please. Tell me how much you need me."

She reached over and turned off the lamp next to the bed, so that the room was in darkness. There was only the sound of his sobs of uncontrolled anguish. "Help me, Susan." His words were indistinct between the animal sounds he was making.

She waited silently.

The door opened and a strong draft of cold night air funneled into the room. She saw him silhouetted in the opening, holding on to each side of the doorframe for support, and then he ran out, oblivious of the cold, unaware of the pain of the gravel under his bare feet. Staggering in a zigzag pattern, his motor senses not functioning, he ran erratically in all directions like a rabid animal.

Susan wrapped herself in a blanket from the bed, closed the door and started to dress. She cried without a sound, without pain, without a distortion of her face. She felt weightless, her consciousness soaring in all directions.

Friday, February 18
Nine-thirty a.m., Airborne
over Chicago

THE HELICOPTER HOVERED over the expressway two miles north of Rolling Meadows. The morning was clear, and the building housing Whiz Crossley's computer was easily visible. The interior of the chopper had been hastily equipped as an arsenal: two long-range rifles, a .50 caliber machine gun and a strange weapon which Frankel had never seen before. The radio was monitored to the control tower at O'Hare Airport. Dirksmith

had secured the call letters of the jet bringing Mendoza to
Chicago, the time it had taken off and its ETA, but its actual
landing time would depend on the air traffic at that hour. Once
on the ground, taxiing instructions would be taken over by Butler Aviation, where all private aircraft landed.

Six of them were squeezed into the cabin. Frankel sat next to
the pilot, the seat with the greatest visibility, two marksmen sat
in the center seats, and Dirksmith and another weapons special-
ist were in the back.

There was no activity around the deserted office building, and
no cars in the parking lot. Frankel broke the silence. "I don't
understand why he hasn't left yet. Mendoza's plane is due at ten-
twenty, and it's going to take Crossley at least a half-hour to get
to O'Hare. Look at the traffic on the expressway."

"Maybe your unimpeachable source is not so unimpeachable," Dirksmith said. He had been difficult ever since Frankel
had called him—hours before—and had used every kind of
pressure to try to persuade him to reveal the source of his
information. "Maybe this is all just a figment of someone's
imagination. Nobody's really sure that Crossley is behind all
this or that he means to knock off Mendoza."

"I'm sure," Frankel said. "What did your men say? Are they
certain that Crossley didn't leave last night after they tailed him
back to the building?"

"Several people left and one person entered the premises, but
none of them was Crossley."

"He could have used a disguise."

"Not likely. He has no reason to suspect that we're on to
him."

Then the building below them exploded. They felt the plane
rock from the turbulent air a split second before the hollow,
booming sound. Debris was flying through the air, the shattered
splinters of the core of the building funneled upward, confetti of
glass, wood, bricks and concrete forming an umbrella and then
showering earthward in slow motion. Now flames appeared,
huge blue-edged, orange-red shapes ascending higher and higher.

Steadying the aircraft, the pilot moved closer to the holo-
caust. In both directions expressway traffic had stopped, and

some cars had been hit by the burning rubble. There was another, smaller explosion followed by dense black smoke that obscured visibility.

Frankel was almost in tears, his emotions raw. "You promised me, Dirlsmith. You promised not to do this until we caught Crossley. You promised."

"We didn't do this, you dumb bastard. Use your head, get a hold of yourself. I had my own men down there. You don't think I would deliberately blow them up."

"I wouldn't put anything past you—anything. You're the coldest son-of-a-bitch in the world, Dirksmith. I thought maybe there was something human about you, but I know better now. You'd sacrifice anyone to get your job done."

"Knock it off, Frankel. Shape up, for Christ's sake. No matter what you think of me, you must know that this isn't our way. We wanted those computers intact. Do you think we'd deliberately destroy evidence? It's those damned Israelis. This is their kind of operation. They love fireworks. They're all demented kids playing with bombs."

"What about Crossley? Do you suppose he was still in the building? He must have been there." He turned to Dirksmith. "Maybe he blew it up himself."

The man next to Dirksmith said, "It was a professional job. Overkill. Whoever planted that bomb was taking no chances."

"Why would Crossley destroy his headquarters now?" Dirksmith asked. "His job wasn't done. He had no way of knowing that we were on to him."

Frankel growled, "We don't have time to jack ourselves off. Call the control tower and have them divert Mendoza's plane. We don't know what's happening and we can't afford to take a chance with his life." Dirksmith did not move. Frankel looked at his watch. "Come on, contact the tower."

"I don't think so," Dirksmith said.

"What do you mean, you don't think so?" Frankel shouted.

"Amateurs always panic, Frankel. You've done your job like a nice Jewish boy; now let the professionals take over." To the pilot he said, "Get over the airport. Don't request permission to land. Stay out of the traffic until Mendoza's plane is ready to land."

"A fucking lot of professionals you are. You'd still be chasing your own ass if I hadn't found Crossley for you."

"The United States Government thanks you very much, Frankel. You've been just peachy."

"Fuck off, Dirksmith."

"If you're going to play cops and robbers on any kind of a permanent basis, I suggest you pace yourself better. It's all in a day's work."

"You think your men blew it, don't you, Dirksmith? You think that somehow Crossley slipped through your surveillance." Dirksmith did not answer. "So do I. I think he's smarter than all of us."

Over the airport they hovered at two thousand feet. From the radio they learned that there had been a momentary hold on all aircraft takeoffs and landings pending a report on the explosion.

The group waiting in the old terminal housing Butler Aviation were unaware of the explosion and the tie-up on the expressway. Susan was posing for pictures with some of the officials who were there to meet Mark Mendoza. Air traffic had resumed, and small planes taxied in and out of the area.

The Israeli consul was at the counter where taxiing instructions were being relayed to the small planes. Now the woman at the radio indicated that Mendoza's plane had landed and was approaching the Butler area. He walked quickly back to the others and led them through the doors toward the runway. Each member of the group was stopped and checked with a metal detector before being allowed through by the regular security force of the airport. In the background, watching every movement of every person, were the grim-faced men of the Israeli Secret Service.

Over forty small planes were parked in the area, forming two straight lines, leaving a wide space in between for maneuvering. A twin-engine Cessna was pulling into the area as the group started out to meet Mendoza, and it taxied to the side and parked, its engines still running. The Lear jet approached, taxiing down the center core, and swung into line directly opposite the Cessna. Two ground crews in carts started down the center lane to service the incoming planes.

The helicopter descended rapidly, hovering thirty feet off the ground, to a position directly above the jet. The motion of its rotors created a sudden downdraft on the group walking toward Mendoza's plane. The men held on to their hats, and Susan put both hands to her hair. Then the door of the jet opened, and the co-pilot appeared and lowered the stairs.

Frankel lurched forward suddenly, grabbed the safety handle on the door of the helicopter, turned it and threw the door open. The wind and the noise of the engine drowned out his voice as he screamed and pointed to the Cessna on the opposite ramp. Off guard, no one reacted quickly enough to understand what was happening. Frankel grabbed the rifle from the man behind him and sighted it on a white-coveralled mechanic standing on the wing of the Cessna. Confused, the marksman tried to grab his rifle back, but Frankel pulled it free again with so much force that only the seat belt prevented him from falling out. As he took aim again, he was distracted by a figure in the open door of the Cessna. Frankel had seen Crossley only once, a staggering figure running in a daze around the half-lit parking lot of the motel, and he couldn't be sure that the crouching figure in the doorway, the barrel of a rifle visible in his hand, was Crossley. He looked from the mechanic on the wing to the man in the doorway. Either one could be the assassin—or both. He sighted on the man in the door, steadying his arm on the structure of the helicopter, trying to compensate for movement, and fired three times in rapid succession. The noise of the rotors obscured the sounds of the shots. Only one bullet came near its mark, tearing through the skin of the Cessna aft of the door.

But another bullet from another gun hit the mechanic precisely in the face, and the man crumbled on the wing, his gun falling to the ground. Then his body fell, and he lay on his back on the tarmac, a bright oval of raw, bleeding flesh where his face had been.

Both the FBI agents and the Israeli intelligence men secreted in the crowd moved quickly toward the plane. There was no time to determine which of the agents had killed the assassin; at the moment it was enough that the attempt had been aborted.

Mark Mendoza, who was standing completely exposed on the top step of the jet, froze at the sounds of the gunshots, then threw himself down and forward for cover, toppling some of the dignitaries waiting for him.

When the helicopter landed, Frankel leaped out first, bucking the wind to rush over to the tangle of bodies on the ground by the Lear. Susan was still standing, protected by a man using his body to shield her. He tried to block Frankel, but he pushed the man aside, grabbed Susan and held her. Then he realized that the rifle was still in his hand and that photographers' flashbulbs were going off all around him.

Other than scrapes and minor bruises, there were no injuries to Mendoza or any of the others. The Secret Service men encircled Mendoza, but when he saw Frankel still holding the rifle, the Israeli broke through, ran over and threw his arms around Frankel, speaking incomprehensible Hebrew words. Now the photographers closed in on the two men, shooting pictures from every angle.

Before Frankel could explain that it was not he who had killed the assassin, Dirksmith was taking over, explaining how Frankel had spotted the man on the wing of the Cessna, and with no fear for his own life opened the door of the helicopter and fired one perfect shot. Frankel tried to interrupt him to explain what had really happened, but there was determination in Dirksmith's eyes and in the set of his jaw, and Frankel realized that it was hopeless to try to correct the story. For some reason Dirksmith wanted everyone to think that he had killed the assassin.

Then he remembered the figure in the door of the plane which evidently no one else in the chopper had seen. He ran to the other side of the helicopter, but the Cessna was gone. He looked out toward the runway and saw several small planes taxiing, but could not identify the right one from this distance. Running back to Dirksmith, he pulled him aside. "Crossley's getting away. We have to stop him."

"What are you talking about?"

"Crossley was in the Cessna—I'm sure of it. It had to be him. The Cessna's gone, and Crossley's in it."

"Wasn't that Crossley on the wing?"

"I don't think so. There was another man with a rifle in the doorway. Didn't you see him? It must have been Crossley. Call the tower and stop the Cessna." Dirksmith took off at a run toward the terminal, and Frankel followed, scarcely able to keep pace with the older man.

In one movement, not even out of breath, Dirksmith broke through the line around the counter, flashed his identification and instructed the woman at the radio to tell the tower to ground the Cessna.

"What call letters?"

"How the hell do I know? It's the Cessna that flew in here just before the Lear jet. It doesn't matter. Call the control tower and tell them to stop all traffic."

"I don't have the authority to do that."

"Get the tower. I'll talk to them myself."

In a minute the woman handed her headset to Dirksmith. "Is there a twin-engine Cessna waiting to take off?"

"This is John Nelson. I'm in charge of the tower here. What's going on?"

"This is Waldo Dirksmith, special agent of the Federal Bureau of Investigation. This is an emergency. I'll verify later. Is there a twin-engine Cessna waiting to take off?"

"I don't know. Just a minute." The voice turned away, but Dirksmith could hear the words. "Hey, Jack, did you clear that Cessna for takeoff?" The answer was inaudible, but within seconds Nelson said, "Sorry, but the Cessna is in the air."

"What about the flight plan?"

"It ought to be over at Butler. We just clear them to take off and land."

Dirksmith handed the headset back to the woman and turned to Frankel. "Are you sure it was Crossley?"

"No, I'm not sure. I only saw him once, and at night. But it had to be."

"I think we'd better have Mrs. Crossley look at the body of the mechanic. If it's her husband she'll recognize him."

"You can't do that to her. There's nothing left of the guy's face."

Three of Dirksmith's men came to the counter then, and he drew them aside and began reeling off instructions.

The Israeli Secret Service had Mendoza and Susan surrounded as they entered the terminal. The rest of the group straggled behind them. The lobby was in chaos as the security force arrived from the main terminal and Chicago police began unloading from squad cars, taking over control and blocking all exits.

"Are you all right, Susan?" Frankel led her away from Mendoza.

"Was the man you shot Whiz?" she whispered.

He shook his head. "I don't think so. I think he was inside the plane and that he got away."

All at once, without warning, she was near tears. "I wish it had been Whiz. I wish it had been. Poor Whiz." Frankel held her. "You don't understand. He was like an animal, Peter, like a mad dog. It would have been an act of mercy to kill him." By now she was crying and unable to say any more.

"We'll find him, Susan. That plane has to land somewhere. Don't worry."

"Stoney!" She screamed her son's name, and the tears stopped as suddenly as they had started. "He'll try to get Stoney."

"Oh, Christ." Frankel turned and broke through the huddle of men around Dirksmith. "We have to get protection for Stoney."

"Who's Stoney?"

"Susan's son. She thinks Crossley may try to get him. She could be right. We have to cover her apartment."

"It is covered," Dirksmith said. "It's been staked out since last night."

"Can you warn your men that Crossley may show up?"

"There's time, Frankel. That plane has to land first."

"There isn't time. Crossley could have landed that plane downtown at Meigs airport by now. It's only a ten-minute run

—fifteen at the most. He could get from Meigs to Susan's apartment in fifteen minutes."

"I'll contact more men," Dirksmith said, "and double the guard on the building."

Frankel returned to Susan. "It's okay. They have your apartment under surveillance. Stoney's well protected."

"I want to get home, Peter. Please, take me home."

"All right. I'd better throw my weight around. Maybe I can commandeer a police car. Wait here."

Friday, February 18
Ten-thirty a.m., Chicago

S~TILL~ ~OUT~ ~OF~ ~BREATH~ from the jump across the roof, the climb down one fire escape and up another, Whiz Crossley wrapped his handkerchief around the heavy wrench he had taken from the plane and smashed the lower pane of the fire door in the kitchen of Susan's apartment. Using the end of the wrench to pry away the wire embedded in the shattered glass, he reached in and unlocked the safety catch he himself had installed when they had first moved in. For a moment he was engulfed by the familiar: the crack in the linoleum, the exposed telephone cable around the back door, the harsh glare of the fluorescent fixture they had planned to replace. The time between did not exist; there was no palace in the desert, no secret computer complexes, no mantras, no dreams. And there were no armed agents to be outwitted at every turn. But the moment was only a moment; then all the dangers were real again.

When he entered Stoney's room, Leonid Tatov was sitting in

a chair, Stoney on his lap, both watching *Sesame Street*. The boy immediately sensed danger and started to get up, but Tatov held him tight, using him as a protective shield. As Crossley started toward them, Tatov revealed the gun he was holding, aimed at Crossley beneath Stoney's arm. Neither man spoke. Again the boy tried to get up, but Tatov's arm held him back.

"I thought you'd try this," Tatov said, "but as you see, it's quite impossible."

"You're Hasad's man."

"I thought you'd seen me that day in Damascus, but I wasn't certain."

"I want the boy."

"There's no way. You can see that. I'd rather not use this gun. It would be a trauma for the boy, don't you agree?"

"I want the boy."

"I've explained that there is no way. I don't want to kill you in front of the child, but I will if I have to."

"Who are you?"

"It doesn't matter, does it? Your only real concern now should be the boy. We'll do quite well together. There'll be horses for him to ride and streams for him to fish. He's all that matters to you, and I swear to you that you need not worry about him. We get on famously together."

Crossley started toward them again, but stopped when he saw the movement of Tatov's finger against the trigger. He squatted on the floor a few feet away so that his face was almost level with Stoney's. Tatov moved the gun, keeping it aimed between Crossley's eyes. "Your name is Stoney, isn't it?" Crossley asked the boy. "Do you like to ride horses?"

The boy looked back at Tatov, whose eyes did not waver from their target. "I don't know. I've never ridden a horse. Leonid says I'll like it. I like to fish, though. My grandfather takes me fishing, and he lets me put on the worms and take off the fish and everything. He says I'm big enough not to get my fingers caught on the hook. I like to go fishing. Do you like it? Leonid does."

"You'd like the desert too, Stoney. Do you know what a desert is?" The boy shook his head. "There's miles and miles of sand. It's like the biggest beach you ever saw, except that there's no water."

"That's funny. Whoever heard of a beach without water?"

"The air is so clear you can almost fly in it. You can be like a bird.' And there's sunshine all the time. You'd like that, wouldn't you?"

"I like to make snowmen. Leonid says we can go skiing in the mountains. You can't ski on sand." He turned his head toward Tatov. "Can you ski on sand, Leonid?"

"No more questions, Stoney. This man has to go. There will be some people here very soon, and I don't think he wants to see them." With his gun, Tatov motioned for Crossley to stand up. When he did, Tatov stood up too, still using the boy as a shield, keeping the gun aimed.

"It's not over," Crossley said. "My time will come. Remember that."

"Go out the back door," Tatov said. Crossley turned and walked out of the room down the hall toward the kitchen, his fingers touching the once familiar walls. Tatov kept pace three feet behind him.

Stoney said, "Put me down," but Tatov held him tight.

"Quoth the spider never more."

"What did you say?"

"Quoth the spider never more," Crossley repeated.

They were in the kitchen. Still with his back to Tatov, Crossley stopped, and again the gun was leveled. Reaching around his neck, Crossley unfastened the chain, held it in his hand for a moment and then tossed it on a counter. "I'm leaving a present for you, Stoney. When you get older you can wear it around your neck. There's a little spider on the end of it. Do you like spiders?"

The boy looked to Tatov for direction. "I don't know," he said.

"When I was a little boy I used to catch them and put them in a big glass jar and watch them spin webs." He opened the back door, then turned to look at his son once more. "I bet that from now on whenever you see a spider you'll think of me."

Crossley walked out into the gray service corridor, where the back stairs, running down seventeen floors, wrapped around the central shaft of the freight elevator. He pushed the button for it. The old mechanism was noisy, and the three of them could hear the door closing on a lower floor and then the sounds of gears and pulleys. When the sound was almost at their level Tatov kicked the kitchen door shut, bolted it and stepped away from it, still holding Stoney. He heard the elevator door open, heard voices, a scuffle and then the sound of men running down the stairs. A moment later there were two shots, their sounds amplified by the hollow shaft.

Tatov hugged Stoney tighter, kissed the top of his head, put him down on the kitchen floor and took his hand. "We're missing a lot of *Sesame Street*. It's probably over."

"What was that noise, Leonid?"

"I don't know, Stoney. Maybe it was the elevator. It sounds funny sometimes." He led the boy down the hall a little faster. "I have a great idea. How about McDonald's for lunch? Let's go play in the park and then go to McDonald's for a hamburger. Did you know that there's a McDonald's in London? Your mother is worried that you might be lonesome when we go to live in London, but it won't be so different, you'll be able to get a Big Mac. You'll like that, won't you?"

Friday, February 18
Eleven a.m., Chicago

THE SCREECHING SOUND of the siren made conversation impossible. Susan sat on the edge of the back seat, one hand gripping the window handle, her eyes fixed on the space between the shoulders of the uniformed policemen in the front seat who were monitoring the dizzy path of the squad car as it wove in and out of traffic. Frankel was holding Susan's other hand, an alternating current of communication between them; he pressing his strength into her and in turn, absorbing the shock of her tensions as her fingernails dug into him. Dirksmith sat back in the seat looking out the window, his face reflecting no emotion.

Six blocks from the apartment building Frankel instructed the officer to turn off the siren and light and slow down. The sudden silence was as deafening as the noise had been. Susan turned briefly to Frankel and he smiled to reassure her.

Dirksmith asked, "Do you have a game plan, Frankel, or are you going to muddle into this in your usual style?"

Ignoring him, Frankel tapped the driver. "Go straight down to Lake Shore Drive, turn left and go west on Banks Street. Drive slow. I don't want to attract any attention." He turned to Dirksmith. "Give me your gun."

"You're out of your league, aren't you, Frankel, or do you have delusions of television grandeur? Who are you today? Colombo? Serpico?" Dirksmith cleared his throat. "Why don't you stop playing cops and robbers and let the pros take over."

"Give me your gun, Dirksmith."

"Your chutzpah is becoming bionic." He handed him the gun.

"Susan, get down on the floor, out of sight." When she turned to him, there were tears in her eyes and her lips were pressed together. "Go ahead, get down." He moved over to the window.

The car turned up the quiet residential street. Nothing seemed out of the ordinary. Then Frankel saw two figures a block away, in front of the apartment building. Frankel lowered the car window, raised the gun and squinted against the glare of the sun. The tall man took the boy's hand and they began to cross the street, walking toward the park.

"Stop the car. Wait."

Tatov and Stoney came into recognizable focus. Frankel lowered the gun and touched Susan's shoulder. "It's all right. Stoney is okay. Tatov has him." Susan jumped up and reached for the door handle, but Frankel restrained her. "Wait until they're near the park." To the driver he said, "Pull up to the playground."

Dirksmith's arms were folded. "What makes you think Crossley won't suddenly materialize. He's done it before."

"I know Tatov. He wouldn't expose Stoney. Your people must have gotten Whiz."

The car stopped. Susan started to get out, then turned back to Frankel. "Peter," she began, but she could say no more. She kissed him on the cheek, squeezed his hand, jumped out of the car and ran toward Tatov and Stoney. Without saying anything, she took Stoney's other hand and the three of them turned into the playground.

As Frankel closed the door, Dirksmith said, "You can't win them all."

The squad continued west, passing a private ambulance that had turned slowly out of the alley behind the apartment building, the siren silent, the red dome dark.

"You win some and you lose some," Frankel said.

About the Author

Born in Chicago, where he still lives, and educated at the University of Chicago, RICHARD HIMMEL combines careers as a novelist, renowned interior designer, discotheque operator, abstract-expressionist painter and suburban husband. On behalf of this mixed-media life, he travels around the world several times a year.